After learning to read aged just two, **Jessica Gilmore** spent every childhood party hiding in bedrooms in case the birthday girl had a book or two she hadn't read yet. Discovering a Mills & Boon novel on a family holiday, Jessica realised that romance-writing was her true vocation and proceeded to spend her maths lessons practising her art, creating Dynasty-inspired series starring herself and Morten Harket's cheekbones. Writing for Mills & Boon really is a dream come true!

On the rare occasions when she is not writing, working, taking her daughter to activities or tweeting, Jessica likes to plan holidays—and uses her favourite locations in her books. She writes deeply emotional romance with a hint of humour, a splash of sunshine and usually a great deal of delicious food—and equally delicious heroes.

Sophie Pembroke has been dreaming, reading and writing romance for years—ever since she first read *The Far Pavilions* under her desk in chemistry class. She later stayed up all night devouring Mills & Boon books as part of her English degree at Lancaster University, and promptly gave up any pretext of enjoying tragic novels. After all, what's the point of a book without a happy ending?

Sophie keeps a blog at www.sophiepembroke.com, which should be about romance and writing but is usually about cake and castles instead.

Michelle Douglas has been writing for Mills & Boon since 2007 and believes she has the best job in the world. She lives in a leafy suburb of Newcastle, on Australia's east coast, with her own romantic hero, a house full of dust and books, and an eclectic collection of sixties and seventies vinyl. She loves to hear from readers and can be contacted via her website: www.michelle-douglas.com.

Happily Ever After...

JESSICA GILMORE

SOPHIE PEMBROKE

MICHELLE DOUGLAS

MILLS & BOON

First Published in Great Britain 2018
by Mills & Boon, an imprint of HarperCollins*Publishers*
1 London Bridge Street, London, SE1 9GF

HAPPILY EVER AFTER... © 2018 Harlequin Books S. A.

His Reluctant Cinderella © 2014 Jessica Gilmore
His Very Convenient Bride © 2015 Sophie Pembroke
A Deal to Mend Their Marriage © 2016 Michelle Douglas

ISBN: 978-0-263-27456-1

0918

MIX
Paper from
responsible sources
FSC C007454

This book is produced from independently certified FSC™ paper to ensure responsible forest management.

For more information visit: www.harpercollins.co.uk/green

Printed and bound in Spain
by CPI, Barcelona

HIS RELUCTANT
CINDERELLA

JESSICA GILMORE

For my parents

To mum, thank you for weekly trips to the library, for never telling me to "put that book down", for the gift of words and stories and dreams.

And to dad for proving that families are more than genes, that blood isn't thicker than water, that nurture totally trumps nature—and for being the best grandpa in the world. I love you both x

CHAPTER ONE

'IF YOU TELL ME where my sister is, I'll give you ten thousand pounds.'

The down-turned head in front of him lifted slowly and Raff found himself coolly assessed by a pair of the greenest eyes he had ever seen, their slight upward tilt irresistibly feline, the effect heightened by high, slanting cheekbones and a pointed chin.

If this lady had a tail, it would definitely be swishing slowly. A warning sign.

He'd never been that good at heeding warnings. He liked to see them more as a challenge.

'I beg your pardon?' Her voice was as cold as her stare. Maybe he should have tried charm before hard cash, but somehow Raff doubted that even his patented charm would work on this cool cat.

Her dismissal should have annoyed him, he was used to people snapping to attention when he needed them, but he had to admit he was intrigued. He smiled, slow and warm. 'Clara Castleton?'

There was no answering upturn of her full mouth as she nodded at the name tag, displayed neatly on the modern oak desk. 'As you can see. But I don't believe you introduced yourself?'

'I don't believe I did.' Raff hooked the wooden chair

out from opposite her desk and slid into it. He knew his six-foot-two frame could be intimidating, used it to his advantage sometimes, but for some reason, standing before her incredibly neat desk, he was irresistibly reminded of being summoned to the headmaster's office.

Although that was where any resemblance to his long-suffering former headmaster ended despite her severely cut suit—her strawberry-blonde hair might be ruthlessly scraped back but it looked as if it was all there and she lacked the terrifying bushy eyebrows. Hers were rather neat lines, adding a flourish to what really was a remarkably pretty face, although the hair, the discreet make-up and the suit were all designed to hide the fact. Interesting. Raff filed that fact away for future use. He sensed he was going to need all the weapons he could get.

He leant back in his chair, keeping his eyes fixed on her face. 'Castor Rafferty, but you can call me Raff. I believe you know my sister.'

'Oh.' Her eyes flickered away from his searching expression. 'I was expecting you a couple of days ago.'

'I've been busy dropping everything and rushing back to England. So, are you going to tell me where Polly is?'

Clara Castleton shook her head. 'I wouldn't tell you if I knew,' she said. 'But I don't.'

Raff narrowed his eyes. He didn't believe her, didn't want to believe her. Because if she was telling the truth he was at an utter dead end. 'Come now, Clara. I can call you Clara, can't I? This short and simple email...' he held up his phone with the email displayed. Not that he needed to be reminded what it said; he knew it off by heart '...tells me quite clearly that in an emergency my sister can be contacted via Clara of Castleton's Concierge Consultancy. Nice alliteration by the way.'

She took the phone and read the message, those intriguing eyebrows raised in surprise. 'Sorry, I have an email address, nothing more.'

'I've tried emailing a couple of times.' Try ten. Or twenty. 'Maybe she'll read it if it comes from you,' he suggested hopefully. 'My original offer still stands.'

'Keep your money, Mr Rafferty.' Her voice was positively icy now. Raff was already finding the anaemic English spring chilly; her tone brought the temperature down another few degrees. 'Your sister has taken care of my fees. She asked me to help settle you in, to continue to make sure the house is cared for. This I can do, it's *what* I do. But unless there is a real emergency I won't be sending any emails.'

It was a clear dismissal—and it rankled, far more than it should do. Time for a change of tactic; he needed to get this right so Polly would be back where she belonged, managing Rafferty's, the iconic department store founded by their great-grandfather.

And he would be back in the field where *he* belonged. He'd barely had a chance to unpack, to assess what was needed, how to play his own small yet vital part in stopping the humanitarian crisis unfolding before him from becoming a full-blown disaster, when he'd received Polly's email ordering him home.

Typical of his family, to think their petty affairs were worth more than thousands of lives. And yet here he was.

Raff looked around the neat, organised room for inspiration. Such a contrast from his last office: a tent on the outskirts of the camp. Even the office before that, situated in an actual building, had been a small room, almost a cupboard, piled high with crates, paperwork and supplies. He couldn't imagine having all this space to himself.

Occupying the corner at the end of the quaint high

street, Clara's office took up the entire ground floor of a former terraced shop, the original lead-paned bow windows now veiled with blinds, the iron sign holder above the front door empty, replaced by a neat plaque set in the wall.

Outside looked like a still from a film set in Ye Olde England but the inside was a sharp modern contrast. The large room was painted white with only bright-framed photographs to alleviate the starkness, although through the French doors at the back Raff could see a paved courtyard filled with flowering tubs and a small iron table and chairs, a lone hint of homeliness.

Clara's very large and very tidy desk was near the back by the far wall, facing out across the room. Two inviting sofas clustered by the front window surrounding a coffee table heaped with glossy lifestyle magazines. The whole room was discreet, tasteful and gave him no clue whatsoever to its owner's personality.

Maybe it was time to try the charm after all.

Raff leaned forward confidingly. 'I'm worried about Polly,' he said. 'It's so out of character for her to disappear like this. What if she's ill? I just want to know that she's all right.' He allowed a hint of a rueful smile to appear.

The look on Clara's face oozed disapproval. Yep, she was still giving out the whole 'disappointed headmaster' vibe. 'Mr Rafferty, you and I both know that your sister hasn't just disappeared. She's gone on holiday after making sure that both her job and home are taken care of. There really is no mystery.

'It may be a *little* out of character.' Was that doubt creeping into her voice? 'I haven't known her to take even a long weekend before—but that's probably exactly why she needs this break. Besides, isn't it your company too?'

Unfortunately. 'Just what has my sister said to you?'

A faint flush crept over the high cheekbones. 'I don't understand.'

Oh, she understood all right.

'She didn't use the words irresponsible or lazy?' Polly's email might have been short but it had been to the point. *Her* point of view. As always, they differed on that.

The flush deepened. Not so cool after all. The colour gave her warmth, emphasising the curve of her cheek, the lushly dark lashes veiling those incredible eyes. An unexpected jolt of pure attraction shot through him. Before she had been like a marble statue, nice to look at but offputtingly chilly. This hint of vulnerability gave her dimensions. Unwanted, unneeded dimensions. He wasn't here to flirt. With any luck he'd hardly be here at all.

'Our communication was purely business,' but she couldn't meet his eye. 'Now, I do happen to have a half-hour free right now. Is this a convenient time for me to show you the house?'

No, Raff wanted to snap. No, actually it wasn't convenient. None of this was. Not Polly's most uncharacteristic disappearance, nor her SOS ordering him home right now. She couldn't expect him to drop everything and step in so she could go on some extended holiday.

Even though he hadn't been home in over four years. He pushed the thought away. He wasn't needed here, not as he was out in the field. Besides, his absence had given Polly the opportunity she had wanted; the two circumstances were entirely different.

Which made this whole disappearing act even odder. If he allowed himself to stop feeling irritated he might start getting worried.

'Mr Rafferty?'

'Raff,' he corrected her. 'Mr Rafferty makes me think I'm back at school.'

Or even worse back in the boardroom, sitting round a ridiculously large table listening to never-ending presentations and impenetrable jargon, itching to get up, stop talking and *do*.

'Raff,' she said after a reluctant pause. He liked the sound of his name on her tongue. Crisp and cool like a smooth lager on a hot summer's day. '*Is* now a convenient time?'

Not really but Polly had backed him into a hole and until he had a chance to work out what had happened he didn't have much choice.

He *was* still joint Vice CEO of Rafferty's, after all. Someone had to take over the reins, stop Grandfather working himself into an early grave; in Polly's absence that person had to be him.

She had planned it well. The contrary streak in Raff wanted to ensure she didn't get her way. To walk away from her home, her company. Show her he couldn't be manipulated.

But of course he couldn't. Despite everything Polly was his twin—and pulling a stunt like this was completely out of character. Polly didn't just quit; she was the hardest worker he knew. The sooner he found out what had happened and fixed it, the sooner they could both return to their lives.

And he was sure that the woman in front of him could help him, if he could just find a way to make her crack, like a ripe and rather inviting nut.

'Okay, then, Clara Castleton,' he said. 'Lead the way.'

'Is there something wrong?'

Clara knew she sounded cold. Raff Rafferty might

have turned on the charm but she preferred to keep a professional distance, especially when her new client owned an easy smile and a devilish glint in blue, blue eyes.

And a disconcerting way of looking at her as if he could see straight through her barriers, as if the suit didn't fool him at all. Her skin fizzed with awareness of his intense gaze—or with irritation at his high-handed ways.

Either way he was dangerous. The sooner she settled him in and got out, the better.

The tall blond man wasn't actually her client but his sister had made sure Clara was fully briefed. The Golden Boy, apple of his grandfather's eye. Clara knew men like Raff Rafferty all too well. It wasn't a type she admired at all. Not any more.

Look at him now, leaning against her van, a smirk playing on those finely sculpted lips.

'This yours?'

Clara held up the keys. 'Why?'

His eyes swept assessingly over the large, practical van, her logo and contact details tastefully picked out on the side. 'I imagined you driving something a little more elegant.'

Clara took a breath, an unexpected flutter in her stomach at the idea of something elegant, that she was featuring in his imagination at all. She pushed the thought resolutely away.

'Save your imaginings,' she said. 'The van is practical.'

'It's practical all right.'

His lips were pressed together; Clara had the distinct impression that he was laughing at her. 'I'm sure it's not your usual style,' she said as evenly as she could. 'If you'd rather walk I can meet you there.'

'Don't worry about me. I'm not fussy.'

'Great.' She was sure that her attempted smile looked more like a grimace. She should make him sit in the back amongst the cleaning supplies and tools. See how fussy he was then.

At least, Clara reflected as she pulled the van out into the narrow main road that ran through the town, he hadn't offered to drive. Some men found it hard to be driven by a woman, especially in a large van like this. Raff was the very definition of relaxed, leaning back in his seat, lean jean-clad legs outstretched.

Practical it might be, but the large van always felt out of place on Hopeford's narrow windy streets. It took all Clara's skills and concentration to negotiate the small roads. The overhanging houses and cobbled pavements might be picturesque enough to pull in tourists and Londoners looking for a lengthy if direct commute, but they were completely ill suited for work vans.

And it was easier to concentrate on the driving than it was trying to make conversation with someone who seemed to suck all the air out of the van. It had always felt so spacious before.

Unfortunately Raff didn't seem to feel the same way. 'How long has Polly lived here?'

Clara negotiated a particularly tight turn before answering as briefly as was polite. 'About three years, I believe.'

He looked about him. 'It seems quiet, not her kind of place at all.'

Clara glanced over at him. She knew that he and Polly were twins and the relationship was obvious. They both had straight, dark blond hair, although his was far more dishevelled than his sister's usual sleek chignon, straight, almost Roman noses and well-cut mouths. But the similarity seemed only skin deep. Polly Rafferty was quiet, always working, whether at home or on her long train journey into the capital. She was reserved and polite; Clara was the closest thing she had in Hopeford to a friend.

On balance she much preferred the sister's reservation to the brother's easy charm and devilish grin. They were dangerous attributes, especially if you had once been susceptible to a laid-back rich boy's style.

Clara knew all too well where that led. Nowhere she ever wanted to go again.

'The town is increasingly popular,' she said, carefully keeping her voice neutral. 'It's pretty, we have good schools and we're on a direct train line into London.'

'Ye—es…' He sounded doubtful. 'But Polly doesn't have kids and last I saw she wasn't that bothered about quiet either. If she wanted pretty there are plenty of places in London that fit the bill. It's not like she's short of money.'

His tone was disparaging and the look on his face as he stared out at the picturesque street no better. Clara gripped the steering wheel tightly. She might moan about incomers flooding the place, driving prices up and her friends out, but at least they appreciated the town.

'You don't have to stay here,' she said after a moment. 'There are plenty of hotels in London.'

His lips tightened. 'The key to Polly's whereabouts is here. I can feel it. Until I know where she is—and how I can get her to come home—I'm staying.'

Polly Rafferty's house was just a short drive away from Clara's office, a pretty cottage situated on a meandering lane leading out to the countryside. It was one of Clara's favourite houses; many of her clients had bought the huge new builds that had sprung up on gated estates around the town, large and luxurious certainly but lacking in Hopeford charm.

'Picturesque.' It wasn't a compliment, not with that twist of the mouth.

'Isn't it?' she said, deliberately taking his statement at face value. 'This is the most sought-after area in town, close to the countryside and the train station. There's a good pub within walking distance too.'

'All amenities,' Raff said, looking about him, his expression one step removed from disdainful.

The condescension prickled away at her. It was odd. She had so many clients who talked down to her and her staff and it never got to her; twenty minutes in this man's sardonic company and she was ready to scream.

Ignoring him, Clara unlocked the front door and stood back to let the tall man enter. He stood there for a second, clearly conflicted about preceding her into the house. She waited patiently, a thrill of satisfaction running through her when he finally gave in, ducking to fit his tall frame through the small door.

He was as out of place in the low-ceilinged, beamed cottage as a cat at Crufts. The house was sparingly and tastefully decorated but the designer had worked with the history rather than against it. Rich fabrics, colour and flowers predominated throughout, a sharp contrast with the casually dressed man in jeans and desert boots, an old kitbag hoisted over his shoulder.

He didn't look much like a playboy. He looked like a weary soldier who wanted nothing more than a hot shower and a bed.

'The bedrooms are upstairs,' Clara said, gesturing towards the small creaky staircase that wound up to the next floor. 'I had the main guest room made up for you.

It's the second door on the right. There's an en-suite shower room.'

She should offer to show him up there but every nerve was screeching at her to stay downstairs, to keep her distance. Noticing the weary slant to his shoulders led to seeing the lines around his eyes, the dark hollows under them emphasising the dark navy blue, leading in turn to a disturbing awareness of the lines of his body under the rumpled T-shirt, the way his battered jeans clung to lean, muscled legs.

She squeezed her eyes shut. What was she doing ogling clients? *Pull yourself together.*

Maybe her mother *was* right: it might be time to consider dating again. Her hormones were clearly so tired of being kept under rigid control they were running amok for the most unsuitable of men.

Clara took a deep breath, feeling her nails bite into her palms as she tried to summon her habitual poise. 'The kitchen's through here,' she said, marching back into the hallway and leading the way into the light spacious room that took up the entire back of the cottage. She had always envied Polly this room. It was made for a family, not for one lone workaholic who ate standing up at the counter. She didn't look back as she continued to briskly outline the preparations she had made.

'I stocked up with the usual order but if there is anything else you'd like write it here.' She gestured towards the memo pad on the front of the fridge.

She turned to check if he was following and skidded to a halt, backing up a few steps as she nearly collided with his broad chest. 'Erm, there's a lovely courgette and feta quiche in the freezer, which will make a nice, simple dinner tonight.' Clara could feel the telltale burn spreading across her cheeks and knew she was turning red. She backed away another step, turning her back on him once again, finding safety in the sleek chrome fridge door. 'If you want your dinner provided then Sue, the regular cleaner, will pop a stew or a curry into the slow cooker for you but you must leave a note on the morning you require it or email the office before ten a.m.'

She was babbling. She *never* babbled but everything felt out of kilter. Her whole body was prickled with awareness of his nearness. She turned, smiled brightly. 'Any questions?'

Raff's mouth quirked. 'Is there anything you don't do around here?'

'Your sister employs me to keep the house clean, the cupboards stocked, to take care of any problems. She's a busy woman,' she said, unnaturally defensive as she saw the disbelief in his face. 'I offer a full housekeeping service without the inconvenience of live-in staff.'

'She pays you to stock the fridge with quiche?' But the smirk was playing around his mouth again. Annoyingly.

'My father's quiche,' she corrected him. 'Don't knock it until you've tried it. There's also plenty of salad, fruit and hummus.'

'Beer, crisps, meat?'

'Put it on the list,' she said, wanting to remain professional, aloof, but she could feel her mouth responding to his smile, wanting to bend upwards.

She needed to get out. Get some air and give herself a stern talking-to. 'The pub does food if you want something different,' she said. 'Or there are some takeaway menus on the memo board. You'll be fine.'

'I usually am.'

'Okay, then.' She paused, made awkward by the intensity of his gaze. With an effort Clara pulled on her professional persona like a comfort blanket. 'If you have any problems at all just get in touch.' She held out her card.

He reached out slowly and plucked it out of her hand, his fingers slightly brushing against hers as he did so. She jerked her hand away as if burnt, the heat shocking her. She swallowed back a gasp with an effort, hoping she hadn't given away her discomfort.

'I'll do that.' He was looking right into her eyes as he said it.

'Good.' Damn, she sounded breathless. 'That's everything. Have a nice evening.'

Clara began to back out of the kitchen, not wanting to be the one to break the eye contact. It was as if he had a hypnotic effect on her, breaking through her usual calm, ruffling the feathers she kept so carefully smoothed down.

'Ouch.' Something underfoot tripped her up and she put a hand out to steady herself, her eyes wrenched from his.

'Are you all right?'

'Yes, thanks.' Steadier in more ways than one, relieved to be free of his gaze. She looked down at the trip hazard, confused by the large hessian mouse. 'Oh, how could I forget? Mr Simpkins' usual routine is biscuits first thing in the morning and more biscuits and some fish in the evening. He has his own cupboard under the sink.'

'Mr Simpkins?' He sounded apprehensive.

'The man of the house.' She smiled sweetly. 'I do hope you like cats.'

And surprisingly cheered up by the horrified look on his face, Clara swivelled and walked away.

CHAPTER TWO

CLARA ALWAYS MULTITASKED. She had to—she couldn't manage the homes and lives of the over-privileged if she wasn't capable of sorting out babysitters, dog walkers and hedge trimmers whilst ordering a cordon bleu meal and cleaning a loo. Usually all at the same time. Driving was the perfect opportunity to gather her thoughts and make mental lists.

But not tonight. Her to do lists were slithering out of her mind, replaced by unwanted images of smiling eyes, a mobile mouth and a firmly confident manner.

Her own personal kryptonite.

Luckily this was probably the last she'd see of him. He would be on the early train to London each morning, return to Hopeford long after she had finished for the night and it wasn't as if she personally cleaned the house anyway.

Besides, Polly would be home soon and he would return to whichever beach he had reluctantly pulled himself away from faster than Clara could change the sheets and vacuum the rug. Things would be safe and steady.

So she had felt a little awareness. A tingle. Possibly even a jolt. It was allowed—she was twenty-nine, for goodness' sake, and single, not a nun. It wasn't as if she had taken vows of chastity.

It just felt that way sometimes. Often.

She should enjoy the moment—and make sure it didn't happen again.

Pulling into her parents' driveway, Clara took a moment and sat still in the fading light. This was usually one of her favourite times, the calm after a full and busy day, the moment's peace before other ties, welcome, needed, unbreakable ties, tugged at her, anchoring her firmly.

The house lights were on, casting a welcoming glow, beckoning her in. She knew she would step into warmth, love, gorgeous aromas drifting out of the kitchen, gentle chatter—and yet she sat a minute longer, slewing off the day, the last hour, until she could sit no more and slid down out of the van onto the carefully weeded gravel.

Clara's parents lived in a traditional nineteen-thirties semi-detached house in what used to be the new part of town. Now the trees had matured, the houses weathered and the new town had become almost as desirable as the old with families adding attic conversions, shiny glass extensions and imposing garages. The Castleton house was small by comparison, still with the original leaded bay windows and a wooden oval front door.

It was ten years since Clara had occupied the small bedroom at the back but the house itself was reassuringly gloriously unchanged.

'Evening,' she called out, opening the front door and stepping into the hallway.

'In here,' her father called from the kitchen and, lured by the tantalising smell, she followed his voice—and her nose.

'Something smells good.' Clara dropped a fond kiss on her father's cheek before bending down to sneak a look inside the oven.

'Spiced chickpea and spinach pastries in filo pastry.'

'I'd have thought you'd had enough kneading during the day,' she teased.

'It relaxes me. Have you got the list?'

'Of course.' Clara produced a neatly printed out list from a file in the cavernous bag she rarely ventured anywhere without. She used her father's deli for her customers' food requests whenever possible. He wasn't the cheapest, although, she thought loyally, he was definitely the best, but not one person ever balked at the hefty bill topped up with Clara's own cut. The prestige of knowing it was all locally made and sourced was enough for most people although she knew many of them also shopped at the local discount supermarket whilst making sure her father's distinctive purple labels were at the front of their pantries and fridges.

Clara put the list down onto the one clear part of the counter and mock glared at her father. 'It would save us both a lot of time if you let me email it to you.'

'Email me,' he scoffed as he pulled a selection of dressed salads out of the cavernous fridge. 'I'll be up making bread at six. When do I have time to read emails? Hungry?'

'For your pastry? Always. I'll be back in a moment.' She shook her head at him. Clara was always nagging her father to get more high tech, to get a website, engage on social media. The delicatessen was doing well, more than well, but with just a little marketing spur she didn't see why it couldn't do better, expand into neighbouring towns. The problem was her father liked to do everything himself.

Pot, kettle, she thought with a grin as she tore herself away from the kitchen and walked into the main room of the house where the sitting and dining room had been knocked through to create one big family space.

A large oak table dominated the back and Clara felt the usual lift in her heart when she spotted a small dark head bowed over a half-completed gothic Lego castle. This was what made it all worthwhile: the long hours, the repetitive work, the nights in alone.

'Impressive,' she said. 'Good day, sweetie?'

The head lifted, revealing a large pair of dark brown eyes. 'Mummy! You're late again.'

And just like that the happiness became swirled with guilt even though the comment hadn't been accusatory. The matter-of-factness was worse. Summer didn't expect her to be on time: she hardly ever was.

'Sorry, Sunshine. How was school?'

'Fine.'

Of course it was; everything was fine. Unless it was awesome, the ultimate accolade.

'I'm just going to eat and then we'll head home. Have you finished your homework?'

'Of course,' her daughter replied with quiet dignity before breaking into a most undignified grin as Clara walked around the table and gathered her in close for a long moment. Summer was getting taller, her head close to Clara's shoulders, the baby plumpness replaced by sharp bones and long limbs, but she still gave the most satisfying cuddles. Clara breathed her daughter in, steadying herself with the familiar scent of shampoo, fresh air and sweetness before releasing her reluctantly.

'I'll be no more than ten minutes,' she promised. 'We might have time for a quick half-hour's TV. Your turn to choose. Okay?'

It was like being a child herself, sitting at the kitchen table with a plate full of her father's trial runs whilst he quietly measured, stirred and tasted and her mother bustled from one room to the other whilst relating a long and very involved story about a dimly remembered school friend of Clara's who was, evidently, getting married. According to her mother the entire single population of Hopeford was currently entering wedlock, leaving Clara as the sole spinster of the parish.

Clara knew her mother was proud of her—but she also knew she would give a great deal to see her married. Or dating.

Heck, her mother would probably be more relieved than shocked if she spent every Saturday night cruising the local nightspots for casual sex.

Not that there were any real local nightspots other than a couple of pubs and even if she wanted to indulge the pickings were slim. A grin curved her lips at the thought of strutting into her local and coming onto any of the regulars. They'd probably call her parents in concern that she'd been taken ill!

'Clara.' The insistence in her mother's voice was a definite sign that she had moved on from a discussion of Lucy Taylor's appalling taste in bridesmaids' dresses and wanted her attention.

'Sorry, Mum. Miles away.'

'I was just thinking, why not leave Summer here with us tonight so you can go out?' Clara repressed a sigh. It was as she had feared. All this talk of weddings had addled her mother's brain.

'Go out?'

'Your cousin is back home for a couple of weeks. I know she's planning to go to The Swan tonight. It would be lovely if you joined her.'

For just one moment Clara experienced a rare shock of envy. That had once been her plan, a job and a life away from the well-meaning but prying eyes of her hometown.

'I've got a lot of work to do—I've promised Summer

some time before bed but then I must spend a fun couple
of hours with the timetables.' She attempted a smile. It
wasn't that she minded working all hours but it didn't
sound very glamorous.

'Come on, love,' her mother urged. 'You never get to
go out. Just one drink.'

It would be so easy to give in. Put the computer away
for the evening, go out and get all the gossip about her
cousin Maddie's impossibly exciting life as a stylist on
a popular reality show. But duty called. She had to remain firm.

She couldn't just drop everything for an unscheduled
night out. No, it was absolutely impossible.

'I've been thinking.' Clara wound her hand around the
half-pint glass, pointedly avoiding her cousin's eyes.
'Maybe it's time I should consider internet dating.'

Clara knew she was fairly stubborn. Unfortunately it
was a trait she had inherited from her mother and passed
down to her daughter. United they were a formidable
team and when her dad had added his gentle voice to
theirs she had been quite outgunned.

Clara had been sent out for fun whether she liked it
or not.

And now she was out, she was beginning to wonder
again whether her mother might be right about more than
Clara's need for a night off.

'Internet dating?' Maddie squealed at a pitch that
could cause serious discomfort to dogs. 'Any dating
would be a good start. Isn't there anyone closer to home
though? I have stories about internet disasters that would
make your hair curl. I know you, one disaster and you'll
give the whole thing up. And there will be a disaster.'
She nodded sagely. 'There always is.'

'Nope. I went to school with, babysat for, employed or have been employed by every single man I know in a ten-mile radius without a single spark. And this way I can profile them first, make sure they're suitable.'

'*If* they tell you the truth,' Maddie said darkly. 'Don't contact anyone without clearing them with me first. I know the language they use.'

Clara laughed, trying to quell the unease Maddie's words conjured up. How would she know who to trust? It had been such a long time ago—and she'd got it horribly wrong then. It wasn't just her pride at stake now; there was Summer too. She'd messed up so badly with Summer's own father, any new man in their lives had to be perfect. Her daughter deserved the best. 'I promise, you get first approval.'

'Ooh, we could have a look now.' Maddie had pulled out her phone and was jabbing away at the screen. 'What are you looking for?'

'Sensible, hardworking with good values.' It didn't take Clara long to think. These things counted for far more than the tilt of a mouth or a warm glint in a pair of navy-blue eyes.

'Very exciting. Any speciality? I have accounts with Uniformly Single, Farmers for You, Country Ladies and Gents and Parents Need Love Too. We could see who is available locally! So, hot fireman, beefy farmer or a fabulous father?'

'They are not all real accounts.' Clara stared at Maddie's phone in disbelief. 'I thought you were happy with Olly.'

'I *am*, but he's an actor. First whiff of success and he'll be off. There's no harm in keeping my accounts open and having the occasional peep.'

'Isn't there anyone, you know, normal?' This was a

bad idea. What had she been thinking, mentioning it to Maddie? She'd meant to do some research first. Approach the whole thing in a sensible businesslike way.

'I still think you're better off warming up on someone you know.' Maddie was scanning around the pub hopefully like a hound on the scent. 'Get back in the saddle before you start galloping. There must be *someone* in here you can practise on.'

It was only Tuesday but that hadn't stopped a constant stream of people popping in for a quick drink or settling in for a longer session. The cousins had bagged a prime position at the corner of the L-shaped room and from her comfortable armchair Clara could see all the comings and goings in the friendly local.

She was out so rarely she felt vaguely guilty, as if she were seventeen again, illicitly consuming half a lager shandy and hoping that the barman didn't ask for ID, jumping every time the door opened in case her parents came in to march her home.

Although these days they would buy her another and beg her to stay.

'Hang on.' Maddie froze as she zoomed in on some unsuspecting prey like the expert hunter she was. 'He looks promising. How about him?'

Clara's chest tightened, an unsettling feeling quivering in her stomach as she saw just who Maddie was staring at. This wasn't who she had been looking for all evening, was it? Wasn't the reason her heart had jumped in painful anticipation each time the door opened?

Stop it, she told herself fiercely.

Raff Rafferty was standing at the entrance looking around the pub. As his eyes swept over Clara they stopped and he smiled slightly, raising one tanned hand in greeting. How embarrassing; he'd seen her staring.

Hoping she wasn't blushing too much, Clara snapped her eyes away, regarding her empty glass with every appearance of absorbed interest.

'You *know* him?' Maddie was still staring in undisguised admiration at Raff. 'Things *have* changed around here, and for the better. You've kept him quiet.'

'I don't actually know him.' Clara was aware how unnaturally defensive she sounded and tried to rein it back in. 'He's new—to town, I mean, but he's not staying for long. He's completely unsuitable.'

'Hot and temporary, sounds perfect for a trial run to me. Sure you're not tempted?'

Clara couldn't quite meet Maddie's enquiring gaze. 'Quite sure. His sister is a client of mine.'

'Oh,' Maddie sighed. 'What a shame he's not a new permanent resident. We could do with some eye candy in this town. Hang on.' Maddie perked up. 'He's coming this way!'

Clara's stomach gave that peculiar twist again. It was a shame that stomachs couldn't qualify for the Olympics because by the feel of the double somersault hers was doing right now she was pretty sure she would score highly on rhythmic gymnastics.

'Clara Castleton.' It was said politely but there was a gleam in Raff Rafferty's eye that unnerved her. As if he was laughing at her.

She looked up as coolly as she could. 'The quiche didn't suit after all?'

'It was delicious,' he assured her. 'But I fancied a drink. Can I get you two ladies a top up?'

Raff turned the full beam of his blue eyes onto Maddie and Clara felt her jaw clench as her cousin beamed back. 'That would be lovely,' Maddie said as Clara blurted out, 'Thank you but we are fine.'

'Come and join us,' Maddie invited, shooting a conspiratorial look at Clara.

'I'm sure Mr Rafferty has somewhere he would rather be.' It was Clara's turn to be signalling her cousin with a meaningful look but Maddie wasn't being very receptive.

'That's a shame.' Maddie smiled up at Raff. 'Do you?'

'I don't think so.' Raff was looking amused. 'I don't have any friends here so I'd love to join you, thanks. I'm Raff.'

'Maddie.' She was positively purring. 'Raff Rafferty, that's an unusual combination. Your parents liked it so much they used it twice?'

He grinned, annoyingly at his ease. 'I wish. No, my mother was into Greek mythology so when she knew she was having twins she decided to name us after the heavenly twins, Castor and Pollux. My sister escaped with Polly. I wasn't so lucky.'

'I like it,' Maddie said. 'It's unusual.'

Clara caught Raff's eye in a moment of shared amusement, an intoxicating warmth spreading through her at the laughter in his eyes.

'You wouldn't like being called Sugar all the time,' Raff assured her cousin. 'After one week at prep school and five fights I changed it to Raff. Now only my grandparents use my real name.'

'It could have been worse.' Clara had been thinking. 'If she'd known you were a boy and a girl you might have been Apollo and Artemis.'

'Good God, literally!' Raff looked horrified. 'I will never despise my name again. What a lucky escape I had. For that I absolutely must get you a drink. What are you drinking?'

Clara opened her mouth fully intending to say no again and more firmly this time, but something extraordinary happened and the words in her head changed as soon as they left her mouth. 'Thank you,' she said. 'I'm drinking the local pale ale.'

Raff hadn't intended to leave the house tonight. It had taken him over two days to get back to England and once the plane had touched down at Gatwick he had headed straight to Hopeford like a homing pigeon aiming for a new world record.

He'd hoped that the key to finding Polly would be right here in the surprisingly shapely form of Clara Castleton or hidden somewhere in Polly's house—and he was going to find it whatever it took.

Only it turned out that being mad with his twin wasn't enough; he simply couldn't invade her privacy. One step into her study and he had frozen. He might not like it but Polly was entitled to her secrets.

For a long time they had only really had each other. Now they didn't even have that. The moment she'd started blaming Raff for their grandfather's blatant favouritism it had all fallen apart and everything Raff did made it worse. Even when he'd finally left, finally had the courage to follow his own path, he couldn't make it right.

He didn't know *how* to repair the damage—if it was even repairable. But whatever she thought, she could rely on him. He'd find out where she was, what was wrong and he'd fix it. Fix them.

So here he was. She'd asked him—told him—to come home and he had. But now what?

His mood had turned dark, exhaustion and frustration making rest impossible, introspection unbearable. Five minutes of television channel hopping later and Raff had had enough. It was time to go and check out the ridiculously quaint town his sister had bequeathed him.

Otherwise he was going to end up having a conversation with the cat. Mr Simpkins knew more than he was letting on; he was sure of it.

It didn't take Raff long to explore. Hopeford defined sleepy small town, was the epitome of privileged. The narrow streets closed in around him, making it hard to breathe. This rarefied atmosphere was exactly what he had been running from the last four years.

He'd breathed a sigh of relief at the familiar sign hanging outside a half-timbered building. A pub, a chance to get his head together, regroup. Four years of changing places, of new jobs, new challenges all had one thing in common. A local watering hole. A place to find out the lie of the land, find some compatible companionship and quench his thirst. The Swan was a little older, a lot cleaner and a great deal safer than his last local but he didn't hold that against the place.

Especially when he walked in and clapped eyes on Clara Castleton.

It had taken a moment or two to recognise her. Sure there was the same feline tilt to her long-lashed eyes, the same high cheekbones but that was where the similarity ended. This version had let her hair down, metaphorically as well as physically, the strawberry-blonde length allowed to fall in a soft half-ponytail rather than ruthlessly pulled back.

Even more disturbingly the lush full mouth was curved in a generous smile.

But none of that mattered. Clara was a means to an end, that was all. Mr Simpkins might not be ready to talk but a friendly night in the pub and he might have Clara telling him anything he needed to know. She must know more than she was letting on—she ran every aspect of Polly's life.

'Thank you for the drink…' oh, no, prim was back '…but I really need to be going.'

Raff glanced at his battered old watch. His grandfather had given him a Breitling for his twenty-first but he preferred the cheap leather-strapped watch he had bought first trip out. Bought with money earned by his own sweat, not by family connections.

'It's still early. Are you sure you don't want to stay a bit longer?'

'It's a work night,' she reminded him. Raff had been doing his best to forget. Tomorrow he was going to have to try and dig up something smart, get up ridiculously early and join all the other pack rats on an overpriced, overcrowded train. No matter he hadn't made this exact journey before. He knew the drill.

The only surprise was whether his particular carriage would be overheated or freezing cold. Unlike Goldilocks, Raff was under no illusions that it would be just right.

'Yes, it is,' he agreed. 'Unless you tell me where Polly is and save me from a day in the office tomorrow?'

She sighed as she got to her feet, gathering her bag and coat in her arms. 'I already told you…'

He'd blown it. He was too tired to play the game properly. He made one last-ditch attempt. 'I'm sorry. Let me walk you home.'

'Why? So you can interrogate me some more?' She shook her head, the red-gold tendrils trembling against her neck.

'No.' Well, only partly. 'It's good manners.' In some of the places Raff had lived you always saw the girl home. Even if it was the tent next to yours.

She shot him an amused glance. 'I think I'll be okay.'

'I won't,' he assured her. 'I'll lie awake all night worrying I failed in my chivalric duty. And I'll have to go to work tomorrow all red-eyed and pale from worry and they will all think I've been out carousing all night. Which will be most unfair as it's barely nine p.m.'

'I don't live far.' But it wasn't a no and she didn't complain as he drained his drink and followed her out, noting the blush that crept over her cheeks as she said goodbye to her cousin, who pulled her close for a hug and to whisper something in her ear.

'Where to?' he asked as he fell into step beside her. She walked just as he'd thought she would, purposeful, long strides in her sensible low-heeled boots.

'I live above the office.'

That wasn't a surprise. 'All work and no play...' he teased. It wasn't meant with any malice but to his surprise she stopped and turned, the light from the lamp post highlighting the colour in her cheeks.

'Why do people think it's a bad thing to concentrate on work?' she asked. Raff didn't reply; he could tell the question wasn't really aimed at him. 'So I work hard. I want to provide stability for my daughter. Is that such a bad thing?'

Daughter?

'I didn't know you were married,' he said and wanted to recall the words as soon as he said them. This wasn't the nineteen fifties and she wasn't wearing a ring.

'I'm not,' she said coldly and resumed walking even faster than before.

Way to go, Raff, nice building of rapport, he thought wryly. *You'll get Polly's address out of her in no time.*

He cast about for a safer topic. 'How old is she? Your daughter?'

'Ten,' she said shortly but he could feel her soften, see her shoulders relax slightly. 'Her name's Summer.'

'Pretty.'

'I was in a bit of a hippy stage at the time,' she confessed. 'Summer says she's glad she was born then because I'd probably call her something sensible and boring now. But it suits her.'

'Does she live with you?'

'I know the flat's not ideal for a child,' she said. Why did she assume every question was a criticism? 'But there's a garden at my parents' and she spends a lot of time there.'

'I spent a lot of time with my grandparents too.' During the school holidays it had been the only home he'd known.

'Polly said they brought you up.' It was a simple statement; there was no curiosity or prying behind it but it shocked him all the same. Polly was confiding in Clara, then. No wonder she hadn't put the welcome mat out for him.

What else had his twin said?

'Do you see a lot of Polly?' The question was abrupt and he tried to soften it. 'We're not really in touch any more. I'm glad she has a friend here.'

'We're both busy but we catch up when we can.' It wasn't enough but he didn't know how to push the issue without frightening her off.

And at least Polly had someone looking out for her. He tried again. 'If you care for all your clients the way you look after Polly, no wonder you're so busy.'

'Not all of them. Some just want cleaners and gardeners, others like to outsource all their home maintenance. Or I can provide babysitters, a shopping service, interior designers. Often it's just putting people in touch with the right services.'

'And taking a cut?'

Clara smiled. 'Of course. But some people need me

on call twenty-four seven, to pick up dry-cleaning, pick the kids up from school, buy last-minute gifts. Whatever they need I supply.'

She sounded so calm, so utterly in control and yet she was what? Late-twenties? A couple of years younger than Raff.

'Impressive.' He meant it.

'Not really.' She sounded a little less sure. 'None of it was really planned.' She had slowed down, her step less decisive, nervously twisting the delicate silver bangle on her wrist round and round. 'I had Summer and I needed to work. Oh, I know my parents would have let us live there. They wanted me to go to university but I couldn't just offload my responsibilities onto them. There's a lot of incomers in Hopeford, busy commuters with no time and a lot of money. I started cleaning for them and things kind of snowballed.'

She made it sound so easy but Raff was in no doubt that building her business up from cleaning services to the slick operation she ran today had taken a lot of grit and determination.

'I'd love Summer to have a proper home.' She sounded a little wistful. 'A kitchen like Polly's and a huge garden. But living above the office is practical—and it's ours. It was a better investment than a house at this stage in our lives.'

Investment, plans. It was like an alternative universe to a man who lived out of a kitbag and changed countries more frequently than he had his hair cut.

'This is me.' Clara had come to a stop outside the leaded bow window. She stood at the door calm, composed. 'Do you think you can find your way back or do I need to walk *you* home now?'

Her face was unreadable and there was no hint of flirtatiousness in her manner. Was she trying to be funny or was she completely serious? Raff couldn't figure her out at all. 'I have an excellent sense of direction,' he assured her. 'So...'

'Goodnight, then.' She offered him her hand, a quaintly old-fashioned gesture. Their eyes met, held; Raff could see uncertainty in her gaze as she stood there for one long second before she abruptly stepped back and turned, hands fumbling with her keys.

And she was gone without even one last backward glance.

Raff let out a long breath, an unexpected stab of disappointment shocking him. *Fool,* he told himself. *You're not here to flirt and, even if you had the time or inclination, since when were ice maidens your style?* He was tired, that was all, the jet lag clouding his judgement.

He had a job to do: find Polly, get her home, return to his real life. Nothing and no one, especially not the possessor of a pair of upwardly tilted green eyes, was going to get in his way.

CHAPTER THREE

WHAT WAS THAT?

Clara looked up as the front door creaked, but it was only someone walking by. Old buildings and narrow pavements equalled many creaks and bangs. It was a good thing she wasn't a nervous type.

Nor was she usually the door-watching type.

But it was getting to be a habit.

First at the pub, now today. And yesterday.

She was pathetic.

Especially as she knew only too well that Raff Rafferty hadn't even set foot in Hopeford in the last three days. He had, she guessed, boarded the train to London on Wednesday morning along with all the rest of the commuters but, according to Sue, the woman who usually cleaned the Rafferty house, he hadn't been back since. His bed was unrumpled, no dishes had been used, no laundry left. Either he was extraordinarily tidy, so tidy even Sue's legendary forensic skills couldn't find any trace of him, or he was staying in London.

This was all Maddie's fault. If she hadn't pulled her aside, told her to invite him in for coffee. 'It's not always a euphemism,' she'd said, mischief glinting in those green eyes so like Clara's own. Only brighter, livelier, flirtier. 'Not unless you want it to be…'

Of course she didn't. And coffee at that time of night was irresponsible anyway—inviting someone in for a cup of peppermint tea was probably never misconstrued. She could have done that. But did she want to? Want that tall, confident man in her flat? Even for one innocent cup of hot herbal beverage?

Because there was one moment when he had looked down at her and her breath had caught in her throat, every nerve end pulsing with an anticipation she hadn't felt in years. If she had stepped forward rather than backwards, if he had put his hands on her shoulders, angled his mouth down to hers, what would she have done?

Clara slumped forward. This all proved that she had taken the whole not-dating, stability-for-Summer thing just a tiny bit too far. If she had allowed her mother to set her up, just occasionally, for dinner and drinks with one of the many eligible men she had suggested over the years, then one measly hour in the pub, one small drink, wouldn't have thrown her so decidedly off kilter.

Raff Rafferty had been a tiny drop of water after a long drought. It didn't mean he was the *right* kind of water but just one taste had reminded her of what she was missing. What it felt like to have an attractive man's attention focused solely on her.

Even if he did have an ulterior motive that had nothing to do with Clara herself.

'That's a fearsome frown. Planning to murder someone?'

After all that waiting she hadn't even heard the door open.

She hoped he hadn't seen her jump, that the heat in her cheeks wasn't visible. 'I exact a high penalty for unpaid bills.'

Clara had been hoping that three days' absence had

exaggerated Raff's attractiveness. They hadn't. He was just as tall, as broad as she remembered but the weary air she had glimpsed last time was unequivocal. He looked as if he hadn't slept for a week.

Dark circles shadowed his eyes, unfairly emphasising the navy blue, his face was pale under the deep tan, the well-cut shirt was wrinkled.

'I need a favour.' He didn't even crack a smile. 'Just how full a service do you offer?'

Clara gaped at him. 'I beg your pardon?'

'I asked…' he spoke slowly, clearly, enunciating every word '…how full a service you offer. I need a girlfriend and I need one now. Can you supply me with one, or not?'

If he hadn't been so tired… If he hadn't been quite so desperate, then Raff might have phrased his request slightly differently. As it was it took a while for the outrage on Clara's face to penetrate the dense fog suffocating what was left of his brain.

'You're not the first person to ask me for extra services,' she said finally, contempt dripping through her words. 'I admit, though, you have surprised me. I would have thought you were quite capable of hiring your own special help.'

Something was wrong, Raff could dimly tell, but he fixed on the positive.

'So you can help me?'

'Normally it's the bored wives that ask for something extra. Someone to help *clean out the guttering, trim the borders.*' She put a peculiar emphasis on the last few words. 'I do like to help them when I can. I usually send Dave round. He might be seventy-three but he's steady up a ladder. They don't ask again.'

Raff tried to sort out her meaning from her words. He was quite clearly missing something. 'Do the gutters need doing?' he asked. 'Surely that's your preserve, not mine. Do what you think best. Look, it's been a long day, a long week. Can you help me or not?'

She looked at him levelly but to his astonishment there was a cold anger in her eyes. 'Not. This is a concierge service not an escort service. Now please leave. Now.'

'What?' Raff shook his head in disbelief as her words sank in. 'I don't want… I didn't mean. For crying out loud, Clara, what kind of man do you think I am?'

'I don't know,' she retorted, eyes hot with fury now. 'The kind of man who walks away from his family, the kind of man who doesn't have to work for anything worth having! The kind of man who wants to rent a girlfriend—'

'Yes! A girlfriend. Not an escort or a call girl or whatever your dirty little brain has conjured up.' Now his anger was matching hers, the righteous fury waking him up. 'If I was looking for someone to sleep with I could find them, don't worry your pretty little head about that, but that's not what I'm looking for. I need someone to come to a few functions with me, to gaze lovingly into my eyes and to convince an autocratic old man that I might just settle down with her. Now, is that something you can help me with?'

If he thought his words might make her feel guilty, get her to back down, then he rapidly realised he was wrong. She uncoiled herself from her seat, rising to her feet to look up into his face, her eyes fixed on his, full of righteous anger.

'This is about fooling your grandfather? Why? So he doesn't cut you off? I have had it up to here with poor little rich boys who live their lives according to who holds the purse strings. I wouldn't help you if I had a hundred suitable girls working for me. Now please leave.'

Raff choked back a bitter laugh. 'I don't have to justify myself to you, Miss Castleton, but for your information my grandfather is ill. He's in the hospital and I am under strict orders not to upset him. So I either start dating one of the unfortunate women on the shortlist he drew up for me, fake a relationship or be responsible for yet another dangerous rise in blood pressure.'

He smiled over at her, sweet and dangerous. 'Tell me, Miss Know-it-all, which do you recommend?'

'A shortlist?'

That had stopped Miss Judgemental in her tracks.

Raff didn't want to let go of the anger and frustration, didn't want to try and tease a responsive grin from that pursed-up mouth, coax a glint out of those hard emerald eyes.

Especially as her words had cut a little deeper than they should. No virtual stranger should have the power to penetrate beneath the shield he so carefully erected yet her words had been like well-aimed arrows piercing straight into his Achilles heel.

Whether it was the lack of sleep, the taut tension in the room or the craziness of the situation, he didn't know but, despite his best intentions, a slow smile crept over his face.

'Do you want to see it?'

Clara's eyes widened. 'You have it with you?'

'I needed something to read on the train. Here.' He pulled the sheaf of papers out of his coat pocket and held them out. 'Names, pedigrees, biographies and photographs.'

She made no attempt to take them. 'Thorough.'

'He means business,' Raff agreed, letting the papers fall down onto the desk with an audible thump. It felt as if he had put down a heavy burden. 'Now do you understand?'

She still wasn't giving an inch. 'Couldn't you just talk to him?'

Raff laughed. 'No one *just talks* to Charles Rafferty. We all tug our forelock and scuttle away to do his bidding. Or run away. Both Polly and I took that route.'

He sighed and picked the papers up again, shuffling them. 'I owe you an apology. It doesn't matter even if you do know where Polly is…' she opened her mouth to interject and he held up his hand '…but I'm sure you don't. She's covered her traces well and I don't blame her.'

The only person he could blame right now was himself. They were so estranged she couldn't, wouldn't confide in him.

Concern was etched onto Clara's face. 'Is she okay?'

Raff shook his head. 'I doubt it. It turns out that great profits and great PR aren't enough. My grandfather showed his gratitude for an another excellent year's trading by telling Polly he was never going to make her CEO, and he is going to sign the company over to me.'

'Ouch.'

Clara sank back into her seat, a sign the battle was over. Thank goodness. Raff had been through enough emotional wars in the last few days. He leant against her desk, grateful for the support. 'That was just the start of it.' Raff ran a hand through his hair. Damn, he was tired. What a ridiculous mess. 'We owe him a lot, Polly and me. It's hard to stand up to him. But this was so wrong I had to say something.' His mouth twisted as he pictured the scene. 'I managed to stay calm but he got completely worked up and ended up collapsing in the most dramatic fashion.'

Raff was aware that he was making light of the situation, but the moment his grandfather had clutched his chest and collapsed was branded in his mind. 'I thought we'd lost him.'

Clara reached a tentative hand across the desk, then pulled it back, seemingly unsure how to react. 'Is he okay?'

'Angina. Apparently he's kept that a secret along with his plans. He's to be kept quiet and not allowed to get worked up, which is a little like telling a baby not to cry. And he is taking full advantage of the situation.' Despite himself Raff grinned. He had to admire his grandfather's sheer bloody-mindedness.

'As soon as I walked through the hospital-room door today he handed me this list.' He held up his hands. 'I know I should have told him the truth right then but seeing as the last time I upset him he collapsed, I didn't. I admit I panicked—next thing I knew I was telling him I had a girlfriend already, it was pretty serious and I was agreeing to bring her along to meet him on Sunday. Two days isn't a long time to find a convincing fake girlfriend, you know.'

Clara leant back in her chair and regarded him solemnly but Raff could swear those cat's eyes of hers were sparkling. 'You seem to be in somewhat of a predicament.'

'I am.' He nodded, trying his best to look downcast as hope shot through him. He needed someone cool, someone professional, someone who understood the rules. She would be perfect, if he could just make her see it.

'I don't understand why you lied in the first place. A

few dates isn't going to kill you, is it?' She was looking stern again.

Raff sighed. It was so hard to explain without sounding like an arrogant idiot. 'I have no intention of sticking around and raising expectations would be unfair.'

'Presumptuous.'

'Hardly.' He laughed but there was little humour in it. 'These women aren't the sort to get carried away, at least not where their futures are concerned. The Rafferty name and fortune is old enough and big enough to put me on several "most eligible bachelor" lists. Why do you think I stay out of the country?'

'Is marriage and a family really so terrible?' For a moment Raff thought he saw sadness shimmering in her face but one blink and it was gone, replaced by her usual cool professionalism.

'No,' he admitted. 'But not for me, not yet. There's a lot I need to do before I'm ready for that kind of commitment.'

If he ever was. He'd seen firsthand just what marriage could do. He still didn't know what was worse: his grandmother staying put out of martyred duty or his mother fleeing as soon as things got tough. Either way it had been hard for Polly and him.

Not that any of his school friends had fared much better. Outside gravy adverts, he still wasn't entirely sure that happy families existed.

'Look, I appreciate that I approached this all wrong but I could really use your help.'

She shook her head. 'It doesn't feel right.'

'Clara, please.' He wasn't too proud to beg. 'You would be perfect: you own your own business, know Polly. My grandfather will adore you.'

'Me!' Was that panic on her face? But there was something else too. She was trying to hide it but she was intrigued.

Raff pressed the point home. 'Look, I'll pay you by the day, even if I only need you for a couple of hours, and I'll owe you. There must be something I can do for you. Don't you need an eligible date at all? Wedding, christening, bar mitzvah?'

'My diary's empty.' But her lush mouth was tilted up into a smile. 'Socially at least.'

'Even better,' he said promptly. 'I'm promising you fine dining, glamorous parties and a clothes allowance. Think of me as a particularly masculine fairy godfather whisking you away to the ball.'

'I can't just drop everything.' But, oh, she looked tempted. 'I have a business, a daughter. What's she supposed to do whilst I'm out gallivanting with you?'

'Gallivanting and drumming up business,' Raff said slyly. Bullseye. Temptation was giving way to interest. 'Think of the contacts you'll make.'

'Contacts in London,' she demurred.

'With your talents it wouldn't matter if they lived in Antarctica,' he assured her. 'You'll be soothing out the wrinkles in half of London's lives in no time. And it won't be for long. I'm hoping to get everything sorted out within a month, six weeks tops. I'm sure your parents won't mind babysitting.'

'No.' She looked down at her computer screen, shielding her expression from him. 'I don't know, Raff. I'd have to call in a lot of favours, for work and Summer. I need to think about it.'

'I'll pay you double your daily rate and cover all costs. And if we're successful a bonus. Ten thousand pounds.'

'That's the second time this week you've offered

me ten thousand pounds.' Clara smiled sweetly at him. 'Burning a hole in your pocket?'

Ten thousand pounds. Small change to someone like Raff Rafferty but not to her. Add the daily double rate and this job looked as if it could be pretty lucrative.

A much-needed cash injection. Sure, things were ticking along nicely, turnover was healthy. But so were her outgoings. She chose her staff carefully and paid them well, used the best products, made sure she had people on call at all hours. She had a brilliant reputation but maintaining it cost money. It made it hard to save enough to expand and she was wary of borrowing.

If this extra job lasted six weeks she could make fifteen thousand pounds more than she had budgeted for. Enough for recruitment and advertising in a wider area, another small van. Maybe she could even engage a part-time PA for the office? She handled so many of the emails and calls whilst she was out and about. Keeping the office open and staffed in business hours would be fantastic.

It would be added security. For her and for her daughter.

But it would mean spending those next six weeks with Raff Rafferty. A man who unnerved her, flustered her. Could she handle it?

He was still perched on her desk, affecting nonchalance, but the tense set of his shoulders was a giveaway. He wasn't as relaxed as he liked to make out. He needed her.

Automatically she tapped at her keyboard, lighting up the dormant screen and clicking onto her emails, the very act beginning to calm her taut nerves. The long list of unread emails in bold might daunt some people but she found them soothing, purposeful and she scanned through the subject lines looking for an answer, a reason to turn him down.

Or an excuse to say yes.

Her inbox was the usual mixture of confirmations, enquiries, queries, staff correspondence and sales, nothing meaty, nothing distracting at all. She was about to close it down when a name caught her eye. Pressure filled her chest, making it hard to breathe, and for one long moment everything, the room, Raff Rafferty, her work disappeared.

An email from Byron.

Clara blinked, unsure whether she was seeing things or if the email was actually there. Her hand hovered over her mouse, unable to click as dizzying possibilities filled her mind. *He was coming over, he wanted to see Summer, to be involved.*

Her daughter wanted for nothing, except for an interested, loving father. Could that be about to change? This was the first time he had contacted her in ten years—that had to be a good sign, right?

'Clara, are you okay? If you don't want to do it that's fine. I'll call in a favour or two. I'd have preferred to keep things professional, that's all.'

'What?' With difficulty Clara fought her way past all the possibilities and emotions swirling dizzily around her brain. 'Sorry, I just need to read this. I'll be with you in a second.'

She noticed detachedly that her hand was shaking as she clicked on the email, the words were dancing in front of her eyes, making no sense at all. She blinked again, forcing herself to concentrate.

Dear Miss Castleton…

The opening line made her reel back, shocked by its formality, but, grimly determined, she read on.

Both Mr Byron Drewe and Mr Archibald Drewe will be visiting London the first week in May and would like to know if it is convenient for you to meet with them to discuss your daughter's future. Her presence is not required at the meeting.

Please send me any dates and times that week that would be convenient for you to meet and I will let you know the final arrangements and venue nearer the time. Any expenses you incur will of course be covered. Please provide the relevant receipts.

On behalf Mr Drewe Jr

Her first communication in years—and it was from Byron's secretary.

Her head was suddenly clear, the dizziness and anticipation replaced with hotly righteous anger. How dared they? How dared they dismiss Summer, summon Clara as if she were a servant? How dared they offer to pay her expenses—as long as she provided receipts like an untrustworthy employee?

Although Byron's father had always thought she was a gold-digging good-time girl, she had just naively hoped Byron believed in her, believed in their daughter. Despite everything.

Byron had spent so much time stringing her along, promising her they would be a family, but he hadn't even had the guts to tell his father about the baby. And once his father found out that was the end.

It was a straight choice: Clara and Summer or his family fortune. Turned out it was no choice at all.

Even then he had lied, promised he'd find a way, that

he loved her, loved Summer. Her heart twisted painfully. He had just wanted her to leave quietly, to not make a scene.

Clara's eyes locked onto the photo that sat on her otherwise clutter-free desk and the anger left just as suddenly as it had arrived. Dark hair, dark eyes, just like her father. Clara's feelings didn't matter here; Byron's behaviour didn't either. Summer was the one who counted and this was the first communication she had had from her daughter's father in years. He wanted to meet. Maybe he wanted to be involved.

Or maybe not. But she had to try. If only she didn't have to do it all alone. Of course her parents would come with her if she asked, but she didn't trust them not to threaten to castrate Byron with the butter knife—or actually do it. Not that he didn't deserve it but it wasn't quite the reconciliation she was hoping for.

Her parents were amazing. Supportive and loving and endlessly giving with their time. Clara couldn't have managed without them. But every now and then she couldn't help but wonder what it would be like to be part of a couple, to have a co-parent. Someone who was there all the time to laugh with at the funny bits, to burst with pride at all the amazing things only a parent could truly understand. To help when things got a little bumpy.

It wasn't that she minded being both mother and father to her daughter, she just wished for Summer's sake that she didn't have to be.

Clara scrolled back to the top of the email and reread it intently. If it were just going to be Byron, then meeting him alone would have been difficult, probably emotional, but eminently doable. His father's presence changed everything. He was a hard, harsh man. Clara sagged. She tried so hard to be strong but she really didn't want to do this alone.

'Here, drink this.' A coffee slid across the desk, rich and dark. 'You look like you've had a shock.'

Clara reached out for the white mug, absurdly touched by the gesture. 'Thanks,' she said, blinking rapidly. *No, don't you dare cry,* she told herself fiercely.

'I make a good listener, you know.' He was back leaning against her desk, cradling a mug of his own, concern in his eyes. 'Besides, you know a lot of my family secrets.'

Clara opened her mouth, a polite rebuff on the tip of her tongue, but closed it as a thought hit her.

Maybe she didn't have to be alone after all?

The memory of his earlier offer hung there tempting, intoxicating. He owed her a favour. Anything she wanted. What if she didn't have to face Byron and his father alone?

'I'll do it.' The words were sudden, abrupt, loud in the quiet office. 'If you guarantee me double time in office hours, treble at evenings and weekends, the bonus at the end of the six weeks and...' she swallowed but forced herself to look up, to meet his eyes '...and you will accompany me to one meeting. Agreed?'

It was Raff's turn to pause, the blue eyes regarding her quizzically, probing beneath her armour. 'Agreed,' he said finally.

Clara exhaled the breath she didn't even know she was holding. 'It's a deal.' She held out her hand. 'I'll see you on Sunday.'

His hand reached out to take hers, folding over it in a gesture that was far more like a caress than a handshake. 'Tomorrow. I'll pick you up at noon.'

'But...' Clara tried to withdraw her hand but it was

held fast in his cool grip '…I thought you needed a date
to meet your grandfather on Sunday.'

He smiled, the devilry back in his eyes. 'I do, but
we need to get to know each other first. You and I are
going on a date.'

CHAPTER FOUR

IT WAS BECOMING an annoying habit, somehow agreeing to the outrageous when she meant to refuse.

She'd felt sorry for him, fool that she was. She'd been lured in by a weary expression, candour and charm. A moment of personal weakness.

And yet there was a certain excitement about getting dressed up, about going somewhere other than The Swan. About going out with an undeniably attractive man.

Even if it wasn't a real date.

It was probably a good thing she had said yes. It was so long since she had been on any kind of date she was bound to be a little rusty, a little awkward. This was an opportunity to practise without any pesky expectations hanging over her.

And that was all this fizz in her veins was. It certainly had nothing to do with Raff Rafferty. It was about a pretty dress, a chance to wear her hair down, to put on a lipstick a little darker, a little redder than she wore for work. A chance for heels.

No, Clara decided, eying herself critically in the mirror, she didn't look too shabby. The vintage-style green tea dress was flattering and demure teamed with black patent Mary Janes and her hair was behaving for once, falling in a soft wave onto her shoulders.

She glanced at her watch. Five minutes. She wanted to be downstairs, sitting at her desk, working when he arrived. She might be all dressed up but this was work. Letting him upstairs, into her private space, was a step far too far.

And there could be no blurred lines.

She took a long look around the small, cosy sitting room. It wasn't the grandest of homes, the fanciest. But it was hers, hers and Summer's. Her sanctuary.

She'd bought it, paid for it, chosen the wallpaper, decorated it. Okay, there was a patch where it wasn't perfectly lined up but it was hers.

Raff would dominate the room, suck all the air out of the space.

Make it unsafe.

The urge to sink onto the overstuffed velvet sofa was almost overwhelming. To play hooky from work, from responsibilities, from this devil's pact. She could curl up with a large bar of chocolate and a Cary Grant film, block out the world for a few blissful hours. She pulled her phone out of her bag—one call and this whole crazy arrangement would be over before it had even begun.

Just one click. So easy.

Her finger moved to the contact list icon and hovered there.

Brrriiiing! The doorbell's loud chime echoed through the room, making her jump.

Panic caught in her throat, making breathing difficult for one long second. Clara put her hand to her stomach and took a deep breath, purposefully clearing her mind, filling her lungs, allowing herself a moment to calm.

This isn't real, she told herself. *This is work. This is my business. I'm happy to clean loos, I'll stock shelves, I even pick up dog dirt. I should be looking forward to a*

few weeks of socialising instead. Any of my staff would
kill to swap with me.

She could do this.

But a part of her would much rather be scrubbing
a room out from top to bottom, picture rail to skirting
boards, than spend any more time alone with Raff Rafferty.

And the other part of her was looking forward to it
just a little bit too much.

'Relax, this is supposed to be fun.' Raff threw an amused
look over at his passenger. Clara sat up ramrod straight,
clutching the seat as if it were her last hope. 'I'm a safe
driver.'

'In a very old car.'

'She's not old, she's vintage.' He patted the steering
wheel appreciatively. 'These Porsche 911s were *the* It
Car in their day.'

'In the middle of the last century.'

'She's not quite that old. This is a seventies' design
classic.' It was the only car Raff had ever owned. She
might be red, convertible and need a lot of loving maintenance but she was a link to his father, the only link
he had.

'The seventies,' Clara scoffed. 'The decade that taste
forgot.'

Raff grinned. 'Sit back, Clara. Enjoy it—the wind in
your hair—if you'd let me put the top down that is, the
green of the countryside flashing by. What's not to love?'

Clara was twisting the silver bangle she was wearing
round and round. 'A date, you said. I thought you meant
a drink in The Swan or, if you wanted to go crazy, a meal
at Le Maison Bleu. This isn't a date. This is kidnap.'

'We are supposed to have been together for a few

months. Mad about each other.' Her body got even more rigid if that was at all possible. Raff suppressed a smile. 'So, we need to create a relationship full of memories in just one day. Now we can do this the easy way and actually enjoy ourselves or we can endure a torturous afternoon full of monosyllables and long silences.' His mouth quirked. 'Now, if we were faking a marriage then the latter would be fine.'

Was that a smile? An infinitesimal relaxation of all those rigid muscles?

'What's your favourite colour?'

'My what?' That made her move. Her head swung round so fast he thought she might get whiplash.

'Your favourite colour?'

She shook her head. 'I don't even...why on earth do you want to know that?'

'I'll go first.' He leant back into the leather seat, enjoying the cold of the steering wheel under his hands, the purr of the engine. 'Okay, my favourite colour is sea blue, the sea on a perfect sunny day. Favourite food is a good old-fashioned roast dinner, which is the boarding school boy in me, I know, but there are times when just the thought of Yorkshire puddings keeps me going. I didn't think I was a cat or a dog person but after three days of Mr Simpkins I am definitely veering towards the canine. You?'

He sneaked a look over at his passenger. She was still gripping onto the seat but her knuckles were no longer white. 'If I'd known there was going to be a quiz I'd have prepared,' she said, but her voice was less frosty.

It took a few long moments before she spoke again. 'Okay, green, I think. Spring is my favourite season. I hate it when the trees are bare. I grew up with cats so I'll stick up for Mr Simpkins. What was the other one?

Food? It's not sophisticated but when I was travelling and eating all this amazing street food I craved cheese sandwiches. My dad's cheese sandwiches. Home-made bread, cheddar so mature it can't remember being young and his patented plum chutney.'

'Just a simple sandwich?'

'As simple as it gets in my house. Dad's a foodie.'

'You went travelling?' That was unexpected. Maybe they had something in common after all. 'I can't exactly visualise you with a backpack! How old were you?'

There was a long pause. 'Eighteen,' she said finally.

'Where did you go?' As Raff knew all too well, most people jumped at the opportunity to recount every second of their travels. It could be worse than listening to other people's dreams. Clara Castleton was obviously the exception; her silence was so chilly it was as if he'd asked her to recite *The Rime of the Ancient Mariner*. Backwards.

'Thailand to start with,' she said reluctantly after the pause got too long. 'Cambodia, Vietnam and then Bali and on to Australia.' She paused again. 'I was there for two years.'

Raff shook his head. 'When I was eighteen I could barely find my own way to university, let alone travel halfway across the world. Your parents must have been worried sick.'

She laughed, a dry hard laugh with no humour in it. 'I was so sure I was invincible I think I had them fooled too.'

Fooled? Interesting word.

'I planned for so long I don't think there was room to worry, really.' She wasn't really talking to him, he realised, more lost in the past. 'My grandfather was in the merchant navy and he had always told me all these stories of places he had been to. I wanted to see it all. Other kids have posters of pop stars on their wall, I had maps and routes and pictures of magical places I wanted to go to. I was babysitting at thirteen, running errands for neighbours and every penny went into my travel fund. I was going to start out in Asia then Australia, New Zealand, on to Japan then South America, finishing off with a Greyhound trip round the States.'

He could picture her. Intent, focused, planning on conquering the world. 'Did you get to go? Did you see all of those places?'

'No.' Her voice was colourless. 'I had Summer instead.'

'Hang on.' He turned and looked at her rigid profile. 'Did you have your daughter while you were away?'

'She was born in Australia.'

He whistled softly. 'That must have been tough. So you cut your adventures short, flew home and became the responsible, capable woman you are today.' He shook his head. 'Quite some achievement.'

He thought he was such a tough guy but his adventures were orderly by comparison. He always knew where he was going to sleep that evening even if it was in a sleeping bag in a shared tent; he had a ticket back arranged, plans for a month of surfing and partying organised. He even got a wage, for goodness' sake. Clara had taken off at an age most people were still figuring out the Tube and had spent three years travelling. Even a pregnancy and a baby hadn't slowed her down.

When she didn't answer he turned to look at her; she was looking out of the window but her body was slumped. It wasn't the posture of someone who had achieved something remarkable. It was more like despair.

'Are you going to tell me where we are going?' she

asked, straightening and turning to him with a polite smile.

The confidences were obviously at an end.

'I don't need to tell you,' he said as he smoothly turned the car through a pair of metal gates, the only break in a sea of barbed-wire fencing that ran along one side of the road screening off the fields beyond. 'We're here.'

'We're what?' Clara twisted in her seat and looked around her, horror on her face as she took in the barbed wire. 'You *are* kidnapping me. Where are we? What is this?'

'*This* is one of the premier activity sites in the country.' Raff flashed her a smile. 'I hope you like mud.'

'You want me to do what?'

Clara wasn't sure what was worse. She ticked the offending items off on a mental list. Lists usually were soothing, bringing order and meaning.

She wasn't sure anything could bring meaning to her current situation.

First, the mud. There was certainly a lot of it, all greeny-brown, glutinous and deep. Second, the outfit. All that time spent wondering what to wear, turned out she needed baggy camouflage trousers, desert boots that had been worn by who knew how many other smelly, sweaty, muddy feet and a shapeless T-shirt that was the exact colour of the mud. Yep, it all came back to mud.

Mud that she, Clara Castleton, was supposed to be trampling, running, heck, apparently she was supposed to be crawling in it. On her belly.

Which brought her to number three. Men. Smirking men. Okay, toned, built men, the kind that actually stretched out their T-shirts in all kinds of good ways, who filled out the baggy trousers with bulging thighs, who wore the mud on their faces with aplomb. Men who belonged here as she most definitely did not.

The most annoying of the men, 'Call me Spiral', as *if* that were really his name, began to repeat the instructions in the same loud bark. 'Run through that trough, climb that rope, go over that bridge, swing across the ravine, crawl under the net, slide...'

'I heard all of that the first two times.' Clara folded her arms and glared up at him, deliberately ignoring the fourth and most annoying thing of all: a palpably amused Raff Rafferty. 'I'm still not clear why.'

'Because I told you to,' Spiral said with no hint of irony. 'Now get your butt over to the starting line.'

'Come on, Clara.' Raff was openly grinning. 'This is supposed to be fun. Where's your sense of adventure?'

Back in Australia. Left behind with her backpack, her travel journals and her well-thumbed traveller's guide.

'*This* is your idea of a date?' She rounded on him. 'What's wrong with a walk, a picnic, doves and flowers?'

'Too obvious. Besides, I had the chance to try this place out and see if I want to hire it for a staff conference. I'm multitasking. I thought you'd approve,' he said with a self-righteous air that made Clara want to smack him—or tip him into the mud that suddenly looked a lot more tempting.

'This isn't just a lousy date, it's a cheap date?'

Raff leant in close, his breath sweet on her cheek. 'It's a fake date and you are on triple time. Enjoy it. Think about what a lovely story it makes.'

Clara gritted her teeth. 'One for the grandkids?'

'In our case one for my grandfather. Do you want to go first or shall I show you how it's done?'

Eying the long trail of ropes, platforms, nets and pits, Clara felt her stomach drop. This was going to be incredibly undignified. But there was no way she was going to look weak in front of him. 'I'll go.'

She refused to look back as she walked to the start line, painfully aware that all the conversation had stopped and every khaki-clad man was staring at her, lips curled with amusement. They were waiting for her to fail. To give up.

They were in for a surprise. She hoped.

'Come on,' Clara told herself fiercely as she stood at the rope marking the beginning and stared out at what looked like miles of hell. The trail started with a long, shallow trough that Clara was supposed to run through. Correction, wade through. The trough was filled with the ubiquitous mud and led to a cargo net that she was sure was higher than her house.

That was just the start.

Weekly Pilates might be good for her stress levels but it hadn't prepared her for this.

'On the count of three,' Spiral roared. 'One, two, three!'

Clara hesitated for less than a second and then, with a muttered curse, pushed herself forward, managing not to yell as she sank calf deep into the cold, gloopy mud.

'Faster,' Spiral yelled. 'Are you a man or a mouse?'

Answering him would have used up more oxygen than he was worth. Clara set her mouth mutinously and forged on. Too slow and she would prove the smirking men right, too fast and she knew she'd pitch face first into the mud. She set herself a steady trot, trying to ignore the cold, clamminess on her lower legs and the sucking noise as she pulled her leg out of the mud and put one hand onto the rope net, ready to pull herself up the impossible height.

Her eyes were focused on each obstacle; there was

no room in her mind for anything but the task. Spiral's encouraging shouts, the cheers of the other staff were just background noise. Clara was aware of nothing but the hammering of her heart, the pounding of the blood in her ears, the burn in her thighs and her arms as she pulled, swung, jumped, waded and crawled. She had no idea how long she had been there. Minutes? Hours?

Heck, it could have been days.

'Come on, Clara.' How on earth had Raff caught up with her? He was breathing hard, his hair damp with exertion, the dark blue eyes alight with life. She should be mad with him; she was absolutely filthy, totally exhausted, every muscle hurt and people kept yelling at her. And yet…

Adrenaline was pumping through her so fast she was almost weightless; the whole world had contracted to this place, this task. She was alive. Really, truly alive.

She reached out for the rope swing, and missed. Immediately Raff was there, one arm steadying her as she leant further forward off the narrow wooden platform, reaching out into thin air.

'Got it!' Giddy with triumph, she grabbed the rope and pulled it back towards her. Putting both hands firmly on it, she wrapped one leg around it and tried to jump on it, slithering back down to the platform as she missed. 'Darn it!'

'Here, let me.'

Clara wanted to tell him no, that she had this, but he was too quick, steadying the rope and, as she jumped again, giving her a quick push up. A jolt of electricity ran through her as his hand pressed against her back but before she could react he had pushed and she was off, swinging through the air.

Her limbs were trembling with the exertion as she

reached the last obstacle, the crawl net. To conquer it successfully she had to lie down, fully face down, in the mud and wiggle her way under ten metres of tight net.

She took a deep breath, the oxygen a welcome tonic to her tired, gasping lungs, and flung herself down into the oozing depths, pushing herself under the net and wiggling through the endless claustrophobic dark, wet mud until she reached the final rope. Once her head was through she gulped in welcome, blessed, clean air before painfully pulling the rest of her out. She lay there collapsed in the mud for five seconds, too exhausted to try and get to her feet.

The mud didn't seem so bad any more. She couldn't tell where it ended and she began. She had turned into some kind of swamp monster.

'That was a very good try.' Spiral's loud tones intruded on the muddy peace and Clara forced herself to pull onto her knees. 'Well done, Clara.'

A glow of pride warmed her. 'Thanks,' she said, drawing her hand across her face, realising too late that rather than wipe the mud off she was adding to it. Spiral held out one meaty hand and effortlessly pulled her to her feet, wrapping a blanket—khaki, of course, she noted—around her shoulders and, grabbing a mug from a plastic picnic table, pressed it into her hands.

Tea. Milky, sugary, the opposite of how she usually liked it. It was utterly delicious.

'You survived.' Raff had eschewed his blanket but was cradling his tea just as eagerly as she was. 'What did you think?'

'That was…' filthy, hard, undignified, unexpected '…exhilarating.'

He broke into an open grin. 'Wasn't it? Do you think

my staff will enjoy it? I thought that it could be the performance award this year. Followed by dinner, of course!'

'That sounds good.' As the adrenaline wore off Clara was increasingly aware of how cold she was; she suppressed a shiver. 'I hope you're going to let them get changed before dinner.'

'I'm kind like that.' He eyed her critically. 'Talking of which, you look freezing. The showers are back in the changing room. Go, warm up, get changed and then I owe you lunch, anything you want.'

Hot water, clean clothes, food. They all sounded impossibly, improbably good. 'You do owe me,' she agreed, putting the mug back onto the table before taking a few steps towards the low stone building where nirvana waited. She paused, impelled by a sudden need to say something, something unexpected.

'Raff,' she said. 'I had fun. Thank you.'

It was the last thing he had expected her to say. Standing there completely covered in mud, the baggy trousers plastered to her legs, the filthy T-shirt clinging to every curve. Raff had expected sulking or yelling, even downright refusal. He didn't expect her to thank him.

He'd known the challenge would shake her up, had secretly enjoyed the thought of seeing prim and judgemental Clara Castleton pushed so far out of her comfort zone—turned out the joke was on him.

'I'm glad,' he said, aware of how inadequate his response was. 'I thought you'd enjoy it.'

Clara smiled. A proper, full-on beam that lightened her eyes to a perfect sea green, emphasised the curve of her cheeks, the fullness of her mouth. She was dirty, bedraggled and utterly mesmerising. The breath left his body with an audible whoosh.

'Liar,' she said. 'You thought I'd hate it. And you were this close…' she held up her hand, her forefinger and thumb just a centimetre apart '…this close to being right.'

'Yes.' The blood was hammering through his veins, loud, insistent. All he could focus on was her wide mouth, the lines of her body revealed so unexpectedly by her wet clothes. What would it be like to take that step forward? To pull her close? To taste her?

Dangerous.

The word flashed through his mind. It would be dangerous; she would be dangerous. Workaholic single mothers were not his style no matter how enticing their smile. Women like Clara wanted commitment, even if they didn't admit it.

They played by different rules and he needed to remember it—no matter how tempted he was to forget.

CHAPTER FIVE

'THAT WASN'T TOO BAD.' Clara's smile and tone were more than a little forced. At least she was trying.

Which was more than his grandfather had.

'It was terrible.' Raff shook his head, unsure who he was more cross with: his grandfather for being so very rude, or himself for expecting anything different.

He *had* expected his grandfather to be terse and angry with him; it would take more than a suspected heart attack and a week in hospital for Charles Rafferty to get over any kind of insubordination even from his favourite grandson. It was the way he had spoken to Clara that rankled most.

'He's not feeling well and it can't be easy being cooped up in bed.'

Raff appreciated what Clara was trying to do but it was no good; her determined 'little miss sunshine' routine wasn't going to fix this.

'He practically accused you of being a gold-digger,' he pointed out. 'I shouldn't have let him speak to you like that.' He had been poised to walk out, stopped only by her calming hand on his arm, holding him in place, the pressure of her fingers warning him to keep still, keep quiet.

'I wasn't going anywhere.' Clara stopped as they reached the hospital foyer; the marbled floor, discreet wooden reception desk and comfortable seating areas gave it the air of an exclusive hotel—if you ignored the giveaway scent of disinfectant and steamed vegetables. 'I've been called worse.' A wounded expression flashed across her face, so fleeting Raff wasn't sure if he had imagined it.

'Thank you.' The words seemed inadequate. Despite his grandfather's antipathy she had been a dignified presence by his side, not too close, not clingy but affectionate and believable. He was torn between embarrassment that she had witnessed his grandfather's most petulant behaviour and an uncharacteristic gratitude for her silent support.

'No problem.' She was saying all the right things but her tone lacked conviction. 'It's my job after all.'

'Come on.' He needed to get out of here, away from the hospital, away from the toxic mixture of guilt and anger, to push it all firmly away. This was why he preferred to be abroad. He could be his own man out in the field. 'Let's go.'

Clara opened her mouth, about to ask where they were going, and then she slowly shut it again. At least they were in the centre of London—it might be a little damp but whatever Raff had in mind it was unlikely to involve mud.

And Raff obviously needed to blow off steam. He was keeping himself together but his jaw was clenched tight and a muscle was working in his cheek. Clara had been treated like dirt before, dismissed out of hand— but her own family had always been there to support her. She couldn't imagine her own grandfather looking at her with such cold, disappointed eyes. Even a teen pregnancy hadn't shaken his love and belief in her.

Polly had called Raff 'The Golden Boy' but it seemed

to her that his exalted position came with a heavy price. No wonder he had needed to employ Clara, to take some of the pressure his demanding grandfather was heaping on as he took advantage of his illness and frailty. An unexpected sympathy reverberated through her—Raff's need to be as far away from his family as possible was a little more understandable.

She kept pace with a silent, brooding Raff as he walked briskly through the busy streets expertly avoiding the crowds of tourists, the busy commuters and the loitering onlookers. Clara rarely visited London despite the direct rail link; if you asked her she would say she was too busy but the truth was it scared her. So noisy, so crowded, so unpredictable. The girl who once planned to travel the world was cowed by her own capital city.

But here, today, it felt different. Friendlier, more vibrant, the way it had felt when she was a teenager, down for the day to shop for clothes in Camden and hang out in Covent Garden where Maddie hoped to be talent-spotted by a model agency whilst Clara spent hours browsing in the specialist travel bookshop. Was it even still there? All her books and maps were boxed away at her parents' house. Maybe she should retrieve some of them, show them to Summer.

'I need to organise a nurse to look after him,' he said, breaking the lengthy silence. 'The hospital won't allow him home without one. He needs to have a specialist diet too, and he is going to hate that.' His mouth twisted. 'At this rate it's going to be weeks before I can talk about the company with him again.'

'Isn't there anyone else who can intercede? Your grandmother?'

Raff shook his head. 'They're separated. She'll have

a go, if I ask her to, but he's never quite forgiven her for leaving.'

Clara knew that Polly and Raff had been raised by their grandparents but not that they had split up. She swallowed, her throat tight; it was becoming painfully apparent how little she knew of Polly's life. They were supposed to be friends and yet she had no idea where she was or why she'd gone.

But was Clara any better? She didn't confide either, happy to keep the conversation light, to discuss work and plans but never feelings, never anything deep. Maybe that was why they were friends, both content with the superficial intimacy, their real fears locked safely away.

'Have they been split up long?'

'Nearly twelve years.' He gave her a wry smile. 'She waited until after Christmas our first year at university. Didn't want to spoil the holidays, she said. We were just amazed she made it that long. She'd wanted out for a long time.'

'I can't imagine your grandfather is easy to live with.' That was an understatement.

He huffed out a dry laugh. 'He's not. Poor Grandmother, from things she let slip I think she was on the verge of leaving when we came to live with them. She only stayed for Polly and me. Now she lives in central London and takes organised trips, volunteers at several museums and spends the rest of her time at the theatre or playing bridge. She's very happy.'

'What about your parents?' She flushed; curiosity had got the better of her. 'I'm sorry, I don't mean to pry.'

'That's okay. We are meant to be dating, after all, and none of this is exactly state secrets.' He didn't look okay though, his eyes shadowed, his mouth drawn into a straight line. 'My father had a stroke when we were eight.'

'I am so sorry.' Tentatively she reached out and touched his arm, awkward comfort. 'That must have been awful.'

'We thought he was sleeping. The ambulance man said if we had called 999 earlier...' His voice trailed off.

Cold chilled her, goosebumping her arms, her spine as his words hit her—they'd found their father collapsed? Her heart ached for the two small children who had to suddenly grow up in such a terrible way.

'The stroke was devastating.' There was a darkness in his voice, the sense of years of regret, of guilt. 'He had to go into a home—oh, the very best home, you know? All luxury carpets and plush chairs but we still knew, even at that age, that it was a place where people went to die.'

Clara felt for the familiar cold curve of her bangle and began to twist it automatically; she wanted to reach out and hold him, hold the small boy who had to watch his father disintegrate before his eyes.

'Our mother couldn't handle it,' Raff continued, still in that same bleak tone. 'She went away for a rest and just stayed away. So my grandparents stepped in, sent us to boarding school and gave us a home in the holidays—and my poor grandmother had to wait ten years for her escape.'

'Her choice.' Clara knew she sounded brisk, the way she sounded when encouraging Summer to sleep without a nightlight, to go on a school trip, to walk to the corner shop on her own. 'It was the right thing for her at the time. There's no point dwelling on what-might-have-beens. You go mad that way.'

She knew all about that. If she hadn't stayed in that particular hostel, hadn't met Byron. If she'd tried harder with his father, if she'd stayed in Australia. 'Our lives are littered with the paths not taken,' she said. 'But if we spend all our time staring wistfully at them we'll never see what's right in front of us.'

'A sick, unreasonable grandfather, a missing twin and an unwanted job?' But the dark note had gone from his voice and Clara was relieved to see a small smile playing around the firm mouth. He stopped in front of her and turned to look at the golden building in front of them. 'We're here. Welcome to the millstone round my neck.'

It had been a long time since Clara had set foot in Rafferty's. The flagship department store occupied a grand art deco building just off Bond Street and, although it was a little out of the way of the tourists pounding bustling Oxford Street and Regent Street, it was a destination in its own right. Discreet, classy and luxurious; just the name Rafferty's conjured up another era, an era of afternoon tea, cocktails and red, red lipstick.

Tourists flocked here, desperate to buy something, anything, so they could walk away with one of the distinctive turquoise and gold bags; socialites, It Girls and celebrities prowled the halls filled with designer items. Anyone who was anybody—and those who aspired to be—drank cocktails at the bar. Rafferty's was a well-loved institution, accessible glamour for anybody with money to spend.

As a child Clara had visited the store every Christmas to see the spectacular window displays, admire the lights, to confide her wish-list to Father Christmas. It had been one of the highlights of her year—and yet she had never brought Summer. She had never even made the seventy-five-minute-long journey into London with her daughter. London was too big, too noisy, too unpredictable.

But as she stood on the edge of the marble steps, remembering the breathless excitement of those perfect days out, Clara's throat tightened. Choosing the perfect gift, admiring the other shoppers, having afternoon tea in the elegant restaurant, those memories meant Christmas to her. How could she not have passed those memories on to her daughter?

To keep Summer safe? Or to keep Clara herself safe?

Maybe, just maybe, she was a little overprotective.

'Are you going to stand there all day or are you actually coming in?'

Clara swallowed. It must be nice to be Raff Rafferty. Adored heir to all this. So sure of yourself, so confident that you could treat life as one big joke.

And yet there were contradictions there. She might disapprove of the lies he was feeding his grandfather—although after the cold, hostile meeting this morning she understood them. But what was he fighting for? The right to live on his trust fund? The right not to do a day's work?

Clara tried to remember what exactly Polly had told her about him. Not much, which was odd in itself; they were twins after all. She said he was spoilt, that she had to work three times as hard and still didn't receive equal recognition. That he was 'messing around abroad somewhere'. Clara had assumed that he was travelling, partying, having fun. After twenty-four hours in his company she wasn't so sure.

He was arrogant and annoying and treated life as one big joke but he didn't *seem* lazy, didn't seem careless of his family's ties and expectations. He had come running the second he'd thought Polly was in trouble and according to the nurse had spent three days and nights at his grandfather's bedside.

Yep, he was definitely a puzzle but, she reminded herself, he was none of her business. And none of this was real, no matter how surprisingly easy it was to forget that.

'I thought you went away to escape Rafferty's,' she said, walking up the famous curved steps to meet him.

'To escape *running* Rafferty's,' he corrected her, escorting her through the famous gilt and glass revolving doors with a light touch on her elbow.

As soon as he took his hand away the spot he had touched felt cold. Clara had to resist the temptation to rub it, to try and get the heat back.

They had entered a massive circular room topped with an ornate glass dome. It was the heart of Rafferty's, an iconic image, immortalised in film, photos and books. Looking up, Clara saw the famous galleries ringing the dome, three storeys of them. Each storey took up the entire block and was filled with a myriad of desirable items: food, clothes, jewellery, books, accessories, pictures, lamps, rugs.

Down here on the beautifully tiled ground floor the world's leading make-up and perfume brands plied their wares, stalls set out in a semi-circle around the foot of the dome. The middle was always reserved for themed displays and, at Christmas, the giant tree that dominated the room.

It was a wonderland. And the man standing next to her wanted to throw it all away.

'It's not that I'm not proud of Rafferty's,' he said, as if he could read her thoughts. 'It was like having our very own giant playground. We could go anywhere, do anything. Polly would walk around talking to all the staff, finding out what they did and how everything worked. I'd usually be hidden away with a stash of sugary contraband in a stock cupboard somewhere.'

'Sounds idyllic.' She could see it too, a cheeky-faced blond urchin charming his way through the store.

'It was,' he sighed, a faraway look in his eye. 'This was our real home. We held every birthday party here. I had my first kiss in this very room with Victoria Embleton-Jones. She was taller than me and a lot more sure of herself. I was in love for a whole week and then she dumped me for an older man with less sweaty hands and a car. I was devastated.'

'My heart's breaking. How old were you?'

'Fourteen. It took me a whole month to get over her. I still get nervous shakes when I meet anyone called Victoria.' His face was solemn but he couldn't hide the gleam dancing in his eyes.

Clara resisted the urge to snort. 'No wonder this place is so special to you, filled with such poignant memories.' She looked around at the bustling, chattering, spending throngs. 'I used to come here when I was a child.' It felt oddly like a confession. 'Afternoon tea was always a highlight of the holidays. I felt so sophisticated.' She sighed at the memory of delicate porcelain teapots and plates filled with cakes. Clara put a hand to her suddenly hollow stomach; it had been a long morning. 'Is that why we're here?' She tried not to sound too hopeful.

'It's not time for a tea break yet, Miss Castleton.' He shook his head. 'I don't know, can't get the staff these days. First we work and then we reward ourselves with as much cake as you can manage.'

'Work?' Heat washed over her; how had she misread the situation so badly? 'If you need a PA I can certainly supply one.'

'I have a perfectly good if rather terrifying PA. She disapproves of me almost as much as you do.' Raff grinned at her flushed and confused denial. 'No, it's time we went shopping.'

'Shopping? I do grocery shopping, as you know, presents as well, but I contract out personal shopping and interior designing...' She was babbling again but couldn't seem to stop.

'Look around, Clara. You're in the world's most famous department store. I could click my fingers and summon a personal shopper for almost anything you could imagine. No, we are going to get you some clothes.'

She gaped at him. 'I have clothes!'

Raff looked her over, sweeping her up and down assessingly. Clara had to fight every individual muscle to make it stay still; the urge to cover herself protectively, shield herself from those keen eyes, was almost overwhelming.

'You have suits,' he said finally. 'Sharp, businesslike suits. Which is great for the office but no use when you're with me. You have jeans and T-shirts and you have a few pretty dresses like the one you are wearing. That's all fine but none of that will do for black-tie dos, for cocktail parties or any of the other dull but apparently necessary events Polly wastes her free time at.'

'Cocktail parties?' The nearest Clara got to a cocktail party was trying to decide between red or white wine at Sunday lunch. 'I didn't expect...'

'I told you it would be time consuming.' His gaze was steely now. 'I also said I would pay you handsomely and make it worth your while in any way necessary. Unfortunately Rafferty's needs to be present at these events. Grandfather can't and Polly won't, until I track her down and beg her to come home. So it's down to me.'

He looked as if he would rather be sitting alone with Mr Simpkins.

'But you, Clara Castleton, are both my secret weapon and my shield. Your very presence will hopefully steer conversation away from dull topics like where I have been and what my plans are whilst simultaneously saving me from match-making mothers and their eager daughters. For that you need clothes. And luckily for you I am temporarily running an establishment that supplies pretty much any outfit you desire.'

'Wait a minute.' She eyed him suspiciously. 'Have you been sneaking through my things?' Raff's assessment of her wardrobe had been depressingly close to the mark.

Raff took another step closer and took her arm, the touch sending a jolt of electricity shooting up, settling at the base of her stomach, his proximity making every nerve buzz. 'I don't need to. I started working here when I was fourteen and spent at least six months in every department.' He shot her an amused grin. 'I was very successful in ladies' wear.'

'That doesn't surprise me,' she muttered.

'So if you're ready…' he ignored the interruption '…let's shop.'

'You will make someone a very good husband one day.' Clara eyed the rail of clothes that Raff and Susannah, the personal shopper he had co-opted to help them, had picked out. 'Forget the name and fortune, any man who can shop like you will be snapped up.'

Raff leant back against the wall. In a stark contrast to the opulence of the outer store the private changing rooms, exclusively for the use of those rich or lucky enough to secure the services of a personal shopper, were a study in sleek minimalism. The walls were a steely grey, the sofas chic, uncomfortable-looking studies in white and black; in this environment the clothes were the stars.

'It's a good thing one of us showed some interest,' he said. 'Poor Susannah certainly earned her commission today. I don't think she's ever met anyone who dislikes clothes as much as you do.'

Clara bit just as he knew she would. 'I like clothes well enough,' she said indignantly. 'I'm just not into fancy clothes or fancy designers or fancy prices.'

Raff suppressed a smile. He might be playing fairy godfather but this Cinderella wasn't at all interested. She'd probably be far more comfortable cleaning the hearth and making the pumpkin into pies than going to the ball.

'Or fancy shoes...' he said provocatively.

'If feet were supposed to be that elevated...' Clara began.

'Then our bone structure would be quite different,' he finished. 'I know, you told me at least three times and poor Susannah twenty. Normally women weep with gratitude after she supplies them with shoes, not lecture her about osteology. Come on, Cinders, enjoy the glass slippers.'

'Cinderella probably almost broke her neck rushing down those stairs in just one shoe.'

She wasn't giving an inch. He shook his head, his grin wide. 'Fairy tales must be a barrel of laughs at your house. It's important that you play the part well and that means dressing the part too. You don't have to keep any of it after we're finished: sell them and give the proceeds to charity, turn them into bunting. They're yours. Personally I'd say enjoy them. There must be a huge demand for sequinned shifts in Hopeford.'

Her mouth tilted upwards. Her smile was irresistible;

maybe it was a good thing she didn't unleash it often. 'Oh, there is. Perfect for a quiet drink at The Swan.'

'We don't have to take them all,' he pointed out. 'I think you need about six cocktail dresses, the same amount in day dresses and shoes and bags as well. Come on, Cinders, the sooner you try them on and make some decisions, the sooner you can have that cake.'

'I think I preferred the mud,' Clara said, but she unhooked the silver sequinned shift and began to carry it to the curtained-off area at the back. She paused at the curtain and turned back, her eyes lowered, cheeks flushed. 'I feel really uncomfortable about this, Raff, you buying me these clothes. It's one thing paying me for my time but this feels a step too far.' She raised her eyes, meeting his with obvious difficulty. 'I can't begin to offer to pay you for them. I'm sure that I can manage with what I have.'

Raff found himself short of breath, unable to formulate any kind of reply. He had been out with enough women to consider that he had a pretty good grip on the feminine mind even if he had been thrust into a single-sex school long before puberty, but he hadn't seen this coming.

Not one ex, from the trust fund socialite to the vegan gardener, had ever turned down a free outfit from Rafferty's.

He wasn't sure whether he admired her pride—or found her stubbornness frustrating. 'Well technically I won't be buying you anything, they're a gift from Rafferty's, but remember I'm not playing Professor Higgins,' he said as offhandedly as he could. 'I'm just ensuring you have the right outfits for the job I have hired you to do. I supply the, what did you call them? Instruments of torture? You wear them.'

She looked at him searchingly for a long moment before nodding, a short reluctant agreement. 'Of course,' she grumbled, 'these clothes aren't designed for real women. If I was a size-zero giraffe I might find this easier.'

Raff ran his eyes over her approvingly. Clara wasn't built like a model, it was true, nor did she eat like one, thank goodness. The year after university, full of pent-up energy he couldn't expel at work, he had partied hard and dated several models and socialites. He had soon got bored with the shallow crowd he was running with.

And women who thought a piece of lettuce meant a full dinner.

No, give him someone like Clara, not too tall, not too small, curves in all the right places. That shift she was holding, for instance, it would fall to mid-thigh, showcase those fantastic legs, cling to the curve of her bosom.

The room felt very small, just a curtain separating him from the area where Clara would be unbuttoning all those tiny buttons, slipping her dress off, replacing it with the short shift.

He took in a deep breath. It was warm in here, roasting in fact. He should talk to someone about the temperature.

'I think you'll look perfect,' he said hoarsely. 'Why don't you get started? I'll just be...' He waved at the entrance. 'I need to get something.' A brandy, a cold shower, some air.

Left alone, Clara felt curiously deflated. There had been something in Raff's eyes. Something hot, something terrifyingly honest. Something that had awakened feelings she had spent so long hiding from: what it was like to be wanted, what it was like to want.

Clara sank down into the hard-backed chair, the sole

piece of furniture in the spacious curtained-off area. For the first time in a really long time she wished she had someone to lean on, to confide in.

Raff, Byron's impending visit, deciding how to best use the money Raff was paying her. There was so much going on she didn't know where to turn.

But there was no one. She didn't want to worry her mother, Summer was too young, Maddie so busy. She had nobody. It hit her like a blow to the stomach as hot, unwanted tears pricked at the backs of her eyes; she blinked them away, wrapping her arms around herself as if she could ward off the unwanted knowledge. She would be so ashamed if her mother or cousin or the handful of friends she kept in contact with guessed just how she felt.

Lonely.

'Come on, Clara, where will self-pity get you?' She hadn't succumbed when she found out she was pregnant, only eighteen, thousands of miles away from home. She had stayed strong when Byron walked out of her life a month before their baby was born.

She wouldn't, *couldn't* give in now. She had a wonderful, healthy daughter, a thriving business. She was lucky, even if it was hard to remember that sometimes.

Slowly, feeling a little punch drunk, Clara rose to her feet and began to unbutton her dress. She was here to do a job. Feelings had nothing to do with it.

The shift was heavy and yet it felt wonderfully cool and soft against her skin, the sequins sparkling as the spotlights hit it. Reflected in the many mirrors that lined the room, Clara gave in to the temptation to pirouette, loving the way the fabric flattered her. Raff was right: annoyingly, she did feel more confident, more sociable in this fabulous, exorbitantly expensive dress.

Muttering, she forced her feet into a pair of strappy

heels. She had thought that pairing silver shoes with a silver dress would be too much, that she would end up resembling a giant glitterball, but she had been wrong. The outfit looked amazing even with bare, pale legs, minimal make-up and a ponytail. Her stomach fluttered at the thought of really going out dressed like this; hair, make-up, accessories. Raff on her arm.

If she could just walk in the shoes that would be a considerable bonus.

A rustle from the other side of the curtain alerted her to another person's presence. Raff must have returned.

Clara took another look in the mirror. Was that really her? So elegant? The shoes added another four inches to her height, giving her legs the illusion of endless length. The urge to hide, tear off this costume and become her own safe self again was almost overwhelming but Clara sucked in a deep breath. She *would* walk through the curtain; she *would* show Raff.

She would hopefully see that heat in his eyes again.

Heart hammering, the wobble in her step not solely caused by the unfamiliar heels, Clara pulled the curtain open, a self-deprecating remark on her lips. But there was no need to utter it.

The room was empty. Another rail of clothes and matching accessories had joined the first one.

Her stomach plummeted as the adrenaline disappeared. It must have been Susannah she had heard. 'Fool,' she muttered. Clara chewed her cheek, indecisive. Should she wait, try on something else, look for him? Unsure, she walked to the door and peeked out, worry turning to irritation as she saw him, right in front of the door, deep in conversation with a small brunette who was smiling up at him.

'Clara?' Darn it, he had spotted her. 'Sorry, I bumped

into an old colleague.' Was it her imagination or did he hesitate over the word 'colleague'?

'Hi, I'm Lisa.' The brunette smiled over at Clara. 'It's so great to see Raff. I thought he was in Afghanistan.'

She thought what? Beach bum or adrenaline junkie, either way Afghanistan was the last place Clara imagined Raff Rafferty.

Or was it? A picture flashed into her mind. That first afternoon, his face grey with weariness, the kind of weariness from hours and hours of travel, sitting in trucks and small airport waiting rooms not from the pampered world of First Class. The battered jeans, the old kitbag.

None of it had added up at the time but she'd been so convinced that she knew the man she was dealing with she hadn't even stopped to consider that her preconceptions might be skewed.

'No, not this time,' he said with a quick glance over at Clara. Was that embarrassment in his eyes? 'I was in Jordan. We're trying to make sure there are some medical facilities in the camps there but I was needed at home so had to take some leave. How about you?'

Lisa blushed. 'I'm based back in the UK at the moment. Did you know I married Mike, Dr Hardy?'

'I had heard. Congratulations. I did a brief stint with him out in Somalia. He's a great bloke.' Again a swift, almost pleading glance at Clara.

Somalia, Afghanistan, Jordan? Polly had said that Raff was abroad, she had been dismissive, giving Clara the impression that he was partying on a beach somewhere, not working in some of the most dangerous places in the world. Wasn't she worried about him?

'Mike is setting up a paediatric programme here in London for kids that just can't be treated in the field so I'm based here too now. It's not the same but there's a lot to do. Actually…' Lisa eyed him speculatively '…this could be a massive piece of luck running into you like this. What are you doing in five weeks' time? Will you still be here?'

'I think so. Why?'

Lisa clasped her hands together and looked up at Raff hopefully. 'We're holding a fundraising ball, all the great and the good digging deep, you know the kind of thing! We had Phil lined up to speak but he had to pull out. Could you speak in his place?'

Raff shifted from foot to foot, his expression one of deep discomfort. Clara watched him with some amusement.

Good, she thought, *let him get out of this.*

'People don't want to hear from me,' he said eventually. 'They want to hear from the medical teams. They're the ones with the real stories.'

'We have doctors and nurses and helicopter pilots and patients,' Lisa assured him. 'But no one understands that without you guys there wouldn't be a hospital—or water or electricity or a single bed. Turning a dusty piece of desert into a hospital? That's the real heroism. We just turn up when it's ready for us. Don't you agree?' she asked Clara.

Clara looked at Raff with her most innocent expression. 'I really do,' she said. 'He'll be there, don't worry. I guarantee it.'

'Really? That's brilliant. Raff, come along to the office this week and we'll sort out slides and I'll let you know how long you have to speak for. Make it funny but real as well, try and make them cry. That's always worth a few more noughts on the cheque!'

'I'll see what I can do.' He slid his gaze over to Clara. 'I'm sure Clara will be happy to help me. You'll have a bit longer to wait for that cake though, Clara. You need a dress fit for a ball, and a pair of glass slippers too.' His eyes dropped to her feet, wobbling in the thin-heeled sandals. 'I'll tell Susannah to bring the highest she can find.'

CHAPTER SIX

CLARA UNZIPPED THE silver shift and let it spill to the floor. She knew Raff was on the other side of the curtain but his silence was absolute.

Fine, if that was the way he wanted to play it, there was no way she was going to be the one to crack.

She bent down and picked up the dress, carefully putting it on the hanger. Still no sound, not even a sigh. Anticipation clenched at her stomach as she slipped the next outfit, a wide-skirted silk affair in a vivid green, off the rail and put it on, barely bothering to check the mirror before wrenching the curtain aside.

'And?'

He was sitting on the sofa, lounging back seemingly without a care in the world. 'The shoes don't go.'

'They go with the other dress. I didn't change them.' Seriously? Shoes? That was what he was thinking? She wouldn't ask, she wouldn't, she wouldn't... 'Okay. Spill.' For goodness' sake, her self-control was legendary. She prided herself on it! But the need to know was burning her and she didn't want to examine why. 'Who was that?'

Raff got to his feet with leonine grace and sauntered over to the rail. 'I think we agreed on the red shoes for that outfit, didn't we? It'll work very well for lunches.

What?' He was regarding her with faint surprise. No wonder. Clara was aware she resembled a fishwife more than a lady-who-lunches, hands on hips and head back. 'I did introduce you. That was Lisa. We worked together.'

'Yes, in Somalia,' Clara said as patiently as she could manage. 'Why were you in Somalia?'

'I worked with her husband in Somalia,' Raff corrected her. 'I knew Lisa in Sri Lanka. I think...' he finished doubtfully. 'It might have been Bangladesh.'

'Mercenary or spy?' The words burst out before she could stop them.

'What?' The look of utter shock on his face was almost comical.

'You keep quiet about what you do, you work in some of the most dangerous places on earth, it has to be one or the other.' It was the only thing that made sense.

'Because spies and mercenaries love to throw fundraising balls?' How she hated that amused smile. He had of course honed in on the only flaw in her thinking.

'Part of your cover.' Okay, not the best idea she'd ever had.

'Interesting theory. I like it. I always fancied myself as a suave, martini-drinking type. Sorry to burst your little fantasy but nothing so exciting.' He paused and handed her another dress, a fifties-style halterneck that Clara secretly rather liked. 'Here, try this on. I'm a project manager for Doctors Everywhere.'

Oh.

Kitbags, dangerous places, fundraising balls, hospitals. That made sense. Reluctantly Clara let go of her visions of chase scenes, fancy cars, an evil mastermind bent on world domination.

'Doctors Everywhere?' she echoed as she obediently accepted the outfit and tottered her way back to the curtain.

Of course she had heard of them; they provided healthcare in the Third World, in refugee camps, in war spots.

They were incredibly well respected. Not the natural playground of playboys. Which meant that every little preconception she had was wrong.

Clara changed on autopilot, so many thoughts tumbling around her brain it was as if her head had joined the circus.

Somehow the emotion she could most easily identify was anger. She pushed away the thought that this might be a little unreasonable. After all, what Raff Rafferty did with his time was really none of her business.

He had made it her business, she argued back as she fumbled with the buttons at the back and cautiously zipped up the tight bodice. Employing her, introducing her to his grandfather, buying her these exquisite, over-priced, really very flattering clothes.

He had made her complicit.

The curtain made a most satisfying swoosh as she pulled it open, and she stomped forward only wobbling twice. Damn, she was still wearing the stupid sliver shoes. No wonder Cinderella had discarded her glass slippers; she was probably in agony by midnight.

'Doctors Everywhere?'

'Yep.' He was still standing up, leaning against the back wall. The plain colour of the backdrop suited him, made the hair a little blonder, the eyes even bluer. Not that she was noticing. Not at all.

Oh, no, she was putting her hands on her hips again. Ten years of careful, calm control and yet one day with this man and she was unleashing her inner harpy. 'Which is obviously such a terrible thing for you to do you had no choice but to lie to your sister and grandfather?' Clara could hear the sarcasm dripping from her voice and tried to calm down.

This wasn't her family. Why did she care so much?

He looked at her for one long moment and Clara thought he wasn't going to answer. After all, the annoying voice of reason whispered, he didn't have to explain himself to her, but after a moment he sighed. 'I didn't lie. They know what I do.'

'They *know*? Then why does your grandfather want you to take over Rafferty's? And why has Polly never mentioned it?' Clara twisted the heavy curtain fabric around her hand and studied him curiously.

'According to Grandfather it's just a phase I'll grow out of. As for Polly...' He glanced away, staring at the stark walls as if the answer would be found there. 'I don't know what she hates more—that Grandfather always wanted me to have this place or that I *don't* want it. I hoped that if I went away she would be able to convince him that she was the better candidate but she accused me of running away. Maybe she was right.'

'Why?' So she was curious; it wasn't a crime.

He pushed himself off the wall and walked over to the small table, which held a jug of iced water and a bunch of grapes, nothing that could mark the valuable clothes. 'Want one?' he offered and she shook her head.

He poured himself a glass. Clara watched as he took a long, deep drink, her eyes drawn to the way his tanned throat worked as he swallowed. He set the glass down and, with a purposeful manner, as if he had come to some kind of internal decision, he turned and faced her squarely, eyes holding hers.

'Because I *was* running away,' he said. 'Away from expectations and responsibility and guilt and family. I was at a really low point, Polly and I were fighting,

Grandfather kept promoting me higher and higher whilst passing her over—and believe me it wasn't on merit—and then I met up with a friend who was volunteering with Doctors Everywhere. He mentioned that they always needed people with good project-management skills and a second language—to be honest I didn't think I had a chance. A pampered boy like me who thought travelling second class was slumming it?

'Nobody was as surprised as me when they took me. But I didn't ever consider not going.' He grimaced. 'I genuinely thought it was a one-off. That I'd be back in three months relieved to be back behind my desk.' His mouth twisted with a wry humour as he remembered. 'I nearly was. That first three months was the most difficult, stressful three months of my life. It made prep school seem like a holiday camp. I couldn't wait for it to be over.

'But I signed up for my next assignment the day after I was released.' He shrugged. 'I didn't know then that I had been broken in easy—an existing brick-built hospital, my own bedroom, not a war zone. Somalia was a horrid shock. But I signed up again as soon as I returned from there, for six months that time. It's like a drug. I think I can walk away any time but I always go back for more.

'Because…it makes a real difference, Clara. Everything I did changed somebody's world. I might not be the person performing the operations—but I was the person making sure that the operations could take place. That we had beds and kits and food and water. It mattered.'

'And Rafferty's doesn't?'

'Not to me.'

Raff heard his words echo around the room. He'd thought them many times but had never said them aloud.

But the sky didn't fall in, the world didn't end, his

grandfather didn't appear in a puff of smoke to blast him away like a vengeful god. He was still the same man, still standing there.

Only everything had changed. He couldn't fool himself or his family any longer. He wasn't working away for a sabbatical or a career break or for an adventure. It was what he *did*, what he needed to do, what he was. And it didn't matter whether his grandfather left him Rafferty's or not, he would just sign it over to Polly. It was hers; she deserved it.

There was no point waiting and hoping that things would work out his way; he had to make them happen.

Clara was still looking at him, that green gaze of hers intent. He didn't know what he had expected. Shock? Disapproval? Horror? It was hard to remember sometimes that to other people Rafferty's was no more than a place to buy beautifully gift-wrapped socks or get an expensive but perfect afternoon tea. It wasn't the centre of everyone's world.

What was it about this woman that made him want to confess, to spill all the secrets that he preferred to keep locked away so tightly? Was it her directness, her transparency? The unexpected way she lit up when she smiled?

Their eyes were locked, the colour rising faint on her cheeks, her breath coming a little quicker. The full mouth parted slightly. Heat rose through him, sudden and shocking. The walls of the room seemed to contract; all he could see was her. The red-gold hair tumbling around her creamy shoulders, delicate tempting shoulders exposed by the deceptively demure halterneck dress, shoulders that were begging for a man to touch them, to kiss the triangle of freckles delicately placed like an old-fashioned patch.

Raff swallowed, blood thrumming round his body, his heartbeat accelerating. She was so very close, green eyes darkening until they resembled the storm-tossed sea. Just a few short steps…

'That suits you.' Raff jumped as Susannah heeled in a third rail. 'Although I don't think those are the right shoes.'

Clara pulled her eyes from his, pulling at the hem of the dress. The room felt a good ten degrees colder and suddenly a lot bigger. 'No,' she agreed, throwing Raff a faint, complicit smile that warmed him through. 'After ten minutes in these shoes I am completely convinced that they are absolutely not the right shoes.'

'Have you made any decisions yet? I've brought a few formal evening gowns as Mr Raff instructed.' Susannah gestured towards the rail. 'He didn't specify but with your colouring I thought greens, blacks and golds might be most suitable. Do you want me to stay and help you try them on?' She picked up a long, dark dress and carried it into the curtained area, hanging it onto one of the silver rails that hung between the floor-length mirrors.

'That's very kind but I think I'll manage, thanks. They all look lovely.' Clara threw the rail a helpless look. 'I'm only on my third dress. I'd better hurry up or I'll never get my reward.'

Cake, she meant cake, Raff reminded himself, fingers curling into a fist as other, equally sweet ways of rewarding her flashed through his head.

Clara took a step back, retreating behind the curtain as Susannah left. Raff paced around the room trying not to interpret every sound he heard. The rustle of a button, the slow, steady zip as the dress was undone, the faint slither of material falling to the floor.

Maybe he should have some more water.

'Have you ever tried to tell them how you feel?' Her voice floated through the curtain.

It took a few seconds for the words to penetrate through his brain, for him to remember the conversation they had been halfway through before time slowed, before his brain had gone into lockdown and his body into overdrive.

'No,' he admitted, running one hand through his hair. It was a relief in some ways to spill the feelings he had carried around for so long, locked inside so tight he barely recognised them himself. Clara was unconnected; she was safe.

In this context at least.

And she was invisible, hidden away behind the curtain; it felt as if he had the seal of the confessional. That he could say anything and be absolved.

'Rafferty's means everything to Grandfather, to Polly too. But it bores me. Merchandise and pricing and advertising and thinking about Christmas in June,' he said slowly, trying to pick his words carefully as he articulated the feelings he barely admitted to himself. 'Polly and I owe my grandfather everything and all he wanted, all he wants, is for me to take this place over. To take my father's place by continuing his work, accepting my great-grandfather's legacy. I didn't know how to tell him I didn't want it. Not ever. What kind of spoiled brat breaks his grandfather's heart?'

She didn't reply. How could she? But her silence didn't feel hostile or loaded.

'I tried.' He leant back against the wall and gazed unseeingly at the ceiling, the long years of thwarted hopes and unwanted expectations heavy on his conscience. 'I really, really tried, worked here after school and every holiday, gave up my dreams of studying medicine and struggled through three years of business management instead. I even did an MBA and I took up the role awaiting me here—and every day, for six years, I hated coming to work.'

He sighed. 'But ironically Polly loved it. I hoped that if Grandfather saw how well she did then he would switch his attention to her. But he's old-fashioned. He doesn't even realise how much he's hurt her by leaving the company to me.'

'You have to tell him.' She sounded so matter of fact. As if it were that easy.

'I know. Unfortunately last time I tried he ended up in hospital.' Raff tried to make his voice sound light but he knew he was failing.

'What's your plan? To spend another six years here hating every moment, you miserable, Polly miserable?'

'No!' he protested. Her words cut a little deeper than he liked. After all, he *had* taken the path of least resistance, hoping it would all work out somehow. He had only postponed the inevitable.

He had run through every possible conversation in his head. None of them ever ended well. If he had to he would just walk away, refuse to be involved, but the old man had lost one son already. If only there was a way to keep the family together and live his own life.

If only he could make his grandfather see...

Unless...

'I could invite him to the ball,' he said, his brain beginning to tick over with ideas. 'Let him see for himself what I've been up to.'

'Will he be fit?' She didn't sound convinced.

There was the flaw. 'It's five weeks away. He'll be back home this week and resting. If I make sure he's escorted at all times, order a special low-fat dinner and keep him away from the wine he should be okay. He never was the sort to dance the night away. I could take a table, fill it with business cronies. He'd enjoy that.'

'And then what?' She still sounded doubtful.

He was over thirty. It was time to be a man, banish the guilt-ridden small boy, eager to please whatever the cost. 'Then, after the ball, when he's seen the difference we make, the difference I make, I'll talk to him again. Honestly and firmly.'

It wasn't a foolproof plan by any means. Nor was it an instant answer. Raff would have to stick around for nearly two months—but he'd planned for that after all, booked Clara for up to six weeks.

It felt like the best shot he had. And regardless of whatever his grandfather decided his own decision was made.

It was only now that he realised just how heavy his burden had been: guilt, expectations, responsibility weighing him down. He wasn't free of it, not yet, but freedom was in sight. It was strange how talking it through with someone, sharing his burden, had helped.

Would anyone have done or was it Clara herself? Raff wasn't sure he wanted to explore that thought any further.

'It could work.' She sounded a little more enthusiastic. 'You better make sure your presentation is spectacular.'

'Our presentation,' he said silkily. 'You're the one who promised we'd be there, agreed to all this. I want your help with every aspect. You don't just get to turn up late and leave early, Cinders. You have to work for your dress and glass slippers.'

Talking of which, she had been a long time getting changed. 'Are you okay in there?'

'Ah…' she sounded embarrassed '…is Susannah there?'

'No, why?'

'Can you find her?' Embarrassment was replaced with curt impatience.

Raff's mouth quirked. 'Are you in need of help? Maybe I can assist? I am fully trained, remember?'

'Raff Rafferty, please find Susannah right now.'

Grinning, Raff sauntered to the door and looked around. No sign. 'I can't see her,' he called. 'I can page her but she might be at the other end of the building, or I can help. Your choice.'

He could almost hear the wheels turning as Clara deliberated her choices.

'Okay. But not one quip, and no looking.'

Interesting.

'I'm a professional,' he assured her. But he didn't feel professional as he walked over; he felt more like an over-eager schoolboy who'd been promised an over-the-bra fumble. Inappropriate, he scolded himself.

And yet he couldn't stop thinking about creamy, bare shoulders and those three little freckles.

Deep breath. Focus on the job at hand. Raff pulled the curtain a little to one side and stepped into the changing room.

Where he stopped still. He didn't want to stare, he knew it was wrong and yet, and yet…

'Well, don't just stand there.' Clara gestured to her side. 'Help me. It's stuck and have you seen the price tag? I can't exactly yank it.'

She was wearing a floor-length strapless dress in a shade of blue so dark it almost looked black.

Revealing both her shoulders and a generous amount of cleavage, the dress clung as tightly as a second skin, emphasising the dip at her waist, the curve of her bottom, the length of her legs. Raff swallowed.

'The zip,' she said with killing emphasis as he remained static. 'It's stuck.'

Trying, with little success, to get some air into his suddenly oxygen-deprived lungs, Raff walked over. It seemed to take an eternity. He was a fool, to think he could walk in here, to the intimacy of a room where clothes were discarded, a room of lingerie and limbs and clinging silks. A fool to think he could step so close to naked arms, inhale the light floral scent she wore, watch one curl tumble down onto a bare shoulder. To touch her.

'Just here.' Hadn't she noticed the effect she was having on him? 'Can you see?'

Raff put one hand onto her ribs, holding her still as with utter concentration his other hand worked at the tiny zip, trying to free it from the thread that held it prisoner. Her skin was hot, burning him through the silk; he wasn't sure whether he could really hear her heart hammering or whether it was his imagination.

Or if it was his heart he heard, deafening him with its beat.

'I think I've got it.' His voice was gruff. 'There!'

As he freed the thread the zip shot down with alarming ease, his hand skimming her waist, her hip, and as it did so the top of the dress collapsed into graceful folds.

It all happened so fast, Clara didn't manage to grab at the dress or shield herself, and he, God help him, he didn't look away.

I'm sorry, he wanted to say, wanting to turn, to walk away, allow her a chance to get herself together but he was glued to the spot, desire hot, sweet and dark burning through him. She was perfect, the swell of her breasts, the dip of her waist, the faint silvery marks on her lower belly a badge of motherhood.

She should pull the dress up, turn away, slap his face,

scream, at least, at the very least she should cover herself up. She didn't even sunbathe topless and here she was, standing like a glamour model, exposed.

Only she was paralysed by the heat in his eyes, warming her through from head to toe, settling in the pit of her stomach, awakening a sweet, insistent ache she hadn't felt for so long. The naked desire in his face provoking pride, need, want.

And she wanted him too. She'd wanted him since the moment he had sauntered into her office, arrogant and demanding, making her think and making her do and making her feel. Not just because he looked so good, was so tall and so broad and so solid, not just because he had eyes that caressed and a mouth that made her knees tremble, but because he was a man who cared, hide it as he might.

But he was a man who was leaving. A man with itchy feet, who lived his life on the edge of civilisation, risking his life every day.

Right now it was hard to remember why that was a problem.

For all the strength apparent in him, held tightly coiled in that strong, muscled body, Clara knew she had all the control here. One look, one word and he would walk away with a sincere apology.

But one move forward and… Anticipation shivered through her.

She had spent the last ten years playing it safe, hiding from any experience that might test her, pouring all her emotions into motherhood. But the moment she had swung off that platform yesterday, the moment she had agreed to Raff Rafferty's offer, a new world had opened up. Not safe, not cosy, unplanned, a world that made her pulse beat and her blood hum and desire swirl sweetly inside her like honey.

And, oh, how she wanted.

Without thinking, without planning, she took another step forward, allowing the dress to fall to the ground as she did so. A wanton part of Clara, long locked away, smiled; the rest of her shivered in anticipation as she took in the expression on his face as Raff drank every inch of her in: fierce, hot need.

She felt utterly desirable.

Another step and she was close, so close. Millimetres separated them. Clara was trembling, tiny, anticipatory shivers running through her every nerve and sinew, her veins humming with excitement. She looked up at him boldly, allowing her want to shine out, and with a muffled growl Raff moved forward, closing the infinitesimal gap, pulling her hard against him. Clara found herself on her tiptoes, straining towards him.

It could only have been a second, two at the most before his lips touched hers but it felt like an eternity and Clara was sure she would explode if he didn't kiss her right there and then. And then his mouth was on hers sure and sweet, his hands were holding her close, one on the small of her back, holding her tight, the other in the nape of her neck and Clara wanted to climb onto him, into him and never let go. The lazy circles his fingers were making on her back, each one teasing hot, sensitised skin to the point of insanity, the way his hand cupped her tender neck, fingers buried in her hair, the way his mouth claimed her, demanding, expecting, giving.

Nothing had ever felt so right.

And when he let her go, staggered back with a look of total disbelief on his face, she was utterly bereft. 'The door's unlocked.' He was breathing hard, his voice ragged.

It took a moment for his words to penetrate her overheated brain. 'Oh.' Anyone could have come in, seen her practically naked, draped all over him. She should feel shamed. But she wasn't; she just wanted to be back in his arms, fused into him.

'I could lock it…'

Her eyes fastened on him, on the question implicit in eyes darkened by desire.

'You could, you probably should.' It wasn't the most eloquent response but it was all he needed. Powerful long strides across the room and the key was turned firmly, the outside world shut away.

Raff turned, eyes glittering dangerously. 'Clara?'

This was it, this was her chance to turn back, to get this relationship back on a professional footing. There was nothing she wanted less. 'I'm standing here in my underwear,' she said as calmly as she could, allowing a purr to enter her voice, tossing her hair back over her shoulder. 'And you're all the way over there and fully dressed…'

'That,' he said grimly, advancing on her with meaningful intent, 'can soon be remedied.'

Clara found herself being walked backwards until her back hit the wall. Panting, she looked up at him, a teasing smile on her lips, a smile he claimed as he swung Clara up in strong arms and she gave in to the sensation of his mouth, his hands, all thoughts drifting away and instinct taking over until she was no longer sure who she was or where she was. All she knew was that right now, in this moment, she was his.

CHAPTER SEVEN

'ARE YOU ENJOYING YOURSELF?'

'Yes, thank you.' Polite, cool, collected. Of course she was, just as she always was.

Clara was playing her part to perfection. His house, his life were seamlessly run by her employees while she stepped into her role as his girlfriend with grace. His employees liked her, she had charmed every business associate he had introduced her to and even his grandfather was showing signs of thawing.

But as soon as they were alone she retreated behind a shield of courtesy and efficiency. A shield he made no attempt to push aside.

It was better that way even if he did keep getting flashbacks of hot kisses, silky skin and fevered moans. After all, he usually kept his relationships short and sweet, superficial. Just not usually this short.

Or this sweet.

'I think we've shown our faces long enough if you want to leave.' Raff liked music as much as the next man but the benefit for ill and destitute musicians was a little out of his comfort zone. 'Unless, of course, you're enjoying it.'

The corners of her mouth tilted up, as close as she had got to a genuine smile in weeks. 'The violinist sounds just like Summer when she's practising,' she whispered, her breath sweet on his cheek. 'I had no idea I was raising a musical genius.'

'He sounds like Mr Simpkins when I've forgotten his evening fish,' Raff retorted. 'I think they're trying to extort money from us with menaces. Pay up or the music continues.'

'The percussionists were good and the harpist wasn't too bad...' She broke off, biting her lip, laughter lurking in her eyes.

'Until she started singing.' Raff glared over at the harp. 'If she isn't some sort of banshee then that voice was genetically engineered for warfare. There's no way those howls could be natural.'

'Come on.' Clara placed her hand upon his arm, just as she had done at every party, every dinner, every benefit over the last few weeks. His blood began to heat up until he was surprised his sleeve didn't burst into flames, but he didn't betray his discomfort by a single twinge.

'Only if you want,' he demurred. 'There's still the Cymbal Concerto to go. I'd hate for you to miss out.'

'So considerate.' She might look as if she were wafting along on his arm but her hand was inexorably steering him towards the open doors. 'Successful night?'

'When it was quiet enough to hear myself speak. Polly must be exhausted, spending her free time at these things.' Raff routinely worked twelve-, fourteen-hour days out in the field but give him those any day over his sister's routine of office by day, business socialising by night. 'I would give anything for a quiet night in The Swan.'

'Me too. You know, I thought my life was in danger of getting into a rut.' Clara breathed in a deep sigh as they left through the double doors that led from the ornate banqueting hall into the equally ornate but much quieter and cooler vestibule. 'But after several weeks of social events I am yearning for my sofa, a film and something really plain to eat. A jacket potato, salad, a piece of grilled chicken.'

'That sounds amazing.' It really did. Canapés and fancy dinners had lost any novelty after just a few days. 'Can I join you?'

It was supposed to be a joke but he made the mistake of looking directly at her; their gazes snagged, held and colour rose over the high cheekbones. 'It would be a rom-com,' she warned him, looking away, her voice light.

'My favourite.' Right then he almost meant it; a night lazing on a sofa, something undemanding on the TV, sounded like paradise. But he could feel the phone in his pocket almost physically weighting him down stuffed as it was with commitments and appointments and functions, all as serious and important and necessary as tonight's. 'I might have a spare evening in, oh, about three weeks.'

Rafferty's had to be represented, had to be seen to be there. This was where business was discussed, decided, where deals were struck. Under the sparkling lights, a glass of something expensive in one hand, a canapé in the other.

'Actually…' Clara sounded almost shy, tentative, completely unlike her usual assertive self '…I wondered if you were free tomorrow morning?'

'On a Sunday?' Raff didn't even try to hide his shock. Apart from that very first week, Clara had kept Sundays sacrosanct. They were her family day, a day she was very firmly off duty.

Did that mean her daughter would be there? Raff rubbed the back of his neck, suddenly a little warm. Just because he and Clara had shared a moment didn't mean he was ready to play at happy families. Especially as that particular moment had been well and truly brushed under the carpet.

And although there were times when he wished it hadn't been quite so rigorously filed under 'let's never mention this again', this was a stark reminder why it had to be.

Families, children, commitment. All very nice in principle, but tying. Even more weighty than the phone.

'I know we don't usually work on a Sunday.' She made the statement sound like a question and Raff shrugged non-committally.

It was chilly outside, cold enough for Clara to pull her wrap around her shoulders as they exited the building and began to make their way down the wide stone steps into the brightness of a London night. If the stars were out Raff couldn't see them, the streetlamps and neon signs colluding to hide the night sky from the city dwellers.

He had arranged to meet their driver on the corner of the street and steered Clara along the cobbled pavement, waiting for the inevitable comment about how much her feet hurt.

It didn't come. 'I have an appointment,' she said instead, looking down at the uneven cobbles. 'I wondered if you would come with me. You said, a few weeks ago…' Her voice trailed off.

'Yes.' He frowned as he remembered. 'Of course.' He *had* said he would attend a meeting with her. Only, that was before.

People *must* be talking about them, about the amount of time they were spending together, about the way he picked her up almost nightly in a chauffeur-driven car— maybe it was his turn to act the graceful escort. Only, it seemed worse somehow. Her family were so close, it felt deceitful.

The thought of getting to know her family, of possibly being accepted by them, twisted his stomach. What if he liked them? Or God forbid felt at home?

'It was the only day they offered me.' She finally looked up, her face pale, her features standing out starkly from the almost unnatural pallor of her skin.

'They?'

She took a deep breath, her body almost shaking. 'Summer's father isn't involved. It's his choice. I really tried.' Raff had to take a deep breath of his own to dampen down a sudden, shocking anger. How could anyone have left her to raise a child on her own?

'I send him photos, videos, school reports, tried to get him to Skype with her. He's never been that interested. But a few weeks ago, the day you asked me to help you out, he emailed.'

'He wants to see you tomorrow.' It wasn't a question.

'He's here with his father. They have money—' She came to an abrupt stop, her throat working.

'So do I.'

She gave him a tiny smile but he wasn't joking. They wanted to play powerful and well connected? He was brought up to play that game.

'Byron's father thought that I, well, it doesn't matter now, but we don't have the best relationship.' She twisted her bangle round. 'I wanted to be strong enough to do it alone.'

Raff's heart squeezed, painfully. It couldn't be easy for her to ask for help. 'Is Summer going?'

She shook her head. 'They don't want her there.'

'Of course I'll be there.' It was just returning a favour, right? The cold, still anger that consumed him when he saw the stricken look in her eyes, heard her voice shake, watched her search for words no mother should have to

say had nothing to do with his decision. It was just a favour. No big deal.

'I've been dreading this,' she confessed, the shadows
under her eyes making them look even bigger than usual.
'All I've ever wanted is for Byron to be part of Summer's
life. And now he's finally here, in London, just an hour
away from her, I'm terrified.' She shook her head helplessly. 'I don't know why. I should be stronger than this.'

Raff stopped and turned her around to face him, tilting her chin up, making her look at him, see the truth of
his words. 'Clara, you are incredible. You raise Summer
alone, you run a business, half of Hopeford relies on you
one way or another. You are the strongest woman I know.'

She stared up at him, doubt in her eyes. 'Really?'

'Really.' He squeezed her shoulders, ignoring the urge
to pull her in a little closer.

She exhaled. 'Thank you, I appreciate it. I really do.'

Raff knew instinctively that it wasn't easy for her to
lean on him; he was honoured, of course, that she had
asked him, had confessed her fears to him. It must have
hurt her to show him the vulnerable side she kept so
locked away. But it was terrifying as well. Physical intimacy was one thing, emotional intimacy, honesty, secrets? Another ballgame altogether.

But she'd been let down enough already. One morning, that was all she was asking. He was capable of that
at least.

As they approached the hotel Clara's demeanour subtly
changed, as if she were going into battle. There was little
outward sign of her stress although her grip tightened on
his arm. Her face was utterly calm as if she were going to
any business meeting, her hair had been ruthlessly tamed
and coiled back in a neat bun, not one curly tendril al-

lowed to fall about her face. It made her eyes look even bigger, emphasised the catlike curve of her cheek; Raff thought she looked vulnerable, a child playing dress up.

She had dressed for battle too, sleek and purposeful in a grey suit.

But Raff could feel the faint tremors running through her body. Her lips were colourless under her lip gloss.

The Drewes were staying at one of the most exclusive hotels in London, an old Georgian town house discreetly tucked away in a square in Marylebone. It was an interesting choice. Not overtly glitzy but it suggested old money, power and taste.

Raff was looking forward to this. He knew all about old money, power and taste. Bring it on.

Clara was all purpose now, marching up the stone steps and through the double doors, turning with no hesitation towards the hotel's sunny dining room.

'Clara.' Both men rose to their feet; although they both wore smiles the brown eyes were alike—cold and assessing.

'Byron, Mr Drewe.' She shook hands in turn, strangely formal considering one of these men was the father of her child. 'This is Raff.' She didn't qualify their relationship. *Good girl,* Raff thought, *keep them guessing.* 'Raff, this is Byron and his father, Archibald Drewe.'

Raff reached over to shake hands in his turn, unable to resist making his own handshake as strong and powerful as he could. So this was Summer's father, this tall, handsome man, whose smile didn't reach his eyes and who wore his privilege with ease.

'Please, sit down.' The elder Drewe looked very similar to his son, the dark hair almost fully grey and the tanned face more wrinkled but with a steely determination behind the affable façade.

Raff pulled out Clara's chair for her, a statement of intent.

'It's been a while,' she said to Byron. 'You've cut your hair.'

'You look great.' The other man was looking at her with open admiration. 'Haven't changed a bit even if you have changed the sarong for a suit.'

He had seen Clara in a sarong. The hot jealousy that burned through Raff at Byron Drewe's words shocked him. Of course he had seen Clara in a sarong—and a lot less too. He was her ex-lover, the father of her child. At some point Clara had been enamoured enough with this guy to have a baby with him.

And at some point he had allowed her to come home, alone. To raise their child alone.

The jealousy ebbed away, replaced with cold dislike and even colder contempt. 'I am trying to persuade her to link her business with mine. But you know Clara.' He smiled at her. 'She has to be in control. Even a name like Rafferty's doesn't reassure her!'

'Rafferty's?' The older man's eyes were now assessing Raff. 'Impressive.'

The contempt deepened. Now they knew who he was his stock had gone up. Raff hated that.

'What do you do now, Clara?' Should Byron Drewe be smiling at her in that intimate way? Raff allowed himself a brief, self-indulgent fantasy of leaning across the table and planting one perfect punch on that perfect nose.

'I run a concierge service.'

'Half of Hopeford couldn't manage without her, including me,' Raff said.

'How interesting.' The older Mr Drewe couldn't sound less interested. Maybe it was his nose that Raff should fantasise about punching.

'It keeps me busy.' If Clara had heard the snub she wasn't reacting. 'And it's thriving. Between work and Summer I don't have much free time.'

Raff bit back a smile as he mentally applauded. *Nicely done, Clara. Remind them why we're here, ignore their put-downs and make sure they realise you're doing them a favour.*

She didn't need him to step in at all. He might as well help himself to the coffee and sit back and enjoy the show.

'And how is Summer?'

Surely Summer's own grandfather shouldn't pronounce her name in that slightly doubtful way, as if he wasn't quite sure it was right.

Or maybe he just didn't like the name. Clara could scrape her hair back and put on a suit but she knew full well that Archibald Drewe still thought of her a teenage hippy with long hair, tie-dye dresses and a happy-go-lucky attitude who had named her daughter accordingly.

She had been that girl once, but it was a long time ago.

'She's good.' Clara pulled out her tablet. 'I have pictures.'

'That won't be necessary, thank you.'

Time stopped for a long moment, the blood freezing in her veins. How could he dismiss her daughter, his own flesh and blood, in that cold, cavalier way?

'She has your hair, your eyes.' She looked directly at Byron, willing him to stand up for her, for his daughter, for once in his pampered life. 'If you ever look at the pictures I send you you'll know that.'

'I look.' He had the grace to sound ashamed. 'She's beautiful.'

'She is, but she is also smart and kind and very funny. You'd like her.'

He shifted in his seat, evidently uncomfortable. Beside her Raff was leaning back, ostensibly totally at his ease, sipping a cup of coffee. But the set of his shoulders, the line of his jaw told her that he was utterly alert, following every word, every intonation.

Every put-down.

Her hands tightened on her cup; it had been like a game of chicken, leaving asking him along to the last possible moment, kidding herself that she might be able to do this alone. Afraid that his presence might make the whole, nasty situation even more humiliating. She'd thought she'd be ashamed, for him to see this side of her. The dismissed, 'unwanted single mother' side. But having him next to her filled her with the strength she needed to battle on. After all, he had his demons too.

She reached over and laid her hand on his forearm, squeezing very slightly, letting his warmth fill her as she lifted her head and stared evenly at her daughter's father.

'I haven't told her you're here but I hope you have got time to meet her.' She wanted to keep it businesslike but she couldn't help babbling a little, trying to sell her daughter to the one person who shouldn't need the pitch, the one person who should be in regardless.

'She has a picture of you in her room and I tell her lots of stories about you and about Sydney. She helps me put the photos together every Christmas, chooses the pictures she wants to send you. She would love to meet you.'

'Clara, I…' Was that pity in his eyes or shame? Either way it wasn't what she wanted to see.

'It's just, while you're here…'

'I'm getting married.'

Clara stared at Byron blankly. This was why they wanted to see her? Did they think she'd be upset after ten years of silence and neglect, that she was so pathetic she still harboured hopes that they would be a family?

The ego of him.

Raff moved his arm so that his hand lay over hers, lacing his fingers through her fingers, a tacit show of support. She should be annoyed at this overt display of ownership but relief tingled through her instead. 'That's great,' she said, injecting as much sincerity into her voice as she could. 'Congratulations, I hope you'll be very happy.'

'He's marrying Julia Greenwood.'

Archibald Drewe obviously expected this to mean something.

'Great!'

'She's heiress to a media empire,' he told her, his voice oozing contempt for her obvious ignorance. 'This is a brilliant match for Byron, and for our business.'

Much better than a penniless English teenager. She'd known she was never good enough for Byron's family. Once it would have hurt that he had allowed them to influence their future. Now she simply didn't care.

As long as it didn't affect her daughter.

'We want you to sign this.' Archibald Drewe slid a sheaf of papers over the table. Aha, this was the real reason for the meeting. Business, the family way.

'What is it?' Clara made no move to take it.

'Byron is about to join together two great businesses, and any children he and Julia will have...' the emphasis here was intentional '...will inherit a very influential business indeed. We don't want anything from Byron's past to jeopardise his future.'

Anything? They meant anyone.

Beside her Raff was rigid, his hand heavy on hers, fingers digging in, almost painfully.

'And what does this have to do with me?'

'I want to make it quite clear…' Archibald Drewe leant forward; obviously the kid gloves were off '…that your daughter has no claim on me, my son or our business. No claim at all. However…' his smile was as insincere as his eyes were hard '…we are not unfeeling. It's not the girl's fault her beginnings were so unorthodox.'

Raff's arm twitched under hers, the only sign he was alive. Otherwise he was completely still. She couldn't look at him, afraid of what might be in his face. She didn't need his anger and she really couldn't handle pity right now.

The room seemed to have got very cold. She knew how Archibald Drewe felt about her; he had made it completely clear ten years ago. She hadn't expected time to soften him; only money and influence could do that.

But, fool that she was, she hadn't expected him to try and wipe his granddaughter out of the family history books.

'We will send no more annual cheques and you will stop with the photos and emails. Julia does not know of your daughter's existence and neither Byron or I wish her to know. If you sign this contract, however, I will give you a one-off payment of one million pounds sterling in complete settlement of your daughter's claim.'

Raff had met people like the Drewes far too many times; with them it always came down to money. What a cold existence they must lead.

'What does the contract say?' Clara's voice was completely still but she was gripping his hand as if he were the only thing anchoring her.

'It says your daughter has no claim now or in the future on our money or any of our business interests. It also states clearly that she may make no attempts to contact Byron or any member of his family.'

'I see.'

'It's a good offer, Clara.' At least Byron didn't try to meet her eye. Coward.

He had promised himself that he wouldn't intercede but it was no good. How dared they treat Clara like this? 'I'll get my lawyer to have a look at it. Clara isn't signing anything today.' Raff made no attempt to keep the contempt out of his voice.

'That won't be necessary.' Clara pushed the contract away and rose to her feet. 'I won't sign away my daughter's right to contact her father or siblings although don't worry, Byron, I'll do my best to talk her out of it. I would hate for her to be humiliated the way I have been today.'

She was amazing. Calm, clear, holding her anger at bay. But it was costing her; he could hear the strain in her voice, see it in the tense way she stood. What if she hadn't asked him to be there, had had to face these two men alone? It wasn't that she couldn't defend herself. She obviously could. No damsel in distress, this lady. But she shouldn't have to.

She should never have been put into this position. They thought their money and influence gave them the right to treat people like dirt. They were everything he despised.

Raff stood up, taking Clara's hand in his as she continued, her eyes as cold as her voice, but he could feel her hand shaking slightly as she held herself together. 'I won't promise not to send you yearly updates—you don't have to open them but she is your daughter and the least you can do is acknowledge that she exists. As for the money, keep it. I work hard and I provide for her. I always have. I've put every cheque you sent away for her future and that's where it stays. I don't need anything from you, Byron, not any more, and I certainly don't need anything from you, Mr Drewe.'

The older man's face was choleric. 'Now don't be so hasty…'

'If you change your mind, if you want to meet her, then you know where I am. Ready, Raff?'

'Ready.' He got to his feet and nodded at the two men. 'I wish I could say it's been a pleasure but I was brought up to be honest.'

It wasn't until they got outside that Clara realised that she was shaking, every nerve jangling, every muscle trembling.

'Come on.' Raff's eyes were still blazing. 'You've had a shock and you need something to eat. And if I stay anywhere near here I will march back in there and tell them exactly what I think of them.'

'They wouldn't care.' She wasn't just shaking, she was cold to the bone. Clara wrapped her arms around herself trying to get some heat into her frozen limbs.

'I'd feel better though.' He shot her a concerned glance. 'Come here.' He pulled Clara into his embrace, wrapping his arms around her, pressing her close. 'You're like ice.'

She had tried so hard to avoid his touch since that afternoon, since she had let down her guard, but the memory of his touch was seared onto her nerve endings and her treacherous body sank thankfully against him.

'Let's get a taxi. We can go to Rafferty's, get you fed.'

'No, honestly.' Clara wasn't ready to face the world yet. 'Let's just walk. I need some air.'

'Whatever you want.' But he didn't let go of her, not fully, capturing her hands in his, keeping her close as they walked. 'I am going to insist on tea full of sugar though. I work in a medical capacity, remember? I am fully qualified to prescribe hot, sweet drinks.'

Clara knew that if she spoke, just one word, she'd start to cry. And she didn't know if she would ever be able to stop. So she simply nodded and allowed him to continue to hold her hands as they ambled slowly through the grey streets.

'You must think I'm a fool,' she said finally. They had continued to wander aimlessly until they had reached Regent's Park. Raff had bought them both hot drinks from a kiosk and they walked along the tree-lined paths in silence.

Raff looked at her in surprise. 'I don't think anything of the sort. Why?'

'Byron.'

He huffed out a laugh. 'If you judged me on my taste in women when I was eighteen your opinion of me would be very low indeed.'

But Clara didn't want absolution. The humiliation cut so deep. 'I thought I was so worldly. I had travelled thousands of miles alone, with a ticket I had saved up for. I had amazing A-level results. I had it all. I was an idiot. An immature idiot.'

She risked looking into his face, poised to see contempt or, worse, pity, but all she saw was warm understanding. 'I didn't really date at school. I was so focused on my future, on leaving Hopeford. So when I met Byron...' She shook her head. 'We were in Bali, staying in the same hostel. He was two years older and seemed so mature. I had no idea he was from a wealthy family. He didn't act like it. It was his suggestion we share a house in Sydney and save to go travelling together. It was his own little rebellion against his father's plans.'

'We all have those.' His mouth twisted.

'At least yours involves saving people's lives.' She wasn't ready for absolution. 'Byron was just playing. But

I didn't see it. I fell for him completely. When I found out I was pregnant I was really happy. I thought we really had a future, travelling the world with a baby. God, I was so naïve.' She stopped and scuffed her foot along the floor, as unsettled as a teenager on her very first date. 'Thank you.'

Raff raised his eyebrows in surprise. 'What for?'

'For standing by me, for allowing me to handle it.'

'Well,' he confessed, 'that wasn't easy. I don't usually resort to violence but I had to sit on my hands to keep from throttling Byron's father when he offered you the money.'

'Why do men keep offering me money? First you and now him. Why do some people think that throwing money at things—at *me*—solves their problems?'

To her horror Clara could hear that her voice was shaking and feel the lump in her throat was growing. *Keep it together, Clara,* she told herself, but there were times when will power wasn't enough.

Clara blinked, hard, but it was too late as the threatened tears spilled out in an undignified cascade. She knuckled her eyes furiously, as if she could force them back.

'Because we're fools?' Raff took her hand in his, his fingers drawing caressing circles on her palm. It wasn't the first time he had touched her today but this wasn't comforting; the slow, lazy touch sent shivers shooting up her arm.

'No, don't.' She pulled her treacherous hand away. 'You don't have to be nice to me. This is all a pretence, isn't it?' The only person she could ask to stand by her wasn't really in her life at all. How pathetic was that?

Her throat ached with the effort of keeping back the sobs threatening to erupt in a noisy, undignified mess, the tears continuing to escape as Raff took hold of her, tilting her chin up so she had no choice but to look him in the eyes.

'Not all of it,' he said, his voice hoarse. 'It's not all pretence, Clara. Is it? I know we haven't talked about it, try and pretend it didn't happen, but it felt pretty real to me.'

'That was just sex.' Easy to say but she knew her tone lacked conviction. There was no such thing as just sex for Clara; she hadn't trusted anyone enough to get close enough for 'just sex' since Byron. Just this man, standing right here, looking down at her with the kind of mixture of concern and heat that could take a girl's breath away.

'I'm on your side, Clara. I'm here for you, whatever you need, whatever you want.'

Hope sprang up, unwanted, pathetic, needy; she pushed it ruthlessly away. 'For as long as we have a deal, right?' Was that sarcastic voice really hers?

'For as long as it takes, as long as you need me.' His hands tightened on her shoulders, his eyes dark, intense as if he could bore the truth of his words into her.

And, oh, how she wanted to believe him. She didn't mean to move but somehow she was moving forward, allowing herself to lean in, rest her head against the broad shoulders, allowing those strong arms to encircle her, pull her close as the desperate sobs finally overwhelmed her, muffled against his jacket. And he didn't move, just held her tight, let her cry it all out. For as long as she needed to.

CHAPTER EIGHT

'You look…' Raff came to a nonplussed stop, trying to find a word, any word, that did Clara justice. It didn't exist.

'Beautiful?' Clara supplied for him. That wasn't the word; it wasn't enough by any measure. 'I hope so. I've spent all day being prodded, plucked and anointed. If I don't look halfway decent at this exact moment in time then there is no hope.'

'Don't worry,' he assured her. 'You're somewhere past halfway.'

The truth was that at the sight of her all the breath whooshed out of his body; in a room full of glitter she shone the brightest. In the end she had eschewed all the designer dresses Rafferty's had to offer and had opted for a vintage dress that had belonged to her great-grand-mother, a ballerina-length full-skirted black silk with a deceptively demure neckline, although it plunged more daringly at the back, exposing a deep vee of creamy skin.

Raff immediately vowed that nobody else would dance with Clara that evening, no other man would be able to put his hand on that bare back, feel the silk of her skin.

'You scrub up nicely as well,' she assured him.

Raff pulled at his bow tie. He'd owned a tux since

his teens but he still felt as if he were dressing up as James Bond.

Or a waiter.

'Nervous?'

'A little,' he admitted. 'Not about the presentation, more how Grandfather will take it. How is he?'

'He's here.' She pulled an expressive face. Her relationship with Raff's grandfather had thawed a little; he was at least polite. But although she told Raff—and herself—that his initial rebuff didn't worry her, she wasn't being entirely honest. It was all too reminiscent of Archibald Drewe's treatment of her, an uneasy and constant reminder of her mistakes.

'Grumpy that he has a special diet and can only drink water but happy he's away from that damned TV and fool nurse. His words not mine.'

'I bet he's glad to be talking work as well.' Raff had mingled business with business and invited some of Rafferty's key suppliers and associates to fill the table he had paid for. It was odd seeing his two very different worlds colliding in this rarefied atmosphere of luxury and wealth.

Opting for something a little unusual, Doctors Everywhere were holding the event in a private garden belonging to the privileged residents of a west London square.

'It's amazing, like a fairy tale.' Clara was looking out at the candlelit gardens, her green eyes shining. Watching the lights play on her hair and face, Raff could only agree.

'We have some very generous—and very rich—patrons,' he said, trying to drag his thoughts back to the business at hand. 'I hadn't even thought about this side of our work. I spend the money, not raise it. I need to talk to Grandfather about allowing them to use Rafferty's for something in the future. We could certainly donate food and staff or raffle prizes.'

And the people he knew could give even more. Helping with the last stages of the fundraiser had been an eye-opener, just not a particularly welcome one.

Raff knew he did a good job out in the field, but anyone with a good grasp of electrics, mechanics and project management could do that. He had other uses that were far more unique: entrée into some of England's richest and most influential echelons and, although he himself didn't value those connections, he knew that no charity could run on good intentions alone. Ensuring the donations came in was a vital role.

But would it be as satisfying? Or would it be a gilded cage just like the one he was working so hard to escape from?

'Is everything set up?' Clara was as cool and collected as ever, on the surface at least, but when he took her arm he felt the telltale tremble.

'Ready to go,' he promised her. 'My mission tonight is to get all these people to remember why they're here and part with as much money as possible.'

And throw the gauntlet down. Show his grandfather that this was where he belonged—and this was where he was staying, no matter what. Only he didn't feel the same burning need to get back out into the field. It helped, of course, that he had been helping to set up the fundraiser, interacting with colleagues, seeing a new side of the charity's work. But it was more than that.

Clara. Everything he didn't want or need in his life. She needed stability and commitment and a father for her daughter, not a travelling jack of all trades whose idea of a perfect day with family meant a day by himself. And yet, and yet...

Somehow she had got under his skin. More than attraction, more than lust. He respected her, admired her strength—but it was those glimpses of carefully hidden vulnerability that really hooked him in. He knew how much she hid it, despised any display of weakness. But she had trusted him enough to lean on him, cry on him, allow him to shoulder her burdens for a short time.

From Clara that was a rare and precious gift. But was he worthy? And was he capable of accepting all that she had to offer?

'They certainly do a lot of good.' Raff's grandfather had been slowly softening throughout the evening, his initial scepticism disappearing when he saw his table companions and the carefully prepared meal that had been specially provided for him. If he still cast a longing look or two at the bottles of very expensive wine that littered the table, he had at least stopped complaining and was sipping the despised mineral water with martyred compliance.

'I had no idea about the sheer scale of their work,' Clara agreed. 'Nor just how desperate things can be. I'll never complain about waiting for a doctor's appointment again.'

Raff and his colleagues spent their lives making sure that people all over the globe, people who lived in poverty, who had fled their homes, who had seen their world turned into warzones still had access to medicine, to doctors. To hope.

He could have taken the easy option, the job provided for him, the family money, enjoyed all that London had to offer the young and the rich. In a way she wished he had; it would be so easy to keep her distance from that man. Much harder to stay away from the man sitting next to her, even though there was no way there could ever be any kind of happy ever after between them.

But in the few days since the meeting with Byron something had changed. They were easier with each other, more intimate. Hands brushed, lingered, eyes met, held. Nothing had happened, not again, but the promise of it hung seductively over them.

Butterflies tumbled around her stomach, a warm tingle spreading through her at the thought.

'I'm sorry.' Raff finally managed to gracefully extricate himself from the conversation he was embroiled in. 'I've been neglecting you all evening.'

'That's okay.' After all, she was being paid for her time.

Not that Clara felt she could charge a penny for tonight; she would ask Raff to donate her fee back to the charity.

Raff pulled a face. 'I'd much rather be talking to you, but I have been promising myself that as soon as the dancing starts I am all yours.' His eyes were full of promise and a shiver ran through her despite the heat in the overcrowded room.

'You didn't say anything about dancing,' Clara protested. 'I can barely walk in these heels, let alone dance.'

'Don't worry.' His expression was pure wicked intent. 'I won't let you fall.'

'You better not. When are you on?'

'In a few minutes. Wish me luck?'

Clara put one hand on his cheek, allowing herself the luxury of touch, rubbing her palm along the rough stubble. 'Good luck,' but she knew he didn't need it. If he managed to get one hundredth of his charm across then he would have the guests clamouring to outbid each other.

The presentations had been spread out throughout the evening. A welcome speech before canapés, then, after the starters, two of the nurses gave an evocative talk that brought their exciting, dangerous and very necessary work alive. A surgeon's visceral yet compelling description of the challenges she faced was an uneasy filler between the main course and pudding.

No one else seemed to notice the incongruity between their surroundings, with the conspicuous display of wealth and luxury, and the poverty and need so eloquently conveyed. Clara saw women wiping tears, the diamonds on their hands and wrists worth more than the total the charity was trying to raise.

'We need to make sure everyone is suitably worked up before the auction,' Raff whispered. 'They'll all be well fed and watered. We want them to go home with their consciences as sated as their stomachs!'

Just the nearness of him, though he was barely touching her, that lightest of contact, sent tremors rippling up and down her body. For so long she had been shut away in a box of her own design, not allowing herself to do or to feel. Constraining herself to the narrowest of lives. And it had worked. She hadn't been hurt, hadn't messed up.

But she hadn't felt either. Hadn't felt this bitter-sweetness ache. That awareness that overtook everything so that all she could see was him; she could feel nothing but his breath on her cheek, sending waves of need shuddering through her.

Clara took a deep breath, trying to regulate her hammering pulse, remember where they were, what he was about to do. 'So it's up to you to seal the deal?'

He grimaced. 'I wish they'd put me on first. Logistics isn't exactly the sexiest subject. They'll be eyeing up the petits fours and coffee and be in a post-dinner slump by the time the auction comes around.'

'Don't be ridiculous.' Clara reached for his hand and squeezed it, trying to quell the absurd jump every nerve gave as her fingers tangled with his. 'If anybody can make logistics fascinating, you can. Go get them.'

Raff turned and looked at her and for one long moment the tent fell away, the people fading away to nothing but a murmuring backdrop to the scorching intensity of his gaze. 'You think?'

'I do.' And she did. This was a new side to the confident, nonchalant playboy—but then wasn't that playboy just a façade? A mask he wore well but a mask nonetheless. And the more Clara saw the passionate, principled man behind it, the more she wanted to retreat, to run away.

She'd thought playboys were her downfall. She'd been wrong. She had survived Byron, left him with her head held high and her heart only slightly cracked. But a man who cared, a man who carried the weight of the world on his broad shoulders? That was a far scarier prospect.

'I think you can do anything,' she said. 'Including make every person here spend three times more than they budgeted for.'

'That's my aim.' The words were jokey but his face was deadly serious. 'Ready to clap nice and loudly?'

'That's my job.'

'I'll make sure I give you a good reference.'

Was it her imagination or did disappointment pass fleetingly over his face at her words? That would be ridiculous, Clara told herself sternly. They both knew what this was. This was a business arrangement. A glitzy, intimate contract maybe but a contract nonetheless. Money was changing hands, favours were being done. That was all.

'Okay, then.' And he was gone, the eyes of half the women in the room following the tall figure as he strode across the marquee.

Clara sank back in her chair, an unaccountable feeling of melancholy passing over her. What had he wanted her to say? She didn't know; she was no good at this. Had swapped flirting for nappies and never quite got her groove back.

'This means a lot to him.'

She jumped. For a moment she'd forgotten where she was, that she was surrounded by people. 'I'm sorry?'

Charles Rafferty was looking up at the stage where his grandson stood, talking to the computer technician. Raff was relaxed, laughing, totally at home.

'I knew he had this ridiculous hankering to be a doctor—it was because of his father's illness, of course, that's why I persuaded him to switch to business; besides, I needed him. But his heart was never in it. When he said he was off to work for these people I thought that a bit of time and freedom would sort him out. That he'd come back to me.'

She had no idea what to say.

Raff was responsible for people's lives every day. He didn't cut them open, administer the medicine, nurse them, but he made that possible. He worked in impossible conditions in impossible countries for an impossibly tiny wage.

And he loved it. It was good that his grandfather was seeing that, acknowledging it.

'He doesn't want to let you down,' she said, aware what a lame response it was.

'No.' The older man looked at her, really looked at her

for the first time in the weeks since they had met. And for once there was no trace of a sneer on his face. Just hollow loss. 'He's aware of his family responsibilities. I made sure of that. He was only eight when his father had the stroke, when it was obvious his father would never recover. Only eight when I anointed him as my heir.'

'And Polly?' Okay, she was going beyond anywhere she had any right to go. But Polly was her friend. And Raff? He meant something to her, something a little like friendship.

'Polly?' He shook his head. 'I made a mess of it, didn't I? I inherited the company from my father and groomed my son to take my place with Castor waiting in the wings. It didn't even occur to me that he might not want it—or that Polly did.'

'Look, he's ready.' Raff had stepped up onto the temporary stage and was gesturing for quiet. He dominated the marquee, tall, imposing, his sheer force of will stopping the chatter as people turned to listen. 'I'm sure you'll work it out,' she said quietly as the main light dimmed, leaving just one spotlight trained directly onto Raff.

The silence was expectant. Clara was aware of nothing but the ache of anticipation twisting her stomach. *Do well,* she urged him silently. *Make them see.* Looking at her hands, she was surprised to see her nails digging into her palms. She didn't feel any pain but when she unfurled her hands there were crescent marks embedded in the soft skin. When had he started to matter so much? When had she begun to care?

It wasn't just because she had helped him, gone over the presentation over and over until it made no sense to either of them.

'I know you are all ready for your coffees.' Raff hadn't raised his voice at all yet every syllable carried to every corner. 'And listening to me talk about project management isn't going to raise your heart rate the way my very talented colleagues did. I have watched them perform surgeries, vaccinate children and deliver babies in every kind of condition you can think of—and I was still blown away by their talks earlier. So no, I can't compete with them. My job now, as in the field, is to enable their work. And this, ladies and gentleman, is how I do it.'

He raised a hand and pressed a button and immediately the room was filled with the sound of drums building up into a crescendo as the screen behind him burst into life.

Raff had elected not to go for a talk and slides, knowing that the previous presentations would be using photos to great effect. Instead he had put together a video, a montage of photos and film showing a 'typical' day in his life, backdropped by fast, evocative music. The film started by panning around a small dorm room, ending in a different if similar room, and took in five different clinics and hospitals, two camps and four temporary clinics during the ten-minute show.

Raff was shown sitting in an office with paperwork piled on top of a crowded desk, spanner in hand, eying up a battered old truck, in a helicopter, setting up a tent, fixing a tap, spade in hand digging a pit, playing volleyball outside a tent, watching a spectacular desert sunset.

But the main focus of the film was the patients and people using the facilities he built, repaired and managed.

As the camera lingered on a queue of women waiting patiently to vaccinate their children, he spoke. 'We need running water, toilets, moving vehicles, electricity, satellite connections, working kitchens, working sterilisers for the most basic of our clinics. The hospitals are a whole other level. It all needs to be brought in on budget and just to add to my woes our staff and volunteers quite like to be fed, have somewhere to sleep and the chance to get to the nearest city to enjoy their time off. It's exhausting, often sweaty and dirty, and involves spreadsheets, but on the rare occasion when everything is working I can stand back and I see this.'

Another image flashed up and stayed there. A small boy beaming at the camera, one leg wrapped in bandages, his arm encased in plaster. 'I see children with a future, families kept together, mothers who will live to watch their children grow up. I see hope.

'Thanks to you we will be able to keep vaccinating, operating, delivering and curing. Your generous donations mean that children, just like Matthew here, have a future. Thank you. I'm now going to give you the opportunity to show just how generous you can be. There are some fabulous prizes in our auction. Dig deep, dig hard and bid as high as you can.'

The spotlight dimmed and the house lights were switched back on as the room erupted into applause. People were on their feet congratulating Raff as he walked around the room.

'That was different,' Charles Rafferty said drily. But, Clara noted, his eyes were moist.

'It was good, wasn't it?' she agreed. 'Luckily Raff blogs a lot when he's out in the field and often embeds video or pictures so he had a lot of footage he could use.'

'If he goes back,' Raff's grandfather said, his eyes fixed on Clara, the intent gaze eerily similar to that of his grandson, 'what about you?'

Clara's mouth dried. She had kind of got used to having him around, sitting on her desk disrupting her, whispering highly libellous biographies of the people they met, raising an approving eyebrow as she made small talk.

She had got used to those moments when their hands brushed, the sensation that time was slowing and that all she could see or hear was him. The swell that seemed to roar upwards, filling her full of awareness of his every movement, his every gesture.

'We've managed so far,' she said as lightly as she could. 'Skype, letters, it works really well. We're both so busy that time apart gives us a chance to breathe. Excuse me for a moment.'

The tent seemed so bright, so loud. The chatter and the music competing with each other, driving up the noise level to a deafening shriek. Each of the myriad lights seemed to shine directly into her eyes, the heat making her stomach roll. She needed air and quiet and dark. She needed some space.

Clara moved quickly across the tent, swerving to avoid the clustered groups, making sure she didn't catch anyone's eye as the announcer returned to the stage to announce the start of the auction. Thankfully, she reached the marquee entrance and slipped out into the grounds.

What was wrong with her? It had been a highly successful night. Raff's presentation had been sensational, the guests all looked ready to start spending and donating lavishly and if Clara had read him correctly then Raff's grandfather looked ready to do the right thing and give the company to Polly.

Even better, she had made some great contacts and, if she dared, was in a great position to expand out of Hopeford.

If she dared. Was that it? Was that the reason for this melancholy that had fallen on her like a damp dusk? Because starting the business had been absurdly simple; it had all fallen into place with surprising ease. But taking it into the big city meant taking risks and that was something Clara just didn't do any more.

Or was it because this adventure was nearly over? She'd thought that she was finished with adventures but maybe that part of her wasn't as dead and buried as she liked to think. As she had hoped. Compared to backpacking around the world it was a tame adventure, true, but a part of her was thrilling to the unpredictability.

And Raff. Clara sighed, feeling the truth exhale out of her with her heavy breath. There it was. Like a fool she was allowing the pretence to take over. Just because they pretended it was a relationship, acted as if it were a relationship, did not make it one. He didn't want or need ties here; he was doing his best to sever the ones he already had.

There was nothing long term for her. She should be sensible. Just as she always was.

'Here you are.' Clara's heart gave an absurd skip at the low voice; clearly the sensible memo hadn't reached it yet. 'Are you okay?'

'A little hot.' That wasn't a lie. 'Shouldn't you be inside for the auction?'

'There's not much call for exotic villas or cases of fine wine out in the field,' he said, walking up behind her and wrapping his arms around her. All thoughts of caution, of taking a step back, fled at his touch. 'I did purchase an obscene amount of raffle tickets, though. You?'

'I don't think there's any point in me competing against any of those platinum cards.' There had been some amazing items on the auction list but the guide prices alone had made Clara take a hasty gulp of her wine. 'I think your grandfather was planning to bid. Maybe we should go back in.'

'He's quite capable of spending a lot of money without

my help.' Raff's arms tightened a little, his breath hot on her neck, burning her, branding her, sending heat flaming through her veins. 'I'm looking forward to spending some time off duty.' He turned her unresisting body round, cupping her face with his hand. 'I just want a night with no more work talk, a beautiful woman on my arm, in my arms. Music, wine, fun. Are you in? Because...' his voice was low, intimate '...there's no one else I want to be with.'

She had spent the last ten years building up a reputation, one she was proud of. She was often called driven, reliable, honest—and she was proud of those attributes. But beautiful? Fun?

Raff thought she was both of them. And tonight, just tonight, Clara thought she might think so too.

'Just one night?' That was what he had said, right? Was it enough? It had to be.

'Is that all you want?'

'Yes.' That was the right answer, wasn't it? She searched his face for answers but he was giving nothing away. Only his eyes showed any expression: heat, want, need. What was she waiting for? 'No. I don't know. You're going away.'

'I work away,' he corrected her.

She stared at him, confused. 'What are you saying?'

He smiled at her, dangerous and sweet. 'I'm saying there's no need to plan ahead.' His hand slid down her shoulder, moved to caress the exposed skin on her back.

Clara felt her stomach drop, her knees literally weaken; she had never realised that could actually happen in real life. Any second now she was going to have to grab hold of him just to keep herself upright.

'Chemistry like this doesn't come along often...' his hand was drifting up and down, scorching a blazing trail along her spine '…but it's more than chemistry. I like you, Clara. A lot. I like how we are together. I like who I am when I'm with you. I think we should stop fighting it and go with it.' He paused, his gaze moving down to linger on her mouth. 'See where it takes us.'

See where it takes us. Somewhere new, somewhere dangerous. But there had been a flash of something in his eyes when he said he liked her. Something heartfelt.

And she liked him too. More than she wanted to admit to herself. He didn't fit any of the criteria she had painstakingly typed into the internet dating sites. He wasn't local, didn't have a steady job, wasn't family orientated. But he made her laugh, made her feel safe—and he made her tremble with need.

Was that enough?

She was over-thinking it. She had said she wanted to try dating again and here was this gorgeous man ready and waiting.

Waiting for her to say yes.

She had to say yes. Raff had never before put himself on the line like that, not for anybody. He didn't know what would happen when he was back out in the field, where they would be this time next year, but he didn't care. Even the thought that they might *be* somewhere next year didn't trigger his usual flight reflexes.

Slowly, his eyes on hers, searching for consent, he reached out and trailed a finger along the feline curve of her cheek, down to her full bottom lip. She stared up at him, eyes wide, endlessly green, questioning.

Whatever she was asking he obviously supplied the right answer because she moved. One small step closer, bringing her full body into contact with his. Raff moved his finger, reluctantly, off the smooth, full lip and followed the curve of her jaw, her skin silky under his touch.

He reached the tip of that pointed little chin and slid his finger under, tilting her face up towards him.

He waited for one torturous second, giving her plenty of time to change her mind before allowing himself to dip his head towards hers for a soft, barely there, sweet leisurely kiss, her mouth opened under his, soft, yielding.

'What do you say, Clara?' he whispered against her mouth. 'Will you come back with me tonight? Come back with me now?'

She leant in and claimed his mouth with hers. 'Yes,' she whispered back. 'I say yes.'

CHAPTER NINE

'I SHOULD HAVE KNOWN I'd find you here. Afraid you'd turn into a pumpkin if you didn't get home before sunrise?' Was that anger in his voice? Clara swallowed, reaching for the hole punch on her desk, settling it back into a perfect line.

'I didn't want anyone to see me leaving.' She couldn't meet his eyes as she answered him. It was the truth, but only half the truth.

She had woken up in the early hours, nestled in his arms, and for one blissful moment had felt happy, sated. Safe. Tempted to wake him up to see if it could be as magical a third or fourth time.

And then reality intruded. How could she face the next morning? The intimacy of early morning conversation, coffee, breakfast—followed by the walk of shame in strappy heels and yesterday's dress. She wasn't sure which scared her more.

She didn't want to be that woman, sneaking out of a bedroom in the dark, shoes in one hand, balled up tights in the other, and yet somehow there she was, tiptoeing through the dark streets until she reached the sanctuary of home and a sleepless night alone in her own cold and empty bed.

'I didn't think you'd mind,' she said in the end. 'I

mean, it's midday and you've only just turned up.' She wanted to recall the words as soon as she'd said them. She didn't want him to know that she'd been watching the door, her phone, her email, half desperately hoping that he would be doing his utmost to track her down.

Half hoping he'd stay well away.

His eyes narrowed. 'I didn't think you were the kind of woman to play games, Clara.'

Ouch. 'I'm not.' Not usually anyway. 'But last night was...' amazing, magical, the best night of her life '...like a fairy tale. I wasn't sure either of us knew what we were doing. Not really.'

They'd spent so much time together, shared so many secrets, danced around the attraction they felt for so long, it was easy to be swept up in the romance. The thought of waking up to regret and apology on his face—or conversely to expectation and hope—was more than she could bear. Far better to run.

She'd never thought of herself as a coward before.

'I knew exactly what I was doing,' he said silkily and she flushed at the sarcastic tone. 'I thought I made it very clear to you that I was in this. With you. But if you can't trust me then there's not really any point, is there?'

'I do trust you.' It was herself she didn't trust; she had got it so very wrong before.

He laughed, a short, hard sound, running his hand through his hair as he shook his head. 'You won't let me in, Clara. You don't want people around here to see us together, to know you stayed over. I haven't met your parents or your daughter. Seriously, when I said I was in, it wasn't as your bit on the side.'

'That isn't fair.' Clara jumped up, sending her chair skittering backwards. 'You told me you liked me yesterday. Yesterday! What does that mean, anyway? We're not in school any more.'

'No, that's why I thought we could try and have an adult relationship.' He sighed. 'Come on, Clara, what do you want? I'm not the kind of guy to offer you hearts and flowers and big romantic gestures. This is new to me too. I thought we could take it one day at a time, find our way into this thing. But if you won't let me in then there's no way it's ever going to work.'

Feel our way in? One day at a time? It was hardly a grand declaration but it was the best he had. Raff wanted this thing, whatever it was, to be honest from the start. His father had treated his mother like a princess, splurged expensive gifts and holidays on her, never allowed her to shoulder a single responsibility. And then the second she had needed to step up she had disintegrated. If Raff was going to try something more serious than a simple fling then it had to be equal.

And that meant honesty.

Damn, he knew relationships were hard but he hadn't expected to feel as bereft as he had this morning. Waking up to find her side of the bed empty, her clothes gone. If it weren't for the faint scent of her perfume in the air he would have thought he had imagined the whole thing.

'I do want to let you in.' She was still standing behind her desk, a physical as well as an emotional barrier between them. 'I'm just not sure how. My parents, Summer, I don't want to let them down again.'

'You think I'll let them down?' Was that really her opinion of him?

'You said yourself one day at a time. How can I risk my daughter's happiness on that?'

Raff huffed out an exasperated laugh. 'All relationships are one day at a time, Clara. Anyone who says otherwise is a liar and a fool.'

He took a deep breath, trying to steady his pulse. 'You want to know why I didn't come rushing round here this morning?' Apart from needing time to calm down before facing her. 'I went to visit my grandfather. To tell him that as much as I love him and appreciate him I can't be who he wants me to be, do what he wants me to do.'

'So you are going back?' She wasn't looking at him, straightening the few items on her desk over and over. He wanted to walk over, remove the stapler and ruler and make her listen. Instead he hung back by the door.

'I was always going back.' He had made that clear right from the start, from the first moment of attraction. 'But it's not full time. We are only ever allowed to do short-term contracts. I could be back in the UK for four months of the year. I've offered to stay on the board at Rafferty's but that's it.'

It hadn't been easy; his grandfather had known all too well what Raff was going to say and had put up some resistance—he wouldn't be Charles Rafferty if he didn't—but in the end he had gracefully bowed down to the inevitable.

It had been a massive relief. Raff didn't want to cut all his ties with his family; imperfect and demanding as they were, they were all he had.

But it didn't have to be that way—if Clara would just allow him in, let them try. Four months a year wasn't a huge amount, he knew that. But it was all he had right now. It was a start.

'And Polly?'

'The company's hers, so all we need is the lady herself. I guess this is when we find out if you've been holding out on me after all.' He meant the words to sound light but they came out dark. Bitter.

Her head shot up. 'Is that what you think?'

'Clara, I don't know what to think.'

She looked stricken, her eyes full of hurt. 'I haven't lied, Raff. All I have is an email address. But she did say to use it if I needed to get in touch so I can send a message letting her know what's happened. If you want me to.'

This could be the moment when he turned around and walked away. He could head back to Jordan completely free. No Rafferty's, no family expectations, no Clara.

Freedom wasn't all it was cracked up to be.

Slowly he moved across the room, his eyes fixed on hers. 'We can do better than this.' His voice was low. 'I wish I could promise you it will all work out but I can't.'

He had reached the side of her desk and held out his hand to her. After a long moment's deliberation she took it, allowing him to draw her out. 'I won't lie to you, Clara. I don't know what's going to happen. And I know four months a year isn't very much. But I think we could be good, if we just tried. If you wanted to.'

'I do want to,' she whispered.

He didn't want to fight with her, didn't want to argue about the future. He just wanted the here and now, to enjoy the present.

He stepped closer, one hand slipping around her waist, the other slipping through the silky tendrils of hair as he finally kissed her good morning. It wasn't the lazy waking-up kiss he had hoped for but right now all he wanted was to taste her, reassure her.

Her mouth was warm and honey sweet; her hands fastened around the nape of his neck, light and cool yet capable of igniting with just one touch. Raff buried one hand in the smooth strands of her hair, anchoring himself to her.

He kept the kiss light, using every ounce of his control to tantalisingly nibble along her bottom lip, resisting her attempts to deepen it, to push it further, harder. Hotter.

His hand splayed out along her waist, tracing the faint outline of her ribs, enjoying knowing that just a couple of inches higher and he would brush against the fullness of her breast, a couple of inches further down and he would brush over the curve of her hips round to her pert bottom. The urge to rush nearly overwhelmed him but he held back with superhuman restraint.

It would be easy, so easy and, oh, so tempting to pick her up, allow those shapely legs to wrap around him, to carry her across the room, lock the door and drop her on one of those plump, inviting sofas.

So tempting. But there was no need to rush. Because part of being an adult meant learning that anticipation was part of the game—and it made the end result all the sweeter.

Slowly, reluctantly, he pulled back. Clara's eyes were glazed, heavy-lidded, her mouth swollen. 'Good morning,' he whispered and was rewarded by a slow, sweet smile.

'Good morning.'

'Shall we start again?'

Her eyes clouded over. It wasn't an encouraging sign. 'Raff…'

Whatever she was going to say was cut short as the front door was flung open, banging against the wall.

Clara jumped back and resumed her official face in less time than it took Raff to register the sound.

'Summer.' She sounded shocked and the look she threw Raff was a mixture of apology and warning. 'What are you doing home?'

Raff turned round and saw a slim girl aged about ten, the pointed chin and high cheekbones clearly marking her kinship to Clara although the dark eyes and hair were her only legacy from her absent father. A stab of anger hit him that Byron had chosen money over fatherhood. The merry-faced girl deserved more.

Every child deserved more.

'Half day.' Summer dropped her satchel onto the sofa. 'Don't you remember?'

'Wasn't Grandma picking you up?' Clara wasn't even looking at him.

'Yes, she dropped me back here though, as I didn't see you yesterday. Who's this?'

Raff watched with interest as the colour rose on Clara's cheeks. 'This is a client of mine...'

'Not any more,' Raff interjected. He smiled at the girl. 'Hi, I'm Raff.'

'Oh.' Summer looked at him with interest. 'The VIC?'

'The what?' Raff didn't spend much time with children. He feared it showed.

'Very Important Client. The reason Mummy has been so busy.'

'That's finished now.' Clara had regained her usual colour. 'Obviously we'll still look after the house but the, er, the project has come to an end. Mr Rafferty has come in to collect his invoice.' She glared meaningfully at Raff.

'And to celebrate.' This was it, the chance to prove to Clara that he was a fit person to be in Summer's life. 'How do you two ladies fancy an afternoon out at Howland Hall?'

'The theme park? Yes, please!'

'I don't think so.'

The two voices spoke at once.

'Mummy, please, I've never been on a roller coaster.' The big eyes turned appealingly to Clara.

'Mr Rafferty, can I just have a quick word?' Clara took Raff's arm and led him to the back of the office, through the French doors and into the courtyard beyond.

'What are you doing?' she snapped. 'This is not okay.'

Unease slithered over him. 'What?'

Clara glared at him. 'Offering to take Summer out.'

He looked at her bemusedly. 'I won a family pass in the raffle last night. I thought it would be nice.'

'You know I don't let Summer meet men I'm dating.' Clara put her hand on her forehead, rubbing distractedly. She looked tired. 'It's not fair on her. What if she gets attached? You're going away.'

'It's an afternoon at a theme park, not an invitation to move in.' What was she getting so worried about? Hang on. 'How many men?'

'What?'

'How many men have you not allowed Summer to meet?' The thought of her out with other men made him lose all focus.

'None yet but there may be. In the future. After all, you said one day at a time...' She didn't finish the sentence; she didn't need to. 'But that's not the point. I don't want Summer going to theme parks and I don't want her going on roller coasters and I don't want her getting attached to you.'

He put his hands on her shoulders. 'Relax, Clara. Every child needs to go on a roller coaster and I promise to be as dull as I can. She'll be so unattached she'll be like a broken jigsaw.'

She chewed her lip. 'I don't know.'

'One afternoon.'

'Roller coasters are dangerous.'

'Not at Howland Hall. They're known for their safety measures. You can't let her grow up without having ever been on a roller coaster. She'll rebel, become a stunt-woman or join the circus. Buy a motorbike for sure.'

'She has promised me she'll never get on a bike!' Clara bit her lip. 'I don't know, Raff.'

'I do,' he said promptly. 'Afternoon of adrenaline-fuelled, gravity-defying fun and then I'll take you both out for dinner somewhere where jeans and trainers are welcomed. If our stomachs can handle it, that is. As a thank-you, to Summer as well. She must have missed you the last few weeks.'

Clara had mentioned that her daughter had found her continued absence difficult; Raff *did* owe her a treat. At least that was what he told himself, pushing away the sudden and unwanted feeling of protectiveness that slammed into him when he thought of her absent father.

Clara twisted the bangle on her wrist round and round, a sure sign she was unsure. 'As long as she knows that's what this is,' she said after a long moment. 'A thank-you. I don't want her getting the wrong idea. And we'll take the van. I'm not letting her into that tiny back seat of yours. I bet it doesn't even have a seat belt.'

'I'll call you Miss Castleton and keep ten metres between us at all times,' Raff promised. 'Now, do you like to be at the front or the back of the roller coaster? The middle is strictly for wimps.'

'This,' Summer said rapturously as she bounced along between Clara and Raff, 'is the best day ever. I only want to do things with VIP tickets, Mummy. It's cool not having to queue.'

'There's nothing wrong with taking your turn,' Clara said, but she didn't even convince herself. Unfair it might be, but there was something to be said for waltzing up to the front of every queue, even though Clara found she couldn't meet the accusing eyes of the people who had been waiting patiently for up to an hour to board one of the world-famous roller coasters.

They had been on the Scorpion twice, Runaway Train three times and the Dragonslayer five times. She'd lost count of how many times they had been on the Rapids. They were all soaked through but luckily as spring slid into summer the weather was complying, and even though she kept checking Summer anxiously her daughter was showing no sign of being chilled.

'I want to go on that one,' Summer said for what must be the twentieth time, pointing over at the Typhoon. Clara shuddered. 'You're too short,' she said firmly.

'I'm not. I'm tall for my age,' Summer insisted.

'Let's go and have a look,' Raff interjected easily. 'There's a height chart just outside and you can have a proper look at it, Summer. You might change your mind when you see how green the people getting off it look.'

It wasn't his place to intercede and part of Clara resented it, but another part of her liked the sharing of the load, the way he interacted with her daughter. The two of them were slightly ahead, strolling along the concrete path. Summer was explaining something involved to Raff, something about roller coasters judging by her expansive hand gestures. It was strange seeing her with a man who wasn't her grandfather, seeing the way she responded to his gentle teasing and laid-back questions.

The old familiar ache twisted around her stomach. She had let Summer down; her daughter needed a father, someone to urge her forward when Clara's instinct was to hold her back, hold her tight.

Raff would be perfect. But would it be fair on Summer when he would be gone so frequently?

Would it be fair to Clara, herself? On the one hand she would keep her independence, wouldn't have to compromise anything in her life. But surely if she was going to take such a big step then there should be some changes.

The theme park was set in the grounds of an old, now abandoned stately home and the owners played up to its heritage. Although there was a vast amount of plastic signage they tried to keep everything vintage-looking; even the food carts and toilets had an Edwardian country-garden look, the staff smart in striped blazers and straw hats,

'It's so cool.' Summer was gazing up at the park's newest ride, her eyes huge. 'Look, Mummy.'

Clara shuddered. 'I feel sick just looking, Sum. How can you want to go on that?' She had never allowed her onto anything faster than a carousel before but there was an adrenaline junkie hidden in her demure daughter. She wanted to try everything.

She reminded Clara of herself when she was young.

'They look like they're flying.'

'If humans were meant to fly, we'd have wings. Honestly, I can cope with any normal roller coaster but this?' The riders were strapped in but their legs were left free, to dangle helplessly as the roller coaster snaked at incredible speed around the twists, turns and loops. That was bad enough but after the first loop the carriages went horizontal, leaving the hapless passengers facing down as the train swooped along the thin rails.

'There's the height sign.' Summer went racing over to it. 'I'm big enough, Mummy, look. Can I go on it, please, please?'

'I don't know.' Her instinct was to say no, just as she

had instinctively wanted to refuse Clara's pleas to go on anything apart from the caterpillar train aimed at the under threes. But she had swallowed down her fears and let her daughter go. And look how happy she was, eyes shining, her face lit up with enthusiasm.

Over the last few weeks it had become painfully apparent just how much she sheltered Summer—and herself—from any kind of physical or mental stress. And that was good, right? Only, maybe, she had crossed the line, just a little, into overprotectiveness.

Better to be overprotective than neglectful. But Summer was growing up, and if she pulled too tightly now she knew it could cause problems later; it was just so hard to let go, even a little.

'I really hate the idea of it, sweetie. I don't think I can.' She'd conquered her own reluctance and gone on every single ride so far, as if sitting by Summer's side would keep her safe, She'd been not so secretly relieved when Summer's age had put a couple of the most terrifying beyond their reach. 'I need to feel something under my feet if I'm travelling at that speed.'

Summer's face fell but she didn't ask again, just nodded in agreement. Despite her good behaviour she couldn't hide her disappointment; her whole body projected it from her drooping shoulders to the tip of her toe scuffing the pavement.

Raff took Clara's arm, pulling her a short distance away, out of Summer's earshot. 'I'll take her on.'

Panic immediately clawed at Clara's chest. 'No, you don't have to.'

He grinned. 'I want to try it. It's meant to be great.'

'You're hanging from a bar looking down at the ground hundreds of feet below and travelling at G-force speeds. How can that be great?'

'Come on, Clara, I know the adrenaline gets you. You're buzzing every time we get off a ride.'

Adrenaline or raw fear? Clara wasn't even sure there was a difference. 'It's not…' She paused. She didn't want to say safe. Not again. Even if every fibre was screaming at her that it wasn't. 'It's not your responsibility.'

'No, but I'm offering. Look, we passed a café just a couple of minutes back up that path. Why don't you go and have a horribly overpriced coffee so you don't even have to watch and we'll find you when we're done?'

'Please, Mummy.' Summer had come dancing over; her eyes pleaded with Clara.

What harm could it do? They had VIP passes so they wouldn't have to join the lengthy queue. In just twenty minutes' time, Summer would be telling her about every twist, turn and scream.

And she would never know that allowing her to go on the ride took far more out of Clara than any roller coaster in the world.

'Okay, then.' She staggered backwards as Summer flung herself onto her with a high-pitched squeal. 'You do everything Raff tells you and remember, if you change your mind just say. No one will be cross or think you're a coward.'

'I won't change my mind. Thank you, Mummy, thank you, Raff. This is totally epic.'

'Totally,' he agreed. 'See you soon, Clara. Enjoy the calm. I think a return to the Rapids after this, don't you? After all, my socks are almost dry now!'

Surely they must be finished now? Clara checked her watch for what felt like the hundredth time. Wanting to block out even the mental image of her daughter queuing and boarding such an unnatural ride, she had opted for a seat at the other side of the café by a large window over-looking a shady pond. Once seated with a latte she had immersed herself in work emails on her mobile. After all, technically it was a work day.

But Sue was proving as ferociously efficient at running the office as she was at running a house and it had only taken Clara twenty minutes to clear the backlog. Without work the old, all-too familiar panic reasserted itself. She swallowed, trying to dislodge the lump in her throat, the clutching sensation at her chest. Summer was fine, she was with Raff, she was on a ride designed to be completely safe despite all outward appearances.

But, oh, if only Summer didn't have to grow up. Maybe the witch in Rapunzel had a point. She was very misunderstood if you ignored the eye-gouging part. In fact, Clara could look up any convenient towers in forests for sale right now and deposit Summer at the top of one.

She sighed. Maybe that was just a little over the top.

Drinking the last bitter, lukewarm dregs, Clara tapped her fingers on the wooden table top. Maybe she should go out there and wait, be at the exit, beaming, ready to welcome her daughter back to solid ground. She needed to hide her fears better, show support for all Summer's whims, schemes and plans just as her parents had for her. Just as they still did.

Mind made up, Clara pushed her chair out and gathered up her bag and jacket and the coats Raff and Summer had left with her. Arms full, she walked towards the exit, deliberately keeping her steps unhurried, hoping if she projected an aura of calm she might even come to believe it herself.

It was only an hour until closing time and the café had been quiet, almost eerily so compared with the hustle and bustle outside. The screams of the riders mingled with the

cries of the hot and overtired toddlers and babies punc-
tuated by screeches and laughter from the school groups
and gangs of older teenagers. The day was still unsea-
sonably warm and the coats were stuffy in her arms as
she walked towards the ride.

It was odd how the noise seemed to dim as she approached the area dedicated to Typhoon. No rattle of
wheels, no Tannoy, no adrenaline-fuelled screams, no
noisy chatter from the queue. It was almost preternatu-
rally quiet, as if she were in some alternate dimension;
in the theme park and yet not of it.

It was as if the ride wasn't running at all...

The blood rushed to her head, pounding loudly in her
ears as she looked up at the twisting circular rails, so very
thin, so very high. But with hideous clarity Clara already
knew what she would see. A train lying like a broken toy
along the curve of a loop, completely still, the passengers suspended high above the ground below, immobile.

It doesn't mean she's up there.

But there was no queue; the waiting people were being
cleared away from the area by efficient staff members.
No jaunty blazers and hats here; they were all purpose
with fluorescent jackets and walkie-talkies and grim,
unsmiling faces.

Clara turned and walked back to the café. They were
meeting her there; she should have waited. Summer
would be disappointed at having missed her turn and
Raff would just be relieved that they hadn't been on that
particular carriage and she would admit that for one terrified moment she had thought they were up there and
Summer would roll her eyes and tell her to stop worrying about everything and they would agree to call it a
day and walk back to the van...

Clara caught her breath. It was all going to be fine.

She walked back into the café, ready to catch her daughter up in her arms and never let her go.

They weren't there. She looked around, her head buzzing with disbelief. They had to be here.

'Are you all right?' The young man behind the counter was looking at her oddly as if he had never seen a woman utterly paralysed by fear, burdened by coats and indecision and terror before.

'Yes,' she said automatically, barely recognising the high, strained voice coming out of her mouth. 'At least, I don't know what to do. I think my daughter is on that train but I don't know who to ask.'

The room was spinning recklessly round, a rushing sound in her ears, and she swayed as if she were on a roller coaster herself, the coats spilling from her arms. Strong arms caught her, sat her down; voices were jabbering at her, asking questions she had no idea how to answer.

She had taken her eye well and truly off the ball and now her daughter was trapped alone except for a man she didn't know at all. And it was all Clara's fault.

CHAPTER TEN

'WHAT'S HAPPENING?'

That was a very good question. Unfortunately Raff wasn't sure he knew the answer. Carefully, making sure he didn't rock the carriage in any way, he turned his head to the side so that he could see Summer. She was holding herself still, her body was unnaturally rigid and the pointed little face was pale but she didn't seem to be on the verge of tears, thank goodness, Raff had never had to deal with weeping children before; doing so trapped two hundred metres in the air would definitely be beyond him.

'I think there's been a problem with the power,' he said as calmly as he could, trying not to dwell on just how uncomfortable it was to be suspended on his back strapped into a leather harness.

Although he believed there were clubs that catered for such desires.

At least the carriage hadn't stopped when they were facing down; there might have been mass hysteria. Instead he could look up at the late afternoon sky and pretend the ground was just a few comfortable feet below.

'Will they rescue us?' Her voice sounded small and scared.

'Of course!' Although goodness knew when. It was

hard to see exactly where they were and what was nearby but the ride extended out well over a kilometre and the entrance platform was a long way back. 'They won't want us cluttering up the park much longer.'

'How?'

'I think they'll use a crane,' he said after some thought. 'Although a helicopter would be fun. Have you ever been in one?'

'No.' Summer sounded wistful. 'Nor an aeroplane. Not even the Eurotunnel. We usually go away with Granny and Grandpa and stay in a cottage and walk.' She sounded less than thrilled.

'That sounds fun,' he said gravely.

'I want to stay in a villa with a pool like Natasha. Mummy says one day when our ship comes in. Although I'd rather fly there.'

Raff wanted to promise her that he'd take her away immediately, anywhere she wanted to go, but he managed to stop the words slipping out. He had no right to promise this child anything.

'Where would you want to go? If you could go anywhere?'

'Well,' she said thoughtfully. 'Natasha always goes to Majorca and that does look epic but I really want to go to Florida and go on all the roller coasters.'

She wanted to what? Raff didn't think he was ever going to set foot on a roller coaster again. 'They have alligators in Florida,' he said.

'Awesome! Have you seen one?'

'Yep, and crocodiles too. Big nasty ones in Africa.'

'You've been to Africa?' Her eyes were big with excitement. 'Did you see elephants and lions and zebras?'

'All of them. There's nothing like lying in a tent and listening to a lion roar somewhere in the distance.' He lowered his voice. 'It makes the hairs on the back of your neck stand up.'

'Ooh.' She sounded envious. 'Have you been to Australia?'

'Actually, no.'

'I was born there,' she said proudly.

'So you've been somewhere I haven't been.'

There was another long pause. 'Raff?'

'Mmm?'

'I'm scared.'

'Look at me.' Raff wiped all tension off his face and smiled reassuringly at her. 'Give me your hand.' Her hand was so small it looked lost in his; he clasped it tightly, giving her a reassuring squeeze. 'I promise you, Summer, we'll be absolutely fine. I am going to be with you the whole time, okay?'

'Okay.'

'Now, where else do you want to go? I've never seen the Northern Lights so that's on my list.' He felt the small hand relax and saw a little colour come back into her cheeks. She was going to be fine; he just hoped that rescue wasn't too far away.

If this was just a tiny proportion of the weight of responsibility Clara carried then no wonder she didn't want her daughter to go anywhere or do anything. If he ever became a parent then he would build a house lined with cotton wool and keep his children confined within. How did anybody do it? Carry that burden? No wonder his mother had run the second she had been left solely responsible for Polly and him.

For the first time Raff felt a glimmering of empathy for his sweet, childlike but ultimately weak mother. Pampered, cossetted her whole life, she had been utterly unprepared for life as a single mother. So she had run away; as he had, as Polly had. It must be in the genes.

But they had been so young, even younger than Summer here, and they had put all their faith and trust in her. She had let them down, badly. He couldn't imagine anything that would induce Clara to abandon Summer—or anything that would induce him to abandon his children if he was ever lucky enough to have any.

Children had never been in his life plan. But lying here, looking up at the stars, cradling a small trusting hand and listening to Summer describe her perfect holiday villa, they suddenly didn't seem like such a terrible idea after all.

'Miss.' One voice seemed more insistent than the rest and Clara forced herself to look up, to try and focus. 'Drink this.'

Tea. Hot, milky and full of sugar, utterly disgusting, but she managed a few sips and the room came back into focus. Clara pushed the still-full mug away but the man pushed it back. 'Drink it up, all of it,' he said and, like a child, she obeyed.

He didn't say another word, not until the mug was half empty. 'Your daughter is on Typhoon?'

'I think so.' She sounded more like herself. 'But I wasn't there. I don't know if she got on that train but she was supposed to meet me here.' Clara looked around. There were a few people staring at her curiously, some more openly than others; she focused on a couple of white-faced groups, possibly also worrying about trapped friends and relatives. 'She's only ten.'

'My name is Steve and I'm a customer service manager here. If you feel up to walking then you could accompany me to the site. The camera automatically photos them as the carriage goes horizontal, for souvenir photos, you know? If your daughter is on there then you'll be able to identify her.'

'Where else could she be?'

'We evacuated the area so she may just be waiting for you at the other side,' Steve said calmly. 'Is she on her own?'

Clara shook her head. 'No, she's with my friend, but his phone is here. I was watching their stuff…' Her voice faltered. Watching their coats, phones, but not them.

She should have been there.

'Okay, then, if you're able to walk, let's go.' Clara nodded numbly. But she didn't need to identify any photos. She knew that Summer was stuck on top of the narrow metal loop in the sky.

The next half-hour was the longest of Clara's life. She managed to phone her parents, relieved when they promised to be there as soon as possible. At least Summer wasn't on her own. Raff would be great in a crisis like this; calm, probably finding ways to make the whole thing a big adventure.

He'd keep her daughter safe.

The waiting friends and families had all been asked to wait in the café where tea, coffee and biscuits were on constant supply.

'They have come to a stop in the worst possible place,' Steve explained to the assembled group as they settled in. A few were in tears, a couple more red-faced and angry, demanding they be listened to and threatening lawsuits, but most, like Clara, seemed dazed. 'It's one of the highest points of the ride and there's no infrastructure nearby we can reach them from. Nor can we safely restart the ride. But we do plan for these worst-case scenarios and help is on the way. We've ascertained that no one is injured…' a relieved murmur broke out at his words '…and although they're not comfortable they're steady and despite appearances they are safe. Specialist rescue workers are bringing in cranes and ropes and we hope to begin freeing them within the hour.'

Clara sank into a chair, her hands cradling one in an endless loop of hot teas people kept putting in front of her. She didn't drink any of them, just held them, letting the warmth travel through her numbness, keeping her anchored in the present, keeping away her fears until she finally heard the news the group had been praying for: the first passenger had been safely brought back down to the ground. The rescue mission was working.

'Mummy!'

At last, at last. Clara was on her feet, pulling Summer close as if she could absorb her daughter back into her, inhaling her in. 'Hi, Sunshine.' Her voice was shaky and she tried to control it. 'I don't think I've ever been happier to see you.'

She stood back a little, anxiously checking her daughter over. There were no signs of strain or tears on Summer's face. In fact, she looked as if she had just strolled over from the carousel next ride over.

'Did you know Raff has been in a helicopter and one of those tiny planes?' Summer tucked herself back under Clara's arm, encircling her waist with her arms and squeezing in tight. 'He's heard lions at night and hyenas. Isn't that the coolest?'

'Totally. Are you okay, Sum? Was it scary?'

'A little,' her daughter confessed. 'But Raff made it all okay. He promised we'd be all right and we were. Wait till they hear about this at school. Natasha is going to be epically jealous.'

'Is she all right?'

Clara's heart missed a beat at the low, concerned voice.

'They took her off first. I just wanted to make sure she was okay.'

'Raff!' Summer left her mother's side and threw herself at the tall, broad man. He stood, awkward for a moment, before wrapping his arms around her and cuddling her back.

A lump formed in Clara's throat, making it hard to speak. This was what Summer should have had, had never had.

'If I ever get stuck on a roller coaster again I want to be stuck with you,' Raff told her daughter seriously. 'You were by far the best-behaved person up there.'

'Some of them were making the most awful racket,' Summer said, hanging onto Raff's arm. 'As if crying was going to make it better.'

'That's why I'm so glad you were there to cheer me up.'

Summer turned to Clara, her face lit up with excitement. 'Can we still go to dinner, Mummy, please? I'm totally okay.'

Clara swallowed. 'Sorry, honey.' There, that was normal, wasn't it? Not a quiver in her voice. 'Granny and Grandpa are just through there waiting to take you home. But I think they mentioned something about fish and chips…'

'I wanted to stay with you and Raff.'

'I'm just going to drive Raff home and then I'll be straight there. Come on, sweetie.'

She hadn't looked at him. Not properly. Raff just stood there as Summer was peeled off him and delivered to her grandparents, still protesting that she was okay and wanted to go out for dinner.

He wanted to placate her, promise her that it would happen some other time. But he wasn't sure about that at all.

'I'm sorry about that.' Clara still wasn't looking at him directly. 'I thought she'd be better off going straight back.'

'I could have driven the van back, if you wanted to go with Summer.'

She paused. 'I wasn't sure if you'd be okay to drive. Besides, I thought we should talk.'

Here it came. Raff was suddenly very tired. There had been a few moments up there when he had been concerned, worried that they'd be trapped for several hours, that the actual rescue process would be dangerous. The responsibility had been heavy.

It was funny; he bore a huge amount of responsibility nearly every day of his life. He had to keep all kinds of facilities going; literally hundreds of lives depended on him. He took that responsibility very seriously, lived for it. But it was nothing compared to the fear he had felt when Clara's daughter was in such terrible danger and there was nothing he could do but sit there, talk to her and hold her hand.

He ran a hand through his hair, aware just how much the accident had taken out of him. All he wanted to do at this point was have a beer, a shower and collapse into his bed, but there was no point putting this off.

Clara would say what she had to say; she had every right to. He had messed up.

They walked away from the building, their steps in harmony but several inches apart, not one centimetre of them touching.

'I'm sorry,' he said after a while, not able to bear the silence any longer. 'You must have been terrified.'

Clara stopped and stood stock still for a long, long moment. Raff could see how unnaturally rigid her shoulders were, the lack of colour in her lips. The defeated look in her eyes.

'You had no right.' Her voice was trembling; he didn't know if she was holding back tears or filled with anger. He feared it was both.

Her throat was burning with the effort of keeping the tears held back. Again. For goodness' sake, she had barely cried in years and now she was giving Niobe a run for her watery money.

'You had no right,' she tried again. 'Inviting us here in front of Summer so I had no choice but to agree, offering to accompany her on the ride. I know I could have said no.' She could hear the volume of her voice rising and took a deep breath. 'I could have but you put me in a really difficult position. I've hardly been around lately, thanks to you. The last thing I wanted to be was a killjoy mother as well as an absent one!'

She expected him to defend himself, to get angry back. Instead he stood, facing her, palms outstretched. 'You're right. I was completely out of line.'

If he thought being calm and reasonable was going to calm her down he was in for a big shock. 'She could have been killed up there!' The words were torn out of her, raw and heartfelt. 'Do you know how it feels to see the one person, the one person you would gladly die for, stuck miles up in the sky and know you are utterly, utterly helpless? Of course you don't!' Was that her? So cold and bitter. 'The only person you care for is yourself.'

Raff's face whitened. 'I care about you.'

She didn't want to hear it. 'Yes, one day at a time.' Was that why she was so angry? They hadn't finished the conversation in her office; Summer had interrupted them before it had been resolved. No, she pushed the uncomfortable thought far out of her mind. It had nothing to do with Raff and his piecemeal approach to relationships; this was all about her daughter.

'She could have died,' she repeated and this time the words really hit home. 'She could have fallen and I wasn't there, Raff. I wasn't there.'

'No, you weren't, but I was.' He ran a hand down her arm, looking intently into her eyes and just like that the anger dissipated. Oh, how she wanted to step forward, lean into him and let him hold her. But she stood firm. 'She wasn't alone. And, Clara? Your daughter was amazing. She's brave and interesting and that is down to you. You are a wonderful mother.'

He was saying all the right things and it would be so, so easy to put this behind her, behind them, and let him into her life properly, into Summer's life. Because this was what Summer wanted, what she deserved. Someone who appreciated just how special she was, someone who made her feel safe.

This was what Clara needed.

But Raff wasn't that man as much as she desperately wanted him to be. He was leaving, soon. And both she and Summer deserved better than a part-time Prince Charming.

'Come on.' She resumed walking, relieved to see the van close by. 'I'll drive you home.'

Raff didn't even try and argue, just slid across to the passenger seat as Clara opened the door and settled herself at the wheel. Neither of them spoke during the short drive back to Hopeford. It was no time at all until Clara drew up in front of the pretty cottage and killed the engine—and Raff still had no idea what to say, how to break the deathly silence.

He had always been able to rely on his charm in the past. Now it wasn't enough, not by miles.

'I know people think I keep her too close.' The words made him jump, unexpected in the long silence. 'But they have no idea what she and I have been through. When I first came back I was so young, other mothers used to think I was her au pair or big sister. I always had to do everything better to prove I was as good as they were.'

'Of course you were.' He could see her. Young, independent, tilting her head coolly as she walked past the whispers, the sneers, the judgement. 'Better.'

'I have to put her first,' she said. 'Always.'

'Clara.' He reached over and took her cold hand. 'I know today was horrible. I can't imagine what you went through. But it doesn't have to change anything.'

She was immobile under his touch, the green cat's eyes remote, shuttered. 'You're leaving,' she said. 'There isn't a future for us, so what's the point?'

Fun? Living for today? Attraction? Raff searched through his usual stock of reasons and arguments and found them wanting.

'I think we could be good together.'

'When you're in town, when you can fit us in? I know how amazing your job is, Raff. I think it's great, that you are a very giving person. I really do. But I can't be second best. And nor can Summer. And I don't think you can give us what we need.'

Ouch. Words like arrows, well aimed and sharp. Raff looked at her and could see no indecision; her eyes were steady, the colour of a stormy sea. 'She deserves better than that, Raff. *I* deserve better. She needs a father figure, someone she can rely on. I know you were great with her up there and I am so grateful but I can't have you in her life. I can't have you in my life.'

Raff wanted to reassure her but what could he say? He couldn't offer her more, couldn't *be* more. His life was elsewhere; his calling was elsewhere. She was right. She deserved so much more than an emotionally stilted runaway could offer her.

'You do,' he said, aware how harsh his voice sounded. He swallowed, shocked at the size of the lump in his throat. 'You both do. I hope you find someone who appreciates just how amazing you are.'

'You didn't promise me anything,' she said, looking down at her hands, twisting the bangle round and round her slender wrist. 'You were always very clear what this was and I thought I knew what I was doing. I guess somewhere along the way the lines blurred for me. That was stupid of me.' She looked up at him, held his gaze. 'But things are clear now. You're a good man, Raff Rafferty. I hope you find whatever it is you're looking for.'

She reached across and opened his door. Her intention was clear. Raff searched for something to say but came up with nothing. All he could do was press a kiss to her soft cheek and climb out of the van and watch as she drove away into the deepening twilight, leaving Raff alone with only the birds' evensong for company.

He was free just the way he liked it. Free of family obligations, free of Rafferty's, free of all ties. It was what he had always wanted.

It should feel so good. So why did he feel as if he had suddenly lost everything?

CHAPTER ELEVEN

'WHAT YOU NEED to do,' Maddie said, 'is get back on the horse.'

'I need to *what*?' Clara stared at her cousin suspiciously.

'Get back on the horse. So you fell. Who can blame you? That man was sex on a stick. I would have quite liked to have fallen myself, if I wasn't with Ollie,' Maddie finished, a little unconvincingly, Clara thought. 'And as a starter to get you back into the swing of things he was perfect. But he was never the main course and you know it, so don't let him make you lose your appetite.' She sat back on the sofa, took a sip of her wine and beamed at Clara.

Clara tried to disentangle Maddie's mix of metaphors and gave up. 'I still don't know what to do about this.' She held up the cheque that had arrived with that morning's post. 'It's twice the amount I was expecting.'

'Which is terrible because?'

Clara gave her a level look. 'Because I was sleeping with him.'

'It's guilt money. He knows he should have stayed and fought for you. He hasn't and he's throwing money at his guilty conscience.'

'I didn't want him to stay and fight for me. I'm not Guinevere.' But Clara could feel her cheeks heating up;

even she didn't believe a single word she was saying. She
knew with utter certainty that they would echo through
her head tonight as she fought off thoughts of him. It
was worse at night, what-ifs and might-have-beens spiralling dizzily through her mind until she finally fell
into a fitful, dream-filled sleep. 'I don't know if I can
accept this. Should I return it, ask for the right amount?'

'Don't you dare.' Maddie sat bolt upright in horror.
'You deserve that money. And as you are giving away
that whole gorgeous wardrobe he bought you...'

'*Gave* me and I'm not giving it away, I'm selling it.
All proceeds to Doctors Everywhere.' She was never
going to wear most of them again; this seemed like the
right solution.

'Every item?' Maddie peeped over from under long
eyelashes but Clara had seen her cousin perform that
trick far too many times before to fall for her beseech-
ing glance.

'Every one.'

'Even the sequinned shift?'

'Even the sequinned shift, well, probably.' She hated
to admit it but she did have a secret fondness for the frivolous, shiny, ridiculously short piece of clothing. Nothing to do with the look in Raff's eyes when she had first
tried it on.

'Bags me it next time we go out!' Maddie was all
smiles again. 'Seriously, Clara, that's one hell of a bonus
for a job well done. Whatever his motivation you put in
a lot of hours—legitimate hours—and he got the results
he wanted. Take the cheque and get yourself signed up
to one of these websites before you retreat back into that
shell of yours.' She patted the open laptop perched between them. 'Right, what are your interests? Fine dining and culture?'

'No!' Clara shook her head, uneasily aware that she was being a little over-emphatic. 'I did far too much of that with Raff.'

'And you didn't enjoy it?'

An image came into Clara's head. Mud. Mud everywhere, Raff hoisting her up onto the rope. The feeling of freedom, of being able to let go. 'I want someone I can do ordinary things with,' she said slowly. 'Walk, talk, read. But when we do them together they become extraordinary.'

There was a long moment's silence. 'Don't we all?' said Maddie softly.

Clara picked up the cheque again, aware she had said too much, revealed too much even to herself. 'I'm not going to sign up yet, no...' as her cousin tried to interrupt '...I don't mean I won't, just not tonight. Not right now. I think I might take Summer away for a few weeks and I'll do it when we get back.'

'But it's term time. You never let her miss school.'

'I think this is a sign.' Clara looked at the cheque. She had already been considering the trip before the cheque arrived. It just made the logistics easier. 'I'll put the amount I was expecting into the business, just as I always planned to. But the extra I'm going to spend doing something I should have done a long time ago. I'm going to take Summer to Australia.'

Australia. Once it had been the promised land—a land of freedom, of exotic, alien landscapes, of opportunity. And then it had all turned to gritty dust. For the longest time she couldn't even hear an Australian accent without a sense of foreboding, of panic. Had put her wanderlust behind her, packed her need for adventure away along with her backpack and guidebooks and dreams.

But in doing so she had denied Summer her heritage. Her daughter deserved to know who she was. And Clara? Clara needed to find herself again. 'I think I was attracted to Raff because he reminded me of how I used to be.'

Maddie snorted. 'You were attracted to him because he was hot.'

Clara smiled. But the painful thump her heart gave whenever she thought of him, the tightness in her chest, had nothing to do with the way he looked, nice as that was. It was the way he made her feel—as if she could do anything. Once she had had that belief in herself.

'That too,' she agreed. 'But if this whole mess has taught me anything it's that I need to figure some things out about me before I can commit to anyone properly. It's a good thing Raff was always going away.' See, that was convincing. She was totally believable. 'I'm not ready for a relationship. Not yet. But I hope to be.' She smiled brightly. An easy, simple relationship. They existed, right?

'And Byron?'

'I hope he'll meet up with us but if he doesn't?' She shrugged. 'I can't force him, Maddie. I used to think if he just met Summer he'd fall for her but now I just don't know. But she should see where she was born, where she spent her first year.'

It was time to lay some ghosts to rest. And when she came back she'd be ready to move on, Raff Rafferty nothing but a pleasant memory. See, she had a plan. Everything was better with a plan. Even a bruised heart.

And that was all this was. She'd allowed herself to believe their own story, that was all. Hearts didn't get broken, not in real life, not after just a few weeks, not when you were the one to walk away, the one with responsibilities.

No, it was just a little bruised. She just needed time,.

Time, distance and a little bit of hope that it was all going to be all right, somehow.

But later, when Maddie had gone and Clara was sitting alone on her sofa, as she always was, that tiny bit of hope evaporated.

She was a strong woman, she owned her own business, her own home, raised her daughter alone. Was it wrong for her to have wanted him to ride into battle for her? Wanted him to try?

She was no fairy-tale princess but right now she would give anything to see Raff on a charger fighting his way through a forest of thorns, scaling a tower, searching the town for the owner of one small slipper. Instead he had turned and walked away without a word.

As Byron had.

Was she that unlovable? Wasn't she worth fighting for? He hadn't said one word to try and convince her to change her mind.

Clara looked around the small room. At the large framed prints and photos she had carefully chosen and hung, the wallpaper she had spent days cutting, pasting and hanging and smoothing out most of the air bubbles.

The sofa she and Summer hung out on, chatted, watched films, read books, cuddled on. The plants she tried not to kill with alternate bouts of love and neglect. The stuffed bookshelves, an eclectic mix of Summer's old picture books, the ones that were too babyish to stay in her room but that Clara couldn't bear to part with, crime novels and business guides. No travel guides though. Maybe it was time to get them out again.

This was her life, the life she chose and worked every minute to maintain. A safe, ordered life. And now it wasn't enough.

She missed him, a huge aching chasm inside her that

hurt more with every day, every non phone call, every non email. She didn't want any of the perfect matches on the dating sites; she wanted Raff.

But he didn't want her.

It was as if the sun had gone out and she didn't know if she was ever going to get used to living in the dull grey gloom. She had to get away. She would take Summer to Australia and while she was there she would forget all about Raff Rafferty.

It was the only way.

'Castor.' His grandfather stood to meet him, every inch the proprietor. He might have been forced into retirement but here, in the world-famous Rafferty tea rooms, he was still king. 'Good to see you.'

'And you, sir.' Raff took the proffered hand and shook it. 'Good to see you out and about.'

'Got no time to play the damned invalid,' his grandfather grunted as he slowly sat down. Raff watched him anxiously but it didn't seem more than the usual twinges of arthritis that had plagued Charles Rafferty for the last few years. He turned to the discreetly hovering waitress. 'We'll have the usual, Birgitte.'

'Should you be eating afternoon tea? Wouldn't the soup be a better option?'

Charles Rafferty scowled. 'I've been eating pap for the last few weeks. A man can't live on soup alone.'

'Nor can he live long on huge amounts of cream and butter, especially after suffering problems with his heart,' Raff reminded him. He turned to the waitress and smiled. 'Can you make sure there is no cream or butter and just a small selection of cakes? Thank you so much.'

'You always did think you knew best.' But to Raff's relief his grandfather made no attempt to countermand his order. Instead he sat back in his chair and turned his trademark sharp look on Raff. The one that had him confessing all his sins instantly. 'Polly returns soon and all this...' he waved one hand at the tearooms '...all this will be hers. Any regrets?'

'Only that it took this long,' he assured him.

'And you? Where next?'

Now *that* was the million-dollar question. Raff's morning meeting at Doctors Everywhere had changed everything and Raff had no idea how he felt about any of it. He waited until the waitress had unloaded the heavy tray, positioning the silver teapot in the middle of the table, accompanied by a silver jug of hot water, a jug of milk, a small bowl of lemon slices and the silver sugar bowl. It was the same design and arrangement as the very first afternoon tea served in this very room nearly one hundred years ago. Rafferty's were big on tradition.

'Jordan,' he said, pouring out his grandfather's tea, knowing he liked it weak, black and with lemon. He wasn't so fussy; in the camps he took his hot drinks as they were served, grateful for the comfort and the caffeine. 'Just for a few weeks.' He stirred his own tea, finding it hard to look him in the eye, not wanting his response to influence him in any way.

'But they want me to consider basing myself back here. Their Director of Philanthropy is moving on and they've asked me to replace him.'

He continued to stir his tea, the morning's conversation still whirling around his brain.

He had gone to the London office to report for duty and organise his next posting, a normal procedure that had quickly proven to be far from standard when he had been ushered, not to the assignments department but into the CEO's office for a long and frank conversation.

'You're one of our best guys out in the field,' the CEO had said. 'But you're replaceable out there. I'd like you to consider working here instead. We completely beat our targets at that ball, and signed up some committed new sponsors; much of that was through your contacts. With you heading up our philanthropy section, combining your business experience with the work you did with us, I reckon we could bring in some serious money—and that means funding some serious work.'

'Obviously you would be good in that role. I trained you myself.' His grandfather was being as modest as usual. 'But you always hated being deskbound. I thought it was the field work you wanted?'

Raff had to fight the urge to squirm. With his grandfather's keen gaze focused on him like this there was no way he could lie to him—or to himself.

'Honestly? I'd been thinking something along similar lines myself,' he admitted. 'It makes a lot of sense, I know. But it will be hard. I love the unpredictability of what I do now. They've promised it won't all be desk work and meetings and events. I'll need to have a good understanding of our needs so I'll still get to spend some time in the field, but it will be site visits from the HQ, not getting my hands dirty and being part of a team, at least not in the same way. But everyone at HQ needs to do at least one field rotation every two years so I wouldn't have to walk away entirely.'

'Is this about the girl? Your grandmother thinks she's the one.'

'When did you see Grandmother?' Raff didn't want to talk about Clara, not to someone who could read him as well as his grandfather did.

'We *are* still married,' his grandfather pointed out as if separate lives and separate houses for the last ten years were a mere technicality. 'But we're not discussing my love life.' Raff choked on his tea. Thank goodness, now *that* would be an awkward conversation in every way. Grandparents weren't supposed to have love lives, especially not ones who were estranged. Bridge partners? Absolutely. Love lives? Absolutely not. 'Wouldn't this new job work much better if you are considering getting engaged?'

'We're not.' With relief Raff turned to the waitress bearing the heavy stand heaped with dainty finger sandwiches, scones and an array of tiny cakes and pastries. 'Thanks so much, Birgitte. Grandfather, don't get up. I'll serve you.'

'Only to make sure I eat brown bread and no cake,' his grandfather grumbled. He looked keenly at Raff. 'I thought things were serious? You've been inseparable for weeks. I admit I wasn't sure at first but actually I quite like her. She's feisty, good thing for a spoilt chap like you.'

Raff took longer selecting each sandwich than was strictly necessary, placing them carefully on the plate. 'It hasn't worked out,' he said, handing him the plate with the elegant flourish a summer working in this very tea room had instilled in him.

'Why ever not? You were smitten.' Charles Rafferty pointed his fork at Raff in a way that would have got either he or Polly sent from the table when they were children.

Smitten. Clara had obviously fooled everyone even better than he had hoped. It helped that he liked her, that he desired her, that he enjoyed getting behind the barriers she put up, making her laugh. He valued her opinion, enjoyed her company—and sometimes the sight of her almost brought him to his knees.

But *smitten*?

'Clara deserves more than I can give her. She needs someone reliable, someone who won't run away the moment things get difficult.' He had told himself this so many times in the last week it sounded as if he were reciting something he had learned off by heart.

'And why is that someone not you?'

Raff opened his mouth to reply and then shut it again, more than a little nonplussed. His grandfather was sitting bolt upright looking expectantly at him, wanting some sort of answer. How could he not know? He was separated from his own wife after all! The Raffertys were all the same: good workers, terrible husbands. Or wives—Polly was no nearer to being settled than he was. They'd probably end up living together in their nineties in a crumbling mansion somewhere and people would call them 'those peculiar Rafferty twins'.

They were impetuous—he had signed up to a crisis organisation on a whim, for goodness' sake—the absolute opposite of the calm, ordered, organised Clara. Raff curled his fingers into his palm. He had to stop thinking about her. She needed a future with someone stable. Someone unlike him.

The honourable, the only thing to do was to respect her wishes, to walk away.

'You did spend six years working in a business you dislike for my sake.'

'I wouldn't say dislike…'

'Four years working for little money in difficult conditions helping others?'

'Well, I…'

'You came home the second your sister needed you?'

'Of course, but…'

His keen blue eyes softened. 'You wrote to your

mother every week even though she never wrote back. Visited your father every weekend even though he had no idea who you were. Rejected invitations to parties, the chance to be in the school team because they clashed with visiting hours.'

How did his grandfather know all this? Know *him* this well? Raff thought he'd done such a good job of keeping it all hidden well away. 'They were my parents.' He coughed slightly to clear his throat, dislodge the unwanted lump that was suddenly lodged there. He hadn't wanted to turn down those invitations, to lose his coveted spot in the team, but what if that had been the week? What if his father had died and he hadn't visited, hadn't told him once again how sorry he was for not saving him?

His mother seldom replied to the letters he dutifully sent. Occasionally parcels would turn up, books or T-shirts or toys. After a couple of years they had become even less frequent—and the toys were too young, the books too easy, the clothes a size or so too small.

'Of course she wants you,' his grandfather said, taking advantage of Raff's introspection to help himself to several of the cakes. 'You're a good man, Castor, loyal to a fault, hardworking, handsome. Well…' his eyes twinkled '…people do say you take after me. The only person who doesn't believe in you, Castor, is you.'

He put his knife down and looked seriously over the table at Raff. 'Don't make the same mistakes I did. Don't walk away because you're too stubborn or too proud or too afraid. You don't want to be my age and full of regrets. They make lonely bedfellows, you know. If I'd tried harder with your grandmother, then maybe…' He sighed. 'I have hope it's not too late for us. You at your age? You should be beating her door down, begging her to take you back.'

Raff saw his grandfather out to his car, his mind whirling. The job, Clara, his grandfather. Clara again. What if he let her down? Couldn't be the man she needed him to be?

There was more than his pride at stake here. More than his heart. He was willing to risk all he was, all he wanted, all his dreams, gamble them on a chance of happiness. But could he risk Clara's, Summer's stability? Their future?

It was so much responsibility. The stakes were far, far too high. Better to fold now than let them lose everything. That was the right thing to do no matter how very wrong it felt.

But try as he might to convince himself a small beacon of hope refused to flicker and die away. What if it wasn't too late? What if he could somehow make things right?

What if this was the chance he'd been waiting for his whole life? Was he just going to sit back and let the opportunity to be part of a family pass him by? He had salvaged his relationship with his grandfather despite all the odds. Maybe, just maybe there was hope for him after all.

CHAPTER TWELVE

IT SHOULD HAVE BEEN utter bliss, lying on a comfortable chaise, the sun blissfully melting into every one of her weary bones and muscles. She didn't even have Summer to worry about; she was currently enjoying a playdate with an old friend of Clara's, an afternoon of beaches, barbecues and rollerblades. She wouldn't be missing Clara at all.

But no matter how comfortable the chaise, how delicious the sun, how novel the lack of responsibility, Clara just couldn't relax. With an exasperated groan she sat up and checked her phone again, hoping someone, somewhere needed her. No, there were no texts, voicemails, emails or any other type of message.

She was utterly alone.

Looking around the lavish poolside area, Clara tried to shake off the gloom. After all, look where she was! Sitting in a comfortable chair, an iced juice on the table beside her, views to die for spread out all around her; blue, blue water overshadowed by the wings of the famous opera house.

She was living the dream, for a few days at least. She had decided to finish their holiday in luxurious style and you really didn't get much more luxurious than her present location.

If she didn't want her admittedly extortionately expensive drink, then she could go for a swim in the rooftop pool just a few feet in front of her, or work out in the lavishly appointed gym, have a nap in the massive hotel room that Summer swore was bigger than their entire apartment or go for a walk. She was just steps from the Rocks Markets and she still had some gifts to buy. If nothing in the touristy stalls tempted her then there were plenty of shops in Sydney's historic heart.

Or she could go to the Botanic Gardens; after all, she told herself, she'd just be taking a walk. She wouldn't be stressing about tomorrow. About the near miracle that was going to occur.

No. Clara slumped back in her chair with a sigh, her eyes unfocused, barely noticing the spectacular scenery. All she could see was the exotic lush greenery of the gardens and the two people who would be strolling there tomorrow. Would they have anything to say to each other? What would be worse: awkward silences or an instant connection?

This was what you wanted, she told herself, as if repeating the words over and over again would somehow make them true. Summer was finally going to meet her father. Clara just hadn't expected to feel so terrified about it.

If she was honest with herself then she might have to admit it wasn't just today, this loneliness. It had been chilling her for weeks even as she had busied herself with preparations for this trip. They had spent the first ten days here in Sydney staying with old friends before heading out to the Blue Mountains, taking in the vineyard where they had lived when Summer was just a baby.

After that they had undertaken the long, exhausting

journey to the farm where one of Clara's friends had moved to, completely in the middle of nowhere. Her daughter had immediately taken to the outdoor life; loving every minute of her first riding lessons, hanging onto a strap as she was bounced around in the back of the truck, swimming in the local watering hole. *Don't,* Clara had wanted to cry out a hundred times. *Look out for crocodiles, for snakes, for spiders, what if the horse bolts or the truck overturns?*

What if?

But she had held her tongue even though it had physically hurt, even though she had been almost doubled up in fear and dread, and she had watched her daughter blossom.

Meanwhile Clara herself found it harder and harder to work out just who she was any more.

The trip had definitely healed some old wounds, but had also brought up new, troubling ones. Even after all the years away she had friends here, people who she could connect with straight away. There was no one outside her family who she had that connection with back in England. No one but Raff.

Damn, she had said his name. If it weren't bad enough torturing herself with images of Summer and Byron getting on so well she became totally redundant, she had to think of Raff. Again.

Truth be told he was often on her mind. The more she tried to forget about him, the larger he loomed.

Because as good a time as she was having, as much fun as it was showing Australia to her daughter, there was a little part of her that knew that having Raff with them would have made everything perfect. He'd have charmed her friends and adored the outback. And if he were here she would feel so much better about tomorrow, if he were distracting her, reassuring her that she was doing the right thing.

She was, wasn't she? Mechanically Clara reached for the bangle at her wrist, turning it round and round, the familiar feel of the silver slipping through her fingertips a reassurance, a grounding.

Typical Byron to leave his change of heart to the last minute, for the grand reconciliation to eat into their last days. But how could she deny him? Well, she would happily deny him anything and everything but this wasn't about him.

Unfortunately though it was about her, because, sitting here alone, she had to admit that once you took away her work and her daughter there was very little left.

She had allowed her worry for Summer, her drive to provide for her daughter, to consume her. Which was laudable. But, there that word was again, it was a little lonely.

Well, things would change. She would date and she would not compare every man to Raff, no matter how tempting. She would have hobbies and friends and relax and soon she wouldn't even remember Raff's name.

Or think about him whenever she looked at the night sky and saw the Heavenly Twins. Thank goodness they had different stars here in the Southern Hemisphere.

Clara eyed her phone again, her pulse speeding up. What harm would one little peek do? He hadn't blogged for a couple of weeks now; she just wanted to know he was all right. It wasn't stalking or being obsessive. It was caring about a friend.

It was almost embarrassing how quickly her browser picked up the Doctors Everywhere website, how it immediately assumed she wanted to go to the section dedicated to field staff blogs. It was almost as if she had been reading it every day. Every evening. When she couldn't sleep…

Not just Raff's blog, all of them. Trying to get an idea of the world he occupied, the people he worked with, his friends, the way he spent his days. The job that was so all consuming he walked away from his family, his heritage, to be part of it.

That he walked away from her without a backwards look.

Her breath caught as she saw the all-too-familiar photo. It was a couple of years old, she reckoned, the hair shorter, more preppy, his gaze wary. Her finger hovered and for one moment she fooled herself that she had a choice before she touched the screen and watched the blog load.

Nothing new. It was the same short entry she had read far too many times detailing his impressions on arriving at the refugee camp. The same matter-of-fact tone as he described families crammed into tents, all their worldly goods reduced to what they could carry, how they were treating pregnant women who had walked for hundreds of miles, malnourished children, broken men.

It was so vivid she could see it; every time the shock hit her anew. His work was so important, how could she compete? What if she asked him to come back and he regretted it, that regret poisoning whatever it was they had?

Or maybe they had nothing and he wouldn't come back at all.

Or what if she risked it? Let him go and welcomed him home in between postings. Shared him with the job he loved so much. Could she do that? Could she be so selfless, live with the uncertainty and the danger and the long months when he was away?

She turned the bangle round and round. That question had become more and more pressing as the weeks went by. She wanted to answer yes...

'Excuse me, miss?' The polite young waiter had returned, a tall glass on his tray.

'I haven't finished this one yet,' she apologised with a guilty look at the still-full drink. It was her third. She dreaded seeing how much money she had wasted on the freshly squeezed juices. But ordering them, sitting here with a drink and watching the world go by was better than sitting in her room and brooding. Just.

'No, miss, this is a new drink. It's a mudslide.'

'A what?' Clara stared at the drink. It looked like a coffee to her.

'A mudslide,' he repeated. 'Vodka, coffee liqueur and Irish cream, mixed with crushed ice.'

A latte with a kick. 'But I didn't order a drink. There must be some mistake.'

'No, miss, the gentleman over there ordered it. He said you were a big fan of mud.'

Clara stared at him. 'He said I...' Was this some strange Australian chat-up ritual? She had worked in a bar not that far from here throughout her pregnancy and for the first months of Summer's life but that was nearly a decade ago. Maybe this was a cultural reference that was totally lost on her.

The only mud she had been near in years was with Raff. Oh!

Don't be ridiculous, Clara told herself. Raff was in Jordan, but her heart was hammering so loud she was surprised the whole pool area wasn't throbbing with the beat. She swallowed, her mouth dry.

'The gentleman?' She could barely get the words out, torn between embarrassment and a longing so deep, so intense it nearly floored her.

'Over at the bar.' The young man nodded over towards the long pool bar the other side of the terrace.

It wasn't him; it couldn't be him. She was setting herself up for a massive disappointment but all the admonishing thoughts in the world couldn't quell the hope rising helium light inside her.

Clara tugged at her skirt as she rose out of the chair, looking over in the direction the waiter had indicated. *Be cool and say no, thank you,* the sensible side of her was whispering. *It'll be some bored businessman seeing you sitting alone. He thinks he'll liven his business trip up with a flirt. That's all it is.*

And just because he has broad shoulders and a shock of dishevelled dirty blond hair and navy blue eyes, even darker with exhaustion, doesn't mean it's him. It can't be him sauntering slowly towards you.

'I thought it was apt.' He nodded at the drink still sitting on the waiter's tray. Raff lifted it off, discreetly passing the young man a folded note as he slunk gratefully back to the bar. 'In lieu of the real thing.'

Clara stood and stared, drinking him in. It was like the first time she had seen him: an old crumpled shirt, battered jeans, skin almost grey with weariness. Totally irresistible.

'I thought you were in Jordan.' Of all the things to say. But conversation had deserted her; she was stuck to the spot like an incredulous statue, unable to move or feel.

'I was two days ago, or was it three? It may have been a week. It feels like I've been travelling for ever.'

'But what are you doing here?' It was a mirage, surely. She was like a traveller in a desert, Raff the welcome oasis. Which made her a truly pathetic human being but all she wanted to do was look at him, relearn every feature for posterity. Instead she stood, a foot between them, too scared to touch him in case he disappeared.

'I wanted to see you.' Clara gaped at him, a mute question in her eyes. 'Maddie told me where you were. Nice surroundings, by the way. Is this how you backpacked as a teenager?'

'Just like this, five star all the way.' She fastened on his words. 'You came to see me?'

'I'm hoping to see a baby koala as well, it seems a shame to come all this way and not see one, but mainly I've come to see you.'

Heat filled her, whooshing up from her toes and filling every atom, every nerve burning. 'Me?'

'And the baby koala…' Raff gestured to the drink. 'Are you going to drink that?'

'Sorry.' It was such a lovely gesture and she was spoiling it. 'I'm not a huge fan of vodka. Or Irish cream.'

He regarded the brown mixture with distaste. 'It sounded better than it looks. Do you want to take a walk?'

'A walk?' For goodness' sake, it was as if she were under a spell. Raff was here. In the swanky terrace bar. Half the way across the world from where she had seen him last, from where he was supposed to be. She should have squealed, thrown herself at him, made some indication that she was pleased to see him instead of standing here gaping.

'I've not been to Sydney before. So far I have seen the airport, the inside of the taxi and this rather nice swimming pool. I have been reliably informed there is a rather impressive bridge and opera house I should take a look at. Where's Summer?'

'With a friend. Tomorrow she's seeing Byron.' It was

such a relief to tell him, the burden instantly slipping off her shoulders.

Raff raised his eyebrows in shock, letting out a low whistle of surprise.

'I know, I told him we were coming and made sure he knew when we would be in Sydney and heard nothing, which wasn't a surprise at all. Then he called last night. Which was a surprise but what could I say?' It was nice to see him, to hear him, to be able to speak to someone who absolutely, intuitively understood.

More than nice.

He grimaced. 'Anything you wanted but, knowing you, I guess you said that of course you could accommodate him at such short notice.'

Clara shrugged, the warmth in his eyes almost too much for comfort. 'For her sake.'

He nodded. 'I know. What time are you taking her?'

She bit her lip. 'He's going to text.'

'Do you want me to come with you?'

Just eight words. Eight simple words. Words that made all the fear and the loneliness and the worry evaporate in the hot Sydney sun.

'Yes, please.' She glanced at him, almost shyly. 'She'll be so happy to see you. She talks about you all the time.'

'I can't wait to see her either. I'm counting on her to teach me all the Aussie slang. And I bet she knows all the best baby koalas.'

'She knows it all.' Clara rolled her eyes.

The lift down was spacious and cool but to Clara it felt tiny, almost claustrophobic. She was sharing it with Raff. Every nerve tingled with the need, the want to touch him but she couldn't, frightened he'd disappear like a genie back into the bottle of her imagination. The lift opened straight into the impressive marble foyer and she mutely led the way to the exit. As they reached the steps the sun hit them bright and hot, as different from an English sun as a daisy from an orchid. Clara automatically began to walk on the harbourside path, the sea sparkling beneath them.

Raff took her hand, an easy, natural gesture. It felt like coming home. Clara allowed her fingers to curl up, to meet his, a lifeline she had thought she could manage without. 'So Cinderella is all alone in the big city? It's a good thing I've come to cheer you up.'

'You're the fairy godmother?'

He squeezed her fingers. 'Or Buttons, but I did have another role in mind.'

The teasing voice had turned serious as he stopped and turned to face her, still holding her hand in his. 'I walked away because it felt like the right thing to do. But it wasn't. It was the cowardly thing to do.' His fingers tightened, almost painfully but she didn't resist, his firm grip anchoring her down. 'I don't really know how families work, how loving someone works. It seems so easy to get it wrong, to let people down so badly it's worse than trying at all.'

Clara clung onto him, her fingers laced tightly through his, her heart hammering. 'I was afraid too,' she said honestly. 'I was losing my way. I spent so many years trying to keep things secure and safe and then you came along.' She shook her head, trying to blink away the tears threatening to fall. 'You made my life look so small. You made me feel small.'

'I didn't mean to.' He stepped forward in alarm, one hand brushing her cheek, collecting her tears as they overspilt. 'I just wanted to see you smile. God, it was presumptuous, I know, but I admit I liked the idea of shaking you up a little. You were so sorted, it made me feel inadequate.' He grimaced. 'That was wrong, sorry.'

'No, it was good,' she protested, holding his hand to her cheek. 'I needed it. If it wasn't for you I wouldn't be here, moving on. I'd just work and look after Summer and kid myself that I was happy with such a narrow life. But I'm not. And if loving you means long absences and worry and sharing you with your work then I can manage. Because that's a lot better than not having you in my life at all. And I do want you, I do love you.'

She'd said it. She'd said it all. The four-letter word she hadn't even admitted to herself on long, lonely, sleepless nights. The world might still be going on around them but here and now it had stopped as the word reverberated around her head.

Love.

She peeked up to see his reaction but Raff's face was unreadable.

'Would it ruin your plans too much if I was around a bit more than that?' he asked. 'If I was around pretty much full time? Thing is…' he grinned ruefully '…and I am being presumptuous again so please bear with me, the thing is I don't know much about being a good husband and father.' Clara's heart twisted at the words. 'But I am pretty sure being away over half the year is not a good start.'

'But you love your job.' It was a half-hearted statement, as her mind raced at his words. Had he really said husband and father?

'I love you more.' Raff trailed his hand along her cheek; every nerve fired up at the light caress. 'They offered me a job in London a few weeks ago and I said I needed time to think about it, but I was just scared. I defined myself through my job. I wasn't sure who I would be without it. But if I'm honest, I'd been thinking about offering my services full time in London anyway. The ball made me realise just how much I can achieve with my friends and connections—it would be pretty selfish of me not to use them. It's a very different kind of challenge but a good one, I think.

'Then when I was away all I could think about was you. Being out in the field wasn't enough any more. In fact...' his finger brushed her lip '...it was pretty lonely.'

'I've been lonely too.' It didn't feel like an admission of failure, not now.

'Suddenly, it didn't feel like such a big decision at all. I was going to take the job and woo you. Only when I hotfooted it to Hopeford you were gone.'

'So you came all the way to Sydney.' Clara smiled at him, a wide, uninhibited grin of joy. 'We leave in two days. You didn't have that long to wait.'

'What's another twenty-four hours of travel?' he said. 'Besides, waiting was making me anxious. I didn't want to lose my nerve. You can be pretty intimidating, you know, Clara Castleton?'

'Me?' She'd worked hard at it but that wasn't who she wanted to be any more. She was sick of keeping the world at arm's length.'

'You can also be funny and warm and sharp and there is no one I'd rather wade through mud with. I told you once I'm not a hearts and flowers kind of guy. I'm the idiot who takes a beautiful woman on an assault course or gets a kid stuck on top of a roller coaster but I promise, if you take a chance on me, I'll always put you first. I'll always try.'

Clara took a step closer to him, finally allowing herself to lean in against that tall, broad body, to lace her

fingers around his neck, to reach up and press a kiss on
that firm mouth. 'I know you will,' she whispered. 'You
always put everyone else first. And I don't need hearts
or flowers or clean and tidy adventure-free dates. I just
need you, Raff Rafferty.'

* * * * *

HIS VERY CONVENIENT BRIDE

SOPHIE PEMBROKE

For Pippa, for everything.

CHAPTER ONE

FLYNN STARED AT HER, a hint of panic in his usually calm and collected brown eyes. Helena gazed back, hoping she looked slightly less like a small wild animal caught in the open by a predator than he did.

She had to admit, though, that was unlikely. This was very new territory for both of them.

'While I know that what we just did was very noble and right and championed the cause of true love and so on... what on earth do we do now?' Flynn asked.

Helena's mind whirred with the possibilities, just as it had been doing since the moment her sister ran out of the door, leaving her holding both the pearl-encrusted ivory wedding dress and the proverbial baby. They didn't have much in the way of options, and one choice kept rising to the top of the very short list.

'Help me out of this dress.' She placed Thea's wedding dress carefully on a padded armchair, then twisted to try and reach the zip at the back of her own flamingo-pink bridesmaid's dress. Not a chance. No one had arms that bent like that.

She looked up at Flynn. He was still staring at her.

Men. Hopeless in a crisis.

Although, actually, before today she'd have wagered that Flynn would be pretty good in an emergency. By all accounts, he'd handled the discovery that his fiancée had slept with his brother less than twenty-four hours before their wedding with remarkable aplomb. He'd managed the news that he was about to inherit sole responsibility for a multinational media conglomerate without breaking a sweat. He'd even let the aforementioned fiancée, Helena's sister, run out and elope with her true love moments before the wedding without looking particularly perturbed.

But apparently Helena in her underwear was pushing him too far.

With a sigh, she turned to present him with her back and the offending zip. 'Just undo me, yeah?'

Flynn hesitated a moment before she felt his warm fingertips against her back. 'Why am I doing this?'

'Because I need to get changed. Into that.' She pointed at the wedding dress and felt Flynn's hands still at her back.

'No. No, you don't. We'll just go down to the church and…'

She spun round to face him. 'And what? Tell every business associate you have plus a nice collection of reporters—not to mention both sets of parents—that the wedding of the year is off?' Helena shook her head. That option was very firmly a last resort. Never mind the tabloid fallout, or the impact on company shares—her father would have a heart attack.

'Surely that has to be better than us getting…' He waved a hand between them and she rolled her eyes.

'Married, Flynn. Go on, you can say it. It's not actually a dirty word. You were all set to do it with my sister, and I suspect you weren't any more in love with her than she was with you. As evidenced by the fact you just told her to elope with Zeke.'

'That was different,' Flynn argued. 'Thea and I had a plan. There was…paperwork.'

The man was completely business bound. Grabbing the file the wedding planner had put together for Thea, Helena pulled out a spare invitation, grabbed the pen from its loop and scratched out her sister's name to replace it with her own. Then, as an afterthought, she scribbled a few lines on the back on it. 'Paperwork,' she said, handing it to Flynn. 'Happy now?'

"'I, Helena Morrison, promise to marry Flynn Ashton purely to avoid the hideous fallout of my sister's elopement,'" Flynn read. 'Helena, this is—'

'Keep going.' Helena reached behind her to try and work the zip down the last few inches, finally succeeding in wriggling the strapless dress past her hips and into a heap on the floor.

Flynn turned his back on her, and Helena bit back a smile. He was so *proper*.

"'Furthermore, I agree to renegotiate this contract once the official Morrison-Ashton company business issue thing is dealt with. Signed, Helena Morrison.'" He placed the makeshift contract carefully on the table as if it were a real and important document. 'Company business issue thing?' he asked, sounding puzzled.

'You know—the whole reason you and Thea were supposed to be getting married in the first place. Whatever that was.' Helena stepped into her sister's wedding dress and prayed to God that it fitted well enough to avoid comment. Thea was taller by a couple of inches and Helena had more in the way of curves, but as long as it did up and she could avoid tripping over the hem she'd probably be okay.

'To join both sides of the business and provide…well, to give the company an heir.'

An heir. A child. Maybe even children, plural. Helena swallowed, then pulled the wedding dress up over her chest. She'd cross that very high and scary bridge when she got to it. Or not. Maybe she could dig a tunnel instead…

Okay, thinking was clearly not her friend today. The exhilaration of Thea's escape, of being the one left behind to fix things, of this whole crazy plan, thrummed through her veins. She felt high on excitement in a way she hadn't since she was sixteen.

What she was about to do might be insane but at least it made her feel *alive*.

For now, at least. 'This doesn't have to be a permanent arrangement, anyway,' she said, manoeuvring herself around to Flynn's side, wedding dress still trailing. 'Lace me up?' No zips for the bride. Apparently corset ties were the order of the day.

He obliged without argument, yanking the ties more than tight enough to keep the dress up and tying them in a very efficient bow at the base of her spine. Apparently she was about to marry the one straight man in Europe more comfortable with putting clothes on a woman than taking them off.

'That wasn't the arrangement with Thea,' he told her.

Helena spun round to face him, a fake smile on her face. 'Yes, well. I'm not Thea, am I?' Something she seemed to have been pointing out to disappointed friends, relatives and acquaintances for most of her life. Mostly her father, first wondering why she couldn't be better behaved, more obedient, less trouble. Until trouble had caught up with her at last and suddenly she was perfectly happy to stay home, stay out of trouble, stay safe.

But it hadn't been enough. Then he'd wanted to know why she couldn't have her sister's drive, or brains, or brilliance. Never mind that she *was* less trouble than Thea at last, that she kept their whole family on an even keel, dealing with the fallout from Thea's latest romantic mishaps.

Just like today, really.

This. This one thing—marrying her own sister's fiancé to safeguard the family name, business and reputation—if this didn't make up for the mistakes of her past, nothing ever would. This was her chance.

She could be enough for Flynn. She might not be Thea, but she was still a Morrison. She could give him what he needed, and maybe marrying him could give her absolution after eight long years in the wilderness.

As long as he never found out why she needed absolution. Flynn, of all people, would never understand that.

Flynn's eyes were serious as she looked into them, steady and firm, and Helena's smile slipped away. He was the ultimate man with the plan, she remembered from overheard business talk and the endless wedding preparations. Could he even do this? Be spontaneous enough to marry a stand-in bride?

'Are you sure you want to do this?' he asked, and Helena rolled her eyes.

'I don't think either of us can be sure about that, given that we've had all of about five minutes to think about it.' There was always a chance that she'd regret this moment, this idea for the rest of her life. But right then…the risk seemed worth it.

'I will walk down there and tell everyone it's off,' Flynn said. 'Just say the word, and you're free.'

Somehow, Helena knew that he'd planned to say those words anyway. That he'd have given Thea a last-minute out too, even if Zeke hadn't come home for the wedding. Flynn was a fair, kind, considerate man. And he might not have been the husband she'd imagined for herself, not least because he was supposed to have been her brother-in-law, but she could have done a lot worse. He was a safe choice. He'd never force her, or trick her or be anything but upfront and honest. It was…refreshing.

This could work, one way or another. Maybe they could make a friendly marriage, for the sake of the family and the business. Or, more likely, it might last a month and then they'd quietly end the whole thing. Either was fine. Flynn wouldn't make a fuss; she knew that much about him. They were the calm two now, the ones who smoothed over rough edges at social gatherings, who kept the joint family dinners his mother insisted on civil, even in the face of insurmountable odds. Between them they'd even hidden the fact that Thea and Zeke had slept together on the villa terrace *during the rehearsal dinner* from the hundred guests inside. Maybe they were meant to be together.

And even if it didn't last, the marriage would have served its purpose as a spectacular PR stunt for Morrison-Ashton and Flynn would be free to find a bride who'd give him heirs by the dozen, if he wanted. Win-win, really.

'I'm sure,' she said, and Flynn smiled.

'Then let's go to church.'

Flynn wasn't his brother. He didn't like surprises, didn't want the risk-taking high, or the buzz from making spur-of-the-moment decisions that Zeke seemed to crave. Flynn liked to work from a plan, to know what was coming and prepare accordingly. His very existence, and the fact of his birth, was the definition of unplanned—but Flynn had always felt that there was no reason his life had to follow the same pattern.

A childhood of believing he was an 'unexpected variable', or just a straightforward 'mistake'—depending on whether he was eavesdropping on his father or mother's conversation at the time—had made it very clear to him how deviating from a plan could screw things up. Never mind that *he'd* been the plan. It was Zeke who had come along and screwed everything up. But Zeke was blood, the true heir they'd really wanted but thought they couldn't have. Not somebody else's unwanted child, brought in to fill a void as a last resort.

If his parents had stuck with the plan and never had Zeke, Flynn's life could have been very, very different.

So Flynn prized structure, deliverables, timescales and, above all, a plan. But today, his *wedding day*, didn't appear to be about what Flynn liked or wanted.

He'd heard that before, from married friends. How the wedding day became all about the bride and her mother and her friends, and all the groom really had to do was show up and say 'I do'. Of course, every single one of those friends had actually married the woman they got engaged to...

Fear had clenched in his chest as Thea ran out of the door, tearing his carefully worked plan to shreds. Three years he'd been planning this, talking with his father, and hers, making sure they used the wedding to its full potential. Two years working on Thea, agreeing terms, gentling her along.

In the end, all the planning in the world hadn't been enough. Thea was gone, and that left him with...Helena.

Helena wasn't part of the plan, not even a little bit. She was another unplanned variable, he supposed. But maybe that meant something. Maybe together they could be more than a list of mistakes, of unexpected consequences.

Either way, she was the closest he was going to get to following his plan for the day.

He couldn't hide the relief he felt when he realised that Helena really planned to go through with her proposal. Yes, marrying his fiancée's sister raised its own collection of problems. And, yes, an argument could be made that any family or business situation that required this level of absurd subterfuge was seriously screwed up. And yet Flynn found himself agreeing that it was the best of a short list of bad options. Maybe it wasn't the original strategy, but it could at least be considered a contingency plan. It wasn't as if he hadn't discussed the possibility with his father, before settling on Thea as the most beneficial to the company.

This wasn't a love match and it never had been. Whichever of the Morrison sisters walked down the aisle on his arm, the purpose was served. Thea might have understood a little better what she was letting herself in for, but Helena wasn't completely ignorant of the situation either.

Morrison-Ashton needed this. Its board, investors—everyone—needed to know that the future of the company was in safe hands.

And hands didn't come safer than Flynn Ashton's.

Flynn had his own reasons for wanting the match, of course, but surely Helena would realise that too. Thea had, quickly enough.

The company needed the PR boost and, even before he'd really believed he might inherit it one day, Morrison-Ashton had always been Flynn's priority. Now he stood to be CEO within the year…and he needed this more than ever. He needed the authenticity the match gave him. Married to one of the Morrison sisters, it wouldn't matter that he wasn't true Ashton blood. His adoption ceased to matter. Even the fact that his adoption had come through just as Ezekiel and Isabella Ashton had discovered that they were expecting their own flesh and blood child, Zeke, lost meaning as anything more than a crippling irony.

As a child, he'd been surplus to requirements, an inconvenience once the Ashtons had what they'd really wanted all along. And, as he'd grown older, he'd been a weapon in his father's hand, used to whip Zeke into shape, to make him earn his inheritance by fighting Flynn for every advantage, every opportunity. But as the husband of Thea—or Helena—Morrison, Flynn would be legitimate. Deserving.

He'd belong at last.

Taking Helena's hand, he led her out of Thea's dressing room, down the stairs and out of the front door into the blazing Tuscan sunshine. With her body close against his, he could feel the tension in its lines and wondered how fast her heart must be beating right now. Maybe even as hard and fast as his.

Because, despite all his rational thoughts, Flynn couldn't quite lie to himself well enough to pretend there wasn't a chance this would prove to be a colossal mistake. *This doesn't have to be a permanent arrangement.* Helena's words echoed around his head. To her, this was only temporary; she was a stand-in bride for the occasion. But temporary didn't fulfil Flynn's needs for this marriage.

He needed permanence, he needed authenticity and he needed heirs. That was the plan and, given everything else that had gone wrong, he had to cling on to those facts. Once he married Helena, she was his for life.

He'd just have to figure out a way to convince her that he could be enough for her, that he was worth staying for. Once they got through this horrendous, confusing day.

Flynn blinked in the sunlight. Everything felt somehow more real outside. The summer sounds on the breeze—insects and dry leaves—disappeared behind a peal of bells from the chapel below.

This was really happening. Maybe not the way he'd planned, but the outcome would be more or less the same. He would have made it at last, the moment Helena said 'I do'. And she would, he was sure. She'd been so fierce, so determined to make this work. Why? he wondered suddenly. What did it matter to her? Or was she just so afraid of their parents' wrath that she'd do anything to appease them?

Maybe he'd ask her. Afterwards.

They walked down the path to the chapel in silence, as quickly as Helena's heels would allow. Flynn glanced down at her feet, catching glimpses of the flamingo-pink satin heels that would have matched her bridesmaid's dress. Thea must have run out in her shoes.

Helena's gaze flicked down and she gave him a rueful smile. 'She took the veil, too. Shame, really. We could have kept my face hidden until it was all over, otherwise.'

Something caught in Flynn's chest. Maybe his wedding to Thea hadn't been a grand epic romance but it had been better than this. Helena deserved better than this.

'I don't want to hide you,' he said, hoping it was enough. 'You're going to be my wife. And I'm proud to have you at my side.' All true, even if he was more proud of her name than her person, for now. But Helena had been a sweet child and, since they'd started the wedding planning, a helpful, cheerful woman. Flynn had no doubt that in time he'd grow even fonder of her. Perhaps they'd even fall in love, if they were very lucky. As he'd hoped to do with Thea.

Helena's smile was a little sad but there was no more time to talk. As they rounded the corner to the chapel Thomas Morrison came into view, waiting to walk his daughter down the aisle.

'Helena! Where on earth is Thea? The mob is getting restless in there...' He stopped, staring at her as he took in the dress.

Flynn stepped forward, ready to jump the first hurdle for the pair of them. 'I'm afraid, sir, there's been a slight change of plan...'

* * *

As the string quartet struck up a new tune, Helena realised that, at the back of her mind, she'd expected her father to call their bluff. To tell them the whole idea was ridiculous and send everyone home. At the very least, she'd thought he'd have put up some sort of argument for reason.

But apparently it didn't much matter to him which of his daughters Flynn Ashton married, as long as he married one of them. Today.

The revelation stung a little more than she'd imagined it would after so many years of not being good enough.

This time, *please, this time,* she was going to be good enough.

'That's our cue,' her father whispered in her ear as the violins picked up the melody.

Helena nodded, focusing on not gripping her father's arm too hard as the church doors swung open.

She was really doing this. Marrying Flynn Ashton. And there was no parent or spurned lover about to run in and yell: *Stop the wedding!* Nobody to tell her she was making a colossal mistake, if she was. How could she tell, anyway? This wedding would get them through today and, right now, that was all that mattered. After that…well, she'd figure out what happened next once all these people had gone home.

It had been too much to hope that people might not notice that Flynn was marrying the wrong sister. From the moment the doors opened and Helena took her first step on to the tiled floor of the aisle, there were whispers. They ran through the pews like a wave, the cool and shady chapel suddenly buzzing with scandal and gossip. Helena couldn't make out the words but she could guess the sentiment.

What's happened? What's gone wrong? How did he end up with her? *What does this mean…?*

There were going to be a lot of questions over the next few hours, days and weeks, Helena realised. They'd got off lightly with her dad because there simply wasn't the time. People were waiting, and Thomas Morrison would not disappoint them. *You came to see my daughter get married? Well, here you go. What do you mean, it's the wrong one?*

Helena tried to suppress a giggle at the thought of her father trying to convince his guests that this marriage was what he'd intended all along, but a small squeak escaped. Her father's hand tightened on her arm and, when she glanced up at him, his expression was grim.

Suddenly, nothing was funny any more. Helena tried to focus on the posies of white flowers tied with satin ribbons at the end of each pew, or the pedestal displays—anything except the truth she saw in her father's face.

She'd thought that this would be enough, that marrying Flynn would make up for the past. But her father's expression told another story. If it didn't matter to him which of his daughters got married today, it didn't mean a thing.

Her slate would never be wiped clean, no matter what she did or how far she went. If eight years of being a perfect daughter hadn't been enough, why on earth had she imagined that marrying Flynn might do it? Thomas Morrison held grudges, and he held on tight. The best she could hope for was that Thea would be in so much trouble that she might eclipse Helena's own mistakes for a while.

Thea. How was she ever going to explain this to Thea?

Thea would have stopped her. But Thea was off chasing her own happy ever after, and Helena had stepped right into the very shoes she'd tried to talk her sister out of just a few days before.

Helena glanced down and caught a glimpse of her bright pink bridesmaid's shoes. Not quite Thea's white satin heels, after all. And this wedding, and everything that would follow, wasn't quite as it would have been for Thea, either. There was less paperwork, for a start. Just a scribbled unofficial contract at complete odds with the thirty-page document that had comprised Thea and Flynn's prenuptial agreement.

But, more than that, Helena wasn't Thea. She wasn't the face of the business and she was neither qualified nor willing to take on her sister's role at the company, presuming that Thea didn't come home to take it back herself. She was still a Morrison, and maybe that was enough for Flynn and his father.

For the first time since she'd entered the church, Helena looked past the flowers, the hats and the gossips and stared at her husband-to-be. Standing there beside the priest, his feet slightly apart, hands behind his back, Flynn looked solid. Calm, reliable, steady. All the things Helena had never thought she wanted in her life until eight years ago. Things she'd thought she'd never be able to find, since.

A casual observer, watching his serene expression, would never guess that the woman he was marrying today wasn't the woman he'd proposed to.

Maybe Helena could earn some of that serenity for herself, by marrying Flynn. If she could be what he needed, then surely he could be enough for her. She just couldn't help but wonder how much he was going to ask of her, before she reached that magical point of *enough*.

Give the company an heir.

Terrifying words—words that sent a shudder through her whole body. But they were just words, part of Flynn's agreement with Thea. Not with her. Never her. Because he couldn't know, wouldn't understand—and so she couldn't tell him what a baby would mean to her. How it might destroy her, this time, just to think about it.

The past only stayed in the past until it got dragged into the present. Hadn't Thea and Zeke proved that?

Too late to question what she was doing now, anyway. He'd given her an out and she hadn't taken it. To run at this point would be worse than if she'd never suggested this stupid idea in the first place. No one would ever forgive her for humiliating Flynn Ashton on his wedding day—for letting it happen twice.

No, she was getting married today and all she could do now was make the most of it, until enough time had passed for a discreet divorce.

Head held high, Helena continued to stare down the aisle at her intended husband until suddenly he looked up and met her gaze. His eyes were steady and serious, just like the man himself. Flynn Ashton was stable, reliable—everything Helena needed in her life. He wouldn't let her screw up again; she knew it.

They reached the front row of seats and Flynn stepped forward to meet them for the ceremonial giving away of the bride. As she disentangled her hand from her father's arm, he leant in towards Flynn. 'She's your problem now, son,' he muttered, and Helena's heart stung.

No, even this wasn't enough for him to forgive her. She couldn't imagine why she'd ever thought it would be. That all of this could be anything except a huge mistake.

'I like to think she'll be my partner rather than my problem,' Flynn murmured back, and Helena's gaze flew to his face in surprise.

Maybe, just maybe, marrying Flynn wasn't a mistake. Maybe it was an opportunity.

Maybe it could even be her future.

With a bright smile, Helena turned, gave her father a dry peck on the cheek, then stepped forward in bright pink shoes to meet it.

CHAPTER TWO

HELENA'S HAND FELT warm in his, an unexpected heat in the cool shade of the chapel. There wasn't a lot of warmth coming from the congregation either. More frosty confusion and comments as sharp as icicles. Flynn squared his shoulders as they took the last couple of steps up to the altar together. He'd known this wouldn't be an easy sell but if there was one thing he'd learnt growing up as the cuckoo in the Ashton nest, it was how to smooth over ruffled feathers.

It was a talent that had served him well in business, too. He was the one they brought in when Ezekiel Ashton had offended an investor or a client. The one who talked secretaries into staying when they'd had the sharp edge of Zeke Senior's tongue one too many times.

But, more than that, he was the one who made things happen. Not by making threats, as Ezekiel did, or taking risks and dares as Zeke would have done, but by gentling people along until they almost thought whatever Flynn wanted was their own idea.

The same way he'd persuaded Thea to marry him, in fact.

But *Helena* was the plan now. He just had to smooth the way forward for them. Make it so that everyone realised that, while this particular wedding was unexpected, it was just what they'd all really wanted all along, even if they hadn't known it.

He'd made a good start at that, he hoped, with his comment to Thomas. After all, Thomas might own half the business but he'd leave it to Helena in the end, once she was married to him. He might even disown Thea altogether after today, not that it made much difference. Zeke had made it clear that he was never coming back to Morrison-Ashton. Flynn would be CEO within the year and he'd have Helena at his side.

Which meant Helena, not Thomas, was the important one now.

Another talent Flynn had learnt young: identify the vital person and focus on them. In a family argument, the vital person varied. Usually it was Ezekiel because he was the head of the household, the ultimate authority. Sometimes it was Isabella because her own power, especially over Ezekiel, couldn't be ignored. Occasionally it was Zeke, but only when two brothers teaming up together could win their parents round to their way of thinking, which wasn't often.

It went without saying that Flynn was never that vital person.

But he wasn't a mistake or an accident, not any more. Not an unfortunate addition or a spare part, to be dragged out when he could be useful. *He* was what the company needed. What the family needed. And all he needed was Helena.

He squeezed Helena's hand, just a small measure of reassurance as the priest smiled at them. Had the old man not realised that there was something amiss today? It was possible. Thea had been out the one time he'd come to call on them. The priest had spoken to Flynn and Helena instead, and had nodded amiably when Flynn had leant forward to murmur their names to him again before Helena walked down the aisle, just to make sure he got it right in the service. It was entirely possible that the man holding the Bible firmly believed that he was joining a young couple in love in the binding act of marriage.

Well, Flynn was on board with the binding part, at least.

As they knelt before the priest, he heard a gasp go up from the congregation behind them. Frowning, he glanced over at his bride and saw her trying to hide a smile behind her hand.

'What?' he mouthed, raising an eyebrow.

Helena gave a tiny shake of her head, but lowered her hand long enough to whisper, 'I think they just clocked the shoes.'

Of course. Those ridiculous pink shoes.

Flynn kept his eyes on the floor in front of him. In all honesty, he quite liked the shoes. Liked the flash of colour and spirit they showed, just like the woman wearing them had when she'd stepped into that wedding dress at the last moment. They were right for Helena.

But they weren't appropriate for a Morrison-Ashton bride, of course. Not for a formal, prestigious event like this. Especially when they were on the wrong feet.

He couldn't let those pink high heels ruin everything. Everything else could go perfectly, Helena could be a perfect blushing bride, and all it would take would be the wrong society matron friend of his mother's saying, 'But did you see those *shoes?*' and suddenly everyone would have permission to pick the whole marriage apart.

As if they weren't going to do that anyway.

Flynn sighed, resigned himself to making the best of a bad day and tried to tune in to what the priest was saying. Before he knew it, they were at the only part of the service that really mattered—the promises and vows.

'Flynn and Helena, have you come here freely and without reservation to give yourself to each other in marriage?' The priest intoned the words with the sort of gravity that made it clear these were serious questions.

Flynn exchanged a fleeting glance with Helena as they both answered, 'Yes.' He wondered if she was thinking the same thing that he was—that he had many, many reservations about this. But he was going to go through with it anyway.

'Will you honour each other as man and wife for the rest of your lives?'

'I will,' Flynn said, Helena's agreement coming just a heartbeat behind.

She'd said it now, and that knowledge filled Flynn with triumph. The rest of their lives. That was exactly how long he needed to prove he deserved this—his place in the family and the business. He knew the board members and the investors. He knew what they needed in order to believe in and respect Flynn's new place at Morrison-Ashton.

Ezekiel Ashton had made it clear for years that Flynn didn't count, that he wasn't a true heir. Even if Zeke hadn't known it, everyone else associated with the business had never doubted for a moment that Zeke was the one who'd inherit.

But not any more. Now that place was Flynn's and the next few moments would cement it for life.

'Will you accept children lovingly from God, and bring them up according to the law of Christ and his Church?'

Beside him, Helena sucked in a breath, just loud enough for him to hear. As if she was steeling herself for something unpleasant. He frowned.

'I will,' Helena said, strong and clear, but Flynn couldn't shake the feeling that he'd just missed something important.

Like saying his line.

'I will,' he said, aware of the priest's waiting gaze.

'Good.' The priest cracked a creaky smile. 'Then, next, we have the vows. Flynn?'

He'd memorised this, had been prepared to stare into Thea's eyes and say just the right words. But now, as he turned to face his bride and take her hand, looking down further than he'd expected to, Flynn realised he hadn't a clue what her middle name was.

His panic must have shown on his face because Helena rolled her eyes and mouthed 'Juliette' at him, allowing his heartbeat to return to normal again.

'I, Flynn, take you, Helena Juliette Morrison, to be my wife.' She smiled as he spoke, and Flynn relaxed into the familiar words. 'I promise to be true to you in good times and in bad, in sickness and in health. I will love you and honour you, all the days of my life.'

He hoped she could hear how much he meant it. Love… maybe that would come and maybe it wouldn't. But honour, constancy and fidelity—those he could give her.

It was the least he could do, given what he would gain from the bargain. She was his now, along with the respectability and the place she brought him. It was done at last.

Flynn couldn't help but think he should feel more relieved about that.

'I, Helena, take you, Flynn Michael Ashton, to be my husband.' The words came out strong and clear, and Helena gave silent thanks that the trembling taking over her insides wasn't visible or audible to the congregation. She'd learnt the vows by heart practising them with Thea; she could recite them with her eyes closed. Which might actually be easier than staring up into Flynn's face, trying to look suitably besotted and loving.

Every single person listening was waiting to see if

they'd really go through with it. Maybe some thought it was a stunt, some crazy PR thing. Maybe they even believed that Thea would appear from the wings to take her rightful place at any moment.

Wow. Those people were going to be *really* disappointed.

Most people, Helena suspected, were just waiting to see if this marriage would really happen, and hoping that at some point over the next few hours they'd find out why.

This was the scandal of the year, and not one of Isabella's friends would rest until they knew what had really happened behind the scenes today.

Isabella. Helena sneaked a sideways look at the front pew as she promised to be true, to love and honour and all the rest of that stuff. Flynn and Zeke's mother sat with a fixed smile on her face, hands clasped around a handkerchief in her lap, the wide brim of her hat shading her eyes. Helena would bet that if she could see any tears in them, they wouldn't be tears of joy.

Explaining this mess to Flynn's parents was not going to be fun. Maybe she'd leave that to him. Refine the art of wifely delegating early.

Her vows done, the priest picked up the baton again. 'What God has joined, man must not divide,' he intoned.

Gosh, that sounded formal. Binding.

Final.

Well, what did he know? He'd happily married the wrong couple without batting an eyelid. There was a pretty strong chance that none of this was even legal. It would be fine.

'Do you have the rings?' the priest asked, and Helena's eyes widened. Did they? What had even happened to them?

But Flynn reached into his jacket pocket and pulled out a ring box, flipping open the lid to reveal two shiny platinum rings. Helena knew those rings, had helped choose those rings.

She also knew there was a good chance that the ring Flynn was about to try and put on her finger wouldn't fit.

As the priest blessed the rings, Helena tried to convey this information to her new husband using only her eyes and eyebrows. Anything else would signal to their audience that there was a problem.

Flynn's forehead furrowed in confusion and Helena resigned herself to losing the outer layer of skin on her ring finger.

'Helena, take this ring as a sign of my love and fidelity.' Flynn took her left hand solemnly and Helena braced herself as the cold metal touched the tip of her finger. 'In the name of the Father, and of the Son and of the Holy Spirit.'

Flynn eased the ring down to her knuckle, where it promptly got stuck. His gaze flashed to hers and she gave him what she hoped was an imperceptible shake of the head.

He understood, thank goodness. His fingers moved down to the base of her finger, but the ring stayed jammed where it was. With a sunny smile, Helena withdrew her hand and hid it in the folds of her dress. She'd ease it further on later, if she could. Otherwise she'd sneak up to her room and find some other ring to serve for the time being.

Flynn's ring slipped on with no problems, of course, since he was actually supposed to be there getting married today. And suddenly the priest was pronouncing them husband and wife and it was all over. Helena blinked out at the applauding crowd and felt grateful that the line 'You may now kiss the bride' seemed to appear more often in movies than at actual weddings.

She was married now. And she did realise that the chances were she'd have to kiss her husband, sooner or later.

It was just that she was voting for later. When her emotions and thoughts weren't spinning like a tornado. When she could sit quietly for a moment and figure all this out, and think about what would happen next.

When she'd had time to prepare herself.

With her hand tucked into the crook of Flynn's elbow, hiding the ill-fitting wedding ring, Helena walked back up the aisle she'd walked down as a single woman. As Helena Morrison.

Now she was Helena Ashton.

She was pretty sure she would never get used to that.

Helena fought to keep her expression bright and happy, tilting her head to brush against Flynn's shoulder as they walked.

'Nearly there,' he murmured as they approached the back of the church. 'Almost over.'

Except it wasn't. Not even a little bit.

The Tuscan sunlight stung her eyes and her skin as they emerged from the cool shade of the chapel. They only had a few moments before everyone else followed, so Helena ripped her hand from Flynn's arm and began to twist Thea's wedding ring over her knuckle. If only she had some hand cream in her bag. Or even her bag.

Brides travelled light, it seemed.

With a pop, the ring slid past the knuckle and into place, and Helena exhaled with relief. One problem down, who knew how many more to go.

As the guests emerged, Helena plastered her best social smile back on to her face. Which, as the first person out was Ezekiel Ashton, was a bit of a waste.

'What, exactly—?' the old man started, only to be cut off by his wife.

'Not here,' Isabella said, her voice quiet but sharp. Helena had no doubt that there would be long discussions about what had occurred that day, but Isabella wouldn't have them happening in front of the guests. 'We have the photos to get through.'

'Forget the photos,' Ezekiel said. 'What do we need photos for?'

'The papers, apart from anything else,' Isabella answered promptly. 'This is still the wedding of the season, regardless of who actually got married.' Her voice dropped low for the last half of the sentence and Helena winced.

Photos. Helena's smile slipped at the thought until Isabella glared at her and she forced it back into place. Where apparently it would stay for the next hour or more, while the semi-famous photographer Isabella had flown over from the States took endless shots of her and Flynn looking happy and slightly shell-shocked.

Oh, well. Wasn't that how all brides and grooms looked on their wedding day?

An hour of endless fake smiles later, Helena's face ached. Still, photos over and done with, she kissed the cheek of the next guest in the reception line, wishing she'd made everyone wear name tags for the occasion. She might know the guest list backwards after helping to put it together, but putting faces to those memorised names was another matter entirely.

Thea would have known them, though. Thea would have wined and dined them as clients in the past, would already have asked them questions about their kids or their pets. No wonder they were all looking at Helena with such confusion and curiosity. She wasn't what they'd expected, or wanted.

She was kind of used to that.

Beside her, Flynn seemed totally at ease, chatting happily with every person who came past. He, at least, seemed pleased with how the day had turned out.

'Such a beautiful day,' a woman in a green hat said, fake smile making it clear that she might well be talking about the weather rather than the wedding.

'Wasn't it?' Isabella said, ignoring the false undertone. 'We're all just so delighted to be one happy family at last.'

'I'm sure,' Mrs Green Hat replied. 'Although you do seem to be missing a couple of members right now!'

Isabella's tinkling laugh gave away nothing. 'Oh, well, we have everyone who really matters right here, don't we?'

'I suppose so. Except you do seem to be missing a best man, at least.' Good grief, the woman was relentless! 'I heard Zeke was home for the wedding, and I was so looking forward to seeing him. Such a bright young man.'

Isabella's expression froze at that, her grin nudging towards a rictus. Leaning between them, Helena plastered on what she hoped was an apologetic smile. 'I'm so sorry to hurry you along, but I'm afraid the line is already out of the door and people are more than ready for the wedding breakfast, I'm sure. Perhaps you and Isabella can catch up a little later?'

Mrs Green Hat looked a little sour at the interruption, as if too much lemon had been squeezed in her gin and tonic, but she nodded politely anyway. No one argued with the bride on her wedding day, did they?

'Of course. Isabella, I look forward to talking with you and *both* your sons later.' She stalked off towards the dining room, not even bothering to acknowledge Thomas at the end of the line, which Helena thought was just plain *rude,* thank you very much. Although, quite honestly, Thomas probably deserved it today. But Mrs Green Hat didn't know that.

Now, if she'd avoided Ezekiel, who continued to glower at every single person he spoke to, she could understand it.

It took forever, but eventually the last of the guests paraded past them and into the dining room. Ezekiel immediately disappeared in the direction of his study without so much as a by-your-leave, but Helena wasn't complaining.

In fact, she let out a sigh of relief and slipped her feet out of her heels for a moment, letting the cool stone floor soothe her toes.

'I don't understand why Thea couldn't at least leave her shoes and veil if she had to run out on us at the last moment.' Isabella peered critically at the bright pink shoes lying on the floor. Thomas must have filled her in on the events of the day, Helena supposed. 'It would be common courtesy, really.'

Rather than not actually running out on her wedding in the first place, Helena supposed. Isabella always did obsess about the details. It wasn't the first time she'd missed the big picture because of it.

'I like the pink ones,' she said, partly just to annoy her new mother-in-law.

'So do I, actually,' Flynn said, standing beside her, and she flashed him a huge smile. Maybe this was why people got married—to have someone on their side when they had to deal with their parents. She'd heard of worse reasons.

Thomas, with a weary sigh, lowered himself into an armchair at the edge of the hallway. 'I suppose we should have known. It's not like she didn't have form. I wonder where they are now.' He stared out of the open front door as he spoke and Helena couldn't help but follow his gaze.

'Zeke and Thea?' Isabella asked. 'God only knows. Probably off somewhere trying to find new ways to destroy our family.'

'They were in love,' Helena said, without even realising she planned to say it. 'They wanted to be together. And we thought…well, we thought this was the best option. Flynn and I.' She reached for him blindly, relieved when Flynn grabbed her hand and held it tight.

'We did,' he agreed. 'Still do, actually.'

Isabella studied her so intently that Helena stared at her toes to avoid her gaze. Her pedicure was the exact same colour as her shoes, she realised with pleasure. She almost wanted to point it out to her mother-in-law, to prove that she was good at details, too.

'Maybe you were right,' Isabella said finally. 'It might all be for the best. At least you're less likely to make a dramatic scene than your sister. If it hadn't been for Thea's place in the company…well, I might have suggested to Ezekiel that he pick you for Flynn instead. I said as much to Thea, actually. So I suppose she knew she had a stand-in, if she needed it.'

'Mother,' Flynn said, the hint of warning in his voice enough to make Isabella stop talking.

But it couldn't stop the icy fingers that crept up the back of Helena's neck at her words. She tugged her hand free from Flynn's. It wasn't just Isabella making it perfectly clear that Helena was second choice, a last resort. She already knew that, thanks. But had Thea really known what would happen? Helena thought not. But it seemed, however cross Ezekiel might be, Isabella wasn't too disappointed with this turn of events. Why would she be? She got a docile, eager to please wife for her son. Flynn had probably been overjoyed when she'd suggested it.

Except, of course, he knew that it was potentially only temporary. Isabella didn't.

But it was only a matter of time before she found out.

Flynn's hand felt suddenly cold without Helena's in it. Curse his mother. Wasn't it enough that *he* had to know that he was an unfortunate backup plan without her driving it home that his new bride was in exactly the same position?

It was time to get the focus back where it belonged—on *their* marriage, rather than the one that hadn't happened.

'Is that all the guests in?' he asked.

'Finally, yes,' Helena said with a small hint of a smile, as if she knew what he was trying to do.

'God only knows how much wine they'll have got through already.' Isabella tucked her hand through Thomas's arm. 'We'll go in and take our seats, then the steward can come and announce you. Is your father coming back?' The last part was added almost as an afterthought, Flynn realised. While Ezekiel might believe this whole day was all about him and his company, as far as Isabella was concerned, this was a social occasion presided over by herself and Thomas. The man she'd never quite left her husband for, but who was more of a husband to her anyway.

Wow, his family was screwed up.

'I'm sure he'll come through eventually,' Flynn said, even though Ezekiel hadn't even mentioned he was leaving, let alone returning to the festivities. It would be just like his father to spite them all after having his plans meddled with. Flynn was pretty certain that, actually, Ezekiel would be perfectly content with Helena as a daughter-in-law. It was just the fact that he hadn't been consulted, or had the final say in the matter, that rankled the old man.

Thomas and Isabella made their way through to the dining room and, rather suddenly, Flynn was alone with his wife for the first time since they'd decided to go through with the marriage. No, not the marriage. That still hadn't been decided, and wouldn't be until they had a document rather more legally binding than a scrawled-on invitation with the wrong name on the front. The wedding, then. That much, at least, they had certainly gone through with.

That much had paperwork.

'I'm sorry about that,' he said apologetically. 'You know my mother.'

'Rather too well,' Helena agreed, and he couldn't help but smile.

'Yes, well. How did you cope with your first official event as an Ashton—the receiving line, I mean? It seemed to go pretty smoothly to me.'

'Yeah, it was fine, mostly. There were a couple of extra-nosy people asking about Zeke—not Thea, of course, that would be too obvious. Your mother and I put them off, for now anyway.' She sighed. 'Although I dread to think what sort of questions they'll be ready to ask after a few too many glasses of champagne.'

She was right, Flynn realised. Sheer politeness might have stopped the bulk of the comments and observations in the church itself, but once the speeches were over all bets would be off.

Which meant the speeches would have to be something quite spectacular, to give them something else to talk about. Or something else to believe, about the way this day had gone.

'We have to change the story,' he said, and Helena's smile turned awkward.

'You got that from Thea,' she said when he raised an eyebrow. 'That's one of her big PR phrases.'

'Well, it applies today. We need to change people's perceptions of what happened here today.' And quickly, since he could already see the steward coming to fetch them.

'Like the fact you married the wrong woman?'

'Exactly that.'

The steward moved to open the door and Helena grabbed Flynn's arm as she slipped her slim feet back into those bright pink shoes.

'Any idea how?' she murmured, as the dining room doors opened and the steward stepped through.

'One or two,' Flynn muttered back.

'Like?'

But then the steward was announcing them as Mr and Mrs Flynn Ashton, and the show was on again. Helena would just have to wait and see. Flynn smiled to himself. Fixing this could be his wedding present to her.

CHAPTER THREE

IT WAS HARD not to be a little bitter. Helena had spent weeks choosing the perfect menu for this dinner, along with Isabella and the wedding planner and even Thea when she'd had time. They'd tasted and sampled all kinds of dishes, weighed up the pros and cons of a fish course against a sorbet between courses, and debated the merits of local versus imported cheeses for hours. And now, here she was, sitting right in the middle of the top table—and she'd barely tasted a mouthful of any of the plates put in front of her.

It wasn't that she didn't want to eat. She was starving, as it happened. But the very efficiently tied corset laces were starting to make breathing a bit more of an issue than she'd like, and she didn't want to strain them any more than she had to.

She stared longingly at the dessert in front of her and resigned herself to just a small taste. And to staying away from the champagne. Bubbles always went straight to her head, and on an empty stomach they'd be disastrous. Especially today. Today, she needed all of her faculties about her.

'Are you okay? You're looking kind of…pink,' Flynn asked, leaning in. Helena supposed to the crowds of guests it looked as if he was murmuring sweet nothings in his

bride's ear. Not asking her why her complexion had coloured to match her shoes.

'It's the corset. It was okay standing up but now it's kind
of…binding.' Which it was supposed to be, really. It was
just that Helena was so very fond of oxygen. And dessert.

Flynn didn't answer immediately. Helena glanced up
to see his cheeks approaching shoe colour, too. 'I'm sorry.
Do you want me to…?' He trailed off, waving a hand behind her back.

Helena shook her head. 'Too late now. It'll be fine. I
just need to make it through the speeches then I'll escape
and find a maid or someone to adjust it.'

'Just don't let any of the guests see you.' Flynn flashed
her a quick grin. 'You'll have the rumour mill announcing you're pregnant in no time.'

Pregnant. Of course. Because she was married now.
And that was what married women did, wasn't it? Gave
their husbands babies.

Isabella probably wouldn't even cry and send her away
this time.

This time, it wouldn't be a scandal, a shameful thing.
It would be wanted, loved. Kept.

And the fact it might break her heart again still wouldn't
matter.

A waiter reached in to clear her barely touched plate
and Helena murmured a thank you, more grateful for the
interruption to her thoughts than the service.

'Time for the speeches next,' she said, visualising the
timetable for the day as she'd seen it on the wedding planner's clipboard.

'And your dad's up first. At least he always makes a
good speech.'

Helena stared at him in disbelief, but Flynn appeared
utterly unaware of what he'd said. 'A good speech?'

'Well, yeah.' Flynn shrugged. 'Doesn't he? I mean, he does all those charity event speaker things, and he always talks well to the board. And I thought he did pretty well last night, at the rehearsal dinner.'

Helena shook her head. 'No wonder Thea slept with Zeke,' she muttered. After listening to their father's speech about her the night before—including, amongst other things, a line about how glad he was that, by agreeing to marry Flynn, Thea had finally made a decision in her personal life as good as the ones she made in business—even Helena had been ready to flee the room. And Flynn hadn't even noticed that his fiancée might have been a bit upset.

She wondered what little gems Dad would have in store for her. Assuming that he'd taken the time to rewrite it from his original speech, as planned for Thea. He might not. They seemed fairly interchangeable to him today— neither one of his daughters living up to what he wanted or expected from them.

She didn't have to wait long to find out. The moment the last of the plates were cleared, Thomas Morrison was on his feet, carefully clinking the silverware against a champagne flute.

'Ladies and gentlemen, friends and family, welcome— welcome to you all!' Thomas smiled broadly around at the assembled company, and Helena wondered exactly how much of the champagne he'd had that afternoon.

'On this very special day, I'd like to thank you all for travelling to be with us, not just on my own behalf, but on behalf of my dear old friends, Ezekiel and Isabella, too. I know that they feel, as I do, that this day would not have been so magical without all of you here to share it.'

Pause for applause. Flynn did have a point, although she'd never admit as much. Her father knew how to play a crowd.

It was just a shame he didn't know how to make his own daughters feel as special.

'This day, this joining of our two families, has been long coming, and long desired. Not just for the obvious reasons of business—although I know several of you very pleased to see your stocks and shares safe for another generation!' Laughter, mostly from a table of middle-aged men in pin-striped suits with much younger wives towards the back of the room. 'No, I have far greater reasons for wanting to see our families irrevocably linked.'

Helena swallowed at the word *irrevocably*, and felt Flynn flinch beside her. Was he thinking about how to get out of this marriage, like she was? Or was he plotting how to keep her in it?

'Helena, my Helena, has always been my golden child. My baby girl. And to see her safe and secure with a man such as Flynn, a man I already trusted with my company, is quite frankly a joy!'

If her cheeks had been pink from oxygen deprivation before, then they had to be bright red and clashing with her shoes by now. As she stared at her full champagne glass, watching the bubbles rise and pop, Flynn sneaked his hand into hers and she squeezed gratefully.

'Flynn—' Thomas turned to address his new son-in-law directly '—you have been given a precious gift today. I expect you to take very good care of it.'

'I will, sir.' Flynn's voice was sure and certain, and the whole room burst into applause again at the sound of it.

'Okay, maybe he's not dreadful at speeches,' Helena murmured to Flynn but, even as she said it, Thomas launched into a long, overdone thank you speech to Isabella for all she'd done in helping to raise her and organise the day. 'Sometimes.'

'Wait until you hear mine,' Flynn teased. But Helena

tensed at the very idea. What on earth was he going to say? *Hi, guys, I know you came to see me marry that other girl but, hey, change of plan and, under the circumstances, this was the best I could do. More champagne, anyone?*

'*This* you're worried about?' Flynn asked, his voice low but amazed. 'Marrying a guy you never even considered as a possible date on no notice in someone else's wedding dress, fine. But the thought of me making a speech makes you tense up? You don't need the corset, your shoulders are so rigid.'

'Not the thought of you making a speech. The thought of you adapting a speech about Thea to suit me on the spot. The fact that everyone here will know you're actually talking about another woman.'

Flynn didn't reply immediately, and when Helena looked up his expression was thoughtful. 'Just wait and listen,' he said finally, just as Thomas asked the room to be upstanding for the bride and groom.

'To Flynn and Helena!' She supposed she should just be glad that most people managed to get her name right.

Flynn got to his feet as everyone else sat down, and Helena gave up worrying about the tightness of her corset laces. It wasn't as if she could breathe while this was going on anyway.

'It's traditional, I know, for the groom to toast the bridesmaids,' he started.

Helena winced instinctively. *That's right—draw attention to exactly what's untraditional about this wedding.*

'But, as you might have noticed, my wife and I don't actually have any today.'

A nervous laugh, and not even the usual cheer at the use of 'my wife and I'. Yeah, this was going to go *brilliantly.*

'A lot of things about today's wedding might not have

been exactly as people were expecting. But, in fact, everything is just as it should be.'

He smiled down at her and something in Helena's chest loosened, for the first time that day.

'All along, we knew we wanted to join our families together, to go into the future as a pair, a team. We wanted to secure our future, and our future happiness. But you can't make a plan for love; you can't schedule romance and desire. You can't outsmart Cupid, as Helena and I learned.'

It was all true, Helena realised. Everything he was saying accurately described Thea and Zeke's discoveries and disappointments of the last couple of days. But the way he said it, the way he smiled lovingly at her as he spoke…it was as if he were telling a different story altogether.

Their story.

'Duty is one thing; family duty something altogether heavier. But true love…well, true love trumps them all.' Women were 'aahing' around the tables, and Helena thought she might even have seen one of the middle-aged men in the pinstriped suits wipe at his eyes. How was Flynn doing this?

'I truly believe that our wedding today is just the first stop on a journey of a lifetime. With Helena, I feel like I have come home at last. Together we, and our families, have a wonderful future ahead of us. And I couldn't be prouder to have my wife by my side as we venture into it.'

Flynn tugged her up to stand beside him, one arm wrapped around her waist, and raised his glass. 'To Helena,' he said, and the room echoed with the repeats.

And just for a moment, standing there in her sister's too tight wedding dress with the wrong shoes pinching her feet, Helena could see the future Thea had planned for herself. A future of acceptance and appreciation, having a man beside her who always managed to say the right thing at the right time.

It almost seemed like the fairy tale it was supposed to be. For a moment, anyway. Until her guests started calling for something more.

'Kiss her!' Mr Teary-Pinstripes called. 'Kiss, kiss, kiss, kiss!' The rest of his table picked up the chant. Then the rest of the room.

Suddenly, Helena almost wished the corset *was* tight enough to make her faint.

Imagining a fairy tale future wasn't the same as kissing the prince. This wasn't how it was supposed to go. They'd managed to avoid it in the church, where at least it would have been expected to be a chaste and swift kiss. Here, now, after all the wine and the toasts…these people wanted the real thing, and anything less was only going to start up rumours again.

She couldn't let that happen. Not after Flynn's speech had tidied away all the talk so neatly.

If they wanted a kiss, she was going to have to give it to them.

She turned to Flynn, eyebrows raised, and he echoed the gesture. 'I never thought my first kiss with my husband would be quite so public,' she murmured, quiet enough that she knew it wouldn't be heard over the chanting.

'It's just for show.' He flashed her a quick smile.

Just a show. Of course. They weren't really in love, whatever Flynn had suggested in his speech. This marriage was only temporary, just until they could sort everything out. It wouldn't—couldn't—last. Not when she couldn't give Flynn what he wanted most.

None of which explained why there seemed to be too much blood in her veins, or why she couldn't look away from Flynn's caramel-brown eyes as he smiled down at her.

Helena's heart raced as he wrapped an arm around her waist and pulled her close, the chanting turning to cheering around them.

It's just for show. The words spun in her head, but all Helena could think as Flynn bent in to kiss her was: *If this is just a show, how am I going to survive the real thing?*

Just a show. That was the key.

Except it wasn't.

Yes, the only reason his first kiss with his wife was taking place in front of a captive audience was to prove a point—to show them that Helena wasn't some sort of poor consolation prize. But that wasn't enough. He had to show *Helena* that too.

And Helena knew the truth.

If he wanted her to stick with this—to believe they had a real future together—well, that future had to start right now. With their first kiss.

'Kiss, kiss, kiss, kiss!' The chanting around them faded into nothing as he leant in closer, his eyes closing as his lips brushed against hers, softly at first, not wanting to spook her. But then, oh, then... Flynn's fingers clutched at her hip, the silk of her dress slipping against his skin as he deepened the kiss.

She tasted like champagne and gold, expensive and sparkling, her mouth warm and willing under his. He'd wanted to prove a point with this kiss but, for the life of him, he couldn't remember what it was. All he could think about was how soft her body was against his, how perfectly it fitted to him.

He opened his eyes, wanting to drink in the sight of her too, wanting to see her reaction, to know if she was as affected as him. But Helena's eyes were closed and, along with his vision, his hearing seemed to return too—or at least his awareness of it.

The chanting had turned to cheering—when, Flynn didn't know. But he was suddenly aware that he was making a spectacle of himself—and Helena—by falling so completely into what was supposed to be a simple kiss. Just a moment to appease the crowd, and a promise of what could follow later.

If their first kiss had knocked him senseless, what would their second do to him? Never mind their third and fourth…

Reluctantly, Flynn loosened his hold on his wife and pulled back, just enough to signal to Helena that the kiss was over. Her eyelids fluttered open and Flynn was gratified to see misty confusion in her bluebell bright eyes, too. At least he wasn't the only one losing his mind over a kiss.

'Well,' Isabella said in a low voice as they pulled apart, 'at least no one here is left in any doubt that you both got what you wanted out of this arrangement.' Flynn couldn't tell if his mother disapproved of that or not. It was often hard to tell with Isabella. He found it easiest to assume that she did disapprove, most of the time.

Not that it made any difference now. He was married to Helena and there was nothing anyone could do about that.

The cheering had turned to chatter and laughter now, after a smattering of applause. Helena's cheeks were pink as she sat down, and Flynn flattered himself that the blush had less to do with her corset than it had.

'Nearly there now,' he murmured to her, reaching to take her hand. She let him hold it long enough for a reassuring squeeze then tugged it away again, giving him a polite, but non-committal, smile.

Flynn frowned. What had changed? She'd been right

there with him in that kiss, he could tell. So why the cool distance now?

As the guests finished their coffees and headed through to the adjoining room, where a bar had been set up for them while the band set up on the terrace, Flynn studied his bride as she sipped tea, and considered.

Helena had been instrumental in the wedding planning, but she hadn't been part of the prenuptial contract discussions. But she *was* Thea's sister. They'd have talked about the terms of the agreement, surely? Which meant that Helena probably knew that marital relations hadn't been contractually required for the first couple of years. Thea had wanted time to settle into married life, and to continue to build up her career, before they started a family. And, since they weren't in love, or even in lust, sex wasn't really necessary until then. At least, on paper.

There was a firm fidelity clause, though. And Thea had changed her mind, just two nights ago, about what she wanted from the marriage in physical terms. She'd wanted them to get to know each other as man and wife, and have that time together first before kids.

Although how much that decision had to do with her trying to hide her feelings for his brother, Flynn suspected he was better off not knowing.

Still, maybe she hadn't discussed that change of plans with Helena. And, even if she had, there was no contract between Helena and him. No carefully debated and worded agreement, no consensus of opinion. Just confusion, lack of clarity and the potential for miscommunication.

This was why the world needed paperwork.

He'd have to talk to her, discuss the situation and what they wanted to happen next. It was useful to have a good idea of their individual needs before they got the solicitors involved, or at least that was what he'd found with her sister.

But that would have to wait until he got her alone. And with two hundred wedding guests still watching them closely—either waiting for another kiss or some sign of what really went down that morning—Flynn didn't see that happening very soon.

A smile crept on to his face as a thought occurred to him. There was one chance for them to be almost alone, if still observed, very soon indeed.

'What are you smiling at?' Helena asked from beside him.

'I'm just looking forward to our first dance,' he answered honestly.

'Well, it can't be any more of a spectacle than our first kiss.' Helena covered her eyes for a moment, obviously embarrassed.

'Don't knock the kiss,' Flynn said, leaning back in his chair. 'I think that kiss might set the tone for our whole marriage.'

Helena's gaze flashed up to his face, uncertainty in her eyes. Flynn tried to give her a reassuring look. She'd feel better once they'd agreed terms. And he'd feel better once he knew she was in this for the long haul. He could persuade her that sticking with the marriage was better for everybody, he was sure.

Even if he had to kiss her a hundred more times to convince her.

'And now, please welcome Mr and Mrs Flynn Ashton on to the floor for their first dance!'

Helena thought her face might crack from all the smiling. Still, she tried to keep up the ecstatically happy bride act as she took Flynn's hand and stepped out into the middle of the ballroom. How had Isabella even managed to *find* a villa with a ballroom? The woman had to have ridiculous magical abilities or something.

Helena just hoped she'd use her powers for good.

'You okay?' Flynn asked as the band struck up the first notes of the first dance. *It Had to Be You.* Thea had picked it after glancing over the band's set list, and Helena still wasn't sure if she'd meant it as a joke. Except Thea wasn't stuck dancing to it for the next three and a half minutes or whatever. Helena was.

'I'm fine.' She smiled up at her husband and hoped he wouldn't notice she was lying. She was a long way from fine.

It was the kiss that had started it. The kiss that had left her knees weak and her brain foggy. Followed by all the sincere congratulations that no one had offered *before* Flynn's speech and a roomful of strangers telling her how this must be the happiest day of her life.

Helena was pretty sure it would go down forever as the most bizarre and confusing. But *happiest*? That really wasn't the right word for it.

Flynn led her around the dance floor without her even having to think about where her feet went next, as if he had a diagram in his head that he just had to follow and everything would be graceful and perfect. Which, actually, knowing Flynn, he probably did.

'So,' he said as the singer launched into the second verse, 'I think we made it through the day without disaster.'

'I guess we did.' After the dancing, all that was left was the sending off. Except she and Flynn weren't going anywhere except upstairs to bed.

Bed.

Oh.

Where were they going to sleep? The bridal suite Thea

had been using, which would have been set up for a romantic wedding night while they were all down at the chapel? Or the smaller room Helena had taken as her own? Or even Flynn's room at the far end of the villa?

And, more importantly, was Flynn expecting that they'd be going to bed *together?*

'About that,' she said, stumbling a little as her shoe got stuck in the too-long hem of her dress. Flynn caught her, strong hands keeping her upright and even still dancing as she found her balance. 'I mean, about making it through the day. And to the night. Um…'

Flynn gave a low chuckle that somehow sounded dirtier than she'd ever imagined he was capable of. 'Don't worry. I don't think anyone is going to be sober enough to notice where either of us sleep tonight. Why don't you take the bridal suite, just in case anyone checks, and I'll stick with my room? I'll have work to do in the morning anyway, and my laptop and files are all set up in there.'

Of course. Work.

Just when she was starting to think that Flynn was a little more enthusiastic about this wedding than she'd expected. But no, it was all just the show, the spectacle, still.

Except that kiss hadn't felt like a show. It had definitely been a spectacle, but it had felt…real. Tingly.

But she wasn't supposed to be getting tingly feelings about this man. Her husband. Stupid as it seemed. She needed to keep this business-like and official until they could sit down and agree a way to get out of it. As she'd told him that morning, this didn't have to be forever.

Couldn't be forever.

If she didn't end this early enough, she'd have to tell him everything, sooner or later. Explain why she couldn't give him all the things he wanted. Had Isabella already realised? Was that why she'd looked so frustrated all day, whenever no one important had been looking?

The band launched into a repeat of the last verse, and Flynn spun her round with a little more enthusiasm. Not enough to be called abandon, of course. And probably planned ahead of time. But the crowd cheered anyway, and Helena tried to improve her mood with the knowledge that this was nearly all over. Another hour or so and they'd serve the cake and light supper buffet, even though no one could possibly be hungry again after the dinner they'd just eaten—except her. And she still couldn't eat because of the ridiculous corset.

Maybe she could smuggle a doggy bag upstairs under her skirts…

The band came to a triumphant finish and Flynn dipped her low over his arm. Helena's heel slid against the wooden floor for a second, then held. Heart racing, she looked up into her husband's eyes and realised her heart wasn't going to slow down any time soon.

Polite applause echoed in her ears as Flynn's smile— a slow private one she wasn't used to—spread across his face and she realised that she was still half upside down with her hair threatening to break free from its pins.

Deliberately, he raised her up to standing again, but his arm tight around her waist kept her upright. Her mind spun—from the dance, from the dip, but mostly from the realisation that she'd thought Flynn was about to kiss her again. Had expected it, almost as her due.

Had wanted it.

And that was dangerous.

With a tight smile, she shuffled back out of his arms. Flynn let her go easily and she tried to stamp down the small swell of disappointment she felt at that.

'I think my father has the next dance,' she said as the band struck up the next tune.

'Of course,' Flynn replied, still smiling. 'And who are we to mess with tradition?'

'Who, indeed?' Helena twirled away, hitching her dress up a little to avoid tripping, and went to find her father. He might not always be her favourite person but he was a great deal safer to be around than her husband right now.

Several hours and considerably more dances later, the evening finally approached its end. Helena had thought about staging a grand departure earlier, but realised that would leave her alone in the bridal suite with her husband and two hundred people downstairs listening for signs of the marriage being consummated.

So not happening.

But at midnight the coaches and cars arrived like carriages on the driveway and the staff efficiently and discreetly persuaded everyone out of the door. Most were staying at hotels down in the town where there would be bars they could abuse all they wanted. But not here.

A few close family and friends of Isabella's *were* staying at the villa, but Helena was optimistic they could avoid them tonight. The bridal suite was at one far end of a wing, with her own bedroom, her father's and Isabella and Ezekiel's suite between it and the rest of the villa. Zeke and Flynn had been roomed at the other end of the building but maybe she could persuade Flynn to take her old room. She could get someone to move his work stuff over now, while no one was looking. It would be much easier to keep up the illusion that they were actually sharing the bridal suite that way.

Helena smiled a gracious goodbye at a passing flurry of guests, then moved away to explain her plan to Flynn—

only to see him exiting the room behind her father and his. Where were they all going?

Frowning, she made to follow and find out, but stopped when a hand slipped through the crook of her arm. To the departing guests, it probably looked like a motherly gesture from her new mother-in-law, but Helena knew differently. Isabella had a grip of steel and if she didn't want Helena going after Flynn she didn't stand a chance of making it.

'Where are the menfolk off to?' Helena asked in what she hoped was an unconcerned tone.

'I believe that Ezekiel and Thomas had some details to hammer out with Flynn, after today's…occurrences.' Helena had never heard a wedding sound so inconvenient.

'Details? What sort of details?'

Isabella waved the hand that wasn't gripping Helena's arm as if to say it was nothing for Helena to worry her pretty little head about. Except Helena did worry. Would worry. Was currently worrying. Pretty much in every tense—especially since she knew beyond any doubt that the three men would be talking about her.

No, not just talking about her. Planning her life. Without any input from her.

'Just little things, I'm sure,' Isabella said lightly. 'Probably what adjustments need to be made to the original marriage contract, for one.'

Yeah, because that wasn't a big thing at all.

'Don't you think I should be in there for that?' Helena asked.

Isabella gave her a disparaging look. 'I can't imagine it would make much of a difference.' Which was, depressingly, very true. But it didn't mean she wouldn't like the opportunity to say her part.

The door had closed behind the men and Helena knew

any chance she had of gate-crashing their summit meeting had passed. All she could do now was wait to see what they decided about her future.

And then choose whether or not she was willing to go along with it.

She allowed herself a small secret smile. They could plan all they wanted, but they weren't in charge of her life. Flynn might be her husband, but he didn't own her. And she hadn't signed any paperwork promising him anything.

Her future was her own and she wouldn't let the men in her life tell her what to do with it.

'I'm going to go up to the bridal suite,' she told Isabella in a sweet, not-causing-any-trouble-here tone. 'It *is* my wedding night, after all.'

'Of course.' Isabella loosened her hold on Helena's arm, studying her face. Helena kept her expression bland. 'I'm sure Flynn won't keep you waiting too long.'

Only until tomorrow morning, given the conversation they'd had while they danced. But her mother-in-law didn't need to know that. 'Well, I'd better go and get ready for him, then.' With a smile, she turned to leave the room, planning to snag a maid to move Flynn's things on her way.

'Helena.' She turned back at Isabella's call. Flynn's mother had a small crease between her eyebrows, as if she were still trying to make sense of everything that had happened that day. Maybe she was. God knew it didn't make any sense to Helena yet, and most of it had been her idea. 'I just wanted to say…maybe things have worked out for the best, after all. Maybe this can be a fresh start for you and Flynn. For you, especially.'

Helena's polite smile tightened until her cheeks ached. 'I hope so,' she said, not even sure if she was lying or not. 'It's about time I was given a second chance around here.'

And, with that, she turned and swept out of the ballroom, leaving her wedding day behind her.

It was time for the wedding night.

CHAPTER FOUR

'Well. That was a day.' Thomas Morrison collapsed into one of the wing chairs by the fire of Ezekiel's study. 'Tell me you keep the good brandy in here, old friend?'

'Of course I do,' Ezekiel answered, his tone irritable. 'Flynn?'

As his father settled himself into the other wing chair, Flynn moved to the hidden drinks cabinet Ezekiel had found within the first thirty minutes of occupying the office and pulled out three of the good glasses. He deserved a drink, after today. More than just a sip of champagne or half a glass of wine with dinner. He'd held it together all day long, turned a potential disaster into a victory, and now he was about to be cross-examined on his actions by his father and father-in-law.

He was *owed* this brandy.

'So.' Ezekiel studied him as Flynn handed out the brandies, placing his own on the low table between them as he dragged another chair over. 'You're a married man now.'

'My son-in-law,' Thomas added, as if either of these facts might have eluded Flynn so far that day.

'This is true.' Sitting, Flynn stretched his long legs out in front of him, feeling the aches from standing too long in thin-soled shoes. Brandy would help with those too, he decided.

'So perhaps you would care to explain *exactly* what you were thinking?' Ezekiel's icy tone would have made a weaker man shiver, but Flynn was used to it. Obviously the old man had been working up to this all day. Better to let him get it out.

'I was thinking about the best course of action in an unfortunate situation.' Flynn kept his gaze steadily on his father's face as he spoke.

'We had a plan! We had a contract, signed and agreed, ready to come into force the moment the girl said "I do"! Now what do we have? A dumb blonde who knows nothing about the company, who can't provide the PR boost we needed, and who you married without a pre-nup so will probably run off with some footballer or something before you even reach your first anniversary!' Ezekiel turned briefly towards Thomas. 'No offence.'

Helena's father merely shrugged. 'None taken. Helena has never been the most reliable of my daughters. But, you have to admit, she did step up today.'

'Yes, she did. And we'd be in a far worse position if she hadn't.' Flynn rubbed a hand across his forehead, suddenly tired. 'Look. Helena has agreed to negotiate a new marriage contract the moment the guests are gone and the buzz dies down. Beyond that…perhaps she doesn't have Thea's business skills, but she has other talents.'

'I bet she does,' Ezekiel muttered darkly. Flynn ignored the implication.

'She's a great hostess, very personable and appealing. And, most importantly, she has the best interests of our families, and the company, at heart. It was her idea to stand in for Thea this morning. She wanted to protect her sister's reputation and preserve this whole wedding of the year spectacle.' Of course, she'd also wanted to avoid having to tell their parents what had happened to Thea and Zeke. Something Flynn had great sympathy with.

'Ah, yes, her sister.' Ezekiel sat back in his chair, fingers steepled in front of him. 'At some point we need to discuss what happened to the unreliable Thea. But what's done is done. What matters now is what we do next. Thomas? What do you think?'

Thomas sighed as he contemplated his daughter. Flynn's jaw clenched at the sound of it.

'Helena's a good girl, mostly. Had her moments, of course, but I hope that we're past those now. Isabella thinks that maybe that's why she took Thea's place. To prove she was ready to put the past behind her.'

'Does she?' Ezekiel nodded. 'Good insight, that woman. One of the reasons I married her.'

And still he didn't find it strange that his wife discussed this with his business partner, not himself, Flynn thought. The relationships between his and Helena's parents still baffled him.

He frowned as Thomas's words sank in. 'What past? What happened?' What was he missing here? His memories of Helena were of the sweet golden child Thomas had talked about in his speech. Maybe she seemed a little more prickly these days, underneath that smooth and charming surface, but Flynn had never really been close enough to investigate further.

He would have to investigate now, though. And he needed all the intelligence he could get going into that.

But apparently he wasn't going to get it tonight.

'Nothing that needs to worry you now, son.' Thomas gave him a kind smile and Flynn tried not to flinch at his use of the word 'son' as an endearment. Ezekiel had never managed that. Not once in thirty years. But then, Thomas had always wanted a son and never got one. Ezekiel had longed for one then got two by accident.

How could he have ever hoped to compete with biology?

'An heir and a spare; that's what a man needs.' The words echoed in Flynn's head from nearly twenty years ago. His father, in another study, with a different glass in his hand, still handing down pronouncements and never, ever listening. *'But you don't ever want to have to use the spare, if you can avoid it. And in this case...well, blood is blood. And yours isn't mine.'*

He remembered the moment so clearly. He'd always known he was adopted; no one had even tried to hide it. But standing there in front of his father as he'd explained exactly why Flynn would never matter, would never be good enough, would never truly count...he could still feel the stabbing pains in his heart now, so many years later.

Flynn rubbed absently at his chest as his father set down his brandy glass on the table and prepared to pass judgement.

'She'll do as she's told,' Ezekiel pronounced. 'And if she doesn't...well, you can always get her pregnant. That tends to calm a woman down. Just make sure she signs the papers before the child is born!' His father's wheezy laugh rattled through him like a curse, and Thomas joined in after only a moment.

I can't sleep with her, Flynn thought, trying to keep his horrified disgust to himself, even as the bile rose up in his throat. It might be the obvious way to keep Helena at his side—crushing any chance of an annulment, for a start, and bringing them together, showing her that there could be something good between them. Something that could maybe even grow into love.

But it wouldn't be fair. He wasn't his father, or even hers. He wouldn't trap her that way until they had some ground rules down. And as much as he wanted a child, an heir of his own, he needed the plan in place before that happened. No child of his would be used as a tool or a weapon.

Not like Ezekiel had used him and Zeke.

'I think I know how to handle my own wife.' Flynn tried to sound amused, confident and true, even though it was a complete lie. Thea, he'd have known how to handle. He'd done the background research, spent time with her, made sure to discuss everything they needed to know about each other.

Except, apparently, the fact that she was in love with his brother.

Still, that aside, he knew Thea. Helena he hadn't got a clue about.

But he was willing to learn. Had to learn, before he could let himself get close. Had to know if she'd stick with him, stand beside him hereafter, before he let himself believe in this marriage. Which meant keeping his hands off her—even after that kiss.

Ezekiel laughed again, sounding even creakier and wheezier than before. 'If you believe that, you're a bigger fool than I took you for. No man ever knows how to truly handle a woman. They thrive on being unpredictable. But you give it a go, if you like. You've got two weeks here on honeymoon together. Get her to sign something binding— the same general terms as we agreed for her sister—and I'll leave you alone to "handle" her. But if you haven't got the paperwork sorted by the time you come back to London, Thomas and I will take it over.'

Flynn's fist clenched against the arm of his chair and the other squeezed his glass so hard that a less expensive vessel would have cracked and smashed. This wasn't just the business they wanted to control. It was him and his future—and Helena's. He'd thought that Zeke forcing their father to name Flynn as CEO within the year would have meant he could finally take on the power and the role he was meant to have. Instead, he didn't even seem to have power over his own marriage.

But what else could he do? If he didn't manage to resolve things with Helena in two weeks he'd look weak anyway. And Flynn knew his father well enough to know he'd use that to his advantage somehow.

'I will do this,' he said, his voice firm and dark. 'Helena is my wife, this is my marriage, and my company before long. I don't need the two of you interfering like a couple of old women.'

The brandy had mellowed them, Flynn realised when they both laughed. Time was he'd have been punished for speaking in such a way. But the balance of power had changed now, whether they liked it or not. They couldn't keep him out, or under their control any longer.

'Then we'll leave you to get on with that,' Ezekiel said, getting to his feet. He placed his empty glass on the table, and Thomas followed suit. 'We're flying out in the morning, but I'm sure your mother will make sure we see you before we go.'

Flynn nodded. Morning wasn't far away now. Not long until it was just him, Helena and the elephant of a post-nup in the middle of the villa. He'd fix this. He had to.

Thomas raised a hand in parting and headed out, but Ezekiel paused in the doorway. 'Two weeks, Flynn. I expect those papers on my desk within twenty-four hours of your return to London, or I'll take steps.'

He closed the door behind him before Flynn could respond. Flynn stared around his father's study, at the inner sanctum that was almost, almost his, and thought about going to talk to his wife.

Then he got up and poured himself another brandy instead. One thing at a time, he decided. And tomorrow, once everyone else had gone, was plenty soon enough.

Especially as he had a sneaking suspicion that Helena wasn't going to like being handled one little bit.

The bridal suite was bigger than she remembered. Or maybe it just seemed smaller when Thea was in there with her. It hadn't even been so bad when the maid was there, loosening the laces of her corset and helping her to step out of the heavy wedding dress.

But now it was just her, alone with the dress hanging from the wardrobe door, and Helena didn't quite know what to do with herself.

A maid had moved her belongings in, presumably during the reception. Helena wondered whether the wedding planner had asked her to do that, or if it had been Isabella. She wondered where Thea's things had gone.

She wondered where Thea and Zeke were right now.

Shaking her head, Helena moved over to the chest of drawers under the window, looking for her nightwear. The third drawer she opened yielded results, and she pulled out the slippery satin negligee she'd packed in a ridiculous fit of optimism.

'Just in case,' Thea had said when they were packing together, back in London. *'You know, a high percentage of engaged people in a recent study said that they met their partners at a mutual friend's wedding. You never know who you might meet!'*

She'd known what Thea meant, though, by the suggestion. That it was time for Helena to move on. To start living that part of her life again. She'd never talked with her sister about the hours spent with the counsellor, talking through the memories, nodding meaninglessly as she was told she couldn't blame herself, that what had happened to her didn't have to define her life. But probably, in Thea's mind, it had been eight years and that was long enough to dwell.

How could she explain that knowing those things was one thing, and acting on them another entirely?

So instead she'd pointed out that the only people she was likely to meet at a Morrison-Ashton wedding were clients, most of whom were either already married or too married to their jobs for Helena to be interested in them.

And now look at her. Married to the almost CEO of the family business, the man who put the 'work' in 'workaholic'. Perfect.

She shoved the fancy nightie back in the drawer and slammed it shut. Returning to drawer number two, she yanked out a pair of workout shorts and a T-shirt instead. It wasn't as if Flynn was going to get the chance to appreciate—or even see—whatever she wore to bed tonight anyway.

Flopping back on to her bed, Helena grabbed her phone from where the maid had helpfully plugged it in to charge and set it on the bedside table. As she stared at the dark screen, a wave of homesick longing flooded through her.

She wanted her sister.

She needed Thea there, to talk through all the craziness. She was the only person in the world who could possibly understand and maybe make sense of all the thoughts and feelings and fears whirling around in Helena's brain right now. Thea would yell, she was pretty sure, and tell her she was an idiot and she didn't have to do this. She'd probably cry and feel guilty, too.

But she'd help her fix it, one way or another.

With a sigh, Helena dropped the phone on the bed cover beside her. That, of course, was exactly why she couldn't phone Thea. For the first time in her life, Thea had chosen to go after what she wanted, what would make her happy, rather than staying behind and helping Helena, or the family, or the business. Helena couldn't jeopardise that by calling her now, throwing her back into the family lunacy. Thea was out and she was happy. And Helena was going to keep it that way.

Which meant she had to fix this herself.

Wrapping her arms around her middle, Helena pulled her knees up and turned on her side, small and insignificant in the oversized room. There was another reason not to tell Thea, of course. A horrible, sneaky, underhand reason. One Helena really hoped wasn't true, but she couldn't promise that, even to herself.

Did I plan for this to happen?

Thea would ask. Maybe not immediately, but eventually it would come up. Thea had to have known about the crippling crush Helena had nurtured for Flynn when they were teens. At fourteen or fifteen, he'd been all she could think about. He was kind, serious, and his eyes had mesmerised her. Not boring blue like hers, but pools of molten caramel. Helena had written embarrassingly awful poetry about his eyes. But, more than anything, he hadn't treated her like 'little Helena' the way everyone else did. He'd seen her as a real person, not just a silly child. A woman, even, with her own dreams and ideas. And he'd encouraged her to go after them.

Of course, he'd been six years older and already away at university then, home only for holidays and birthdays. Maybe that was part of it—he wasn't around her enough to be irritated by the little hanger-on, the way Thea and Zeke had been. It had also ensured that Flynn had remained completely oblivious to her affections. And Helena wasn't about to let him find out now.

But Thea must have realised. Isabella certainly had. And since that was still…before, she'd been sympathetic, even caring and protective of Helena's feelings.

That crush was a decade old, of course, but the thought still lingered. Had she manipulated things so that she was the one who ended up in the wedding dress? She didn't think so—and, even if she had, she didn't think Thea and Zeke would be complaining. But she'd certainly jumped into that dress quickly enough.

She'd told Flynn, and herself, that it was all to save face, to protect the family—even to protect Flynn from any embarrassment. But, at the heart of it, had she married him because a part of her had never truly moved on from that crippling teenage crush?

Helena wasn't sure.

But she knew a crush wasn't enough of a reason to stay married, and neither was family loyalty. Just as she'd told Thea. And she already knew she wouldn't be able to give Flynn the future he wanted.

Still…

Maybe it was the champagne talking or the lack of food, but Helena couldn't shake one lingering thought. Even if it wasn't forever…could she really pass up the opportunity to live out the wedding night her fourteen-year-old self had dreamed of so often?

Her stomach clenched at just the idea of it. Could she even try? Thea, the counsellor—everyone had told her she had to move on with her life. Had to open up to intimacy again. And she'd tried, of course she had, but it had never felt quite…safe.

Flynn was safe. A laugh bubbled up as she remembered her father calling him 'a safe pair of hands'. But he was right. Flynn would never hurt her, or make her do anything she didn't want. And he was enough of a gentleman that if she changed her mind she was pretty sure he'd not just let her go but never even mention it again.

And he was her husband. Even if she wouldn't—couldn't—give him children, she could give him this. Give them this. And didn't they deserve something good at the end of this horrendous day?

It would be good, she knew. Better than good. She might not have a lot to compare it to, but that kiss…she'd almost melted at his feet right then. How could anything that led on from that kiss be less than spectacular?

Helena swallowed, made herself sit up. This was the rest of her life, starting today. She'd done her part and now they were all even. She wasn't going to waste any more time trying to make up for things—she'd done everything that she could. And maybe she and Flynn wouldn't make this marriage last longer than it took the ink to dry on the divorce papers, but didn't that mean there was all the more reason to mark the occasion?

She was moving on from everything that had led them to this day. And sleeping with her husband would prove that.

Pushing herself up off the bed, Helena padded across to the chest of drawers and opened the third drawer again, holding the negligee up against her body for a moment as she summoned up every bit of courage she possessed.

Time for a fresh start.

Flynn was halfway through the second brandy when the knock came. He blinked, confused, for a moment. This was his father's study. Who would come looking for him here at long past midnight? And it felt so weird to be the one about to call for whomever it was to come in. As if he should be sitting on the other side of the big old desk, staring censoriously at someone.

A second knock. Flynn shook his head, blamed the brandy for his thoughts and said, 'Come in.'

The door creaked open, slow and loud, and Flynn put down his glass and sat up straight as Helena's blonde waves appeared around the edge of it.

'Oh, good,' she said with an unfamiliar smile. 'You're alone. This could have been embarrassing otherwise.'

'Embarrassing?' Flynn asked, confused. But then Helena stepped into the room and he understood all too well. 'Oh.'

The pale satin of her negligee clung to curves he'd barely realised she had until he'd glimpsed her in her underwear that morning. Somehow, even if this ensemble covered more, it seemed worse. He could almost make out the dark tips of her nipples through the thin fabric, and his whole body was suddenly heavy with desire.

Helena bit her lip and Flynn knew he should set her at her ease, reassure her about…something. But he couldn't find the words. Any words. Could barely remember the English language, in fact.

'So, I was sitting up in the bridal suite and I got to thinking.' Turning, she closed the door behind her and Flynn's eyes focused automatically on her bottom, lush and curved and perfectly highlighted by the satin. Oh, he was doomed.

'Thinking,' he repeated dumbly, very aware that he had absolutely no idea what was happening here and, given the circumstances, probably little chance of figuring it out even if she explained it in words of no greater than two syllables. 'Uh…what about?'

'Us, mostly.' Facing him again, she flashed him a smile—a bright and happy smile like he remembered from Helena of old. Helena at fourteen, following him around the house all Christmas Day, her new camera in hand. Except Helena at fourteen had worn taffeta dresses his mother picked out and had never, ever rendered him speechless like this.

'You mean the wedding?' Flynn asked, feeling proud of himself for managing that much in the face of satin nightwear.

'More…the marriage.' Moving over to the drinks cabinet he'd left open, Helena poured herself a brandy, then brought the bottle over to top up his glass. Because obviously what he needed at this point was *more* alcohol. The two brandies he'd already had appeared to have addled his mind completely.

Or maybe that was just her.

She sat down in his father's abandoned chair and crossed her legs, slim ankles showing under the hem of her negligee. Flynn had always felt that ankles were fairly safe parts of the female anatomy to look at, until now. Now, all he could think about was encircling one of those neat ankles with his fingers, trailing them up under all that satin until she uncrossed those legs and parted her thighs for him…

No. Hadn't he already decided he couldn't risk getting any closer to his wife until they agreed terms? He needed her tied to him for good before he risked anything— pregnancy or worse. He couldn't take the chance that he'd grow attached, start imagining their future together, if she might walk out on him at any moment. And he wasn't about to let brandy and satin derail the only part of his plan that was still intact.

'Did you want to talk about the marriage contract?' he asked, straightening himself in his chair and placing his full glass out of easy reach on the table. All he was feeling right now was lust. Nothing to worry about—as long as he didn't act on it. A one-night stand would be one thing, a temporary release—and wow, did he want that right now.

But a man couldn't have a one-night stand with his own wife. That wasn't how this worked.

'Not exactly.' The smile she gave him now wasn't a memory at all. It was all new—teasing and tempting and tantalising. The sort of smile Flynn Ashton would never have been allowed to see if he hadn't married this woman that morning.

Suddenly, the whole fiasco seemed worthwhile, just for a glimpse of that smile. Even if he couldn't do anything about it—yet.

Yet. That was the key. He didn't need to close this door forever, didn't need to shut down what this could be completely. He just needed to put it on ice until they got the details sorted. Who knew, the anticipation might even make the final outcome all the sweeter.

He just needed to exercise a little patience, that was all. And who knew patience better than him? The man who'd spent his life waiting to belong, for a place in the family, to be trusted with the business. He was so close now and he couldn't let his libido screw that up for him.

'I was thinking that there could be certain perks to this being married thing,' Helena went on, and Flynn focused very hard on not imagining those perks.

'I'm not sure—'

'I mean, we have this great opportunity to get to know each other better, for one thing.' Helena folded her legs up under her so she could lean over the arm of the chair, bringing her closer to him. He could smell her skin. She smelt like roses, and it was going to kill him.

'I've known you since you were born,' Flynn pointed out. 'I think we know each other pretty well.'

'Maybe.' Helena's answering smile was brief, and shaded. Almost sad. Flynn frowned; he'd known earlier, talking with her father, that he was missing something about Helena's past. That sad smile just made him want to know what even more. 'But we're different people now.'

'Than when we were children?' Flynn laughed, but he knew it sounded forced. 'I should hope so.'

'We're different people than we were this morning, Flynn,' Helena said, her beautiful face suddenly serious. 'You're a husband now, and I'm a wife. I'm Mrs Flynn Ashton now, remember?'

Sobered, Flynn nodded his agreement. 'I know. And that's…it's a big change for both of us. And that's why I think we need to spend some time figuring out what that means, for *our* futures, not just the family or the business.'

Helena blinked and sat back a little. 'I'm glad you feel that way.'

'What did you expect?' Flynn asked, not sure he wanted to hear the answer.

'Well, you disappeared from our wedding to hole up with my father and yours—presumably to discuss how our marriage impacts on the shareholders or something.' Helena shrugged. 'You can understand my belief that the human part of this marriage comes second.'

'It's not that,' Flynn assured her. 'But our parents are flying out tomorrow morning and I wanted to deal with them before they go. So that we don't have to think about them at all while we enjoy our honeymoon.' Instead, he could focus on getting Helena to sign the blasted marriage agreement so that when they got back to London he could put his energies into taking over as CEO of Morrison-Ashton, rather than firefighting whatever actions his father decided to take to solve the problem.

'Our honeymoon…' Helena's tongue darted out to lick her lips and Flynn's mind flew from business back to their first kiss. The way she'd melted against him, how his hands had clenched at her hips. How all he'd wanted in the world was to draw her closer and closer to him…

Not helping.

'I had some ideas about our honeymoon,' Helena went on. 'And getting to know each other better during it.' She leant in again and Flynn forced himself to pull back, to keep a distance between them, even if it was somehow actually physically painful.

'I had some thoughts too,' he said. 'I think the first thing we need to do is get the paperwork sorted.'

Helena blinked at him then shifted back, away. 'Paperwork.'

'I think it's important that we both know where we stand in this marriage.' He kept his gaze fixed on hers as he spoke. He wasn't hiding away from her, or pretending he didn't know what she was offering. But he needed to be plain about the way things were going to be.

No sex until they had the papers signed. Even if it felt as if it might kill him.

'You mean your father wants to make sure I've signed away my rights to anything worthwhile before I get my feminine claws into you.' Helena got to her feet, shaking her head. 'You know, he really doesn't have to worry. I don't want your money or your business. I don't even want this stupid ring, but I can't get it off my fat finger.' She waved her left hand in front of his face and Flynn reached out to grab it.

'You agreed to this marriage.' He ran his finger over the band, soothing the red skin there, and after a moment she stopped trying to pull it away again. Progress. 'You even pushed this ring into place. Nobody forced you into anything, and the only thing you signed before we said our vows was a meaningless invitation.'

'I know that.' She sounded irritable now. Flynn never

imagined that could be a step up from seductive but, under the circumstances, he was happy to go with it. 'And I know we need the paperwork so that we can get out of this whole mess neatly when the time comes—'

'That's not why.' They were married now. It was time to disabuse her of any notion that this marriage was a temporary thing for him. 'We need it so that you can be my wife, completely, without any of this confusion or people talking about us. We need it to make us official. Legitimate.'

Helena's eyes narrowed and she pulled her hand from his, but he could still feel the phantom memory of the cool metal of her ring against his fingertips.

'You mean to make you legitimate,' she said, her glare accusing. 'You need the paperwork to prove you're really part of the family. You think it'll make it easier for you as CEO when your dad steps down, now Zeke's gone.'

'That's part of it,' Flynn allowed. 'But not all.'

Helena stood, shifting so her weight was on one leg and her hip cocked out for her hand to rest on it. It emphasised the curve of her waist in a way Flynn really shouldn't be thinking about right now, and he tried to focus on the unhappy curl of her lips rather than anything below them.

'Really?' she asked, sounding unconvinced. 'Then tell me this. If you'd married Thea today, would you be down here drinking brandy alone? Or would you be in bed with her right now?'

CHAPTER FIVE

HELENA ALMOST DIDN'T want to hear the answer. It was a stupid question—one that neither of them could escape from now it'd been asked. Maybe that was for the best. If things had gone to plan, Flynn would have married her sister today. She knew that Thea hadn't loved him, but she'd never really given much thought to how Flynn felt about Thea. She'd just assumed, given his usual pragmatic, spreadsheet-based approach to the whole thing, that it was a business convenience.

She'd even wondered idly once or twice if Flynn was gay and his marriage to Thea an elaborate cover to hide the truth from Ezekiel. Heaven knew the old man was hidebound and rigid about everything else. No reason to assume that he'd deal with a son who liked men any better than he'd dealt with a son who ran out and abandoned the family business like Zeke had.

Flynn wasn't gay. No gay guy could have kissed her the way he had at the reception. And, besides, she knew when a guy wanted her—and Flynn's eyes when she'd walked in had spoken volumes. Lusty volumes of erotic poetry.

He wanted her. But he wasn't going to take her, even offered up on a plate. In Helena's experience, there were limited reasons for that sort of restraint—and they usually came down to being faithful to someone else.

What if Flynn had really loved Thea? What if he was heartbroken right now, drowning his sorrows in brandy while she swanned in wearing white satin and tried to seduce him?

Could she have made a bigger mess of this? But there was no going back now. She needed to know the truth.

'Tell me honestly, Flynn. Would you have slept with Thea tonight?' she asked again, and Flynn's gaze slipped away from hers.

'Probably.' His shoulders lifted slightly then slumped. 'We'd talked about…well…getting to know each other as man and wife, from the start.'

Helena's jaw tightened. She could almost imagine the conversation, probably squeezed in between a meeting about the quarterly projections and a client presentation. Thea, cool and calm and business-like, the way she only ever was when she was working, not dating. Flynn, as un-flappable as ever, giving equal gravity to the budget and his sex life.

One of them had probably even said the words: *in the interest of mutual satisfaction* or something.

'But it was different with Thea,' Flynn said, a hint of apology in his voice. 'We were…well, I was…'

In love, Helena finished for him in her head. And that was something Helena couldn't match up to. She'd thought she could be enough for him, for now. But not if he was in love with her sister.

Flynn sighed. 'We had paperwork,' he said in the end, as if that explained everything.

For Flynn, it probably did.

'That's all you want from this marriage? Paperwork?' Helena gripped the back of the chair she stood behind, keeping it between them like a shield. A screen, at least. How humiliating to be having this conversation in almost see-through nightwear. How had this ever seemed like a good idea?

'No.' That was his firm voice. His don't-mess-with-me business voice. She'd heard of it, mostly from Thea, but he'd never used it on her before. They'd never been close enough for him to have the opportunity, not since she was fifteen.

'Then what *do* you want?' She didn't care if she was pleading. She needed to make sense of this if she hoped to have any chance of sleeping tonight. She swept a hand down the side of her negligee. 'You don't want this. You don't want happily ever after. But you don't seem to want a quickie divorce either. Whatever happens next, we're stuck with each other for at least the next two weeks. So tell me—what is it you *do* want?'

'I want a wife. I want paperwork. I want something to follow the plan just *once*.' He grabbed his glass and downed the remaining brandy. Helena just stared at him. Was that Flynn losing his temper? she wondered. She'd never seen it before. And still, it seemed so…insubstantial.

'I'm sorry,' he said, as if he'd thrown the glass at her or something. 'It's just…it's been a long day, and not one bit of it has gone the way I expected. I'm still…adjusting.'

To being married to the wrong woman. To losing the woman he'd actually *wanted* to marry. She couldn't even blame him.

'Right,' she said, as if her life hadn't been turned upside down a couple of times in the last twenty-four hours, too. 'I can understand that.'

Flynn looked up, his eyes red and tired. 'For you too, I know. It's been…'

'One hell of a day.'

'Yeah.' They stared at each other for a long moment, and Helena felt the knowledge that she was tied to this man, for better or for worse, sinking into her bones in a way it never had when she'd said the words.

This was her future, whatever happened next. He'd always be her husband, even if he became an ex. They were joined—and she didn't understand the first thing about him.

This Flynn, the one she'd seen tonight, was nothing like the one her fourteen-year-old self had thought herself in love with. He wasn't kind, noble and knowing. He wasn't even the unfeeling, emotionally detached man she'd assumed he had to be to deal with his fiancée running out on him. This Flynn cared. He felt. He hurt.

And this was the man she'd married. The man she intended to keep secrets from until they could *un*marry.

'I should…' She wiggled her fingers towards the door. 'Sleep would probably help. Both of us.'

'Yeah.' Flynn sighed. 'I'll head up in a moment, too. I just have one phone call to make.'

'Now? It's two in the morning, Flynn.'

'I know. But this can't wait.'

'I'll never understand that,' she admitted. 'You and your dad—and Thea. The way you're married to the business. I mean…' She winced as she realised what she'd said.

But it didn't seem to register with Flynn. 'This isn't business.'

Not business? Then who would take his call at two a.m.? Unless…was he phoning Thea? She didn't want to know if he was.

Helena turned to leave, but paused in the doorway as she remembered her original plan for their sleeping arrangements—before the negligee and the discovery that her husband might well be in love with her sister, even now.

'I thought…maybe it would be a good idea for you to sleep in my old room? Tonight, at least. I had the maid move your things. It's right next to the bridal suite, so it makes it a little less likely for you to be caught out on the other side of the building in the morning, when you're supposed to be ravishing your new wife.'

He actually flinched at the words and Helena swallowed down the spike of pain she felt at that. No, she definitely wasn't enough for Flynn Ashton, even after everything she'd done today.

'Okay. I'll do that then. I'll see you in the morning, Helena.' He said it kindly, a sop to her poor hopeful ideas of a night with her husband.

'Yeah. In the morning.'

Maybe things would look brighter with the sunrise. They sure couldn't look much darker.

Flynn didn't sleep much.

He'd woken his solicitor up the moment Helena left and asked him to book a flight over to discuss the new marriage contract. Explaining why that was necessary hadn't been fun, and he rather suspected he'd have to do it again in the morning anyway, once Henry was properly awake. Even the best contract solicitor in London needed a little time to surface from sleep before his brilliance began to shine.

That vital task performed, he'd headed up to bed, pausing at the top of the stairs while he considered his options. Helena had a point; sleeping in her old room would make the chance of discovery in the morning less likely. And since apparently his stuff was already there anyway, he'd trudged off in the direction of the bridal suite, letting himself into the room next door. And if his body tugged him towards another door, another bed, another body, well, he resisted. Just.

But lying in sheets that still smelled of her perfume, of

roses, of her skin, made it impossible not to think of Helena. His wife.

He'd hurt her tonight, he'd seen it in her eyes, even if he wasn't sure exactly what he'd said wrong. Everything, probably. He was out of practice at dealing with women. For the past few years, it had only been Thea for him, and that wasn't exactly a normal relationship. One of the most reassuring parts of it was being able to discuss things openly and clearly, without misunderstandings.

But with Helena…they didn't have that grounding. And so he'd miscalculated and caused her pain. So now he needed to try and find a way to fix that and make sure it didn't happen again.

Henry's arrival should solve the second part of that. Once they had their expectations down on paper, things would get easier between them. But making things up to her…that was all on him.

Flynn eventually drifted off thinking of ways to improve relations with his wife, only to be awoken by his internal clock a mere three hours later. Six a.m. on the dot; he knew without checking his phone. It always was. He'd been waking up at six for so long now he couldn't sleep in if he wanted to.

Actually, today he wanted to. If he could sleep, he would miss the departing parents and family. Helena could get over last night with coffee and breakfast, and by the time he finally emerged the world would be stable and right again.

Flynn sighed, rolled out of bed and headed for the shower. Heat and steam were the next best thing to sleep, anyway.

Clean and awake, Flynn towelled off and reached for his usual suit before remembering that he was on holiday.

More than that, he was on his *honeymoon*. It might not resemble what other people expected from a honeymoon, but it was the best he was going to get. And he certainly wasn't going to wear a suit for it.

Even if he suspected that today, his first day of marriage, would look very similar to every other day that had come before it. He had work to do, as ever. And he had to review the marriage agreement he'd had with Thea before Henry arrived.

But first he had to make sure his parents actually left for London. At least, with them gone, he wouldn't have to worry about Ezekiel meddling or Isabella upsetting Helena.

Of course, with the departure of everyone else, it would just be him and Helena left together. Alone.

And that, Flynn decided, could get very interesting indeed. At the very least, it would give him a solid chance to make things up to his new wife.

All the more reason to make sure that Henry got there soon.

Helena woke the morning after her wedding, just as she'd gone to bed: alone. Why on earth did that feel like a surprise? she wondered as she lay back on the luxurious sheets and stared at the ceiling.

Here she was, the first day of her honeymoon, and she wasn't sure she was going to see her husband at all. Wasn't sure that she wanted to either.

Except their parents were leaving that morning. He'd have to be there to see them off, right?

And if Flynn was there, did she really have to be there too?

Helena sighed. Sadly, yes, she did. This was the first full day of the charade that was set to take over her life for the next however long—the act of being a devoted and dutiful wife. At least, with the remaining guests and family gone, the only people she'd have to keep it up for were the villa staff—until they got home to London, anyway.

Dragging herself out of bed, she showered and dressed quickly before heading down to the entrance hall, her still damp hair curling around her shoulders.

'The car for the airport is here,' Flynn said, walking in through the front door just as she came down the stairs.

'Unlike the people it's here to transport.' Helena looked pointedly around the empty hallway, trying to ignore the way her heart jumped, just a little, at the sight of him. Could she be more pathetic? He might have married her, but he'd made it very clear that all he wanted was the paperwork.

They stared at each other for a long moment and Helena felt the cool stone walls pressing in as the silence between them grew. She'd never had a problem finding things to talk to Flynn—or anyone else—about before, but all of a sudden it was as if the rings they wore had sucked all the small talk out of them.

We're good at this, she reminded herself desperately. *We're the ones who keep the conversation going, who smooth over the awkward silences and the embarrassing comments!*

But apparently that skill only worked with people they weren't married to. Or when one of them hadn't turned down a wedding night in the marital bed, at least. Great.

'Maybe I should go and check on them,' Flynn said eventually, moving towards the stairs. Helena tried to dodge out of his way, but miscalculated, her foot slipping on the bottom few steps.

She reached for the banister but Flynn was there first,

grabbing her around the waist with both arms to keep her upright.

Helena waited for her heartbeat to return to normal speed now she was safe. It didn't.

Looking up, she saw honest concern in Flynn's golden caramel eyes. His very close eyes. Not far from his very close lips. So close, in fact, that she'd only have to move a centimetre or two and they'd be kissing. Like they'd done after the speeches. And that kiss had hinted at so much more…

Until he'd turned down her advances just a few hours later. The memory of his dismissal settled over her like a cold shower.

'Just look at you two lovebirds! *Such* a beautiful sight.' Isabella's voice rang out across the hallway, echoing off the stone walls as she descended the stairs. Flynn pulled away so quickly that Helena ended up grabbing the banister anyway. *So much for chivalry.*

'Let me help you with that, Mother.' Flynn jogged up the stairs to take his mother's suitcase from her and carried it down. 'Where are Dad and Thomas?'

Isabella rolled her eyes. 'In the study, I believe. Last-minute business meeting before our flight.'

Helena saw the look of irritation that crossed Flynn's face, but Isabella either missed or chose to ignore it. Feeling left out, was he? She supposed she'd better prepare herself for two weeks of him sloping off to check his email and taking business calls during lunch.

That was if they spent any time together at all. What if he just intended to work all through the honeymoon?

Helena shook away the thought. She had to look on the bright side or she was going to go mad. So what if her husband had better things to do on their honeymoon than spend time with her? That just gave her more opportunities to go exploring, to see more of the country, maybe go back to that pretty jewellery shop she'd found with Thea in the nearest town. She could treat herself to something pretty then have lunch in that little *trattoria*. Maybe flirt with a nice Italian man… The thought stopped abruptly.

She couldn't do that any more, could she? Not now she was married. And especially not once she signed Flynn's blasted paperwork with its ironclad fidelity clause. Not that she had any particular plans to go out and pick up a guy or anything. It wasn't really her style, was it? But she did *like* men, had several close male friends and enjoyed the warm buzz she got from flirting with them, just a little, even knowing that they would never do anything about it.

But that was off the table now. Flynn would probably have private detectives following her around, photographing her having lunch and researching every man she ever spoke to. And if he didn't, his father certainly would.

Yeah, she really hadn't thought this whole thing through.

A door opened just down the corridor and she heard her father's laugh as he and Ezekiel emerged from their conference, dragging their cases behind them.

'All ready?' Flynn asked the men. 'The car for the airport is here.'

Ezekiel nodded and one of the villa staff darted forward to take their cases out to the car. Flynn followed with Isabella's. Helena stood awkwardly, waiting for whatever happened next. The moment they left, everything would change again and she was beginning to fear that her bright attitude wasn't going to last a full two weeks.

'Well, have a good journey home, all of you,' she said. 'And we'll see you in London in a fortnight, I guess.'

Isabella nodded and leant in to kiss the air beside Helena's cheeks. 'We'll have the house all ready for you both. Then you and I can sit down and discuss your social calendar.'

Social calendar? 'Great.'

Ezekiel nodded his own farewell then walked out of the front door with his wife, leaving Helena alone with Thomas.

'You've got two weeks here, Helena,' he said, studying her face with serious eyes. Helena's breath caught in her throat. She and Thea had always known that their father was easy-going and affable—but only to a point. When he turned serious, they knew it really mattered. 'Use them wisely. You've made your choice and you need to stick with it now. So make this work.'

He didn't really need to add the *or else*, Helena supposed. She knew well enough what happened when she disappointed her father.

'And if you speak to your sister,' he added, pausing by the door, 'tell her we need to discuss her future. Sooner rather than later.'

Helena nodded stiffly. She didn't envy her sister that conversation.

But then, Thea probably wouldn't envy Helena two weeks in Tuscany trying to 'make things work' with a husband who didn't want her, either.

Well, if all Flynn wanted was a paperwork wife, Helena could give him that. Watching as he waved to their parents' departing car from the front step, Helena made a decision. If this was all business anyway, she'd let Flynn get on with his—while she focused on her own life. She'd cleared her calendar for the month around the wedding, knowing things would be manic enough without adding any new projects for her burgeoning interior design business into the mix. But here she was with time on her hands, her laptop and freakishly fast Internet access, given their location. It was the perfect chance to get on with the new website she'd been planning for months.

Time for her to get on with her own future for a while.

Their married life had slipped into a routine surprisingly quickly, Flynn realised a few days later. Every morning he woke, went for a run, returned to the villa to shower and dress, then sat down for breakfast. Helena usually joined him then and they made polite, if sparse, conversation over the English papers he'd arranged to have delivered.

Then Flynn would settle into his father's study to work while Helena did…whatever it was she did all day. Sometimes they'd see each other for lunch, sometimes not. Dinner they usually took together in the dining room, and Helena always turned in for bed first.

There had been no repeat of her wedding night offer, something for which Flynn was profoundly grateful as Henry had been held up in London and wasn't able to get out to Tuscany until the end of the week. As much as he wanted the paperwork sorted before he allowed himself to really invest in the marriage, he knew his own limitations. No man had willpower strong enough to resist Helena in that negligee night upon night, whatever the stakes.

Still, he thought as he took his morning run on the fourth day, he didn't want the distance between them to grow so much as to be insurmountable, either. Once Henry arrived he needed Helena on side, ready to work with him, ready to make this marriage real.

With an extra burst of energy he took the last stretch up the drive to the villa at a sprint, the thought of a calendar entry he'd barely registered the day before spurring him on.

Back in his room, he checked his phone as he caught his breath again. He smiled. Right there, scheduled neatly in his personal calendar by his PA, who'd been put in charge of all the honeymoon plans, was exactly the right way to make things up to Helena. A romantic tour of a Tuscan vineyard, complete with wine-tasting, lunch and perhaps a drive through the countryside. Perfect for the honeymooning couple.

It would mean taking the whole day off to do it properly. If he'd been with Thea, as planned, they'd have spent half a day there then both headed home to catch up with emails, he imagined. But Helena, he suspected, required a different hand. After four days of distance, this needed to be all or nothing.

And Flynn was going all in.

Helena ignored the first three knocks on her door. She'd stayed up late after dinner working again on the new website and had planned to catch up on her sleep with a well-earned lie-in—especially as it meant she stood a better chance of avoiding her husband at breakfast. The endless awkward pauses and stilted conversations over the dining tables were becoming more than she could bear. Would it be like this in London? She hoped not.

But the fourth knock she couldn't ignore, especially as the door opened seconds after it.

'Helena…you're not up?' Flynn closed the door behind him and stared at her, a frown line deepening between his eyebrows.

'It's only nine-thirty.' Helena shuffled into a sitting position, glad that she'd slept in her comfortable shorts and T-shirt instead of the ridiculous negligee. 'We're supposed to be on our honeymoon. I'm maintaining the happy couple illusion.'

'The car's picking us up in half an hour. You might want to get up.' Flynn crossed to the bathroom while Helena just blinked at him in confusion. 'I'll get the shower running. Give it a chance to warm up for you.'

'I can run my own shower,' Helena protested, swinging her legs over the side of the bed. Apparently she was getting up. 'And, anyway, what car?'

She heard the sound of water running and Flynn re-emerged. 'The car to take us on our vineyard trip. Didn't it get put on your calendar? I've got it all arranged for us.'

Helena felt that same chill that had overtaken her on her wedding night begin to snake its way through her veins, despite the steam from the shower seeping into the room and the warm summer morning outside.

'You mean you had it all arranged for you and Thea.' She was not jealous of her sister, Helena reminded herself. It wasn't as if she was in love with Flynn either. She just liked to know where she stood, that was all.

'I arranged it for my wife and me. That's you, in case you'd forgotten.'

'Not likely,' Helena muttered.

Flynn headed back towards the door. 'Car will be here at ten. I'll meet you in the foyer.'

And then Helena was alone again, with only the sound of falling water to keep her company.

A vineyard tour. Presumably that included wine-tasting, so things could be worse. Maybe there'd even be lunch. Taking a deep breath, Helena decided to focus on the positive. Paying attention to the good things in life, she'd found, was sometimes the only way to avoid drowning in the despair of all the bad things.

So—good things only.

The sun was shining, the new website was going well enough that she'd earned a break, and she would have wine and food in the sunshine today. Maybe she could even talk the maid into coffee and something resembling breakfast before they left, if she was quick.

Lots of good things to distract from the one awful thing. It was going to be a good day.

Forcing a smile, she hopped in the shower, washing away her bad mood with the soap suds. By the time she emerged again, the maid had left coffee and a pastry on the chest of drawers and Helena sipped and nibbled happily as she flicked through her wardrobe to find something suitable for a newly married woman on her honeymoon, taking a tour with her husband.

She really hadn't packed for this. Mostly, she'd just been working in shorts and a T-shirt so far. But today's trip seemed important to Flynn, so she guessed it should be important to her, too. Maybe they'd even manage to learn how to speak to each other again. That kind of milestone required more than a pair of shorts, Helena decided.

In the end, she settled on a sunny yellow cotton dress, patterned with daisies around the hem, and slipped her feet into white sandals. She twisted her wet hair into a knot at the back of her head, knowing it would dry quickly enough in the sun and give her pretty waves when she let it down that evening. Even with ten minutes to add sun protection and a little light make-up, she was still ready well before ten.

Grabbing her straw hat and bag, she headed down the stairs to find Flynn already in the entrance hall.

'You were quick,' Flynn said with a smile. 'I thought I'd be waiting a while for you.'

'Shows how little you know me.' Helena arched her eyebrows. 'I'm very efficient—when I want to be.'

'Well, thank you for your efficiency.' He glanced away for a moment before meeting her gaze again. 'I'm sorry we haven't had much time to spend together so far this week. With Zeke's surprise coup, getting Dad to make me CEO, things are frantic at work, making sure everything's in place.'

'I understand,' Helena said as coolly as she could. 'I had work to do too, anyway.'

Flynn blinked and Helena realised he probably hadn't even known she had a job, beyond helping out with his wedding. Irritation rose in her chest. Rosebud Interiors might not be much compared to the might of Morrison-Ashton, but it was still her company.

'That's good, then,' he said. 'Maybe you can tell me more about it over lunch?'

Some of the irritation faded away when she realised he did sound honestly interested. 'Yeah, okay.'

'Great. Well, then, let's get going.' Flynn held out an arm for her. After a moment she took it and was rewarded by a warm private smile. 'I'm looking forward to a day out with my wife.'

Helena beamed back, an unexpected warmth blossoming inside her despite herself at the words 'my wife'. Maybe this day wouldn't be *all* bad.

CHAPTER SIX

As THE CAR flew through the Tuscan countryside, Flynn settled back into his seat and ran through his plan for the day again in his head.

Main objective: to make Helena comfortable with this marriage in time for Henry's arrival. Or was the main objective to get Helena to sit down and sensibly discuss the marriage contract? One led to the other, admittedly, but a firm objective was the first step of any plan. So, which was it?

Maybe he needed a broader plan. Make the objective a signed contract before they headed back to London. In which case, today's steps broke down into—

'Oh, wow!' Helena wound down her window and stuck her head half outside the car. 'Look at this place, Flynn!'

Resisting the urge to pull her back inside, where a passing car was less likely to lop her head off, Flynn tried to look around her at what had made her so excited. Whatever it was, it fitted nicely with his plan, at least. Coaxing Helena into a better mood was definitely step one.

Outside, field after field of grapevines sunned themselves as they ripened and, up ahead, Flynn could see the farmhouse from the photo his PA had attached to the diary entry. This was the right place then, at least.

'It's gorgeous.' Helena ducked back into the car, her

smile far more authentic this time. 'This is where we're doing the tasting?' she asked as the driver took another twist in the rough driveway at considerable speed.

'This is the place.' Flynn made a mental note about a raise for his PA as he pulled out his phone and checked the notes on the diary entry again. 'A tour of the vineyards, followed by a tasting with antipasti, then a drive to a nearby *taverna* for lunch, where I believe they serve the wine from the estate.'

'Sounds perfect.' She flashed him a quick grin that showed her neat white teeth. 'Very romantic.'

'I think that was the plan.' He tucked his phone back in his pocket as the car reached the top of the drive and slowed to a stop. 'At least, that's what I asked my PA to organise.'

'You asked her to organise romance?' Helena asked, eyebrows raised. 'Isn't that a little counter-intuitive?'

'I don't see why.' The driver opened Helena's door, so Flynn opened his own and stepped out into the late morning sun. 'Most things can be improved by a little planning.'

'Still...romance needs a certain sort of spontaneity. Don't you think?'

She really wasn't anything like her sister, Flynn mused. Although, given Thea's own last-minute change of plan for love, perhaps they had more in common than he'd imagined.

'I think that people like to think that the good things in life are natural, that they just happen,' he said. 'But in my experience a lack of planning tends to lead to unfortunate outcomes rather than good ones.'

Helena stared at him over the bonnet of the car. 'Boy, have you been having the wrong experiences.'

Maybe she was right. But not about the planning. And if they wanted to get along equably enough as man and wife… Mentally, Flynn added: *Convince Helena of the merits of forward planning* to his schedule for the day.

He had always liked a challenge.

'Mr and Mrs Ashton! Welcome. I'm Gia.' The dark-haired woman stepped forward on to the driveway and shook Helena's hand enthusiastically before moving on to Flynn.

'Call me Flynn,' he said, taking her hand in both of his. Her husband looked far more relaxed in the company of this stranger than he did in hers, Helena thought.

'And I'm Helena,' she added with a little wave. 'So… is this your home?'

Gia laughed, a low, mellow sound. 'It is! It belonged to my great-grandparents, then my grandparents, then my parents. And when they retired three years ago I took it over with my husband.'

'And began producing some of the most renowned Chianti in the region,' Flynn said. Gia's gaze moved to him, her eyebrows raised. Helena would have done the same, were it not Flynn the Planner talking. 'I read the website in the car,' he added with a shrug.

'It's good to have a truly interested visitor,' Gia said. 'Now, why don't you come inside with me and have a coffee before we start our tour?'

'That sounds like a fantastic idea,' Helena agreed, even as she saw Flynn check his watch. Good grief, the man was going to have to learn to find flex in his schedule to allow for coffee or they were never going to make it through the fortnight without killing each other.

The coffee was dark and rich, the farmhouse kitchen shady and cool—both a welcome respite after the air-conditioned swerving of the car. Helena felt her stomach settle and her shoulders relax as she sat and peppered Gia with questions about the house and the vineyard.

'I was working in America—California, in fact—until five years ago,' Gia said, pushing a plate of *biscotti* towards Helena.

'Making wine?' Helena asked, helping herself.

Gia shook her head. 'Real estate, believe it or not. But I toured plenty of the vineyards out there with clients. But then one year I came home for Christmas and, over dinner, my parents told me it was time for them to retire. They didn't want to interrupt my career, so they were planning to sell the vineyard.' She gave a small shrug and reached for a *biscotti*. 'I couldn't let them do it.'

'So you took it on yourself instead,' Flynn said. 'Very brave.'

Gia gave him a lopsided smile. 'I don't think I realised the risk I was taking until later. I came here with no plan, no real training, no idea what I was doing. But I learned fast and I studied hard. I took courses, asked questions and paid attention to *everything*. My parents stayed on to help for the first year or so, then I met my husband and he came on board, and between us all we found a way to make it work.'

Helena raised her eyebrows at Flynn across the table, sipping at her coffee while she waited for him to notice. Even he had to acknowledge everything Gia had built here without a plan.

But Flynn merely raised a single eyebrow in return then turned his attention back to Gia. 'I imagine you needed to work up a business plan and so forth once you took it over?'

'Of course. But that initial decision—that first jump. I never for a moment planned that, until that Christmas Day when I suddenly couldn't imagine doing anything else.'

Like her, on the morning of their wedding, Helena realised. She'd never really, truly imagined stepping into Thea's place if she decided not to go through with the marriage. But once she'd left, and she'd seen Flynn standing there…she couldn't imagine not marrying him in her place. Even though it was utterly, utterly crazy and unplanned.

Of course, Flynn would probably argue that marrying Helena was the closest thing to following his plan that he could manage on short notice.

Not exactly romantic.

'Come on,' Gia said, jumping to her feet. 'If you've finished your coffee, let's take a look around the vineyard.'

Helena gulped down the last mouthful of her coffee, grabbed another *biscotti* for the road and followed their guide out of the back door. She had a feeling that Gia was a woman who would appreciate the spontaneous aspect of romance. And she had an idea Gia might be able to help her with—if she could get her alone for a moment.

Flynn watched Helena as she skipped between the vines, peppering Gia with questions at every step. Gia, for her part, answered every one thoughtfully, following Helena at a more careful pace. Eventually Flynn tuned out of what they were saying altogether and just studied his wife.

She was golden in the sunlight, shining with—no, radiating—life and energy. Now they had escaped the villa, she seemed to have come to life. She'd been lovely in her borrowed wedding dress, gorgeous in that slippery silky thing on their wedding night, and pretty in the simple tailored shorts and tees she'd been wearing around the villa—but today, in a simple sundress and sandals, she was beautiful. She was *alive*.

Absently, Flynn pulled his phone from his pocket to check if Henry had sent through his flight details yet. The sooner they got this contract sorted, the sooner he could start making this marriage everything he'd planned for it to be. But there were no messages from his solicitor, or his PA, and as Flynn frowned at the screen Helena turned around to scowl at him.

'No working on honeymoon,' she said, plucking the phone from his hand and dropping it into her ridiculously large straw bag.

Gia's face tensed behind Helena. Flynn suspected she'd seen this between guests before, and that it didn't always end well. Except he and Helena weren't most guests, were they?

'I hope you can find that again in there,' he said mildly. 'It's got all the rest of our honeymoon activities scheduled on it.'

'All of them?' Helena asked with arched brows, and Gia laughed.

'Perhaps not all,' Flynn allowed.

'Good.' Helena twirled back to face Gia. 'Because I might have one or two surprises to add to it.'

Flynn's body tightened, just a little, at the warmth and promise in her voice that had been so absent the last few days, and he took a moment before following the women along the path. Maybe he'd plan a few surprises for Helena, too. The moment he had that contract signed.

Gia ended their tour right back where they had begun— at the back door to the farmhouse. Flynn wasn't sure if he'd learned very much about growing grapevines, but he was certainly ready for the wine-tasting.

As Gia opened the door to let them back into the kitchen, a man's voice floated out over a babble of childish nonsense. 'Trust me, *baba*, you won't like that one.'

'Is he after the salami or the wine today?' Laughing, Gia crossed the kitchen to give both man and baby a kiss on the cheek. 'Helena, Flynn. This is my husband, Roberto, and our son, Casper.'

'Pleased to meet you,' Flynn said, glancing over at Helena. She stood, mesmerised by the child, her lower lip trapped between her teeth. Was she thinking of the child they might have soon? He hoped so. 'I'm Flynn Ashton, and this is my wife, Helena.'

Breaking her reverie, Helena smiled suddenly and waved at Casper. 'Hi.'

'We'll get out of your way now,' Roberto said. 'Everything should be set out. We'd have left already if somebody hadn't got a little hungry.' He held up a small bowl with some fresh fruit cut into baby-sized pieces. 'Come on, Casper. Let's see what birds we can spot from the terrace today.'

As Roberto and the baby wandered back out again, Gia watched them go. They were a nice family, Flynn thought. Obviously working together to keep everything—childcare and wine-making—running smoothly. He admired that.

He wanted that for himself. He'd discussed it with Thea, of course, although he'd planned to do so in greater detail after the wedding. He didn't want a wife waiting at home for him, organising parties and social events while sending her children off to boarding school, the way Isabella had done. He wanted a family where every member belonged and felt at home.

Watching Helena in the sunlight, he'd almost been able to picture it—more so even than he'd ever managed with Thea. It was possible, he thought with a smile, that losing his fiancée on his wedding day might turn out to be the best possible thing for his future. Whatever Helena said about their union being temporary, if they wanted, her behaviour said otherwise. If she didn't intend for it to last, why would she have accosted him in that negligee on their wedding night? No, Helena wanted this to work as much as he did—seeing her staring at the baby only confirmed that for him.

They'd talk, just as he planned. Maybe over lunch. Once she understood what this marriage meant to him, the contract negotiations were bound to go more smoothly. And then they could get on with properly enjoying the honeymoon.

He smiled again at the thought, before realising that Helena had already sat down at the tasting table and Gia was pouring their first wines. He slipped into the seat beside his wife and thought, just for a moment, about taking her hand.

But when he looked across, he saw a frown line marring her forehead and realised that the sunny, happy, teasing Helena he'd admired outside had gone—and he had no idea what had changed.

But he planned to find out.

Helena barely remembered anything from their tasting, later. She hoped she'd nodded in the right places, and said the right things, but she had no real idea. Flynn hadn't said anything, so perhaps she'd managed to keep up the show. To pretend that everything was fine and normal. That seeing Casper hadn't sent her mind spiralling back eight years.

Normally she was better at this—at being around babies and children. But today, with Flynn there beside her, a hopeful look in his eyes…all she'd been able to think about was the baby girl she'd given away.

Eventually, Flynn checked his watch and gave Gia an apologetic smile. 'This has been absolutely fascinating. Thank you so much for taking the time to show us around, and letting us taste your wonderful wines.'

'It's been my pleasure,' Gia said, beaming.

Roberto and Casper came out to wave them off and Helena tried to ignore the tug that still pulled at her middle, even after all these years. Instead, she plastered on a smile as she waved back then got into the car.

As the driver pulled away from the farmhouse, Helena handed Flynn back his phone, tipped her head back against the headrest and closed her eyes. But her mind still filled with babies.

Casper was a beautiful child, she thought, remembering his pudgy fingers clenched around a piece of apple, and his big brown eyes under dark curls. Nothing at all like the girl she'd given away eight long years ago, with her fine, pale baby down on her head and her unfocused blue eyes. There was no reason for him to remind Helena of her own child, except that every baby she saw did.

Probably always would, she'd realised by now.

But the life her daughter lived…she hoped that was like Casper's. Happy and full of family and laughter in a way it never could have been if Helena had kept her.

She'd done the right thing, however much it hurt. And sometimes that was all she could cling on to.

Squeezing her eyes tighter for a moment, willing away any tears, any signs of weakness, Helena tucked away all those feelings, all the regrets and what-ifs that rose up when she least wanted them, and returned to the present day. To her husband. Blinking a few times, she watched the Tuscan countryside flashing past the car window, all greens and reds and yellows and bright, bright blues.

How could she be sad when the world around her was so beautiful?

Composed again, she twisted in her seat to look at Flynn. He was engrossed in his phone screen so she gave it a few moments before clearing her throat. Still nothing.

'Where are we going for lunch?' she asked.

'Hmm?' Flynn's head moved as if he were paying her his full attention, but his gaze remained attached to the screen in front of him. Helena almost laughed, but decided not to encourage him.

Instead, she snatched the phone from his hand again and selected his calendar app. 'Let's see...'

Flynn's fingers closed over the screen, warm against her own hand. 'I thought you wanted spontaneity and surprises with your romance.'

'Not when you already planned it. Or your PA did.'

'It's a surprise to both of us that way,' Flynn pointed out.

Helena rolled her eyes. 'I really don't think you understand spontaneity.'

'It doesn't matter now anyway,' Flynn said, taking the phone from her and tucking it in his top pocket as the car slowed to a stop. 'We're here.'

She'd known she wasn't getting that phone back.

The driver opened her car door and Helena stepped out into the sunshine again, her head a little heavy from the drive and the wine-tasting. The *trattoria* they'd arrived at looked almost like someone's house, with its beautiful window boxes overflowing with flowers and the painted shutters thrown open. Helena spun slowly around to take in the view; nothing but fields and sunshine for miles, and the glint of a village a few miles down the road.

'You like it?' Flynn asked. He'd put on his sunglasses and Helena wished she could see his eyes. Surely even he had to admire the romance of a place like this.

'It's beautiful.' This was the sort of place she could imagine living—or at least designing. Nothing quite as grand as the villa they'd borrowed for the wedding, but cosy and homely and filled with good food and red flowers. It wasn't just beautiful; it was perfect.

'Then let's go in.' Flynn held his hand out to her and, after staring at it for a moment, Helena took it. She couldn't help but wonder, though, if it was a planned or spontaneous gesture. Either way, his hand felt warm and right in hers, so she decided not to ask.

Inside, parts of the restaurant's stone walls had been left bare, while others had been plastered and painted a creamy white that reflected the sunlight. Helena smiled at the happy mix of rustic and modern, finished with bright blooms in hand-blown glass vases, crisp table linen and an oversized clock hanging over the stone fireplace.

It was almost exactly how she'd have chosen to decorate it, given the chance.

They were shown to their table by an olive-skinned Italian girl in a neat black and white uniform. It wasn't a huge place—the ground floor had been mostly knocked through to make a large dining area, with the kitchen added on at the back of the house, as far as Helena could tell. Still, the fact that almost every other table was already occupied, considering such an out of the way location, gave Helena great hopes for the quality of the food. Despite the bread and antipasti she'd enjoyed at Gia's vineyard, her stomach started to rumble.

'What are you in the mood for?' Flynn asked as Helena cracked open the menu.

'Everything,' she answered, feasting on the lists of dishes printed on creamy paper in front of her. There was just the right amount of choice, she decided. Not too much, or it became impossible to decide, but enough that she felt she could consider each dish individually before picking her absolute favourite.

Flynn laughed. 'You like food, don't you?'

'Who doesn't?' The only question was: did she feel in the mood for meat or fish? And should they have a separate pasta course or just starters and mains? She reached for an olive from the bowl on the table between them to help her think. 'Everyone needs to eat.'

'Yes, but for some people it's just fuel. You really enjoy it.'

Helena glanced up to find his gaze settled on her, as if she were something to be studied, catalogued and understood. It was unnerving. But then, didn't she want to do the same to him? Understand where he came from, and where they were going? Maybe Flynn's thoughts had followed a similar thread, in which case the rest of the meal might go easier than she'd expected.

Closing the menu—she was settled on the *porcetta* anyway—Helena returned Flynn's interested gaze.

'What about you?' she asked. 'Do you cook? Or do you survive on takeaway Chinese like Thea when she's working?'

'I cook.' Flynn settled back in his chair. He hadn't even looked at the menu, she realised. 'Not often, but I can when the mood strikes me. I like eating fresh.'

'Me too. Fresh and in season always tastes better than pre-packaged.' She flashed him a grin. 'So, we do have some things in common, then. That's good.'

'It is,' Flynn agreed. 'But really, given our families, I never doubted we'd find some common ground.'

Helena gave a slight shrug. 'I don't know. I never really felt like a typical Morrison, not like Thea. I mean, I didn't go into the family business or anything.'

'No, but you grew up with the same expectations and weight of that family name,' Flynn said, more insightfully than she'd expected.

'And you grew up with those of the Ashton name.'

'Not really.'

A waiter approached before she could ask him to elaborate. Flynn ordered them wine, then asked for recommendations for food and ordered them without ever opening the menu, which Helena respected. For herself, she took the suggestion of *risotto alla Milanese* to start, but stuck with her *porcetta* for the main course.

As soon as the waiter had cleared the table, though, Helena pressed the point. 'What do you mean—not really?'

'Hmm?' Flynn had his phone out of his pocket again, but placed it face down on the table when she spoke.

'You said "not really" when I talked about you growing up with the expectations of the Ashton name. What did you mean?'

Flynn shrugged. 'Just the obvious. I'm not a real Ashton.'

'Of course you are! I mean, I know your father...' She trailed off. How exactly could she describe the way Ezekiel Ashton treated his sons? 'I know he wasn't always exactly even-handed with you and Zeke.'

'You mean he played us off against each other.' Flynn's voice was still even, but he stabbed at the nearest olive rather forcefully with the little stick. 'I know exactly why he gave me the job that was always promised to Zeke when I graduated. He wanted Zeke to have to fight me for it.'

'Except Zeke left instead.'

'And I stayed.' Another olive suffered a violent and pointy end.

'Why?' She'd wondered before, of course. Not originally, but ever since Zeke came back. She'd never got the full story, although she suspected Thea had. But either way, what had happened between Zeke and their father had influenced Flynn's life hugely. If she wanted to understand her husband, she had to understand that.

Flynn paused, a poor, defenceless olive halfway to his mouth. 'Where else would I go?'

'Anywhere, I suppose. Zeke did.'

'No. I...owed my father. Whatever else he did, and whatever his reasons, he took me in and gave me a home and a future when my real parents offered me neither.' A chill settled around Helena's heart at his words. 'I always knew that my place would be working at Morrison-Ashton, wherever I could be of most use.'

'You don't…' Helena swallowed, imagining a younger version of Flynn, always so neat and sensible and *kind*. Was it all because of a sense of debt? Had his adoption really coloured his whole life that way?

Had her daughter's?

And how would Flynn react when he found out about her past?

'You shouldn't have to sacrifice your own life and happiness to the company, though,' she managed in the end. 'Wasn't there ever anything else you wanted to do?'

Flynn shrugged. 'I never really considered it.'

'That's…that's awful.'

With a gentle smile, Flynn shook his head. 'Not really. Finding a place at the company…that was always the key for me, the way to assure my place in the family, too. But, in the end, that wasn't enough. Even Zeke turning the CEO role over to me… Our father had spent so long making it clear that it was meant for Zeke, that it had to stay in the family, it wouldn't have been enough.' He looked up and met her eyes, and Helena felt the warmth from them before he took her hand between his. '*You* made it possible for me to be a part of the family. Marrying you…you have given me the place I always wanted. And I need you to keep it.'

CHAPTER SEVEN

THOSE BLUEBELL EYES were so very wide Flynn wondered if he might have pushed too far. But it was important that Helena understood exactly how serious he was about making this marriage work, even if it meant partially explaining why.

He didn't want her pity, or to spill his bleeding heart story all over her. But if they were going to make a future as husband and wife, she had to know him. As he needed to know her, he supposed. And, after today, he hoped he was getting closer to that.

'Look. Zeke gave me the position that was always meant to be his, and our father had to accept that. I don't expect him to like it, ever, but it is now a fact. Before long there'll be contracts—'

'And we all know that paperwork is king,' Helena interjected, a wry smile on her lips.

'Indeed. The world has changed now, and so has the company. I want to be...worthy of that. I want to use this opportunity to bring Morrison-Ashton fully into the twenty-first century, build it up to even greater heights. I want to make our fathers proud. I want to make my wife proud.'

She glanced away at that, but her fingers tightened around his just for a moment. Almost, Flynn thought. He almost had her, and all he'd had to do was tell the truth.

'You've got it all planned out,' she murmured.

'I like to know where I'm going,' he said with a shrug. 'I find it helps make up for never knowing where I came from.'

Her eyes widened, and her gaze fixed on his face. 'Do you really feel that?'

'Sometimes.' Flynn frowned a little. 'Why?'

'I don't know. I just…' She took a breath, and he could almost see her trying to calm herself. But why? His adoption had never been a secret and, living as closely as their families had, none of this could really be considered a surprise. 'I always knew you were adopted, and I realised before I was very old that it made Ezekiel treat you differently. But you were always one of the family to me—to us. Even to Isabella, I think. And Zeke…'

'I've made my peace with Zeke,' Flynn said, remembering the last conversation he'd had with his brother before he left. Before he took Flynn's bride with him.

'Even now?'

'Especially now.' He stroked the back of her hand lightly, just enough to remind her that they were connected now. 'Zeke didn't take Thea; she chose to go. And yes, that might not have been in my plan. But, as a result, I got to marry a beautiful, bright, wonderful woman. One who always considered me family, which means more than you can know. Trust me, I'm happy with how things turned out.'

'Oh!' It was more a surprised squeak than a word, and Flynn would have laughed at the shock on her face if it wouldn't have ruined the mood.

He released her hand and leant back as the waiter appeared with their starters. He had a feeling the conversation wasn't done yet, but he'd said what he needed to. She knew where he stood now. All he needed was for her to join him.

Easy.

He took a bite of his *crostini di fegato* while she toyed with her risotto, her fork twirling through the rice grains without ever making it near her mouth. She'd talk when she was ready, he decided, and set about enjoying his starter instead.

He was halfway through when she said, 'The other night…' then stopped and winced.

Of course. Their wedding night. Of course she'd want to talk about that in a crowded restaurant where he couldn't do anything to persuade her that his reluctance to take her to bed had nothing to do with lack of interest.

'It had been a long day for both of us,' he said as neutrally as he could.

She waved a hand at him across the table, dismissing his words as unnecessary or irrelevant, he wasn't completely sure which. 'That night, I thought for a moment that you might have been in love with my sister.'

Flynn blinked at her in confusion. 'Why on earth would you think that?'

The burst of laughter Helena didn't quite manage to contain by slapping her hand to her mouth drew the attention of every other diner in the room. Flynn steadfastly refused to look at or acknowledge them, keeping his gaze on Helena as she simmered down to a giggle.

'You realise how ridiculous that is, right? You were supposed to marry her four days ago, and you can't imagine how I might have got the impression that you were in love with her?'

Put like that, he supposed she had a point. 'Except you knew that the marriage was a business arrangement.'

'For her, yes. But I'd never spoken to you about how you

felt. Still haven't, actually.' She paused in a way that suggested he was supposed to remedy that. Immediately. Except at that point the waiter returned to clear their starters, followed by another server carrying their main courses.

Flynn sighed and picked up his wine glass, taking the opportunity to consider his answer. Once they were alone again, he said, 'Marrying Thea was the plan because it gave us both what we wanted—or at least what I thought she wanted. Business and personal security, a future together and the possibility of children. Plus a good boost for the company PR. She got to escape her ridiculous failures with men, and I got to earn a real place at the family table. It worked.'

'So, nothing about love at all?' Helena pressed her fork into her *porcetta*, cut a sliver and popped it into her mouth. 'Mmm, this is delicious.'

'I'll admit I hoped that one day we might come to love one another. But no, I wasn't in love with her.' And it was painfully obvious to all and sundry that she hadn't been in love with him either. That was the only part that still smarted, just a little. Flynn turned his attention to his main course, mostly to pretend that it didn't.

'But you'd spoken about…children. And you admitted that you would have slept with her already, if she'd gone through with the marriage.' Her neutral tone gave nothing away, no hint of the right answer for him to give. Even if she hadn't really asked a question.

'For me, and for Thea, I think, we wanted to make this a real lasting marriage. Even if it didn't start out from a place of true love or anything. She's an attractive woman,' he added, watching Helena's face closely as he spoke for any sign of a negative reaction. Sometimes when women said they wanted honesty, in his experience, they wanted anything but. 'And we had an iron-clad fidelity clause.

If either of us ever wanted to have sex again, it had to be with each other.'

Helena sat back and studied him, sipping from her own wine glass. 'I like our story better,' she said after a moment.

'Our story?'

'Yes. It's more…dramatic. Romantic. Spontaneous.'

'Of course.' Flynn's shoulder muscles relaxed a little now she hadn't thrown wine in his face for talking about sleeping with her sister. 'And you like romance and spontaneity.'

'Who doesn't?' She gave a small shrug. 'But you two would have gone into that marriage with a heavy weight of expectations—written and signed in blood.'

'I like to think of it as more of a plan,' Flynn said mildly.

'You mean a schedule.' Helena shook her head. 'But life doesn't work like that. What if you slept together and it was dreadful?'

Flynn *really* didn't want to talk about this, but apparently he didn't have much of a choice. 'Then we'd have…I don't know. Practised, or something.' Could this be more awkward?

'What if she couldn't have children?' There was something behind Helena's eyes as she spoke, something he'd have missed if he hadn't been watching so closely. Was she trying to tell him something? He really hoped not.

'Then we'd figure something out. IVF or surrogacy. Adoption, maybe.' As a last resort. If he ever had to adopt, though, he'd do it differently. It would be about giving another lost child the sort of chances he'd had—but without the baggage. Not about what that child could give him.

'What if she fell in love with someone else?'

'Then she'd probably run away with him on our wedding morning.' A joke, but only just.

Helena rolled her eyes. 'I mean after the wedding.'

'Then we'd have…' The thought had never really occurred to him. The marriage was such an escape for both of them, to put them in a position where they didn't *have* to take the risk of love, that he couldn't imagine either of them looking for it outside of their union. 'We'd have talked about it. Sorted something out.'

'Like we're talking now,' Helena said. 'And since you're married to me, not her, I suppose we need to make some decisions about these things.'

And there it was. Everything he wanted, needed and he hadn't even had to ask for it. By the time Henry arrived with the new marriage contract, she'd be ready to sign, Flynn was sure of it.

'Just when I was celebrating our story for being different,' she said with a sigh.

He could afford to give her a little ground now, Flynn decided. He wanted her to be happy, after all. 'What did you like best about our story?'

'Oh, I don't know. The…immediacy of it, I guess. That we got married on a moment's notice, without all that paperwork and advance planning. If we were actually in love, it would be the most romantic thing ever. As it is…I guess it wasn't incredibly sensible.'

'Maybe not,' Flynn allowed. 'But I like to think it can work.'

'Yeah?' She'd finished eating, Flynn realised, and pushed her plate aside. The bottle of wine was almost empty too.

Maybe it was the wine that gave him the confidence to say, 'I want with you everything I ever wanted with Thea. Maybe even more. I want us to have a real marriage, and I hope that we will fall in love. But I need to know that you'll stick with it. That you'll give us a chance.'

Helena's bluebell eyes were wide and he could see the indecision in them, even if he couldn't fathom her reasons for holding back. She worried her lower lip with her teeth for a moment, and Flynn realised he was actually holding his breath. Waiting for his own wife to tell him she wanted to be married to him.

How had it come to this?

'I will,' Helena said eventually, so soft he almost didn't hear. Then she added, stronger this time, 'Yes, Flynn Ashton, I will stay married to you.'

This time, Flynn was pretty sure it was relief, rather than the wine, that caused his words. 'In that case, let's get out of here. I've got the perfect way to celebrate.'

A spur-of-the-moment idea, spontaneous and romantic—she was going to love it.

And suddenly that mattered an awful lot to him.

Flynn didn't let go of her hand all the way out to the car. Helena couldn't decide if the feel of his fingers wrapped around hers was comforting or terrifying.

What had she just done?

The whole idea was to stay married long enough to negate any scandal then get out, quick—preferably before Flynn discovered anything about her history that might ruin their friendship forever. Exes could be friends as long as they didn't screw up the marriage—or each other—too badly.

But now…now she was promising to stay with him? To try and fall in love—as if that were even a thing people could do—and have a real life—a family!—with him. Everything she'd been avoiding for years.

As Flynn shut the car door after her, letting go of her hand long enough to whisper something to the driver before getting in the other side, Helena closed her eyes and let her head fall back.

Why? What had possessed her to do it?

Well, that one was probably easy enough. Guilt more than anything. Hearing Flynn talk so honestly about what he wanted from this marriage and why... How could she not want to give him that? To give him a place in their family. To give him the one thing he'd always needed most and never had—a place to belong.

Maybe it was partly a decade-old crush, partly that he'd always been a friend to her. But a large chunk of it, she knew, had to do with a tiny baby girl she'd never even been allowed to hold.

Flynn could never find out about the daughter she'd given away. He'd never understand. And if he wanted a family...well, he'd said himself that he'd consider surrogacy, or even adoption. He hadn't sounded thrilled at the idea, but still. Maybe she'd never even have to explain how the idea of another child growing inside her made her feel physically sick and her body start to shake.

Maybe he'd never need to know what she'd done.

Or maybe, just maybe, he'd understand. Not immediately, of course—she was under no illusion about that. But he wanted this marriage, wanted real love to grow between them.

Maybe all she needed to do was to build a relationship strong enough to withstand the truth, when it finally came out. Not an easy task, admittedly. But maybe not completely impossible.

'You okay over there?' Flynn asked, and when she opened her eyes he was leaning across the middle seat in the back of the car, looking at her.

She forced a smile. 'I'm fine. Where are we going?'

'It's a surprise.' Flynn sat back, looking smug. 'A spontaneous, unplanned, romantic surprise.'

'That your PA planned?' she guessed.

But Flynn shook his head. 'Nope. This one is all me. And I think you're going to love it.'

She probably would, Helena thought. It seemed that Flynn Ashton could convince her of whatever he set his mind to. And she couldn't deny the spark of pleasure that Flynn doing something off schedule, just for her, gave her.

She didn't realise where they were going until the car started over the bridge into the town nearest their villa. She'd been there before with Thea, had planned to come back and do some shopping herself. But she still couldn't imagine what Flynn planned for them to do there.

Maybe they were checking into a hotel. Maybe he'd decided to celebrate their new arrangement by consummating their marriage and didn't want to do it in the bed he was supposed to have shared with her sister.

Helena glanced over at Flynn. He didn't look like a man anticipating having sex within the hour. And, if she was honest, he didn't seem like the type to drag her off to a hotel without discussing it first.

One thing she'd learned in less than a week of marriage—her husband liked to talk things through. Who knew?

The car pulled into a row of parking spaces right by the central *piazza* and the driver opened her door. Helena stepped out, just as Flynn arrived to take her hand again.

'Now can you tell me?' she asked, but he shook his head.

'Soon,' he promised. Tugging on her hand, he led her across the *piazza*, towards a little side street, dodging cars speeding round corners and pedestrians too busy talking on their phones to look where they were going. The air smelled of strong coffee and sunshine, and it was almost enough for Helena to put all her worries aside.

The shade of the side street soothed her warm skin and

Helena's eyes widened in delight at the array of tiny shops, each selling everything from watches to leather goods to dresses and scarves. But Flynn obviously had a very clear idea of where he was going and allowed no time for window-shopping.

Even off-plan, Flynn Ashton didn't dawdle. Helena sighed. Maybe she could teach him.

'Here,' Flynn said and stopped so suddenly that Helena barely avoided crashing into him. As it was, she found herself staring into a shop window with her side pressed up against his, their joined hands tangled between them. She blamed his closeness for the long moments it took her to realise what she was looking at.

'A jewellery shop?' she asked, tearing her gaze away from the sparkly treasures in the window to look up at her husband.

'Yes. I thought…well, the romantic and spontaneous nature of our wedding meant that you never got an engagement ring. I thought we could choose one together, to celebrate.' He shuffled ever so slightly, from one foot to the other. Was he…no, really, was he nervous? Maybe that was why he avoided spontaneity—in case it went wrong.

An engagement ring. A little after the fact, but still. It would be something just for her—something that wasn't Thea's first.

She really liked that.

'I think that's a lovely idea,' Helena said, squeezing Flynn's fingers between her own. Then, impulsively, she stretched up on her toes to kiss him—not on the cheek like the sort of brother or friend he'd always been, but right on the lips. It was short but sweet, and enough to let him know that she was embracing her new role, she hoped. 'Let's go in.'

Inside, the cramped little shop felt too warm despite

the dim lighting and shady spot. Laid out in glass counters sat tray after tray of diamond solitaire rings, varying slightly in design and shape and style, but all very clearly appropriate engagement rings.

'I spotted this shop walking through town the other day,' Flynn murmured as Helena took in the racks of sparkles. 'I just remembered it at lunch. Looks like it's just the place for what we're looking for.'

'It does,' Helena agreed, even as disappointment tugged at her belly. How was she supposed to pick one ring to symbolise their whole future life together when they were all basically the same? Which tiny variation might make the difference to her happy ever after?

A neatly dressed woman stepped out from a back office behind the counter and smiled as she offered to let Helena try some on. Flynn smiled his encouragement as the shop assistant unlocked the cases and took out the first tray.

Helena blinked as more diamonds than she'd ever imagined caught the light and sparkled up at her.

Well, maybe she'd just have to try some on. Surely she'd know the right one when she found it?

Somewhere around tray three, or ring thirty-six, Helena began to doubt her theory. Flynn had wandered off to the other side of the shop, leaving Helena and the increasingly bored assistant to wade through all the diamonds alone.

'They're all beautiful,' Helena said apologetically, for what must have been the sixth time. 'I just…I'm looking for one that feels right. You know?'

'Of course,' the assistant said in her thick Italian accent. 'You will wear this ring forever. It must be perfect.'

'Exactly,' Helena said, her fingers clenching at the word 'forever'. She sighed. 'Why don't we try this one again?' It *was* beautiful. Simple, elegant… Helena couldn't figure out what was wrong with it.

Flynn appeared over her shoulder, frowning. 'Not that one,' he said. 'Looks too much like—'

'Thea's,' Helena finished, the problem suddenly clear. Slipping the ring off again, she placed it back in the tray and moved over to the next one.

'Hang on,' Flynn said. Helena glanced up—he was across the other side of the tiny shop again and this time he had the assistant with him, unlocking another cabinet. 'I want to try something.'

Helena frowned, but waited as instructed. Grinning, Flynn crossed the room with his fist clenched tightly around something. 'Close your eyes.'

'Really?'

'Yep.'

He looked so pleased with himself that she couldn't help but do as he asked. She felt him take her left hand and slip a ring on to the fourth finger.

'And it even fits perfectly,' Flynn said. 'Okay, open your eyes.'

Helena stared at the jewel on her finger. 'That's not a diamond.'

'Well, no. I mean, obviously, if that's what you want, there's plenty to choose from here. I just thought…'

'No, no. I mean—it's not a diamond! I couldn't figure out why the other rings weren't right, but now I get it. I wasn't looking for a diamond.' Helena grinned. It all seemed so obvious now that Flynn had solved it for her.

The shop assistant muttered something in Italian that Helena couldn't understand but guessed probably meant: *Why couldn't she have figured that out half an hour ago?*

Relief flooded Flynn's features. 'Oh, good. I just…that one made me think of you. I don't know—maybe it's because it's blue.'

'Sapphire,' Helena said.

'Whatever. It reminded me of your eyes. And I know it's not traditional, but neither is buying the engagement ring after the wedding.'

'It's perfect.' Helena tilted her finger to make it sparkle in the dim overhead lights. 'I love it.'

'Great. Then hand it over.' He held out his hand, palm up.

'What?' Helena curled her fingers in to keep her ring right where it was, thank you very much.

'You can't wear it yet,' Flynn said with exaggerated patience. 'I need to propose properly with it.'

'You also need to pay for it.' The shop assistant gave them a not entirely patient smile, and Flynn laughed.

'Very true. Perhaps we can have a ring box?'

As the shop assistant rang up the total, Helena reluctantly slipped her sapphire off her finger and placed it in the velvet box on the counter. Everything about this marriage might be backwards, she thought, but that didn't mean it couldn't work.

Flynn had picked out her perfect ring when she didn't even know what she was looking for. What other marvels might he work in her life if she gave him the chance?

They were almost home when his phone rang.

'I'm sorry,' Flynn said, yanking it out of his pocket. 'Do you mind?'

Helena shook her head. 'Go on. I think you've earned at least one business call today.'

He flashed her a smile as he answered. He knew that the engagement ring idea was a good one. When in doubt, buy jewellery—his mother's entire contribution to his education about how to treat women might not have been lengthy, but it worked.

'Henry. I hope you're calling with good news.' And

flight numbers, preferably. He wanted everything he and Helena had discussed down on paper before anything changed. And especially before they had to go back to London and deal with their families again. If anything was going to screw things up between them, Flynn would place money on it being Ezekiel Ashton—even if he didn't mean to.

'Afraid not.' Henry sounded harassed. Henry never sounded anything other than cool and collected, even when Flynn woke him up at two in the morning. This was not a good sign. 'Can you talk?'

The car swept up the driveway of the villa, stopping right by the front door. 'Yeah, I can talk. Just one moment.'

'Let me guess,' Helena said as the driver cut the engine. 'You need to work.'

'Just a little. But we'll have dinner together?'

'Definitely.' Helena grinned. 'You've got something to give me later.'

'That's right, I do.' Once again, jewellery saved him from himself. 'I'll see you for dinner.' Opening the car door, he stepped out and strode towards the villa. 'Henry? I'm here. What's happening?'

'I need you to make a decision about priorities,' Henry said as Flynn let himself into the villa and headed for the room his father had been using as his study. Ezekiel wasn't there any more and it only made sense for him to use it. The symbolism of taking over his father's desk was purely accidental, if rather satisfying.

'Priorities?' Flynn sat himself in the desk chair. With his laptop and files set up down there it already felt more like his own space. He'd already spent a decent amount of time there and, with another week or so of their honeymoon to go, the chances were he'd be spending a lot more. Just not so much as to alienate Helena.

See? He had his priorities straight.

'Which is more important to you: your post-nuptial agreement or the contracts for the sale of This Minute to Morrison-Ashton?' Henry asked.

'You mean the contracts that compel my father to make me CEO, in return for Zeke selling us his company,' Flynn clarified. They both knew his interest in those contracts of sale had less to do with the digital media company his brother had built up and more to do with his own future at Morrison-Ashton. 'Why? What's gone wrong with them?'

'Your father is contesting rather a lot of the details.' Flynn got the impression that Henry was understating things there. Ezekiel Ashton would fight tooth and nail to retain control of that company until they put him in his grave. But Flynn had faith in Zeke. He'd said it was a done deal and that meant it would be, eventually—however hard and long their father fought it. 'Your brother's legal team are doing an admirable job, but I think you might want me here to help smooth the path from our side. Just to make sure that he doesn't manage to slip anything in there that could hold up his stepping down from the CEO position.'

'Henry, are you trying to get out of a paid holiday in Tuscany for a couple of days?' Flynn kicked his feet up on the desk and leant back in his desk chair.

Henry laughed. 'I might be trying to not gate-crash your honeymoon, but only for business reasons, I promise you.'

'Well, I'm afraid you're going to have to gate-crash,' Flynn told him. 'We've got to get that marriage contract signed.'

'Things going that badly, huh?' Henry asked, his tone sympathetic.

'The opposite, actually.' Flynn let himself remember the look on Helena's face when she'd seen her ring. 'It's going very, very well. And I don't want to give my father the chance to ruin that.'

'You think he will?' Henry sounded surprised. 'I know he wasn't entirely happy about you marrying the wrong sister, but does it really make that much difference?'

'Do you know, Henry, I think it will. To me, anyway.' He couldn't say how. It had been less than a week. But already his relationship with Helena felt more like a...well... relationship than things with Thea ever had.

'You're sounding smitten, my friend.'

'I'm a newlywed,' Flynn joked. 'I'm supposed to be besotted with my wife. Whoever she turns out to be.'

Henry laughed. 'Well, okay, then. But if things are so hunky-dory with the new Mrs Ashton, what's the worry?'

'It was made very clear to me by my father and his esteemed business partner that unless I return from this trip with a signed and notarised post-nuptial agreement, they would take it into their own hands to get one. I want this marriage to be on my terms—mine and Helena's. That means we need you here to make that legal.'

'Fair enough.' Flynn heard the clicking of a mouse on the other end of the line. 'Best flight I can get has me with you tomorrow mid-morning. Will that work?'

'Perfect.' That gave him tonight to wine and dine Helena, propose, kiss her goodnight. Just one more frustrated night in his own bed and then they could sign the papers and make this a real marriage at last.

'I'll get it booked,' Henry promised. 'But, Flynn...make sure you're both on the same page before I get there, yeah? You know these things always go more smoothly when there are no surprises.'

'I know. Don't worry. Helena and I aren't the secretive types.' Compared to Thea, Helena was an open book. And he didn't have any more brothers for her to declare undying love for, so he figured he was probably safe there too.

'Then I'll see you two lovebirds tomorrow,' Henry said and hung up.

Flynn dropped his phone on to the desk and pulled the ring box out of his pocket, opening it to admire the deep blue stone at the heart of the ring. He'd clear his emails and then still have time to shower and change before dinner.

He smiled to himself. Just another hour or so and it would be time to propose to his wife.

CHAPTER EIGHT

HELENA WOUND THE last string of lights along the beams of the terrace and stood back to admire her handiwork. Not bad, if she did say so herself. The table for two—complete with white linen napkins and flickering candlelight—was all prepared, and the fairy lights she'd found left over from the wedding decorations were perfect for giving their little terrace dinner table the right romantic atmosphere—far better than they'd managed in the formal dining room the last few days. The flowers climbing the stone walls added a heady, spicy scent in the last of the day's sunlight, and the air was still warm enough that she didn't need the wrap she'd brought out with her.

She smoothed down her blue silk dress and tucked a blonde curl behind her ear. She was ready, the table was ready. The wine she'd brought from Gia's vineyard was open on the table, ready for pouring, and the cook had promised her that dinner would be ready at exactly seven-thirty.

It was the perfect night to get engaged.

All she needed now was her husband.

She turned to let the warm evening breeze brush over her skin as she stared out across the beautiful Tuscan countryside. It was almost a shame to have to go back to London at all, she thought. Out here, all things seemed possible.

Possible enough that she'd put on her best lingerie under her dress, anyway.

'Okay, this kind of spontaneous romance I am absolutely in favour of.'

Helena turned at the sound of Flynn's voice and found him leaning against the doorway between the terrace and the house, his gaze fixed not on the romantic trappings she'd set up, but firmly upon her.

'Actually,' she admitted, 'this is the kind of romance that takes planning. I got Gia to smuggle the wine into the car when you were preoccupied with your phone earlier.'

'So, you were planning this even before our ring-shopping expedition?' Flynn stepped closer and Helena could feel her skin warming and the little fine hairs on her arms standing up as he grew nearer. How had she never known how he affected her until she married him?

'Long before. Can't a girl want a romantic night in with her husband?'

'She most certainly can.' He put a hand on her waist and Helena only just resisted the urge to snuggle up close against his chest. 'Especially when she wears a dress like yours.'

'You like it?' She stepped back far enough to give him a quick twirl, the silky pleats of her dress rising up a little around her thighs as she turned.

'I adore it. You look beautiful. Even more beautiful than you did in the vineyard earlier, with the sun in your hair and your gorgeous bright smile.'

'You thought I was beautiful then?' That had also been before their conversation in the restaurant—before she'd agreed to stay with him. Maybe he had more reasons to want her to stay than just his plans for the future.

Maybe he did really want *her* to stay, not just any girl bearing the right surname.

'I couldn't believe I'd never seen quite how beautiful you are before.' His gaze locked with hers as he spoke, and his irises seemed lit up by the fading sunlight until they looked like poured caramel. Helena swayed closer to him without thinking, as if there was simply nowhere else she should or could be. He caught her around the waist, arms strong and warm as he pulled her near.

'You know, I had a big lunch…' Helena trailed off as she licked her lips, and watched Flynn's Adam's apple bob as he swallowed.

He wanted her. He wanted her as much as she wanted him and, whatever his reasons for sending her to bed like a child on their wedding night, tonight, this night, he was hers. One way or another she was taking her husband to bed—before she lost her nerve completely.

Or so she thought until he dropped his arms from her waist and stepped away.

'Dinner is served!' The maid stepped on to the terrace, plates in her hands, and Flynn strode across to pull Helena's chair out for her.

Helena pouted at him, and he laughed. The maid, forehead creased, wisely placed their meals on the table and disappeared back into the villa.

'Come on, sit down.' Flynn rattled her chair a little against the stone of the terrace. 'I want to do this properly.'

'I suppose.' Helena took her seat, let Flynn push her chair in. At least she'd asked the cook for just a pasta main and a pudding, since they'd had lunch out already. Maybe they could take the dessert up to bed with them…

The long strands of pasta, wrapped in a deeply savoury *ragu*, were delicious, Helena had to admit. As she twirled them expertly around her fork and sipped at the gorgeous red wine, courtesy of Gia, she thought there were worse ways to spend the evening.

'So, is London missing you, then?' she asked, thinking of the phone call that had dragged him from her earlier.

'Oh, I expect they're enjoying the peace, quite honestly.' Flynn gave her a half smile. 'Apart from my solicitor, who I woke up at two o'clock the other morning.'

'So *that's* who you were calling. I did wonder who could be important enough to let me go up to bed alone...' Helena watched his face closely as she spoke and yes, there it was. A hint of uncertainty, an uncomfortable twist of the mouth.

She put down her fork.

He'd asked her to spend her life with him. They'd bought a ring. He'd called her beautiful...and he still didn't plan to sleep with her tonight.

There was definitely something odd going on here.

'That's who was calling earlier, too,' Flynn went on, as if Helena hadn't just uncovered a problem of major proportions in their marriage. 'Apparently my father is being difficult about the contracts for the sale of This Minute, as expected. Nothing to worry about, though. Zeke's legal team are, by all accounts, very capable.'

'That's good.' Somehow, she had a feeling that the people Zeke would have put on the job wouldn't just be capable. They'd be relentless, and they'd take Ezekiel Ashton for everything they wanted before they gave him what Zeke had promised.

She didn't have a problem with that, actually. Especially after her conversation with Flynn at lunchtime.

No, Helena's only problem so far this evening was a husband who didn't want to sleep with her—or wouldn't let himself want it. And that was far more important right now than a manipulative father-in-law with a Zeus complex.

They finished their pasta in companionable silence, but Helena barely tasted it. Any moment now, she knew, Flynn was going to get down on one knee and present her with the most perfect ring and ask her to share her life with him.

But how could she promise to do that without finding out if they were compatible in bed? If she could relax enough to let herself be with him? Or if there was some reason she should know about that meant they might never even find out?

The maid cleared their dishes silently. Flynn smiled at her and said, 'We'll wait a moment on dessert, if that's okay. I'll call you when we're ready,' and Helena knew this was it.

She'd dreamt, as a younger girl, about proposals—maybe even more than she'd dreamt about weddings and wedding nights. She'd imagined herself falling in love, having some handsome man drop to his knees and beg her to marry him. She'd even thought about the perfect way to respond—amazed joy, she'd decided, was best. Hand to the mouth, perhaps, and an enthusiastic, *Of course I will!*

She'd never imagined it would be like this.

'I know this isn't going to come as much of a surprise to you.' Flynn reached into his pocket and pulled out the ring box, grinning at her all the while. 'But I want you to have the full experience. So...' He stood up, moved around to her side of the table and gracefully lowered himself to one knee. 'Helena Juliette Ashton. Would you do me the incredible honour of agreeing to remain my wife and live our very own happily ever after together?'

Amazed joy, Helena tried to remind herself. Enthusiasm. Happiness. Saying yes.

But instead, what came out of her mouth was, 'Why don't you want to sleep with me?'

'What on earth could have given you that idea?' Flynn asked, his hand still holding out the open ring box. Helena merely raised her eyebrows at him and watched as his gaze slid from her face down to that perfect sapphire. 'Trust me—I want to make love to you very much.'

Helen frowned. He was telling the truth. Hadn't she seen it in his eyes, felt it in his touch, known it even when he'd kissed her after the speeches on their wedding day? So maybe she was asking the wrong question.

'Okay then, why won't you?'

'Is this really the time you want to have this conversation?'

'I think it's something that shouldn't wait any longer,' Helena said. 'But you can, you know, stand up if that's easier.'

'Right. Because that's the biggest problem with this conversation.' Nevertheless, Flynn pushed himself up to standing then dragged his chair across to sit beside her.

'So?' she asked when he sat looking at her, not saying anything.

Flynn sighed. 'So. Of course I want to sleep with you. You're my wife. You're beautiful. I care about you and I hope to have a future with you. But...'

Oh, no. Where was this going? Even in her panic, Helena didn't believe for a second that he hadn't done it before, and she knew he wasn't in love with Thea, so what was it? Even if he had some purity, 'waiting until marriage' thing going on, they were already married!

'Before we take that step, before we start something that will hopefully lead to a deeper affection between us, I think it's important that we agree certain things about our future together.'

Helena blinked. 'Isn't that what we did at lunch? What we're doing now, with the ring and all?'

'Partly,' Flynn said. Why wasn't he meeting her eyes? 'But, for it to be truly official, we do need the post-nuptial agreement to be signed and filed. Should anything happen, it's important that these things have been formalised.'

Helena stared at him. 'Flynn. Please, please tell me that you're not refusing to sleep with me because of *paperwork*.'

Dropping his head to stare at his hands, Flynn gave a sort of half laugh. 'It does sound that way, doesn't it?'

'Wanna try and make it sound a different way?' Helena suggested.

'Okay.' Flynn sucked in a deep breath and sat back in his chair, letting the air out slowly. A delaying tactic, Helena recognised. He was figuring out the best way to say whatever he had to say, which meant she probably wasn't going to like it.

'The other night, before you came in wearing that incredible satin thing—that's still upstairs, right? I really want to see you in that again some time when I can appreciate it properly.'

'It is.' A faint warmth hit Helena's cheeks. So far he wasn't doing so badly.

'Good. Anyway. Before that, I had a meeting with our fathers that left me in a...not great mood. But it also got me thinking.' He looked up, his serious eyes focused on hers. 'The moment we sleep together, we've changed the game. There's no hope of an annulment when we get back. You have to be sure that it's what you want.'

'An annulment?' Helena shook her head a little to try and make sense of it. 'You were refusing to sleep with me to make sure I had an out?'

'That was one reason.'

'What was the other?'

'My father suggested that, should I have any problems getting you to agree to the same terms as Thea for the marriage, I should just get you pregnant to tie you to me, then make sure you signed before the child was born.'

Helena's heart froze in her chest. 'What did my father say?' she asked. Because Ezekiel probably never knew what she'd been through, and she expected that kind of callousness from him anyway. But her own father...

'He... Helena, he laughed. He said something about you making up for the past by marrying me, and he laughed when Dad told me to get you pregnant.' He ran a shaking hand through his hair, and Helena wanted to hold him, to soothe him. To have him soothe her. But all she could hear in her mind was her father's laughter, dismissing the most important thing—the worst thing—that had ever happened to her as a joke.

She'd known that she and Thea were often more useful than loved. She'd understood that this marriage was a business deal, convenient and lucrative rather than something to be celebrated.

But until this moment she'd never realised quite how little her father thought of her. And suddenly her heart felt as if it had been torn apart.

'I couldn't bear it.' Flynn was still talking, and Helena tried to pay him proper attention again. 'They were just so casual about the idea—about a child's life. And I knew I couldn't risk that. That we had to be sure, that everything had to be agreed before anything like that could happen.'

Helena swallowed and it felt as if there was a rock stuck in her throat. He hadn't wanted her to be trapped, hadn't wanted any child to be unwanted, or used, like he had been. Her soul ached for the boy Flynn must have been, and for the man he'd become. Her own battered heart reached out for his. Maybe they really could give each other what they'd lacked so far, all their lives—love.

He wanted so badly to do this right, to make a perfect future for them. And so what if he planned it out moment by moment? His reasons were good. His heart was good.

And Helena wanted that heart for her own. More than she'd ever done as a fourteen-year-old child. More even than when she'd envied her sister her golden, good fiancé. More than when she'd stepped into that borrowed wedding dress, and more certainly than when she'd propositioned him in her negligee on their wedding night. More still than when he'd chosen her the perfect engagement ring.

She was in love with her own husband, and it scared her and filled her more than she'd ever known anything could.

'I think you should ask me that question again now,' she said, nerves making her whole body feel as if it was vibrating from the inside out. She needed to tell him the truth, needed to confess. But if she did…it could destroy the cautious happiness they were building together. Once they were home, once the paperwork was signed, maybe then she could talk about what had happened to her, what she'd done. Maybe then she could make him understand.

But first she had to make him love her.

Flynn smiled up at her, already on his knees again. 'Helena. Will you be my wife? In every way there is?'

'Yes,' she breathed and felt that amazed joy flooding through her.

Flynn swept her up in his arms the moment she spoke. He owed her a proper kiss, after their first public one, and that was what he intended to give her. Lowering his mouth to hers, he tried to convey everything he felt—every hope, every dream—through a kiss.

From her eager response, he hoped he had got pretty close.

It amazed him to think that just last week he hadn't known this woman—not really. He knew Helena, Thea's sister, or Helena, Thomas's daughter. But he had no idea of the wonder, the humour, the warmth and the beauty that lay beyond those labels.

'I can't believe I came so close to marrying the wrong woman,' he murmured against her lips, and felt rather than saw her smile in response. 'This is it. This is exactly how it was meant to be all along.'

'I know,' Helena said, and he could hear her happiness in the words. 'I know. And we so almost didn't…'

'But we did. We have each other now.' It might not be love yet, Flynn thought, but he could see the pathway there. Could see every step between here and their future.

Helena pulled back a little, still smiling, her eyes glistening with unshed tears. 'You haven't even put the ring on me yet.'

'I haven't?' Flynn blinked, and saw it sitting on the table beside them. Pulling it free of its velvet box, he lifted Helena's left hand and slipped it on next to her wedding ring. 'There.'

'There,' Helena echoed, staring down at her hand. 'It really is the most beautiful ring I've ever seen.'

'For the most beautiful woman,' Flynn said, knowing it was corny and not even caring. Somehow this moment, alone on the terrace, felt more permanent, more official than the big church ceremony and the signed register. This was the moment he'd remember as their true wedding. The moment they understood each other and committed to their future.

Helena smiled up at him, then caught her lip between her teeth, the way he already knew she always did when she was deciding whether or not to say something.

'Go on,' he said. 'You may as well say whatever it is. After your response to my initial proposal, it's unlikely you can come up with anything worse.'

'True. And I do think you'll like this one more.' Swaying

closer, she wrapped herself tighter around his body, pressing herself against him until it felt as if even air couldn't squeeze between them. His body began to react immediately, even before Helena rose up on her tiptoes, brushing against him every slow inch of the way, and whispered in his ear, 'So, do you want tiramisu for dessert? Or me?'

He swallowed, trying to cling on to the composure he was so famed for in the boardroom. The plan was to wait. He'd already pushed so far up against every line he'd drawn for himself. And there was more than business on the line here, he admitted to himself, more than money. He had to be sure he could risk his heart. 'Are you sure? The contract—'

'Paperwork's a formality,' she murmured against the skin of his neck, placing kisses between each word. 'I'm yours now, whatever happens. So take me.'

The words ripped through the last of his self-control and Flynn hauled her up his body into another kiss, this one harder, more desperate, more wanting.

'Upstairs,' he managed, just, as her hands clutched at his back. 'Now.'

He didn't need to say it twice.

It was several hours later, with the sky dark outside the bedroom window, that Flynn tugged her closer against his naked body and said, 'We never did get that tiramisu.'

Helena laughed against his skin, her hands still roaming over his chest. 'You never got me in that negligee, either.'

'Maybe tomorrow night,' Flynn said, yawning.

'Maybe,' Helena agreed, although she knew they'd never make it that far. By tomorrow night they'd be too desperate for each other again, too consumed with want that they'd forget all about her fancy nightie. Just as they had done tonight.

It had been more than she'd dreamt it could be. The way he moved against her, within her...the way he touched her, with a sort of reverence she'd never imagined a man could have for her body. As if he were drinking in every detail of her, and each one intoxicated him.

She should never have worried about them being compatible, and she almost laughed when she thought that, until a couple of hours ago, she'd honestly been afraid he hadn't wanted her.

She'd been scared, she admitted to herself, lying in the darkness in her husband's arms. She'd not wanted to think about it, but there had been very few men since she'd fallen pregnant at sixteen, and none that made Helena feel the way that Flynn did. She'd worried whether she'd be enough for him, worried more about protection until he'd pulled a condom from his wallet, and worried most that he'd be able to tell her secrets with one glance at her body.

He hadn't, though. And since his eyes and hands and mouth had covered every inch of her, she didn't imagine he would now.

Her past was locked away until she chose to share it with him. He'd be hurt, she knew, that she'd kept it from him, but she liked to think he'd understand. Especially now—they were already so close, and after so little time. By the time it mattered, when they talked again about children, they'd be a proper unit. A family, even. He'd understand.

And he'd understand, she thought, if she told him she wanted to adopt. He might even welcome it. As long as she got the timing right, they would make it work, she was sure of it.

They had to. She'd committed now, and so had he. There wasn't any room to step back any more.

'What are you thinking about?' Flynn asked, his voice

sleepy as he kissed the top of her head. 'You're keeping me awake with all those thoughts.'

'I'm just thinking how happy I am,' Helena replied, and hoped he didn't know her well enough yet to tell when she was lying.

He didn't. 'Good,' he said, turning on to his side and pulling her back against his chest. Soon, his breathing evened out and she knew he was asleep.

But Helena lay awake almost until the sun crept over the window ledge, thinking about the things she'd done and the choices she'd made.

When Flynn awoke the next morning he knew instinctively that it wasn't six a.m. The sun sat too high in the sky, sending beams of warmth and light that cut across the bed. They hadn't shut the curtains the night before, he realised, and still he'd slept in well past his normal waking hour.

It had to be the exercise, he thought, stretching out aching muscles as far as he could without waking the woman sleeping in his arms.

His wife.

She'd been everything he'd dreamt she could be, and more. If he'd needed any extra proof that things had worked out for the best, he had it. As the mid-morning sun glinted off the sapphire on her finger, he knew that Helena was the one for him, for life. Whatever happened next—with his father, the company, even with Zeke and Thea—it would be him and Helena against the world. They had their own family. His hand slipped down to rest against her stomach for a moment. And one day, not yet, but once things were settled with the CEO role, that family would grow a little bigger.

He couldn't wait.

Flynn toyed with the idea of waking Helena to remind

her again just how good they were together, but then his eye caught on a piece of card tucked in the edge of the mirror on her dressing table, just under the window. Squinting, he made out the words printed on the front and smiled when he realised what it was.

His wedding invitation. His and Thea's, defaced by Helena to turn it into theirs. And on the back, he knew, would be that impromptu contract she'd scrawled across it.

The contract. Henry was arriving today. Would be arriving—Flynn glanced at the clock next to the mirror—any moment now.

Reluctantly, he disentangled himself from Helena's pale limbs, smiling when she reached for him without waking. Tucking the blanket around her, he pulled on yesterday's jeans and headed for the room next door, where the shower wouldn't disturb her. He'd get dressed, hunt out some breakfast and meet with Henry. If they were quick, he could have the whole contract ready for signatures before Helena even woke up.

By the time he made it downstairs, Henry had not only arrived but had also befriended the maid and the cook. Flynn found him settled into one of the armchairs in the large hall area, a cup of coffee and a plate of pastries at his elbow. He folded the paper he was reading as he saw Flynn descending the stairs and tucked it away in his briefcase.

'Am I to assume that the urgency with which you required me to dance attendance on you has now passed?' Henry asked, a mocking smile on his face.

Flynn couldn't help but smile back. Henry had known him a long time, had worked with him almost since he'd started at Morrison-Ashton, and knew Flynn better than most. If anyone was going to be happy for him, it was probably Henry.

It was another sign of how little input he'd had on the

wedding planning and guest list that Henry hadn't been invited. Maybe they should throw some sort of spectacular first anniversary party next year and invite all the people they'd have actually liked to be there. Poor Helena hadn't been allowed to invite *anyone* to her own wedding.

He should really make that up to her.

Flynn dropped into the chair opposite his friend and helped himself to one of the pastries. 'We still need the contract,' he said. 'But you're going to have to wait for my wife to wake up first. She's not good at mornings.' He tried to keep his expression blank as Henry studied him, but apparently failed as Henry shook his head and laughed.

'Oh, you lucky, lucky—' He broke off before the curse. 'Only you could get dumped on your wedding day and still end up with a beautiful bride you're madly in love with.'

'I didn't say love,' Flynn argued, but he couldn't help the grin that came at the thought, 'yet.'

'A couple of years' time, you're going to be running the company, making millions and have chubby toddlers chasing around after you. It's going to be sickening.'

'Perhaps,' Flynn agreed. 'Doesn't sound too bad to me.'

'It wouldn't. You're not the one who'll have to deal with you being so insufferably smug about it.' Henry flashed him a grin. 'Seriously, though, I'm happy for you. Nobody deserves this more than you.'

Was that true? Flynn suspected not. But the fact his friend thought so…that meant something. Maybe, after every bad start, everything he'd had to fight to get here, maybe this was his time to be happy at last.

He hoped so.

'Come on.' Flynn got to his feet. No point lingering on the sentimental when there was paperwork to deal with. 'Let's go through to the study and get started. I'll have the maid bring us some more coffee. I'd like to get this agreement put to bed before Helena wakes up, so she can sign it and forget it.'

'You mean so you can take her back to bed again,' Henry said.

'That too.'

'You know I have to go through all the details with her too, right? You can't just tell her to sign here and have done with it—however desperate you are to get her naked.'

Pretty desperate, Flynn had to admit. But not enough to ignore the law. 'I know. But I want to try and keep this one simple, if I can. Helena's not a huge fan of paperwork.'

Maybe, once Henry had gone, he'd take her over his father's desk in the study. Maybe that would endear her to paperwork a little bit more.

'And she married you?' Henry asked in mock astonishment. 'Heaven help her.'

Flynn ignored him. It was going to be another glorious day.

CHAPTER NINE

HELENA WOKE UP ALONE, stretching out in the bed like a starfish to work out the kinks and aches that her muscles had built up over the night. She wasn't used to sharing her space while she slept, although she was happy to learn if it meant sharing the bed with Flynn.

Where was Flynn, anyway?

Checking the clock, she saw it was already late morning, which meant he'd probably sloped off to work. Maybe she'd surprise him in his study, persuade him to come back to bed for a while. They could rerun the events of their wedding night, only with the right outcome this time…

She showered quickly, fixed her hair and cleaned her teeth, then dressed in the satin negligee Flynn had so wanted to see again. Then, just in case she ran into any or all of the household staff on her way down, she slipped on a light matching robe which made the whole ensemble *almost* decent.

Yawning, she opened the door and headed for the stairs, wondering if maybe she should stop for coffee first. No, husband first, then coffee. She could send him out to bring some back to the room afterwards. Ooh, breakfast in bed! That was what honeymoons were for. Well, amongst other things…

When she reached the study, she didn't bother to knock and didn't even register the two voices inside until she'd already opened the door.

'Oh! Sorry.' She pulled an apologetic face at Flynn, who smiled reassuringly. The man sitting across the desk from him, a laptop between them angled so they could both see the screen, laughed. It was a nice laugh, though, Helena thought. Not cruel or mocking, just amused.

'Don't worry,' he said, getting to his feet. 'We were actually waiting for you. I'm Henry, Flynn's solicitor.' He held out a hand for Helena to shake.

She frowned as she took it. 'Solicitor? Is there something wrong?' Then she realised, and groaned. 'Seriously, Flynn? Paperwork, at this time in the morning?'

'It's practically lunchtime,' Flynn pointed out.

'In his defence, I think he mostly wanted to get it sorted so that you could both get back to enjoying your honeymoon,' Henry said.

Rolling her eyes, Helena dropped into the third chair set around the desk. 'Fine. But I'm going to need coffee.'

It turned out that most of the post-nuptial agreement—which sounded like a stupid name to Helena, but was apparently what the thing was called—was pretty boring. Flynn and Henry had already been through the document and updated the original to reflect the slight change in wedding plans. Helena found some comfort in knowing that these were things that Thea had agreed to, even agreed with. It made nodding along as Henry talked her through it much easier.

Their finances, the business; that was all straightforward in the end—the lengthy negotiations between Thea, Flynn and their fathers had already hammered all that out. So the contract mostly came down to the relationship between her and Flynn.

That part, at least, she understood.

'So, you're both still happy to live in the London townhouse we arranged, right?' Henry asked, and Helena nodded. 'Great. Next up, charitable and social obligations.'

Helena sighed. She really should have just stayed in bed. Flynn would have come and found her eventually.

When they reached the part about sexual relations, Flynn stared at the ceiling and Helena couldn't help but laugh.

'I'm guessing we can strike the part about negotiating the initiation of sexual relations in one year's time?' Henry asked, clearly unable to hide the amusement in his voice.

'Yeah, I think that ship has pretty much sailed,' Helena said with a grin.

'It was a stupid clause anyway,' Flynn added, his gaze still focused on the ceiling.

'Okay, then. In that case, the next bit is the declarations,' Henry said, scrolling down to the next page.

'Like the sickness and health part of the wedding?' Helena asked.

'Not exactly. Basically, we just need you to sign this section to say that you've never been married before, are not in a partnership with anyone else at this time, that you don't have any children by a previous relationship—things that would affect your finances or inheritances mostly.'

Helena's whole body trembled as if she had no control over it. She couldn't speak—every word she thought of stuck in her throat. Her skin burned as if she'd stepped too close to the fire—and maybe she had, in a way.

She'd known last night that she had to tell Flynn about her daughter, but not like this. Not now and not here, not with Henry listening in.

Not when everything was finally going so well.

'Helena? What's wrong?' Flynn was at her side now—

when had he even moved? He took her hand, squeezing it gently, and Helena wanted nothing more than to cling on to it and never, ever let go. She'd come so close to getting everything she'd ever wanted.

And now one mistake from eight years ago was going to wreck it all.

In her mind, the film of the night she'd told Thea ran over and over. Her sister's tears, followed by her father's shouts. The ugly accusations, the hatred. And then the pity in Isabella's expression when she'd arrived, as she always did, to support Thomas above all else. Not just pity, though. A sense of inevitability, as if they'd all known Helena would screw up irrevocably in the end; it had only been a matter of time.

Thea was the only one who'd listened, who'd understood what had really happened that night. And their father had just blamed her for letting Helena out that night at all. As if Thea were more to blame than Helena, and Helena more to blame than the boys who—she stopped that thought. She couldn't relive that. Not now.

Instead, she remembered the coldness in her father's eyes as he'd told her they would fix this. That she would do exactly as she was told. He and Isabella had a plan and she would follow it to the letter. And, if she did, she could come home and live her normal life again. Afterwards.

As if she could ever be the same, after.

'Do you want me to call for someone?' Henry asked, sounding concerned. 'Get some water or something?'

'Yeah, there should be someone in the kitchen.' Flynn placed the back of his hand against her forehead. 'Helena, talk to me. What is it? Are you feeling faint? I should have got you a proper breakfast. Let me ask Henry to—'

'No.' She couldn't take it any more. She couldn't let him carry on being so kind to her, not when he didn't know the truth. 'I don't need anything. But I can't…' She stumbled over the words as she tried to get to her feet. Her legs felt too weak to support her body, but she forced them to move, to take her away from here. 'I can't sign this.'

And then she ran, the image of Flynn's horrified face imprinted on her memory.

Okay, this…? This was *not* the plan.

Flynn stared after his wife as Helena stumbled out of the study and raced up the stairs. From the doorway, he could just about see the way she clung to the banister as she climbed, that stupid satin nightgown flapping around her legs.

'What happened?' Henry asked, striding across the hall-way with a glass of water in his hand.

'I have no idea,' Flynn replied, gaze still locked on the now empty staircase. 'But I'm going to find out. Stay here.'

They had an agreement, he fumed silently as he took the stairs two at a time. They'd talked about everything, he'd opened up to her in ways he'd never imagined he'd be able to with anyone. He'd married her! He'd given her that blasted ring and taken her to bed. He'd let her in, let himself hope, believe that he could have the future he'd dreamed of. That he was enough for her…and now? Now she said she couldn't sign.

No. That wasn't the way this plan went at all.

He thumped his fist against the wood of the bridal suite door, but didn't wait for her to tell him to come in. She had to know he'd follow, had to know he'd need an explanation.

'Flynn, I…I'm sorry.' She looked so small curled up on the bed, her knees under her chin and her arms wrapped tightly around them.

'Then come downstairs and sign the agreement.' Maybe

this was just last-minute nerves. Some fear of paperwork he didn't fully understand.

But Helena shook her head. 'I can't. I'm sorry.'

'I don't want apologies. I want reasons.' He hadn't even moved from the doorway, he realised. There was no point staying if she wouldn't explain. He wasn't sure, but he thought his grip on the door handle might be the only thing keeping him upright while he waited for her answer.

'I can't sign it because it's not true. The declarations.'

Flynn blinked at her, his mind foggy with incomprehension. 'What? You're already married?' She shook her head. 'You're in love with someone else?' Both sisters? Surely that was too cruel a joke for the universe to play, even on him.

'No. Not that.' Her words came out almost as a croak. As if her throat didn't want to let them leave.

And then her meaning sank in, and he wished he'd never heard her at all.

'You have a child.' There was no emotion in his voice, he realised, because it was all swirling inside him. Every possible negative feeling—betrayal, horror, pain and everything in between—ran through his blood, his muscles, his organs, causing them to seize up and scream in silent pain. 'Where is it now?'

It. He'd married the woman and he didn't know she had a child—and even now he could only call the poor thing 'it' because he didn't know enough to know if it was a girl or a boy.

'She was adopted,' Helena whispered, and every single drop of those awful emotions prepared to come tumbling out of him.

'You gave her away.' He couldn't look away, couldn't focus on anything except her face. He'd thought that she'd let him in, thought they were planning a life together.

When all the time she'd been holding back, keeping him at a distance as he'd tumbled headfirst into love with her. His plan wasn't hers, and never would be.

'It was a mistake. I was sixteen and I was so, so scared.' Her words were tumbling out over each other, but he was barely listening. He was still trying to make sense of this horrific reality he now found himself in. One where the woman he loved was a woman who lied, who left people behind. And to think he'd believed her when she'd promised she'd stay, that they could have a life together. He was an idiot. After thirty long years, didn't he know better than to believe any person who said they'd take him into their heart, love him and keep him as their own?

'When I told Thea—'

'Thea knew.' Of course Thea knew. Who else would Helena turn to? And why would Thea mention it to him? She could never have imagined that Helena would jump into her place so fast. No, he couldn't blame Thea for this one. Only Helena. 'Who else?'

'Um…my father. And Isabella.' Not his father, of course. If Ezekiel had known, this would have come up sooner, the moment the old man had realised they were married. He'd have rubbed this in just to cause Flynn pain.

But Thomas. Thomas had known and he'd stood there and nodded when Flynn explained that he and Helena were getting married. Had laughed when Ezekiel talked about Flynn getting Helena pregnant—and had never mentioned that he wouldn't be the first.

'They sent me away,' Helena said, those bluebell eyes still wide but somehow no longer so innocent. 'As soon as they found out they got me out of town, somewhere I couldn't be a scandal or a bother.' She sounded so broken, so distraught, he almost wanted to take her in his arms and comfort her. But he knew that he was still seeing her as *his* Helena. And she wasn't any more. She was a stranger, one who'd lied about who she was, what she could be to him. What he could be to her.

If she'd truly loved him, if she'd really wanted their future together, she'd have told him about her baby. And if she'd told him before he fell…at least he could have discussed it rationally, seen if there was still a chance for them to make this work. Maybe not with all the hearts, flowers and romance they'd hoped for, but a pragmatic business marriage as originally planned.

But she'd let him fall in love with her then torn his heart out by telling him that his whole image of her was a lie. That she wasn't the person she'd promised to be.

He'd told her everything—how it had felt, growing up as the spare part in the Ashton household, knowing he wasn't wanted or needed any more, once his parents had Zeke. She must have known exactly what it would do to him, knowing that she'd done that to her own child—given it away to an uncertain fate. And she'd kept it from him until it was too late.

Until he loved her.

It was calculated, cruel, and the Helena he'd fallen for would never have done it. That was what he needed to remember. The Helena he loved didn't really exist. Instead, all he was left with was a wife he barely knew and would never, ever understand.

'This is what your father meant, isn't it? When he said you were making up for past mistakes.' Flynn lowered his head and laughed, all bitterness and no humour. 'What? You think marrying one poor adopted boy makes up for the girl you gave away without a second thought?'

'No! Of course I don't. You don't understand—'

'You're right—I don't understand!' Flynn roared, tearing himself away from the door as he strode across to the bed when she sat. He wouldn't touch her—couldn't bring himself to—but he wasn't going to keep a safe distance either. Helena scooted up to cower against the headboard anyway. Another sign she'd never known him at all.

'I don't understand how you could have sat there at lunch yesterday and listened to me telling you how I wasn't wanted—by my birth parents or my adoptive ones—and promised to make a better life, a better family with me, when all along you were no better than any of them.' The shame of the secrets and feelings he'd admitted to this woman burned. Maybe she hadn't been laughing at him all along, but she'd still let him spill his guts while she gave up nothing at all.

She'd still lied to him about the person she was.

'I thought I knew you. Thought we knew each other,' he said. 'But the woman I bought that ring for could never give away her own child.'

Helena's face paled, spots of bright red blazing on her cheekbones in contrast. Tearing her engagement ring from her finger, she threw it across the bed towards him. It clattered off the edge and on to the floorboards, but he made no move to retrieve it. What would he do with such a thing now, anyway?

'You thought you knew me? All because you could pick out a ring I liked?' Helena hurled the words at him as if he were in the wrong. As if she had any grounds to argue at all.

'Because I thought we'd been open and honest with each other!' Gripping the end of the bed frame, Flynn tried not to remember how close he'd felt to her, here in this very room.

Helena shook her head, her blonde hair curling wildly in the air. 'No. You thought you'd found someone who fitted your plan, your schedule. You thought you could make me the wife you needed. You married me for my name, remember, nothing more. I was just your convenient stand-in bride.'

'You know that's not all you were.' If that were so, why would it hurt so much now to know the truth?

'Wasn't I? Then why were you so desperate for me to sign my life away to you?'

'I wanted a future with you! A family!' He was shouting, he knew it, knew everyone in the house must be able to hear them. He didn't care. Not any more.

'But you never asked me if that was what I wanted!' Helena yelled back, up on her knees now as she faced him. 'You say you wanted a family, but all you really wanted was an heir. Something to legitimise you as a real Ashton, to give you full control of the company. Why else were you so set on marrying Thea? And why did you marry me with no contract, no agreement?'

'Don't you dare.' Cold fury ran through him like a wave. 'You think you can tell me why I wanted a child of my own? You, of all people? Who had that and just gave it away. Gave her away. You called her a *mistake*.'

Helena reared back as if he'd slapped her. 'You have no idea what you're talking about.'

'Oh, I think I do,' Flynn answered. 'I imagine it went something like this. Poor little rich girl, doesn't get as much notice as her clever older sister. Wants Daddy to pay her some attention too so she starts acting out—the usual teenage rebellion. Dates inappropriate boys, stays out partying—all the classics. But one day she goes too far, realises she's pregnant. Maybe you didn't even know who the father was.' She flinched at that, and he knew he'd hit a nerve. Part of him took a vicious pleasure in the fact. 'So you go crying to big sis, make her tell Daddy for you. And Daddy fixes everything, right? Sends you away to have the baby then palms it off to somebody else—no harm, no foul. No damage done—except to that poor kid's life.'

She jerked back at his words, as if they caused physical pain.

Good. He wanted her to hurt. Wanted her to feel the same pain he did.

If he couldn't love her any more, he had to break things between them altogether. Their marriage would never be anything more than a convenience, from this day forward.

It was all over for them now. It had to be.

Helena stared at him, horrified. How could this be the same man she'd shared this bed with the night before? Or even the man she'd worshipped at fourteen for his kind understanding? This Flynn was someone she barely recognised. 'You're right. You don't know me at all.' No more than she knew him, apparently.

'On the contrary, I believe I've finally got a glimpse of the real you.' Flynn's mouth twisted in a cruel sneer. 'And the sight sickens me.'

He didn't know, Helena told herself. He didn't know the truth of what had happened to her that night. But he wouldn't listen either. Just like her father never had.

She couldn't forgive him for that.

'Trust me, the feeling is mutual.'

'What did you expect, Helena?' Flynn threw his arms wide, the injured party, hurt and wounded at her hand. And he was, she knew. She should have told him the truth from the start, let him make his own choice with all the information. But things had moved so fast, and she couldn't bear the thought of losing him so soon after he'd finally become hers. She'd wanted them to build a relationship that could survive the truth.

Great job, Helena.

'Did you think you could keep it a secret forever?' Flynn asked. 'Or at least make me fall so in love with you that it wouldn't matter what horrific things you'd done in your past?'

She felt the colour rise in her cheeks, warm and humiliating. That was, of course, exactly what she'd thought. Or hoped, at least.

She should have known better. People didn't ever really forgive, not when it mattered. Even taking her sister's place and marrying Flynn hadn't been enough for their father to forgive either of them. Why should Flynn be any different?

'I thought you'd respect me enough to listen to me when I told you. To hear my reasons and try to understand.'

'You want me to listen? I'll listen. Tell me, Helena. How did it feel to give away your own child to a total stranger? Did you feel bad for a whole day, or just until your daddy gave you your credit card back so you could go shoe shopping?'

He didn't have a clue. Didn't know her or care for her enough to give her the benefit of the doubt, even.

'It's all black and white to you, isn't it?' she said, staring at the man she'd thought she loved. 'On-plan or off-schedule. Right or wrong. Us and them. It doesn't occur to you that people might have reasons or beliefs or feelings different to yours, does it? You can't imagine any scenario in which I might have done the right thing.'

'The right thing? How can giving away a child ever be the right thing?' Flynn stood gripping the frame at the foot of the bed, his arms stretched out to the sides as he loomed over her. Helena swallowed, her mouth dry as the image of him there, so much stronger and more powerful than her, took her back to another awful day. The worst of her life from the day her mother died until now.

Two other men, barely more than boys, that same look

in their eyes. The look that told her she didn't matter to them, that what she wanted, the decisions she made, didn't matter at all. She meant nothing.

She had put herself there in that room with them. She'd made her choice and now she would pay for it.

'You can't tell me you thought you were giving her a better life,' Flynn went on, and Helena flinched at just the accusation in his voice. 'You come from one of the richest families in the country. You could have given that child everything it ever needed and you chose not to.'

'No.' It wasn't loud, but Helena put every bit of feeling she had behind the word. 'No, I couldn't. I couldn't give her what she needed most.'

'And what was that?' Flynn asked, a bitter mocking tone in his voice.

'Love.' She looked up and met his eyes then, took every glimmer of hatred and disgust he had to give. 'I couldn't have loved her the way she needed, the way she deserved. And so I agreed when they told me I had to give her away.'

'You couldn't...' Flynn shook his head in disbelief. 'You really are a piece of work, aren't you? Have you honestly convinced yourself that you did what was best for that child?'

'You tell me.' Helena got up from the bed. She needed to be equal with him for this, couldn't let him glare down at her any more. He still had almost a foot of height on her, but at least she didn't feel quite so helpless. She fisted her hands at her hips and stared him down. 'You grew up in a family like mine—our families were practically one and the same for years. You tell me, how did it feel to grow up there without being wanted or loved? Because if it felt anything like my childhood did after my mother died, you wouldn't wish it on anyone.'

For a moment he looked stunned, and she wondered

if this was her opportunity. Her one chance to make him truly understand what had happened that night and how it had changed her. How knowing it was all her own fault had only made everything that followed a thousand times harder.

Could she make him understand the depths of despair she'd hit? How it had felt as if her soul had been torn apart the moment she'd realised she could never look at or think of her own child without remembering the night that she had been conceived? Without feeling that same pain over and over again?

But then his expression changed and the repulsion in his eyes grew greater than ever.

'If that's truly how you feel, Helena, perhaps you should ask yourself something. How are you any different from your father or, worse, mine? And what kind of *monster* can't love their own child?'

Monster.

The word hit her in the gut and she wrapped her arms around herself as she doubled over, as if he'd hit her with bullets not insults. He was right. He didn't understand and he wouldn't listen, but he was still right.

But if he thought she could ever forgive herself for the decisions she'd made, then he hadn't got a clue about her.

'Do you think I don't live with that knowledge every day?' she asked. 'Why do you think I held out against the agreement? I know you want kids and I know I can't have them. We could have adopted, perhaps, but the thought of carrying another child...I couldn't do it. Even for you.'

'Do you think I'd want you to, now? Do you think I can even imagine touching you?' Revulsion shadowed his face. 'You say you live with it every day. Well, so will I, now. Because you talked me into marrying you, into *sleeping with you,* and now we're stuck with each other.'

'You want a divorce?' Helena asked. 'I'll give you one, and gladly. We can both be free. You can find another way to find that legitimacy you crave. Except there isn't one, is there? You've run out of Morrison sisters now. It's me and my sordid past or nothing at all. Entirely up to you.'

Hatred burned from Flynn's eyes, and Helena realised that they could be making each other unhappy for the rest of their lives. That knowing how happy they could have been would only make their misery more bitter.

Maybe this was her punishment, at last. Or her atonement.

Either way, she thanked God no children would have to live through it with them.

The air between them crackled with anger, frustration and helplessness, and Helena couldn't look away from him if she tried. She needed to know. Would he choose this hell of a relationship, just to keep the company? Or would he walk away with his integrity intact?

But she didn't find out. Because, just then, Henry knocked on the open door.

'I hate to interrupt,' he said in a tone that said he was glad to have a reason to separate them right now. 'But I just had a call from London. I'm so sorry, Helena, but your father has been rushed to hospital. Heart attack. We need to get back to London. Immediately.'

CHAPTER TEN

HELENA KEPT HER silence all the way to London.

She felt as if she'd spoken all the words inside of her already; that if she tried for any more all that would come out would be gibberish. She had no more angry barbs to throw at Flynn, no more defences to try, no more arguments to make. And she was still too far from understanding what her father's heart attack meant, or how she felt about it, to even begin to speak on the subject.

So she grabbed her most important things in silence, forcing them into her carry-on bag, knowing that the villa staff would pack up and send on the rest. She dressed as comfortably and casually as she could manage, needing the sensation of soft cotton and warm cashmere against her skin, now she couldn't rely on her husband's touch.

She slipped her sunglasses on, nodded goodbye to the maid at the door and climbed into the back of the car Henry had hired at the airport, ignoring the two men in the front.

And then she headed home.

It was dark by the time they reached the hospital. Henry had asked—not Flynn, of course; he'd barely looked at her for the last thousand miles—if she wanted to go home first, to change, to sleep, whatever. But Helena had shaken her head, and he'd asked the taxi driver to go straight to the hospital.

Drizzle misted the windows of the cab, familiar, damp and chill. Suddenly, Helena was glad to be back home. Tuscany had felt like such an escape, such a fairy tale, until today. But she knew it could never be that for her again. And to stay another moment would only ever have reminded her of what she'd lost.

She didn't wait for Henry or Flynn to follow as she strode into the hospital. Flynn had called his mother from the car and Helena had heard enough to know where her father was, so she headed straight to him.

Isabella seemed to have aged a decade in just a week. She stood, leaning against the wall outside Thomas's room, her make-up faded and her hair no longer fixed in place. She looked up as Helena approached and her face crumpled.

'Is he…?' Her first words for a thousand miles, Helena thought, and she couldn't even finish the sentence.

Isabella shook her head. 'The doctors say the surgery went well. They've done…' she gulped in air and Helena realised she was trying to keep from crying; Isabella, the icy matriarch, had actual tears in her eyes '…something,' she finished. 'They'll tell you all about it. I don't…I don't understand it all. Not at all.'

It was the day for it, Helena thought. Nothing at all made sense today.

Flynn and Henry caught up at last, Flynn wrapping his arms around his mother in a way Helena was sure she'd never done for him. Did he know, she wondered, about Isabella and Thomas's decade-long affair? She'd never asked. One more secret between them, she supposed.

Ignored, Helena moved to the door, pushing it open to step inside her father's room. He looked smaller there in the bed, hooked up to machines and tucked under crisp white hospital sheets. He wouldn't even know she was there. And if he didn't recover, if something else happened…he might never know how her past had come back to screw up her present. That he'd been right that night eight years ago when he'd told her she'd wilfully ruined her life.

'Oh, Daddy.' Her throat thickened as the tears welled up. Clenching her fists, Helena tried to stop them, tried to keep at bay all the feelings that threatened to wash her away in their flood.

'Helena?' Henry's cautious voice came from behind her, but she didn't turn. 'Are you okay? Do you need… anything?'

No, she wasn't okay. She might never be okay again. She hurt so deep she thought her bones might crack, and she feared that anger might be the only thing holding her together—anger at her father for almost dying, at Flynn for not understanding, at those not quite men who had almost destroyed her, and at herself for letting them.

Henry couldn't fix any of that. But there was one thing he might be able to do.

'I need my sister,' she told him.

It took an hour of persuasion to get his mother to leave the hospital and, even then, she wouldn't go home. Instead, Isabella insisted on being taken to Thomas's town house, saying she wouldn't be able to sleep anywhere else.

Flynn supposed this meant that the polite charade of ignoring the fact that his mother had been sleeping with his father's best friend for the last ten years was over. Everybody's secrets were being exposed today, and it left Flynn feeling as if he'd been scraped raw.

Helena wouldn't leave her father's room, and Flynn had refused to even try to persuade *her*.

Henry waited for him in the cab while he got his mother settled, then asked, 'Where to now?' as soon as he returned.

Flynn wished he had an answer. A bar was tempting—somewhere he could drink away the memory of the last week. But when he sobered up nothing would have changed, and a hangover wouldn't help anything at all.

He wasn't facing his father tonight, not while his mother was sleeping at another man's house. So that left him with the house he'd had prepared for himself and his wife to come home to after their honeymoon. It probably wasn't even fully furnished yet but it was *his* and Henry had the keys.

'Let's go to the town house. See if they've delivered the liquor cabinet yet.' Because, while a night of whisky in some dive bar was off the cards, there was no way he was getting to sleep without a drink tonight.

Henry gave the address to the driver and Flynn tipped his head back against the headrest and tried not to think until they arrived there.

The house loomed out of the darkness like a mausoleum. Flynn forced images of how he'd imagined his life in this place from his mind as Henry fumbled with the keys, and made his way straight to the library as soon as the door swung open. Boxes of books sat unopened on the floor, surrounded by empty shelves awaiting them. His desk had been placed at the wrong angle in the corner, but next to it sat his liquor cabinet. It was empty, of course, but a short search turned up the box containing his collection of fine malts and Henry soon tracked down the tumblers in the kitchen.

Flynn pulled the two wing chairs into position on opposite sides of the empty fireplace, ignored the mess around them and poured them each a double measure of his favourite Scotch.

Henry waited until his whisky was halfway down the glass before he spoke, which Flynn appreciated.

'So. What happens now?'

The question he'd been avoiding all night. 'I have no idea.'

'Okay. Well, I guess you don't need to figure it all out tonight. You both need time, and with her father sick… Helena's asked me to find Thea. Get her home.'

Flynn looked up at his friend, noting that the concern in his voice was echoed in his expression. 'How much did you hear? Earlier.'

'Enough.' Henry's voice rang heavy and he stared into his glass.

'I can't…I can't comprehend any of it right now.'

'The reasons you wanted this marriage—enough to marry the wrong sister, even. They haven't gone away.' He was playing devil's advocate now, Flynn knew. The consummate solicitor, Henry always could make both sides of any argument.

'I know.'

Henry sighed. 'I'll leave you the agreement anyway—the draft version. Read it through again. Maybe it'll help you come to a decision.' He pulled the thick stack of paper from his laptop bag and placed it on Flynn's desk. 'I'd better go. I'll call tomorrow, see how things are.'

Flynn nodded, more to show that he'd heard him than in agreement.

'And, Flynn?' Henry said from the door. 'Try to sleep, yeah?'

He didn't even bother nodding that time. Instead, he sat and stared at the contract that was supposed to ensure his future, his family. He sipped his Scotch and when it was gone he poured himself another.

When he finished that one, he stood, grabbed the stack of paper and tossed it in the empty fireplace.

It could be the first thing to burn when he unpacked the matches.

CHAPTER ELEVEN

HELENA HADN'T WANTED to go home—not least because she wasn't entirely sure where home was. But by mid-morning the next day, after Helena had spent the night sleeping in a very uncomfortable armchair next to her dad's bed, Isabella was back, looking well rested, immaculate but still with an edge of fear in her eyes.

'Helena, darling, go home and take a shower. Flynn will be waiting for you—you haven't even seen your new marital home yet!'

'I'm fine here, really,' Helena said, wishing she couldn't feel the creases on her face where she'd fallen asleep against a striped cushion. 'Besides, all my stuff is still at Dad's house.' That was a thought. Maybe she could just nip back there long enough to shower and change, now she wouldn't have to share the space with Isabella.

'No, it isn't.' Isabella laid down the words like a trump card. 'I had everything packed up and moved over to the town house the moment we returned from Italy. All your clothes, books, personal belongings—they're all there waiting for you in your new home.'

Along with a husband who couldn't bear to look at her. Perfect.

'I want to wait until Dad wakes up.'

Isabella's expression grew concerned again, and she

turned to tug Thomas's sheet a little higher over his chest. 'Shouldn't he have woken up already? The doctors don't seem concerned, but even here I don't feel you ever really have one-on-one attention, do you?'

'They're taking good care of him.' Helena tried to sound soothing, and also tried to forget that she was talking to her father's married lover. 'The best care. And they say he shouldn't wake up until this evening, so—'

'So you have plenty of time to go home, shower and see your husband,' Isabella finished for her, leaving Helena to realise, too late, that she'd been outmanoeuvred by her mother-in-law.

She spent the cab ride to the town house rehearsing what she'd say to Flynn in her head, but it proved unnecessary. Whether he'd gone to the office or his parents' house, or even back to Italy, Helena had no idea, but Flynn was not home. Not in their home.

She wandered the half unpacked rooms, filled with unfamiliar possessions, taking in the trappings of what should have been her future. In what she assumed was supposed to be the library she found two empty crystal tumblers and a bottle of Scotch—the only real evidence so far that Flynn had even been there at all.

She dropped into one of the chairs, bone-weary, and wondered if this was where he'd sat the night before. Wondered if he'd ever speak to her again, if she'd ever get the chance to explain herself. If it would even make a difference.

She frowned, squinting at the fireplace in front of her. What was that? Leaning forward, she fished out the papers and immediately wished that she hadn't.

As she flicked through the pages of what should have been her post-nuptial agreement, Flynn's plan for their future, she felt the tears begin to fall at last, hot and thick against her cheeks. And, as the words blurred in front of her, she began to rewrite them in her mind, to imagine them the way they should be.

A future she'd want to live. Not one based around who got what or a schedule they had to follow. But a future that grew organically, from the love between two people.

She didn't want a piece of paper compelling her to live her life bullet point by bullet point. And if Flynn thought that was what he needed...he was wrong. He'd spent his whole life so far trying to place order on an existence that had started in chaos—with not belonging, with bad timing, with uncertainty and manipulation. But he couldn't do that forever. Life didn't work that way.

She only had to look at her father in his hospital bed to know that.

Or think about the moment she'd crossed out her sister's name on that wedding invitation.

Life leapt out at you when you least expected it, and all you could do was hold on for the ride. And someone needed to teach Flynn Ashton that fact.

Maybe even her.

Wiping her tears away with the back of her hand, Helena reached into her handbag and pulled out a pen. Deliberately, and with several thick black lines, she crossed out the boring legalese title and replaced it with her own.

A Manifesto for a More Spontaneous Marriage.

She smiled at the words for a moment, her mind suddenly filled with ideas and possibilities and a world of impulsive romance. Of amazed joy.

And then, starting on the back of page one, she began to write out every hope and dream she had for her future.

Even if she had to accept it would never have Flynn in it.

* * *

Flynn couldn't stay in the house so he went to the only place he really ever felt at home. The office.

He arrived while the place was still abandoned and dark, even the most conscientious employees still tucked up in their beds. He turned on his computer, settled back in his chair and lost himself in emails and memos and contracts for as long as he could.

By the time the sun was fully up, he'd caught up on everything that had happened since he'd left for Italy. He almost wished he hadn't spent so much time keeping on top of his emails when he was away—it would have given him more of a distraction now, when he needed it.

And more time to spend with Helena, before everything he'd thought they were building together came crashing down.

'So, you made it back.' His father's creaky voice jerked Flynn out of his own dark thoughts. He looked up to see the old man standing in his doorway, staring down at him the same way he'd always done when Flynn's school reports came in, however good they were. 'I heard tell you'd cut short your honeymoon. I assume you got your wife to sign the papers, as we discussed?'

Of course, that was all he was concerned about. His best friend and business partner was in hospital, his own wife hadn't left the man's side, but all Ezekiel Ashton cared about was paperwork.

Exactly what Helena had accused Flynn of.

'Helena's father just suffered a massive heart attack. Last I heard, he still hadn't woken up. Forgive me for not pressing her on the formalities just yet.' His voice sounded icy-cold, even to his own ears, but Flynn wondered how much he was speaking to his father and how much to himself. He wanted this sorted as much as the old man did.

He wanted it finished so he could move past the ache that never seemed to leave his chest.

'I understand that Thomas has the only woman he needs dancing attendance on him already.' There was bitterness in Ezekiel's voice, deeper than Flynn had heard from him before. 'I'm sure his daughter is superfluous to the proceedings.'

'She's in love with him, you know. Mum, I mean.' Flynn didn't say it to wound. Just to see if his father would react. If he could even feign surprise this late in the game.

'Of course she is,' Ezekiel scoffed. 'Any fool could see that for the last ten years or more. But she never left me, did she? She always knew I could give her more.'

Flynn thought about his mother's face, careworn in a way he'd never seen it as she'd brushed her hand against Thomas's cheek. 'She might now, I think.'

'Then she's more of a fool than your brother and your runaway bride put together.'

'Actually,' Flynn said, 'I'm starting to think that Thea and Zeke were the only ones to get things right in all this.'

Ezekiel's blank expression told Flynn all he needed to know. His father would never understand love—not the way that Flynn hoped to understand it one day.

'Get that post-nuptial agreement to me by the end of the week,' Ezekiel said before turning and walking away.

Flynn stared after him long after he had gone. Whatever happened next with him and Helena, it wouldn't be about paperwork, not any more. It wouldn't be a schedule or a plan.

He couldn't love a woman who couldn't love her own child; it was as simple and as hard as that. Couldn't trust a woman who had lied, and left a helpless baby behind, not to do the same to him when it suited her. And no amount of planning or paperwork could change that.

* * *

Helena awoke from dozing in her chair at the sound of a phone ringing. It took a moment for her to identify it as hers, and longer to find and answer it.

'Helena? It's Henry. I wanted to let you know that I got hold of your sister. She'll meet you at the hospital as soon as her flight gets in tonight.'

'I'll be there.' She wiped the sleep from her eyes and tried to focus. 'Thanks, Henry.'

Dropping the phone into her lap, she stretched her arms up above her head, trying to relieve the ache in her shoulders. It was almost six; Flynn would be home before too long, she assumed, and she wanted to be out of the way again before that happened.

She bit her lip and stared at the mass of paper in her lap, no longer neatly clipped together and numbered, but loose and covered in her messy scrawl that grew less intelligible by the word. It would probably never make sense to another person, and she wasn't even sure she could take it with her and look at it every day without remembering the day she hadn't signed it. But she'd written it, and somehow that felt like enough.

Leaving the agreement on Flynn's desk, Helena grabbed a few of her things, packing a bag with some changes of clothes and the basic necessities. She'd need to come back sooner rather than later, but it would see her through the next day at least. Isabella might have moved her stuff here, but Helena knew she couldn't stay. She'd figure something else out.

So, with only a brief glance back at the manifesto she'd written, Helena Ashton straightened her hair and clothes and silently slipped out of the house that should have been her home.

It was time to move on.

* * *

The hospital room looked almost exactly as she had left it. Thomas still lay peacefully sleeping, the heart monitor beeping at his side, and Isabella sat in the armchair beside him, pretending to read a magazine. Helena thought she might still be on the same page she'd been staring at that morning.

'No change?' she asked from the door, and Isabella's head jerked up at the sound of her voice.

'He woke up earlier. Not for very long. But he seemed himself. He…was glad I was here.' The relief in Isabella's voice was palpable and Helena felt the knot in her middle start to loosen, just a touch.

'That's great. That's…wonderful.' Helena sank down into the other, less comfortable chair in the room. She might not be sure how she felt about her father right now—beyond furious and hurt—but she wasn't ready to lose the only parent she had left. Not yet. And not before she'd figured out what to make of her relationship with him.

'Henry called earlier,' Helena said, smoothing down the edge of Thomas's sheets, even though they didn't need it. 'Thea's on her way—presumably with Zeke; I didn't ask. She'll be here tonight.'

Isabella froze, the lines of her shoulders and neck suddenly sharp. 'I must admit, I didn't expect to see them again so soon.'

'I imagine they feel the same.'

Helena had assumed that everyone would have had time to get over the wedding fallout before they were all together again. That she and Flynn would be happily living their lives and Thea's runaway bride act could become a near-miss, a funny story to tell at dinner parties. *Can you believe how wrong we nearly got this? Thea almost married Flynn! Isn't that crazy?*

But not now. Now, those conversations would go very differently indeed. And Helena had been so preoccupied with the idea of having her big sister here, where she belonged, where she needed her, that she hadn't even thought about what she was going to say. How she was going to explain what had happened since she'd left.

Or how other people would feel to see her.

Their father had been furiously disappointed in Thea. But surely that would change now? Now that he was lying in a hospital bed with an uncertain future, of course he'd want both his daughters there.

Helena had to believe that or there was no hope for her family at all.

'I'm going to get coffee,' Helena said. 'Do you want coffee?'

Isabella nodded, but her eyes were already fixed on Thomas's face again.

Three cups of coffee later, Thea arrived in a flurry of activity, sweeping through the hospital as if she were back in her power suit and high heels instead of the floaty sundress she was actually wearing. Zeke followed in her wake, grim-faced and suitcase in hand.

Their father was sleeping again, so Thea quizzed his doctors more thoroughly than Isabella or Helena had managed. Helena waited outside while Zeke spoke with his mother and Thea asked more questions.

Then they stepped out of the room again and Helena felt the weight on her shoulders start to lift.

'You're here.' Helena stared at her sister across the hospital corridor. 'You came.' And then she burst into tears.

'Okay, so I was gone less than a week,' Thea said, putting her arm around Helena's shoulders. Helena resisted the urge to snuggle up to her like a toddler, but only just.

'Explain to me exactly how everything went up in smoke in my absence?'

'Firstly, it is not my fault that Dad had a heart attack,' Helena said. 'Or that Isabella appears to have left Ezekiel and moved into Dad's house.'

Thea blinked. 'Okay, well, that's a start. What is your fault, then?'

This was the big one. Helena almost wished she didn't have to tell her. Thea looked so relaxed, so happy—and at least five years younger. It was amazing what love could do, Helena thought, as Zeke brought over more coffee and a couple of plates of sandwiches. The hospital dining area was nicer than Helena had imagined it would be, even in a private hospital. Too nice, in fact, for the scene she was pretty sure it was about to witness.

She took a breath.

'I married Flynn.'

'You what?' Zeke swore as he spilt boiling coffee over his hand. 'Give a guy some warning for that kind of news, will you?'

'Sorry.' Helena flashed him a quick smile then turned her attention back to Thea.

Her sister's eyes were wide and disbelieving. 'Why? Did Dad make you? Or Isabella?'

'It was my idea,' Helena told her. 'All mine. After you left, when I thought about actually having to go down there and tell everyone the wedding was off, this seemed like a better option.' It sounded stupid out loud, Helena thought.

'A…better option? After you spent weeks—months!— telling me to get out, that I couldn't marry someone I didn't love.' Thea sounded outraged at the very idea.

'I know. I know. But it was different for me.'

'Different—how?' Zeke asked, frowning. But Thea's

eyes had gone wide and sad, and she touched her finger-tips to her lips as she said, 'Oh, Helena. You loved him.'

Helena shook her head. 'Not at the start. It wasn't that simple. I mean, maybe I never got over that crush I had when I was fourteen, not totally, but I wasn't planning on basing a marriage on that. I thought, since there was no contract, we could just get a quiet little divorce once the scandal died down. I knew he wanted kids and I… can't think about that. So I knew it couldn't work out. But then…he convinced me it could be more. That we could have a future together, have everything he was supposed to have with you.'

'Want me to kill him?' Zeke asked Thea conversation-ally. 'I gave that man everything he wanted—the company, mostly, admittedly—and he took Helena too. I can kill him.'

'I'd…rather you didn't,' Helena said. 'Even after everything.'

'Tell me about "everything",' Thea instructed. 'And, Zeke, stop interrupting.'

'I don't even know how to describe it. I can't say what changed. We talked a lot. I learned a lot—about him, about how he grew up. He bought me a ring.' Her gaze jumped down to her left hand, where only the too tight wedding band remained. 'I fell in love.'

'So what went wrong?' Thea asked. 'Because, given that this all happened over the course of the last week and you've been crying pretty much constantly since I arrived, I'm figuring it has to be big. Tell me, so I can fix it.'

Helena gave her a watery smile. 'You can't fix this one, Thea.'

'Watch me try.'

'I couldn't sign the post-nuptial agreement Henry brought over. It had a line in it…I had to swear that I had no children.'

'Oh.' Thea's eyes closed as she listened.

'So I had to tell him about…' Helena swallowed. 'I told him I was sixteen, I had a baby and I gave her away.'

'What did he say?' Zeke asked, his voice tense.

'He called me a monster.' Helena shrugged. She figured that covered the basics.

'Okay, now I really am going to kill him.' Zeke was on his feet before Thea grabbed his arm and pulled him back down.

'Did you explain? What happened to you?' Thea's gaze focused so tightly on Helena's face that she squirmed under the attention.

'I didn't get into details, no.' Helena sighed. 'I don't think it would make any difference, anyway.'

'If he knew you were raped?' Zeke shook his head. 'You're wrong. My brother might be an idiot but…it makes a difference.'

'Does it really?' Helena wasn't sure if she was asking them or herself. 'I put myself in that position. I went there, I got drunk and they told me I said yes. And I know, in my head, that they were wrong—that they abused me and they committed a crime. I know that, I do. But…'

'But?' Thea pressed when Helena stopped.

'But I was the one who couldn't love that child, no matter how she came into the world. And that's what I know he'll never forgive me for.'

The tears came again then. Thea wrapped her arms around her, and Helena clung to her big sister like a lifeline.

Thea couldn't fix this one, she knew. But maybe having her there would be enough to help her through it.

'You need to tell him, sweetheart,' Thea murmured against her hair. 'He deserves to know everything.'

'I know,' Helena whispered back. Because not telling Flynn everything had got her into this mess. And maybe it wouldn't make a difference—maybe she didn't even want it to. But if she ever wanted to move past this, she had to get it all out.

And then leave it behind.

'I'll go with you,' Zeke said. 'We can pick up the rest of your stuff while we're there.'

Helena nodded, grateful to have someone else making the decisions for a while.

'You can do this.' Thea tucked a finger under Helena's chin, making her look up into her eyes. 'And I will be right here for you, every step of the way.'

Helena gave another shaky nod. Thea was right.

She'd survived worse than this, with her sister beside her. And she'd survive it again.

She turned to Zeke. 'Then let's go and get this over with.'

CHAPTER TWELVE

FLYNN IGNORED THE knock on the door the first time. He'd already spoken to Henry at the office, dealt with his father and phoned his mother. Anyone else could go jump as far as he was concerned.

But, by the third knock, even Flynn had to admit that whoever it was didn't seem to be going away.

He wrenched the door open and found he couldn't even muster up any surprise at seeing his brother on his doorstep—or Helena standing just behind him.

'We've come for Helena's things.' Zeke glanced at Helena, who seemed to shrink back further, then turned back to Flynn, his jaw set and eyes full of fury. 'And while she's packing, you and I are going to have a word.'

The anger that had never been more than a moment away, ever since Thea and Zeke had left, simmered up closer to the surface. 'I suppose that's logical. You run off with my fiancée on my wedding day, and you think now is the time to talk.'

Zeke stepped inside and from the corner of his eye Flynn saw Helena slip in behind him, heading for the staircase. He wanted to stare, to take her in one last time, but he wouldn't let himself. He had to cut her out of his life completely. It was *good* that she'd come for her things.

'Nothing about this situation is logical. Flynn—' Zeke started, but Flynn couldn't let him finish.

'So what? You don't like the mess you left behind so you're here to whisk Helena away too? What's wrong with you? Is one sister really not enough?'

He felt the punch before he saw it, the blossoming throb of pain radiating from his cheekbone as Zeke pulled his fist back. The surge of adrenalin had him wanting to return it, to break his brother's face for coming here after everything that had happened, for acting so righteous. His hands balled up into weapons as he prepared to strike—

Until a small hand grabbed his arm and yanked it back.

'Stop it. Both of you. Idiots!' Helena's cheeks had spots of red in them as she glared at them both. 'Zeke, I thought you were coming here to support me?'

'And I thought you were going to do the talking,' Zeke countered.

Helena's jaw tightened and Flynn couldn't help but wonder what it was she still had to say. How could there be anything left?

'Fine.' She grabbed a bag from behind her and thrust it into Zeke's hands. 'In that case, you go and pack. We'll be in here when you're finished.' She jerked her head towards the door of the library.

Inside, Helena seemed perfectly at home in a room he hadn't even realised she knew existed. With decisive strides, she made her way to the desk and, grabbing two tumblers, poured them both a whisky. Turning, she handed one to Flynn and he could see the uncertainty in her eyes, even as she ran the show.

She thought he would reject her again, even though she'd sent Zeke upstairs to pack so she could leave him, once and for all. How many more ways were there for them to show each other they weren't meant to be?

'Okay, look, this is what's going to happen here,' Helena said, clutching her own glass with both hands as she sat down in the chair nearest the desk. Raising his eyebrows, Flynn followed suit, settling into his own chair. 'I am going to tell you some things. Not because I think you deserve to hear them, and not because I think they'll change anything.'

'Then why are you bothering?' Flynn asked because he had to try and remember which Helena this was now. It was just harder with her sitting right there, blonde and lovely and tired and hurt.

'Because it matters to me. Because I need to have the full truth out there before I can move on.' She gave a light shrug. 'And because Thea told me to.'

'Then by all means,' Flynn said with excessive courtesy, 'talk away.' It wouldn't make any difference. It couldn't, not now.

Helena sucked in a breath then paused as if she hadn't expected the permission to be granted so easily. She took a sip of whisky before she started to talk.

'When I was sixteen, I snuck out of the house to meet an older boy, one I knew I wasn't supposed to see. He took me over to his friend's house, said we'd have a little party.'

Flynn shifted in his seat. He didn't want to hear this, didn't need to hear this. 'And you were all about the parties, right?'

Helena ignored him. 'When I got there, they gave me a drink, then another one. And another—maybe more. I wasn't used to alcohol so it affected me quickly. But I wasn't so drunk that I didn't tell them to stop when they tried to take my top off. I wasn't so far gone that I didn't scream when they raped me, one after another. I knew they were lying when they said afterwards that I was plastered, that I'd said yes and I just couldn't remember. But I was too ashamed to argue.'

The glass toppled from Flynn's hand, rolling across the rug and leaving Scotch in its wake. Flynn watched it go, a solitary focus in a world that was shifting around him, spinning until he didn't know which way was up any more.

Maybe you didn't even know who the father was. He'd said that and she'd winced. Because she hadn't known. Because two men had taken that away from her. Had taken everything. And now she sat here relating the story in a perfectly matter-of-fact voice, as if she were putting herself apart from the memory so it couldn't hurt her any more.

He wanted to reach out to her, to touch her, to tell her he was listening now, but what right did he have? And what good would it do when she was leaving him anyway?

'I knew there was a chance I wouldn't have been able to look at my daughter without remembering that night, without reliving it.'

'And that's why you thought you couldn't love your own child.' The words rasped in his dry throat and Flynn grasped tight on to the arms of his chair to try and stop his world from tilting so far it tipped him off.

'After that day, I wasn't sure I'd ever be able to love anyone or anything again,' Helena said, and when her gaze flashed up to meet his Flynn felt it all the way deep in his soul. 'But I did. I fell in love with you, even when it was the craziest, riskiest thing I could do. And it still wasn't enough.'

Flynn swallowed, unable to find the words to respond. Helena drained the last of her whisky and put the glass next to a stack of paper on the desk before getting to her feet.

'I gave up my child, did everything our parents wanted, and it still wasn't enough for them. Eight years later, I married you to try and make up for my past mistakes and *that* wasn't enough either. So, you know what? I'm done trying to be enough for anyone else. I'm good enough for me. I'm not a monster, whatever you think.'

'Helena—I didn't—' Flynn started, but she held up a hand to stop him.

'No. You're not talking. You're listening, and then I'm leaving.' She swallowed and he could see the tears forming in her eyes. Fine. She wanted him to listen? He'd listen. And maybe some of this crazy mess would start to make sense to him at last.

'I was a child, and I was taken advantage of,' Helena went on. 'I did the best I could then, and I'm doing the best I can now. And if that's not enough for you? It's your loss, Flynn. Because I didn't want you as a CEO or as an heir. I wasn't going to push you aside because I found a better option. I just wanted you. I wanted the future you painted for me in your wedding speech. You talked about how you can't plan for love or schedule romance—and then you went and tried to do just that. But I didn't want some spreadsheet setting out when we had sex, or had kids, or when you should buy me flowers. I wanted a real marriage—love. And that's so much more than anyone else has ever offered you.'

I just wanted you.

The words echoed in his brain until he could hear nothing else. Grasping at the arms of his chair, he tried to push himself up, to reach her, reason with her. 'Helena. I…'

'No.' She shook her head, blonde waves flying, and he knew again that he loved her. He'd used her lies and the adoption as an excuse to push her away before she could hurt or leave him. When all along she'd offered him everything he'd ever wanted—and never believed he'd deserve. 'I can't…' She bit back a sob and Flynn felt like the worst man who had ever lived. 'Look, read this. Then we can talk.' She thrust the stack of papers from his desk into his hands and he stared at it, confused.

By the time he realised what he held, the door had swung closed and she was gone.

He wanted to follow, wanted to fix things, but he didn't know where to start. And Helena had just given him the best clue he was likely to get.

Their marriage contract, except now it was covered in Helena's handwriting. The same loopy scrawl he'd seen on the back of that invitation on their wedding day, promising they would figure everything out once they were married.

Well, now that time was here.

Pouring himself another whisky, Flynn settled down to read and hoped against hope Helena's words would tell him how to make this right.

It was five days before the doctors finally agreed with Thomas's protestations that he was ready to go home.

Ever since he woke up the first day he'd been demanding to be let out, but Isabella kept telling him, 'I almost lost you, Thomas! So you are staying here until the doctors say it is time to go home.' The tone in which she said this ranged from calming to almost hysterical, depending on how belligerent he was being that day.

Helena had stayed back, letting her mother-in-law deal with him, knowing that she was the only woman he'd listen to anyway. But she'd visited every day and even managed some short civil conversations with her father. Thea's first visit had elicited rapid beeping on Thomas's heart monitor as he'd berated her, but Thea had taken everything he'd thrown at her without losing any of the serene calm she'd come to possess since running away with Zeke.

Then she'd told him in no uncertain terms that she was happy, living her life the way she wanted to, and anyway, had Isabella told Ezekiel she'd left him yet or were they waiting for him to guess?

That shut him up for almost half an hour.

But once they were all back living in the Morrison house again, it was harder to ignore the fact that Helena was there and Flynn wasn't. Or that Isabella wasn't leaving and no one had spoken to Ezekiel. Helena knew that sooner or later this all had to blow up in their faces, but she was happy to ignore the fact for as long as possible.

Until, in fact, Isabella decided she wanted to throw a party.

'It can be a welcome home party for Thomas, to celebrate his…well…'

'Survival?' Zeke suggested when his mother trailed off. 'Continued health? Heart attack?'

'His life,' Isabella said firmly. 'We could make it an engagement party for you and Thea too, perhaps,' she added with a sideways look at them.

Thea and Zeke exchanged a glance that only lasted a moment, but appeared to convey a whole conversation.

'Actually,' Zeke said, 'it's a bit late for that.'

'A bit…late?' Isabella's eyebrows rose.

'After we left Italy…we took a flight to Vegas,' Thea explained, and Helena clapped a hand to her mouth to hold in a whoop of laughter.

'*Las* Vegas,' Isabella said for clarification, in the tone that Helena imagined she'd probably use to say 'a *brothel*'.

'Please tell me you were married by an Elvis impersonator!' Helena thumped her brother-in-law on the arm. 'And I can't believe you didn't tell me immediately!'

'She nixed the idea of Elvis, unfortunately,' Zeke said. 'But yes, we got married.'

'Well.' Isabella appeared at a loss for words, which Helena thought might be a first. It also didn't last very long. 'In that case, we'll have to make it a rather larger affair. We'll have it out at the estate, rather than here in town. I'll go and call the planner right now.' She started to head for the door, then paused and turned back to face the three of them. 'I know I...well, I might not have always showed this, but I think you did the right thing. All of you. Sometimes love is bigger than propriety and gossip. And sometimes you don't know how long you have... Anyway, I would like to celebrate the marriages of my sons.'

Thea stepped up and kissed Isabella on the cheek. 'Thank you. That means a lot.'

'When are you going to tell Dad you're leaving?' Zeke asked.

Isabella gave him a sad smile. 'If he hasn't noticed that I've gone by now, he probably never will. But yes, I have a meeting with him and my solicitor tomorrow. We'll keep everything civil and low-key. We all owe each other that much.'

It was hard to imagine, Helena thought, after all these years, that Isabella would officially step into the role and life she'd been living secretly for so long. Maybe it was a good thing, maybe not—but she wouldn't wish her father on anyone else so maybe it was just inevitable.

Isabella had always loved Thomas more than her sons, or his daughters. But until now she'd valued her social standing and reputation more than love. That shift alone... could it be the making of a new Isabella?

'Helena,' Isabella said, breaking her out of her musings. 'You did the right thing too. It might not feel like it yet, but I believe that it will.'

Helena tried to smile but the sadness within her wouldn't let her. Flynn hadn't called in the days since she'd left him in the library of what was supposed to be their home. The truth hadn't made a difference in the end. So even if marrying Flynn *had* been the right thing, for him it was still outweighed by all the wrong things she'd done before.

And no fancy party was going to change that.

'Your mother has left me.' Ezekiel entered Flynn's office without knocking and dropped into the visitor's chair. 'I just met with her and a divorce solicitor.'

Flynn wondered if this was really news to his father, whether he'd honestly thought that Isabella would come back once Thomas had recovered. 'I'm…sorry?'

Ezekiel waved a hand to dismiss Flynn's apology, as if the dissolution of his marriage was nothing but a mere inconvenience. 'It shouldn't affect things here. Thomas and I have been business partners too long to let something like this tear down everything we worked so hard to build up.'

Of course that was his concern. Business before everything else, just the same as always.

'I'm glad things will be…amicable.' What else could he say?

'In fact, she's throwing a party this weekend. You should have an invite somewhere in there.' He pointed to Flynn's in-tray. 'Celebrating your brother's quickie wedding in some Vegas casino, apparently.'

Flynn smiled as he flicked through the stack of papers. Of course Zeke and Thea had got married, and as irreverently as possible. Finding the envelope, he ripped it open and read the invitation.

Isabella and Thomas invite you to celebrate life and love with them.

They certainly weren't wasting any time at all. And apparently his mother had given up worrying what other people thought. He approved, he thought.

Even more, he approved of this party—because Helena would be there. He'd done as she asked. He'd listened, he'd thought and he'd spent a lot of time considering her manifesto.

His mother's party would be the perfect time to show her how well he'd learned, and listened. And to tell her his new plan for their future.

As Ezekiel ambled back out of the office, Henry rapped on the door.

'You got a moment?' Henry asked.

'Of course.' Flynn gestured to the seat across the desk. 'What's up?'

Henry sat, holding a brown file tightly between two hands. 'I have the information you asked me to find. Are you sure you still want it?'

Flynn's chest tightened. 'I'm sure,' he said, even though he wasn't. 'Thank you for doing this for me.'

Henry shrugged as he handed the file across. 'I'm just grateful you decided to look up your birth mother, rather than asking me to find the monsters who hurt Helena. After that first phone call…let's just say I had visions of having to defend you in court if you'd found them.'

'I'm trying to look to the future, not the past. And, you know, not get arrested.' Flynn held the file lightly between his fingers but didn't open it. Did he really want to know? And did it matter? Was it enough to just acknowledge that perhaps his real mother had reason to believe that he would have a better life without her, whatever happened next?

'If you want me to make contact, I can,' Henry said, nodding at the file. 'When you're ready.'

'Maybe.' He'd thought this was what he needed, to prove to Helena that he'd moved on. But the more he'd studied her manifesto, the more he'd realised this wasn't about adoption—his, or her daughter's. It was about them finally allowing themselves to be happy.

He opened his bottom desk drawer and slipped the file inside. 'Not just yet,' he said. 'But soon, I think.'

'Okay.' Henry shrugged. 'Anything you want me to do in the meantime?'

Flynn smiled. 'How would you like to come out to the family estate for a party this weekend?'

'Sounds good,' Henry said. 'What's the catch?'

'I need you to go and pick something up for me first. From Italy.'

CHAPTER THIRTEEN

'YOU LOOK BEAUTIFUL.' Thea finished zipping up Helena's deep blue cocktail dress and stepped back. 'Flynn won't know what's hit him.'

'Zeke, last I saw,' Helena joked. She didn't know how much Zeke had told Thea about their visit to Flynn, but she'd seen Thea cooing over his bruised hand afterwards.

Thea sat on the bed, smoothing out her own bright red dress. Isabella had wanted her to wear white, but Thea had been adamant that she had already done the wedding thing. Almost twice.

'Are you going to be okay down there tonight? With him here, I mean?' Thea asked.

Helena shrugged. 'I don't think it matters if I am or not. Even if he wasn't my husband, he would still be Zeke's brother, Isabella's son. He's going to be around, always. I'm going to have to get used to it some time or another.' Not to mention the fact that she'd met with Isabella's divorce solicitor the day before. At some point, she'd have to sit across a table from Flynn and discuss what happened next. She wasn't looking forward to it but if Isabella could do it, so could she.

Thea checked her watch. 'It's time. The first guests are probably already arriving.'

Zeke met them at the top of the stairs and they headed

down together. It was strange, Helena thought. It had been so many years since the four of them had been at a party together in this house. So very much had changed in the years since Zeke had left home but, in lots of ways, it felt like just another party.

At least she was old enough to drink at them these days.

'There you all are!' Isabella called from the hallway. 'Come get a glass of bubbly and say hello to some people.' Helena and Thea exchanged a glance, grabbed champagne flutes and headed in.

The party was in full swing by the time she caught her first glimpse of Flynn. Isabella had collared him by the door and was holding his arm tightly as she spoke close to his ear. Helena had no idea what she was saying but she suspected she didn't want to hang around and find out, either.

With so many people in attendance, it wasn't too hard to keep moving between the crowd and stay out of Flynn's way. It was entirely possible he was doing the same thing, of course. She was under no illusion that he'd be desperate to talk to her, either. If he had been, if he'd moved past his anger and disgust, he would have called by now.

People would talk, of course, if they weren't seen together tonight—but people would talk anyway, the moment the divorce was announced. Maybe it was better to get the rumours started now so it wouldn't be so shocking later. They could even bury the news under the announcement of Thea and Zeke's wedding.

Helena looked around for Thea and her husband. This was their night, after all—theirs and Isabella's and Thomas's. She'd celebrate with them and then she'd disappear upstairs for an early night when no one would notice. Thea could tell people she had a headache if anyone asked.

There. She had a plan. Flynn would be so proud.

The minutes ticked by unbearably slowly, but eventually Helena figured it had to be safe to escape. She was halfway across the room to let Thea know she was going when she heard the sound of metal on glass.

'Ladies and gentlemen, if I could ask for your attention, please?' Flynn's voice rang out across the party and stopped Helena in her tracks. 'My mother has asked me to say a few words.'

Of course she had. Of course Isabella would be behind this.

And of course she'd be grabbing hold of Helena's arm right now.

'Come on,' she said as she dragged her closer to where Flynn was making his speech. 'I don't want to miss this.'

I do, though! Helena sighed and allowed herself to be dragged. But after this she was going to bed.

'As you probably all know, my mother and Thomas asked us here tonight to celebrate life and love, in its many and wondrous forms. We are all, as I know you are, giving thanks for Thomas's swift recovery and hoping for plenty more life for him to enjoy yet. And we're celebrating a marriage—yes, another one!' A smatter of laughter at that, and Helena felt too many eyes on her.

Not Flynn's, though. He hadn't even glanced in her direction.

'Thea and Zeke's wasn't a conventional wedding, by all accounts, but, since nothing else about their relationship was conventional either, it seems only right that it happened this way.' Flynn looked out over the crowd as he spoke, as if he was meeting every person's gaze individually. 'There's no point pretending you don't already know the story. Thea and I were, only last month, intending to marry each other—until Zeke drove back into our lives and reminded us all of something important. The power love has to override all plans, make a mockery of any schedule and lead us to places we never thought we'd want to go.'

Helena's heart clenched at his words, so similar to the speech he'd made on their wedding day. The tightness in her chest only grew when Flynn turned to gaze directly at her as he spoke again.

'Since my own marriage, I seem to have learnt a lot about love, and about life. Far more than I ever knew before. And that is entirely down to my beautiful wife, Helena.' He motioned towards her and Helena blushed at the 'ahh's from the crowd.

What was he doing? Keeping up the charade? Making it impossible for her to walk away? Or was it just possible that this was something else? Something more?

Helena held her breath and allowed herself a moment to hope.

'In fact, I needed so much education that my wife wrote me a memo, to help me make sense of it all.' The crowd laughed as, from a side table nearby, Flynn picked up a stack of paper and held it up. Helena's eyes widened. Her manifesto!

She'd poured every hope and dream she had into that pile of paper. Every small detail and moment that would make her future happy. And Flynn had read it, and carried it with him tonight. Did that mean…did he want them to have another chance?

'I won't read this aloud, although I think every married couple should have a copy. In fact, I have a photocopy here for you, Zeke!' More laughter, and Helena grasped at her skirt with clammy hands. She wanted this over. She wanted to know what this was, what he was doing. She wanted to *understand*.

'But I did want to quote just a couple of lines.' He

flicked through the pages to a sheet towards the end, and Helena held her breath. 'Helena wrote: "Love is about more than where it can take you or what it can provide—a marriage, a home, a family, status or money. Love is about experiencing any or all of those things with the one person who makes them worthwhile. Who makes life meaningful."'

Flynn lowered the paper and gazed out over the crowd at her again, and the hope that had budded tightly in Helena's heart began to blossom.

'Helena is the only person who could ever and will ever bring that meaning into my life, whatever our future brings. And I feel so incredibly lucky to have realised that, at last.'

He looked away, smiling out at his audience again, but Helena didn't mind. *Those* were the words she hadn't even known she needed to hear.

'Life doesn't follow a plan, any more than love does,' Flynn went on. 'Sometimes the best things in life just happen—and so do the worst things. What makes it harder is that sometimes you can't even tell which is which. But life doesn't go backwards, and neither does love. You can't switch love off or pretend it never happened. All you can do is love and live in the now, and look to the future with amazement and joy. And that, my friends, is what I wish for my brother and his wife, and for my mother and Thomas. And, most of all, for Helena and me.'

He stepped down to wild applause, but he didn't seem to hear it. Instead, he walked straight to Helena, took her hand and placed something in it, folding her fingers over it before she could see. But she knew from the shape, the feel of it, exactly what Flynn had given her.

And she smiled and let him take her other hand and lead her outside.

* * *

Flynn's heart beat double time as he walked Helena out to the outdoor seating area behind the house. There was a slight drizzle in the air, which he'd normally hate, but tonight it just meant that they were able to be alone.

'My manifesto,' Helena said. 'You know that was just a sort of joke, really.'

'No, it wasn't,' Flynn said, and tried not to focus on how long it had been since he'd seen her, and how much he had hurt her. 'It told me everything you felt and wanted. It let me know you, see you clearer than I ever had. That and finally hearing the full story about what happened to you.'

She looked away and Flynn reached out to rest his palm against her cheek, to keep her eyes on him. 'Why didn't you tell me in Tuscany?'

'Because it wouldn't have made any difference,' Helena said, and her mouth twisted up into an almost smile. 'Everything you said was still true.'

'No,' Flynn said, as firmly as he could. He had to make her believe this. 'I judged you as the person I thought you were, without even thinking about you as the woman I'd fallen in love with. I…before I read what you'd written, I was angry with myself for falling in love with you. For loving someone who had done something I considered unforgivable. But now…now I feel I know you better. And I know, even if you don't, that the woman who wrote this doesn't have it in her not to love. You think you wouldn't have loved that child? You're wrong.'

'In which case, I still did the wrong thing by giving her away.' Helena pulled away. 'So nothing changes.'

'I changed,' Flynn said quietly. 'You changed me. I thought…I thought I had to follow a plan, my rules, my schedule. That anything outside of them was wrong. By my rules, what you did was wrong, yes. But you don't live by my rules—or anyone else's. You made the decision you had to make at the time, with the best information you had. And that decision had a big part in shaping who you are today, in making you the woman I love.'

'So…you're saying you forgive me?' Helena chewed on her lower lip as she looked up at him with those big bluebell eyes.

'I'm saying that you don't need my forgiveness. You need to forgive yourself.'

She couldn't stop the tears, didn't even want to. And, as Flynn pulled her into his arms and held her against his chest, she knew she'd come home again, at last.

'Do you forgive me?' Flynn asked against her hair. 'The things I said…they were unforgivable, I know. But do you think…?'

'Yes,' Helena said. 'I forgive you.' But if forgiveness was the start for them, she knew it wouldn't be everything. They had a long way to go yet.

'But, Flynn,' she said, leaning back to see his face, 'I can't just forget—any of it. You, or what happened to me. That's going to take time.'

'I have all the time in the world for you.' Flynn set his cheek against her hair and Helena sighed. It felt right. She wanted it to be right. And yet…

'I can't promise you anything,' she said. 'Well, nothing beyond the fact that I'm apparently always going to love you. Can't seem to shake that one.'

'Good.'

'But I don't know if I'll ever be ready to have children.' It hurt to say the words, hurt to think it. She'd been happy, imagining her life without kids, until she'd married Flynn. Now, it stung—not just because she couldn't give him what she knew he wanted, but because for the first time she wondered if she might want it too.

Flynn loosened his arms from around her waist and took her hands in his instead, rubbing his thumb over the knuckles of the fingers, still wrapped around the object he'd placed in her palm.

'I promise you this,' he said, his expression solemn. 'There is no schedule for our life together, no plan. Not any more. If it happens one day that you turn to me and tell me you're ready to try for a baby, I'll be the happiest man on earth. And if it doesn't?' He shrugged. 'I'll still be the happiest man on earth because I'll be married to you.'

Slowly, he dropped to his knees and Helena bit back a sob. Could he really be giving her everything she'd ever wanted? And could she forgive herself enough to accept?

Peeling back her fingers, he took her engagement ring from her hand and placed it at the tip of her ring finger. 'Helena Juliette Ashton. Will you do me the honour of being my wife?'

Through her tears, Helena giggled. 'Isn't this where we came in?' she asked as he slid the ring home.

'It's the only place I want to be,' Flynn said, and tugged her down for a kiss.

EPILOGUE

THE TUSCAN SUN shone down as bright as ever, and Helena pulled the brim of her straw hat down to shade her eyes as she watched her niece and nephew chase each other through the grapevines, racing after their new friend Casper.

It had been five years since she and Flynn had first visited Gia's vineyard, but Helena still felt exactly the same sense of home as she had the first time.

Up ahead, Thea and Zeke quizzed Gia about her growing methods, about how the wine was made, and Gia answered patiently the questions she must have been asked a thousand times before.

Helena tuned them out and focused instead on the warm sun on her shoulders, the buzz of summer insects in the air, and her husband's hand in her own.

'This is a wonderful place for a family, don't you think?' she asked, and Flynn murmured his agreement.

'I'm so glad we got to bring Thea and the kids here,' she went on. 'It's good to share this place with them.'

'It's been a great holiday,' Flynn agreed, but Helena knew he was barely listening—too languid and lazy in the sun.

'Maybe we'll come back again next year with our own child,' she said as casually as she could.

Flynn stopped walking and Helena grinned, ducking her head so he couldn't see.

'Helena. Are you saying…? Do you think you might be ready to maybe…?' It wasn't often Flynn fell over his words. It was kind of nice to hear.

She beamed up at him, loving the amazed wonder on his face. 'I'm saying it's a little late for that conversation.'

His eyes widened further. 'You mean you're already…? And you're okay? Do you want to talk about it?'

'I'm fine,' Helena assured him, taking his hand and placing it on her still flat stomach. 'We're fine.'

'We said we'd talk about this if you ever changed your mind. I don't want you to feel—'

'All I feel is happy—' Helena interrupted '—happy and grateful and loved.'

Flynn let out a long breath. 'You're sure?'

'I'm sure.' She grinned. 'And you did say you wanted to be more spontaneous.'

'I couldn't have planned this any better,' Flynn said, and kissed her.

* * * * *

A DEAL TO
MEND THEIR
MARRIAGE

MICHELLE DOUGLAS

For Greg, who brings me glasses of red wine whenever I need them and supplies hugs on demand—the benchmarks of a romantic hero. :)

CHAPTER ONE

THE FIRST PRICKLE of unease wormed through Caro when the lawyer's gaze slid from her to Barbara and then down to the papers in front of him—her father's will, presumably. The lawyer picked up a pen, turned it over several times before setting it back to the table. He adjusted his tie, cleared his throat.

Even Barbara noticed his unwillingness to start proceedings. Turning ever so slightly, her stepmother reached out to pat Caro's hand. 'Caro, darling, if your father has disinherited you—'

Caro forced a laugh. 'There'll be no *if* about that, Barbara.'

It was a given, and they both knew it. Caro just wanted all the unpleasantness over so she could put it behind her. Her father was about to utter the last words he ever would to her—albeit on paper. She had no expectation that they'd be any kinder in death than they had been in life.

'Mr Jenkins?' She prodded the lawyer with the most pleasant smile she could muster. 'If you'd be so kind as to start we'd both appreciate it. Unless—' she pursed her lips '—we're waiting for someone else?'

'No, no one else.'

Mr Jenkins shook his head and Caro had to bite back a smile when the elderly lawyer's gaze snagged on the long, lean length of Barbara's legs, on display beneath her short black skirt. At thirty-seven—only seven years older than

Caro—Barbara had better legs than Caro could ever hope to have. Even if she spent every waking hour at the gym and resisted every bit of sugar, butter and cream that came her way—which, of course, she had no intention of doing.

The lawyer shook himself. 'Yes, of course, Ms Fielding. We're not waiting for anyone else.'

'Come now,' she chided. 'You've known me my entire life. If you can't bring yourself to call me Caro, then surely you can call me Caroline?'

He sent her an agonised glance.

She made her smile gentle. 'I *am* prepared, you know. I fully expect that my father has disinherited me.'

She didn't add that the money didn't matter. Neither Mr Jenkins nor Barbara would believe her. The fact remained, though, that it had never been money she'd craved but her father's approval, his acceptance.

Her temples started to throb. With a superhuman effort she kept the smile on her face. 'I promise not to shoot the messenger.'

The lawyer slumped in what had been until recently her father's chair. He pulled off his spectacles and rubbed the bridge of his nose. 'You have it all wrong, Caro.'

Barbara clasped her hands together and beamed. 'I *knew* he wouldn't disinherit you!'

The relief—and, yes, the delight—on Barbara's face contrasted wildly with the weariness in Mr Jenkins's eyes. Cold fingers crept up Caro's spine. A premonition of what, exactly…?

Mr Jenkins pushed his spectacles back to his nose and folded his hands in front of him. 'There are no individual letters I need to deliver. There are no messages I need to pass on nor any individual bequests to run through. I don't even need to read out the will word for word.'

'Then maybe—' Barbara glanced at Caro '—you'd be kind enough to just give us the general gist.'

He slumped back and heaved out a sigh. 'Mr Roland James Philip Fielding has left all of his worldly goods—all of his wealth and possessions—to...'

Caro braced herself.

'Ms Caroline Elizabeth Fielding.'

It took a moment for the import of the lawyer's words to hit her. When they did, Caro had to grip the arms of her chair to counter the roaring in her ears and the sudden tilting of the room. Her father had left everything...*to her*? Maybe...maybe he'd loved her after all.

She shook her head. 'There must be a mistake.'

'No mistake,' the lawyer intoned.

'But surely there's a caveat that I can only inherit if I agree to administer my mother's trust?'

Her father had spent the last twenty years telling her it was her duty, her responsibility...her *obligation* to manage the charity he'd created in homage to her mother. Caro had spent those same twenty years refusing the commission.

Her father might have thought it was the sole reason Caro had been put on this earth, but she'd continued to dispute that sentiment right up until his death. She had no facility for figures and spreadsheets, no talent nor desire to attend endless board meetings and discuss the pros and cons of where the trust money should be best spent. She did not have a business brain and had no desire whatsoever to develop one. Simply put, she had no intention of being sacrificed on some altar of duty. End of story.

'No caveat.'

The lawyer could barely meet her eye. Her mind spun...

She shot to her feet, a hard ball lodging in her chest. 'What about Barbara?'

He passed a hand across his eyes. 'I'm afraid no provision has been made for Mrs Barbara Fielding in the will.'

But that made no sense!

She spun to her stepmother. Barbara rose to her feet, her

face pinched and white. Her eyes swam but not a single tear fell, and that was somehow worse than if she'd burst into noisy weeping and wailing.

'He doesn't make even a single mention of me?'

The lawyer winced and shook his head.

'But…but I did everything I could think of to make him happy. Did he never love me?' She turned to Caro. 'Was it all a lie?'

'We'll work something out,' Caro promised, reaching out to take Barbara's hand.

But the other woman wheeled away. 'We'll do nothing of the sort! We'll do exactly as your father wished!'

Barbara turned and fled from the room. Caro made to follow her—how could her father have treated his young wife so abominably?—but the lawyer called her back.

'I'm afraid we're not done.'

She stilled and then spun back, swallowing a sense of misgiving. 'We're not?'

'Your father instructed that I give you this.' He held out an envelope.

'But you said…'

'I was instructed to give this to you only after the reading of the will. And only in privacy.'

She glanced back at the door. Praying that Barbara wouldn't do anything foolish, she strode across and took the envelope. She tore it open and read the mercifully brief missive inside. She could feel her lips thinning to a hard line. She moistened them. 'Do you know what this says?'

After a short hesitation, he nodded. 'Your father believed Mrs Fielding was stealing from him. Valuables have apparently gone missing and…'

And her father had jumped to conclusions.

Caro folded the letter and shoved it into her purse. 'Items may well have gone missing, but I don't believe for one moment that Barbara is responsible.'

Mr Jenkins glanced away, but not before she caught the expression in his eyes.

'I know what people think about my father and his wife, Mr Jenkins. They consider Barbara a trophy wife. They think she only married my father for his money.'

He'd had *so much* money. Why cut Barbara out of his will when he'd had so much? Even if she *had* taken the odd piece of jewellery why begrudge it to her?

Damn him to hellfire and fury for being such a control freak!

'She *was* significantly younger than your father…'

By thirty-one years.

'That doesn't make her a thief, Mr Jenkins. My father was a difficult man and he was lucky to have Barbara. She did everything in her not insignificant powers to humour him and make him happy. What's more, I believe she was faithful to him for the twelve years they were married and I don't believe she stole from him.'

'Of course you know her better than I do—but, Miss Caroline, you do have a tendency to see the best in people.'

She'd been hard-pressed to see the best in her father. She pushed that thought aside to meet the lawyer's eyes. 'If Barbara did marry my father for his money believe me: she's earned every penny of it several times over.'

Mr Jenkins obviously thought it prudent to remain silent on the subject.

'If my father's estate has passed completely to me, then I can dispose of it in any way that I see fit, yes?'

'That's correct.'

Fine. She'd sell everything and give Barbara half. Even half was more than either one of them would ever need.

Half an hour later, after she'd signed all the relevant paperwork, Caro strode into the kitchen. Dennis Paul, her father's butler, immediately shot to his feet.

'Let me make you a pot of tea, Miss Caroline.'

She kissed his cheek and pushed him back into his seat. 'I'll make the tea, Paul.' He insisted she call him Paul rather than Dennis. 'Please just tell me there's cake.'

'There's an orange syrup cake at the back of the pantry.'

They sipped tea and ate cake in silence for a while. Paul had been in her father's employ for as long as Caro could remember. He was more like an honorary uncle than a member of staff, and she found herself taking comfort in his quiet presence.

'Are you all right, Miss Caroline?'

'You *can* call me Caro you know.' It was an old argument.

'You'll always be Miss Caroline to me.' He grinned. 'Even though you're all grown up—married, no less, and holding a director's position at that auction house of yours.'

In the next instance his expression turned stricken. 'I'm sorry. I didn't mean to mention that bit about you being married. It was foolish of me.'

She shrugged and tried to pretend that the word *married* didn't burn through her with a pain that could still cripple her at unsuspecting moments. As she and Jack had been separated for the last five years, 'married' hardly seemed the right word to describe them. Even if, technically, it was true.

She forced herself to focus on something else instead. 'It's not *my* auction house, Paul. I just work there.'

She pulled in a breath and left off swirling her fork though the crumbs remaining on her plate.

'My father has left me everything, Paul. *Everything*.'

Paul's jaw dropped. He stared at her and then sagged back in his chair. 'Well, I'll be…'

His astonishment gratified her. At least she wasn't the only one shocked to the core at this turnaround. To describe her relationship with her father as 'strained' would be putting it mildly. And kindly.

He straightened. 'Oh, that *is* good news Miss Caroline. In more than one way.' He beamed at her, patting his chest just above his heart, as if urging it to slow its pace. 'I'm afraid I've a bit of confession to make. I've been squirrelling away odd bits and pieces here and there. Things of value, but nothing your father would miss, you understand. I just thought… Well, I thought you might need them down the track.'

Good grief! Paul was her father's thief?

Dear Lord, if he knew her father had written Barbara out of his will, thinking her the guilty party… *Oh!* And if Barbara knew what Paul had done…

Caro closed her eyes and tried to contain a shudder.

'Paul, you could've gone to jail if my father had ever found out what you were doing!'

'But there's no harm done now, is there? I mean, now that you've inherited the estate I don't need to find a way to…to get those things to you. They're legally yours.' His smile faded. 'Are you upset with me?'

How could she be? Nobody had ever gone out on a limb like that for her before. 'No, just…frightened at what might've happened,' she lied.

'You don't have to worry about those sorts of what-ifs any more.'

Maybe not, but she still had to find a way to make this right. 'It's only fair that I split the estate with Barbara.'

A breath shuddered out of him. He glanced around the kitchen pensively. 'Does that mean selling the old place?'

What on earth did she need with a mansion in Mayfair? She didn't say that out loud. This had been Paul's home for over thirty years. It hit her then that her father had made no provision in his will for Paul either. She'd remedy that as soon as she could.

'I don't know, Paul, but we'll work something out. I'm not going to leave you high and dry, I promise. Trust me. You, Barbara and I—we're family.'

He snorted. 'Funny kind of family.'

She opened her mouth and then closed it, nodding. Never had truer words been spoken.

'Will you be staying the night, Miss Caro?'

Heavens, where Paul was concerned, *Miss Caro* was positively gushing—a sign of high sentiment and emotion.

From somewhere she found a smile. 'Yes, I think I'd better.' She had her own room in the Mayfair mansion, even though she rented a tiny one-bedroom flat in Southwark. 'Hopefully Barbara will… Well, hopefully I'll get a chance to talk to her.'

Hopefully she'd get a chance to put the other woman's mind at rest—at least about her financial future.

'Mrs Fielding refuses to join you for breakfast,' Paul intoned ominously the next morning as Caro helped herself to coffee.

Caro heaved back a sigh. Barbara had refused to speak to her at all last night. She'd tried calling out assurances to her stepmother through her closed bedroom door, but had given up when Barbara had started blasting show tunes—her father's favourites—from her music system.

'You will, however, be pleased to know that she did get up at some stage during the night to make herself something to eat.'

That was something at least.

'Oh, Miss Caroline! *You* need to eat something before you head off to work,' he said when she pushed to her feet.

'I'm fine, Paul, I promise.' Her appetite would eventually return. Although if he'd offered her cake for breakfast…

Stop thinking about cake.

'I'm giving Freddie Soames a viewing of a rather special snuffbox this morning.' She'd placed it in her father's safe—*her* safe—prior to the reading of the will yesterday. 'After that I'll take the rest of the day off and see if I can't get Barbara to talk to me then.'

As a director of Vertu, the silver and decorative arts division at Richardson's, one of London's leading auction houses, she had some flexibility in the hours she worked.

She glanced over her shoulder at Paul, who followed on her heels as she entered her father's study—*her* study. 'You *will* keep an eye on Barbara this morning, won't you?'

'If you wish it.'

She bit back a grin, punching in the combination to the safe. Ever since Paul had caught Barbara tossing the first Mrs Fielding's portrait into a closet, he'd labelled her as trouble. 'I *do* wish it.'

The door to the safe swung open and—Caro blinked, squinted and then swiped her hand through the empty space.

Her heart started to pound. 'Paul, please tell me I'm hallucinating.' Her voice rose. 'Please tell me the safe isn't empty.'

He moved past her to peer inside. 'Dear God in heaven!' He gripped the safe's door. 'Do you think we've been burgled?'

Something glittered on the floor at her feet. She picked it up. The diamond earing dangled from her fingers and comprehension shot through her at the same moment it spread across Paul's face.

'Barbara,' she said.

And at the same time he said, 'Mrs Fielding.'

She patted her racing heart. 'That's okay, then.'

'She'll have been after those jewels.'

'She's welcome to those jewels, Paul. They're hers. Father gave me Mother's jewels when I turned twenty-one.'

He harrumphed.

'But I really, *really* need that snuffbox back—this instant.'

She sped up to Barbara's first-floor bedroom, Paul still hot on her heels. She tapped on the door. 'Barbara?'

'Not now, Caro. Please, just leave me in peace.'

'I won't take up more than a moment of your time.' Caro swallowed. 'It's just that something has gone missing from the safe.'

'That jewellery is *mine*!'

'Yes, I know. I'm not referring to the jewellery.'

The door cracked open, and even the way Barbara's eyes flashed couldn't hide how red they were from crying. Caro's heart went out to the other woman.

'Are you accusing me of stealing something? Are you calling me a *thief*?'

'Of course not.' Caro tried to tamp down on the panic threatening to rise through her. 'Barbara, that jewellery belongs to you—I'm not concerned about the jewellery. Yesterday I placed a small item in the safe—a silver and enamel snuffbox about so big.' She held her hands about three inches apart to indicate the size. 'I have to show it to a potential buyer in an hour.'

Barbara tossed her hair. 'I didn't see any such thing and I certainly didn't take it.'

'I'm not suggesting for a moment that you did—not on purpose—but it's possible it was accidentally mixed in with the jewellery.' Behind her back she crossed her fingers. 'I'm *really* hoping it was. Would you mind checking for me?'

Barbara swept the door open and made a melodramatic gesture towards the bed. 'Take a look for yourself. *That's* what I took from the safe.'

The bed didn't look as if it had been slept in. Caro moved tentatively into the room to survey the items spread out on the bed. There was a diamond choker, a string of pearls, a sapphire pendant and assorted earrings and pins, but no snuffbox. Her heart hammered up into her throat.

'It's not here,' Paul said, leaning over to scan the items.

Caro concentrated on not hyperventilating. 'If...if I don't find that snuffbox I'll... I'll lose my job.'

Not just her job but her livelihood. She'd never get another job in the industry for as long as she lived. In all likelihood legal action would be taken. She'd—

Breathe! Don't forget to breathe.

Barbara dumped the contents of her handbag onto the bed and then slammed her hands on her hips. 'Once and for all—I haven't taken your rotten snuffbox! Would you like to search the entire room?'

Yes! Though of course she wouldn't.

Her gaze landed on a tiny framed photograph of her father that had spilled from Barbara's bag. An ache opened up in her chest. How could he have treated Barbara so badly? She understood Barbara's anger and disappointment, her hurt and disillusionment, but she would never do anything to intentionally hurt *her*—of that Caro was certain. She just needed to give the other woman a chance to calm down, cool off...think rationally.

'Did you not sleep at all last night, Barbara?'

Barbara's bottom lip wobbled, but she waved to the chaise lounge. 'I didn't want to sleep in the bed that I shared with...'

Caro seized her hands. 'He loved you, you know.'

'I don't believe you. Not after yesterday.'

'I mean to split the estate with you—fifty-fifty.'

'It's not what *he* wanted.'

'He was an idiot.'

'You shouldn't speak about him that way.' Barbara retrieved her hands. 'If you're finished here...?'

'Will you promise to have dinner with me tonight?'

'If I say yes, will you leave me in peace until then?'

'Absolutely.'

'Yes.'

Caro and Paul returned to the study to search the room, in case the snuffbox had fallen during Barbara's midnight raid on the safe, but they didn't find anything—not even the partner to that diamond earring.

'You didn't take it by any chance, did you, Paul?'

'No, Miss Caroline.'

'I'm sorry. I thought I'd just check, seeing as…'

'No offence taken, Miss Caroline.' He pursed his lips. '*She* has it, you know. I'm not convinced that the second Mrs Fielding is a nice lady. I once saw her throw your mother's portrait into a closet, you know.'

Caro huffed out a sigh. 'Well… I, for one, like her.'

'What are you going to do?'

She needed time. Pulling her phone from her purse, she rang her assistant.

'Melanie, a family emergency has just come up. Could you please ring Mr Soames and reschedule his viewing for later in the week?'

The later the better! She didn't add that out loud, though. She didn't want to alert anyone to the fact that something was wrong—that she'd managed to lose a treasure.

Her assistant rang back a few minutes later. 'Mr Soames is flying out to Japan tomorrow. He'll be back Thursday next week. He had asked if you'd be so good as to meet with him the following Friday morning at ten o'clock.'

'No problem at all. Pop it in my diary.'

Friday was ten days away. She had ten days to put this mess to rights.

She seized her purse and made for the door. Paul still trailed after her. 'What do you mean to do, Miss Caroline?'

She wanted to beg him not to be so formal. 'I need to duck back to my flat and collect a few things, drop in at work to pick up my work diary and apply for a few days' leave. Then I'll be back. I'll be staying for a few days.'

'Very good, Miss Caroline.'

She turned in the entrance hall to face him, but before she'd swung all the way around her gaze snagged on a photograph on one of the hall tables. *A photograph of her and Jack.*

For a moment the breath jammed in her throat. She pointed. 'Why?' she croaked.

Paul clasped his hands behind his back. 'This house belongs to you now, Miss Caroline. It seemed only right that you should have your things around you.'

Her heart cramped so tightly she had to fight for breath. 'Yes, perhaps… But…not that photo, Paul.'

'I always liked Mr Jack.'

'So did I.'

But Jack had wanted to own her—just as her father had wanted to own her. And, just like her father, Jack had turned cold and distant when she'd refused to submit to his will. And then he'd left.

Five years later a small voice inside her still taunted her with the sure knowledge that she'd have been happier with Jack on *his* terms than she was now on her own terms, as her own woman. She waved a hand in front of her face. That was a ridiculous fairytale—a fantasy with no basis in reality. She and Jack were always going to end in tears. She could see that now.

Very gently, Paul reached out and placed the photograph facedown on the table. 'I'm sure there must be a nice photograph of you and your mother somewhere.'

She snapped back to the present, trying to push the past firmly behind her. 'See if you can find a photo of me and Barbara.'

Paul rolled his eyes in a most un-butler-like fashion and Caro laughed and patted his arm.

'The things I ask of you…'

He smiled down at her. 'Nothing's too much trouble where you're concerned, Miss Caro.'

She glanced up the grand staircase towards the first-floor rooms.

'I'll keep an eye on Mrs Fielding,' he added. 'I'll try to dissuade her if she wants to go out. If she insists, I'll send one of the maids with her.' He glanced at the grand-father clock. 'They're due to come in and start cleaning any time now.'

'Thank you.' She didn't want Barbara doing anything foolish—like trying to sell that snuffbox if she *did* have it. 'I'll be as quick as I can.'

Despite the loss of the snuffbox and all the morning's ker-fuffle, it was Jack's face that rose in her mind and mem-ories of the past that invaded Caro, chasing her other concerns aside, as she trudged across Westminster Bridge.

The sight of that photograph had pulled her up short. They'd been so happy.

For a while.

A very brief while.

So when she first saw his face in the midst of the crowd moving towards her on the bridge, Caro dismissed it as a flight of fancy, a figment of her imagination. Until she realised that blinking hadn't made the image fade. It had only made the features of that face clearer—a face that was burned onto her soul.

She stopped dead. Jack was in London?

The crowd surged around her, but she couldn't move. All she could do was stare.

Jack! Jack! Jack!

His name pounded at her as waves of first cold and then heat washed over her. The ache to run to him nearly undid her. And then his gaze landed on her and he stopped dead too.

She couldn't see the extraordinary cobalt blue of his eyes at this distance, but she recognised the way they narrowed, noted the way his nostrils flared. She'd always wondered what would happen if they should accidentally meet on the street. Walking past each other without so much as an acknowledgment obviously wasn't an option, and she was fiercely glad about that.

Hauling in a breath, she tilted her head to the left a fraction and started towards the railing of the bridge. She leaned against it, staring down at the brown water swirling in swift currents below. He came to stand beside her, but she kept her gaze on the water.

'Hello, Jack.'

'Caro.'

She couldn't look at him. Not yet. She stared at the Houses of Parliament and then at the facade of the aquarium on the other side of the river. 'Have you been in London long?'

'No.'

Finally she turned to meet his gaze, and her heart tried to grow bigger and smaller in the same moment. She read intent in his eyes and slowly straightened. 'You're here to see me?'

His demeanour confirmed it, but he nodded anyway. 'Yes.'

'I see.' She turned to stare back down at the river. 'Actually…' She frowned and sent him a sidelong glance. 'I don't see.'

He folded his tall frame and leaned on the railing, too. She dragged her gaze from his strong, hawk-like profile, afraid that if she didn't she might reach across and kiss him.

'I heard about your father.'

She pursed her lips, her stomach churning like the currents below. 'You didn't send a card.'

He didn't say anything for a moment. 'You send me a Christmas card every year...'

He never sent her one.

'Do you send *all* your ex-lovers Christmas cards?'

She straightened. 'Only the ones I marry.'

They both flinched at her words.

In the next moment she swung to him. 'Oh, please, let's not do this.'

'Do what?'

'Be mean to each other.'

He relaxed a fraction. 'Suits me.'

She finally looked at him properly and a breath eased out of her. She reached out to clasp his upper arm. She'd always found it incredibly difficult not to touch him. Through the fine wool of his suit jacket, she recognised his strength and the firm, solid feel of him.

'You look good, Jack—really good. I'm glad.'

'Are you?'

'Of course.' She squeezed his arm more firmly. 'I only ever wanted your happiness.'

'That's not exactly true, though—is it, Caro?'

Her hand fell away, back to her side.

'My happiness wasn't more important to you than your career.'

She pursed her lips and gave a nod. 'So you still blame me, then?'

'Completely,' he said without hesitation. 'And bitterly.'

She made herself laugh. 'Honesty was never our problem, was it?' But the unfairness of his blame burned through her. 'Why have you come to see me?'

He hauled in a breath, and an ache started up in the centre of her. 'Hearing about your father's death...' He glanced at her. 'Should I give you my condolences?'

She gave a quick shake of her head, ignoring the burn of tears at the backs of her eyes. Pretending her relationship with her father had been anything other than cold and combative would be ridiculous—especially with Jack.

'You don't miss him?'

His curiosity surprised her. 'I miss the *idea* of him.' She hadn't admitted that to another living soul. 'Now that he's gone there's no chance that our relationship can be fixed, no possibility of our differences being settled.' She lifted her chin. 'I didn't know I still harboured such hopes until after he died.'

Those blue eyes softened for a moment, and it felt as if the sun shone with a mad midday warmth rather than afternoon mildness.

'I am sorry for that,' he said.

She glanced away and the chill returned to the air. 'Thank you.'

The one thing the men in her life had in common was their inability to compromise. She couldn't forget that.

'So, hearing about my father's death...?' she prompted.

He enunciated his next words very carefully and she could almost see him weighing them.

'It started me thinking about endings.'

Caro flinched, throwing up her arm as if to ward off a blow. She couldn't help it.

'For pity's sake, Caro!' He planted his legs. 'This *can't* come as a surprise to you.'

He was talking about divorce, and it shouldn't come as a shock, but a howling started up inside her as something buried in a deep, secret place cracked, breaking with a pain she found hard to breathe through.

'Are you going to faint?'

Anger laced his words and it put steel back in her spine. 'Of course not.'

She lifted her chin, still struggling for breath as the knowledge filtered through her that just as she'd harboured secret hopes of reconciling with her father, so she had harboured similar hopes where Jack was concerned.

Really? How could you be so...optimistic?

She waved a hand in front of her face. The sooner those hopes were routed and dashed, the better. She would *never* trust this man with her heart again.

She lifted her chin another notch against the anger in his eyes. 'You'll have to forgive me. It's been something of a morning. We had the reading of my father's will yesterday. Things have been a little...fraught since.'

He rubbed a fist across his mouth, his eyes hooded. 'I'm sorry. If I'd known, I'd have given you another few weeks before approaching you with this.' His anger had faded but a hardness remained. His lips tightened as he glanced around. 'And I should've found a better place to discuss the issue than in the middle of Westminster Bridge.'

She had a feeling her reaction would have been the same, regardless of the where or when. 'You've just been to my flat?' she asked.

He nodded. 'I was going to catch the tube up to Bond Street.' It was the closest underground station to where she worked. 'But...'

'But the Jubilee Line is closed due to a suspicious package at Green Park Station,' she finished for him. It was why she was walking. That and the need for fresh air. 'I'm on my way to the flat now. We can walk. Or would you prefer to take a cab?'

Jack didn't like Caro's pallor. Rather than answer verbally, he hailed a passing cab and bundled her into it before the motorists on the bridge could start tooting their horns. The sooner this was over, the better.

Caro gave the driver her address and then settled in her seat and stared out of the side window. He did the same on his side of the cab, but he didn't notice the scenery. What rose up in his mind's eye was the image of Caro when he'd first laid eyes on her—and the punching need to kiss her that had almost overwhelmed him. A need that lingered with an off-putting urgency.

He gritted his teeth against it and risked a glance at her. She'd changed.

It's been five years, pal, what did you expect?

He hadn't expected to want her with the same ferocity now as he had back then.

He swallowed. She'd developed more gloss…more presence. She'd put on a bit of weight and it suited her. Five years ago he'd thought her physically perfect, but she looked even better now and every hormone in his body hollered that message out, loud and clear.

After five years his lust should have died a natural death, surely? If not that then it should at least have abated.

Hysterical laughter sounded in the back of his mind.

Caro suddenly swung to him and he prayed to God that he hadn't made some noise that had betrayed him.

'I hear you're running your own private investigation agency these days?'

'You hear correctly.'

Gold gleamed in the deep brown depths of her eyes. 'I hear it's very successful?'

'It's doing okay.'

A hint of a smile touched her lips. She folded her arms and settled back in her seat.

'Calculating the divorce settlement already, Caro?'

Very slowly her smile widened, and his traitorous heart thumped in response.

'Something like that,' she purred. 'Driver?' She leaned

forward. 'Could you let us out at the bakery just up here on the right? I need to buy cake.'

Cake? The Caro he knew didn't eat *cake*.

The Caro you knew was a figment of your imagination!

CHAPTER TWO

'JACK, I FIND myself in a bit of a pickle.'

Caro set a piece of cake on the coffee table in front of him, next to a steaming mug of coffee. She'd chosen a honey roll filled with a fat spiral of cream and dusted with glittering crystals of sugar.

Jack stared at it and frowned. 'Money?'

'No, not money.'

He picked up his coffee and glanced around. Her flat surprised him. It was so *small*. Still, it was comfortable. Her clothes weren't cheap knock-offs either. No, Caro looked as quietly opulent as ever.

She perched on the tub chair opposite him. 'You seem a little hung up on the money issue.'

Maybe because when they'd first met he hadn't had any. At least not compared to Caro's father.

Don't forget she was disinherited the moment she married you.

She hadn't so much as blinked an eye at the time. She'd said it didn't matter. She'd said that given her and her father's adversarial relationship it was inevitable. And he'd believed her.

He bit back a sigh. Who knew? Maybe she'd even believed the lie back then.

'Perhaps we should clear that issue up first,' she continued.

'You didn't have to buy cake on my account, you know.'

He wished she hadn't. Her small acts of courtesy had always taken him off guard and left him all at sea. They'd oozed class and made it plain that she'd had an education in grace and decorum—one that he'd utterly lacked. It had highlighted all the differences between them. He'd lived in fear of unknowingly breaking one of those unknown rules of hers and hurting her.

You hurt her anyway.

And she'd hurt him.

He pushed those thoughts away.

Caro gazed at him and just for a fraction of a second her lips twitched. 'I didn't buy cake on *your* account.'

She forked a mouthful of honey roll to her lips and while she didn't actually close her eyes in relish, he had a feeling that deep inside herself she did.

'This cake is very good. Jean-Pierre is a wizard.'

That must be the baker's name. She'd always taken pains to find out and then use people's names. He'd found that charming. Once. Now he saw it for what it was—a front.

'But if you don't want it please don't eat it.'

He leaned towards her, his frown deepening. 'You never used to eat cake.'

'I know! I can't believe what I was missing.' Her eyes twinkled for a moment and her lips lifted, but then she sobered and her face became void of emotion. 'But people change. Five years ago you wouldn't have been at all concerned with the threat of me taking you for half of all you owned.'

He'd worked hard during the last five years to make a success of his security and private investigation firm. Such a success, in fact, that if he were still alive even Caro's father would sit up and take notice. He sat back. It seemed he'd been making money while Caro had been eating cake. It summed them up perfectly.

'Five years ago I didn't have anything worth taking, Caro.'

She looked as if she might disagree with him, but after a moment she simply shook her head. 'Let me waste no further time in putting your mind at rest. I don't want your money, Jack. I never did. You should know that yesterday I was named as my father's sole beneficiary.'

Whoa! He straightened. Okay...

'As we're still married I expect you could make a successful claim on the estate. Do you wish to?'

His hands clenched to fists. 'Absolutely not!'

She shrugged and ate more cake. '*You* haven't changed that much, then. Earlier today I'd have staked the entire estate on you not wanting a penny.'

Damn straight! But her odd belief in him coupled with her utter lack of concern that he could have taken her for a financial ride pricked him. 'So, this *pickle* you're in?'

She set her plate down, clasping her hands to her knees. 'Jack, I'd like to hire you for a rather...delicate job.'

He tried to hide his shock.

'But before we continue I'd like an assurance of your discretion and confidentiality.'

'You wouldn't have asked me that once.' She'd have taken it for granted.

'True, but when you walked away from our marriage you proved my trust in you was misplaced. So I'm asking for an assurance now.'

He glanced down to find his knuckles had turned white. He unclenched his hands and took a deep breath. 'I should warn you that if this "delicate" matter of yours involves murder or threats of violence then I'm honour-bound to—'

'Don't be ridiculous! Of course it doesn't. Don't take me for a fool. I'm a lot of things, but I'm not a fool.'

He bit back something very rude. Bending down, he

pulled the divorce papers he'd had drawn up from his satchel and slapped them onto the coffee table.

'I don't want to do a job for you, Caroline. I simply want you to sign the divorce papers and then never to clap eyes on you again.'

Her head rocked back, hurt gleamed in her eyes, and that soft, composed mouth of hers looked so suddenly vulnerable he hated himself for his outburst.

She rose, pressing her hands to her waist. 'That was unnecessarily rude.'

It had been.

She glanced at her watch. 'As interesting as this trip down memory lane has been, I'm afraid I'm going to have to ask you to leave. I have to be somewhere shortly.' She picked up the papers. 'I'll have my lawyer read over these and then we can get divorce proceedings underway.'

'And you'll draw the process out for as long as you can to punish me for refusing this job?' he drawled, rising too.

Her chin came up. 'I'll do nothing of the sort. You can have your divorce, Jack. The sooner the better as far as I'm concerned.'

A weight pressed down on him, trying to crush his chest. It made no sense. She was promising him exactly what he wanted.

With an oath, he sat again.

Caro's eyes widened. 'What are you doing?'

'Finishing my coffee and cake. Sit, Caro.'

'Really, Jack! I—'

'It's hard, seeing you again.'

Her tirade halted before it could begin. She swallowed, her eyes throbbing with the same old confusion and hurt that burned through him.

The intensity of emotion this woman could still arouse disturbed him. It was as if all the hard work he'd put in over the last five years to forget her and get his life back on track could be shattered with nothing more than a word or a look. He couldn't let that happen. He straightened. He *wouldn't* let that happen.

'No woman has ever made me as happy as you did.' He sipped his coffee. 'Or as miserable. I wasn't expecting the lid to be lifted on all those old memories. It's made me... testy—and that's why I said what I said. It was a mean-spirited thing to say. I'm sorry.'

Finally she sat. 'It doesn't make it any less true, though.'

'It's not true. Not really.' He didn't look at her as he said it. 'I expect things will be more comfortable once we put this initial meeting behind us.'

'I expect you're right.'

She frowned suddenly and glanced a little to his left. With a swift movement she reached down and picked up... *His cufflinks!*

Jack bit back a curse. They must have fallen from his case when he'd pulled out the divorce papers. He could tell from the way her nostrils suddenly flared that she recognised the box. They'd been her wedding present to him when he'd said he'd prefer not to wear a ring—rose gold with a tiny sapphire in each that she'd claimed were nearly as blue as his eyes. He'd treasured them.

His glance went to her left hand and his gut clenched when he saw that she no longer wore her wedding ring.

Without a word she handed the box back to him. 'You really ought to be more careful when you're pulling things from your bag.'

He shoved the box back into the depths of the satchel. 'Tell me about this job you'd like me to do for you.'

He didn't owe her for her signature on their divorce papers, but if by doing this he could end things between them on a more pleasant note, then perhaps he'd find the closure he so desperately needed.

'And, yes, you have my word that I will never reveal

to another soul what you're about to tell me—unless you give me leave to.'

She stared at him, as if trying to sum him up. With a start he realised she was trying to decide whether to trust him or not.

'You don't trust my word of honour?'

'If you're after any kind of revenge on me, what I'm about to tell you will provide you with both the means and the method.'

He didn't want revenge. He'd never wanted revenge. He just wanted to move on with his life.

And to kiss her.

He stiffened. *Ridiculous!* He pushed that thought—and the associated images—firmly from his mind.

'I have no desire to hurt you, Caro. I hope your life is long and happy. Would it ease your mind if I didn't ask you to sign the divorce papers until after I've completed this job of yours?'

She leaned back, folding her arms. 'Why is this divorce so important to you now?'

'I want to remarry.'

She went deathly still. 'I see.'

She didn't. It wasn't as though he had a particular woman in mind, waiting in the wings, but he didn't correct the assumption she'd obviously made. It was beyond time that he severed this last tie with Caro. He should have done it before now, but he'd been busy establishing his company. Now it was thriving, he was a self-made success, and it was time to put the past to rest.

If Caro thought he'd fallen in love again, then all well and good. It would provide another layer of distance between them. And while he shouldn't need it—not after five years—he found himself clinging to every scrap of defence he could find.

'Well…' She crossed her legs. 'I wish you well, Jack.'

She even sounded as if she meant it. That shouldn't chafe at him.

'Tell me about this job you want to hire me for.'

He bit into the cake in an effort to ignore the turmoil rolling through him and looked across at her when she didn't speak. She glanced at the cake and then at him. It made him slow down and savour the taste of the sweet sponge, the smooth cream and the tiny crunch of sugar.

He frowned. 'This is really good.'

Finally she smiled. 'I know.'

He'd have laughed at her smugness, but his gut had clenched up too tightly at her smile.

She leaned forward, suddenly all business. 'I'm now a director at Vertu, the silver and decorative arts division at Richardson's.'

'Right.' He didn't let on that he knew that. When they'd married she'd been only a junior administrator at the auction house.

'Yesterday I placed into my father's safe a very beautiful and rather valuable snuffbox to show to a client this morning.'

'Is that usual?'

She raised one elegant shoulder. 'When selected customers request a private viewing, Richardson's is always happy to oblige.'

'Right.'

'When I went to retrieve the snuffbox this morning it wasn't there.'

He set down his now clean plate, his every sense sharpening. 'You have my attention.'

'I put it in the safe myself, prior to the reading of my father's will.'

'Which took place where?'

'In my father's study—the same room as the safe.'

He remembered that study. He nodded. 'Go on.'

Her expression was composed, but she was twisting the thin gold bangle on her arm round and round—a sure sign of agitation.

'The fact that I am sole beneficiary came as a very great shock to both Barbara and I.'

He raised an eyebrow. 'Your father and Barbara have remained married all this time?'

'Yes. I believe she loved him.'

Jack wasn't so charitable, but he kept his mouth shut.

'When Barbara retired to her room, the lawyer gave me this letter from my father.' She rose, removed a letter from her purse and handed it to him. 'More cake?'

He shook his head and read the letter. Then he folded it up again, tapping it against his knee. 'He thought she was stealing from him.'

Knowing Roland Fielding, he'd have kept a very tight rein on the purse strings. What kind of debts could his lovely young wife have accrued that would have her risking being caught red-handed with stolen goods?

'He was wrong. It wasn't Barbara who was pilfering those bits and pieces. It was Paul.'

'Paul is still working…?' He blew out a breath. 'Shouldn't he have retired by now?'

She pressed her hands together. 'My father wasn't a man who liked change.'

That was the understatement of the year.

'And, to be fair, I don't think Paul is either. I suspect the thought of retirement horrifies him.'

The bangle was pushed up her arm and twisted with such force he thought she'd hurt herself.

'He and Barbara have never warmed to each other.'

'And you're telling me this because…?'

'Because Paul was putting all those things he'd taken—'

'Stolen,' he corrected.

'He was putting them away for *me*.'

Jack pressed his fingers to his eyes.

'He was as convinced as I that I'd be totally written out of the will. He thought that I might need them.'

He pulled his hand away. 'Caro, I—'

She held up a hand and he found himself pulling to a halt.

'If Barbara finds out why my father wrote her out of the will and that Paul is responsible, she'll want him charged. I can't let that happen—surely you can see that, Jack? Paul was doing it for *me*.'

'You didn't ask him to!'

'That's beside the point. I know Barbara has been wronged, and I mean to make it up to her. I intend to split the estate with her fifty-fifty.'

He let the air whistle between his teeth. 'That's very generous. You could probably buy her silence for a couple of million.'

'It's not generous and I don't want to "buy her silence"! I want her to have half of everything. Half is certainly far more than I ever expected to get, and I'm fairly certain she won't begrudge me it.'

Was she?

'Where does the snuffbox come in?'

She hauled in a deep breath. 'During the middle of the night Barbara removed the jewellery from the safe. As it's all hers she had every right to remove it.'

He straightened. 'Except the snuffbox went missing at the same time?'

She nodded. 'When I asked her about it she claimed to not have seen it.'

'But you don't believe her?'

Her fingers started to twist that bangle again. 'She was upset yesterday—understandably. She wasn't thinking clearly. I know she wouldn't do anything to deliberately hurt me, but my father has treated her so very shabbily and

I suspect she panicked. I fear she's painted herself into a corner and now doesn't know how to return the snuffbox while still maintaining face.'

'And you want me to recover said snuffbox without her being aware of it?'

'Yes, please.'

It should be a piece of cake. 'What happens if the snuffbox isn't restored to Richardson's?'

'I'll lose my job.' She let out a long, slow breath. 'I'll never work in the industry again.'

He suddenly saw what she meant by revenge. Her job had been more important to her than starting a family with him. Now he had the potential to help destroy all the credibility she'd worked so hard to gain in one fell swoop. The irony!

'Worse than that, though…'

He lifted a disbelieving eyebrow. 'Worse than you losing your job?'

Her gaze didn't waver. 'Richardson's prides itself on its honesty and transparency. If I don't return that snuffbox there will be a police investigation.'

'The scandal would be shocking,' he agreed.

'For heaven's sake, Jack—who cares about the scandal?' She shot to her feet, hands on hips. 'Barbara does *not* deserve to go to jail for this. And Paul doesn't deserve to get into trouble either.'

They were both thieves!

'This mess is of my father's making. He forces people into impossible situations and makes them desperate. I won't let that happen this time around. I won't!' She pulled in a breath and met his gaze squarely. 'I mean to make this right, Jack. Will you help me?'

He stared at her. This woman had dashed all his most tightly held dreams. Five years ago she'd ground them underfoot as if they hadn't mattered one iota. The remembered pain could still make him wake up in a lather of sweat in the middle of the night.

He opened his mouth.

His shoulders slumped.

'Yes.'

Since when had he ever been able to say no to this woman?

Caro tiptoed past the disused pantry, and the butler's and housekeeper's offices—both of which had been vacant for as long as she could remember. The kitchen stretched all along the other side of these old rooms, with the small sitting room Paul used as his office on the other side of the kitchen. She'd chosen this route so as to not disturb him, but she tiptoed just the same. The man had bat-like hearing.

Lifting the latch on the back door, she stepped out into the darkness of the garden, just as she'd promised Jack she would. She glanced around, wondering in what corner he lurked and watched her from. Feigning indifference, she lifted her head and gazed up at the night sky, but if there were any stars to be seen they were currently obscured by low cloud.

She knew from past experience, though, that one rarely saw stars here—the city lights kept the stars at bay and, as her father had always told her, star-gazing never got anybody anywhere in life.

'Tell that to astronomers and astronauts,' she murmured under her breath.

'Miss Caroline?'

Paul appeared in the kitchen doorway. Caro wiped suddenly damp palms down her skirt. No one was supposed to see her out here.

'Dinner will be ready in ten minutes.'

She turned towards him. 'Are you sure there isn't anything I can help you with?'

'Certainly not.'

In his youth, Paul had trained as a chef. With the help of an army of maids, who came in twice a week, Paul had kept this house running single-handed for nearly thirty years. Although, as her father had rarely entertained, the position hadn't been a demanding one.

When she was a child she'd spent most of the year away at boarding school. So for nearly fifteen years—before her father had married Barbara—it had just been her father and Paul rattling around together in this big old house.

Some sixth sense—a hyper-awareness that flashed an odd tingling warmth across her skin—informed her that Jack stood in the shadows of a large rhododendron bush to her left. It took all her strength not to turn towards it. She'd wanted to let Paul in on their plan—his help would have been invaluable, and for a start she wouldn't be tiptoeing through the house in the dark, unlatching doors—but Jack had sworn her to secrecy.

And as he happened to be the surveillance expert…

She reached Paul's side and drew him to the right, away from Jack, pointing up at the steepled roofline. 'Did you know that one night, when I was ten, I walked all the way along that roofline?'

Paul glanced up and pressed a hand to his chest. 'Good grief!'

'I'd read a book about a cat burglar who'd made his way across London by jumping from roof to roof.'

'Tell me you didn't?' Paul groaned.

She laughed. From the corner of her eye she saw a shadow slip through the door. 'Mrs Thomas-Fraser's Alsatian dog started up such a racket that I hightailed it back to my room before the alarm could be raised.'

'You could've fallen! If I'd know about that back then it would have taken ten years off my life.'

Caro shook her head. 'I can hardly believe now that I

ever dared such a thing. Seriously, Paul, who'd have children?'

He chuckled and patted her shoulder. 'You were a delight.'

To Paul, perhaps, but never to her father.

'Come along.' He drew her into the house. 'You'll catch a chill if you're not careful.'

She wanted to laugh. A *chill*? It was summer! He was such a fusspot.

'I don't suppose I could talk you into joining Barbara and I for dinner?'

'You suppose right. It wouldn't be seemly.'

Seriously—he belonged in an England of a bygone age. 'Oh, I should go and lock the other door.'

'I'll take care of it.'

To insist would raise his suspicions. 'Paul, do we have any headache tablets?'

He pointed to a cupboard.

When he'd gone, she popped two tablets and unlatched the kitchen door—just in case. This sneaking around business was not for the faint-hearted.

Barbara sliced into her fillet of sole. 'Caroline, do I need to remind you that if your father had *wanted* me to inherit any portion of his estate, he'd have named me in his will?'

Caro swallowed. 'You only call me Caroline when you're cross with me.'

Barbara's gaze lifted.

'I didn't know he was going to do this, Barbara. I swear. I wish he'd left it all to you.'

Her stepmother's gaze lowered. She fiddled with the napkin in her lap.

'And if he *had* left it all to you,' Caro continued, 'I know you'd have made sure that I received a portion of it.'

'Of course—but that's different.'

'How?'

'This money has been in your family for generations. It's your birthright.'

Twaddle. 'I mean to give Paul a generous legacy too. He'll need a pension to see him through retirement.'

'That man's a rogue. I wouldn't be surprised if he hasn't weaselled enough bonuses out of your father over the years to see him through *two* retirements.'

'Even if he has, he'll have earned every penny.'

The other woman's gaze narrowed. 'You and your father—you never could find any common ground. You didn't understand each other. You never brought out the best in him. And—you'll have to forgive me for saying this, Caro, darling—you were never at your best when you were around him either.'

Caro opened her mouth to dispute that, then shot her stepmother a half smile. How could Barbara still defend him after he'd treated her so shabbily? 'Okay, I'll concede that point.'

Where was Jack at this very moment? Was he in Barbara's room, scanning its every hiding place? Had he found the snuffbox yet?

The thought of Jack prowling about upstairs filled her with the oddest adrenaline rush—similar to the one she'd had as a ten-year-old, when she'd inched across the mansion's roof. It made her realise how boring her life had become.

Not boring! Predictable.

She stuck out her chin. She *liked* predictable.

'Caro?'

She snapped her attention back to Barbara.

'You had the oddest look on your face.'

Jack had *always* had that effect on her. 'Just trying to work out the morass that was my father's mind. *And* yours.'

'Mine?' Barbara set her fork down. 'Whatever do you mean?'

'If our situations were reversed you'd be happy to share my father's money with me. Why aren't you happy for me to share it with you?'

Barbara picked up her clutch purse and rose. 'I find my appetite has quite fled. I really don't wish to discuss this any further.'

Caro nearly choked on her sole. *Jack!* If Barbara should happen to find him in her room…

'Please don't go! I—' She took a hasty sip of water. 'I'm tired of feeling lonely in this house.'

Barbara's face softened. She lowered herself back to her chair. 'Very well—but no more talk about your father and his money.'

'Deal.' Caro did her best to eat her new potatoes and green beans when all the while her stomach churned.

Please be careful, Jack.

She glanced over at her stepmother. 'Paul tells me you've barely been out of the house lately? Don't you think you should get out more? Being cooped up like this can't be good for you.'

Barbara sent her a tiny smile. 'On that subject we happen to be in complete agreement, darling. Lady Sedgewick has invited me down to their place in Kent this very weekend. She's having a house party. I thought I might accept her invitation.'

'Oh, yes, you should! The Sedgewicks are a lovely family. I was at school with Olivia. Do go. You'll have a lovely time.'

It was beyond time that Barbara started enjoying herself again.

Caro tiptoed into her room ninety minutes later. 'Jack?' she whispered into the darkness, before clicking on the light.

Her room was empty. She tried to crush the kernel of disappointment that lodged in her chest. He hadn't said that he'd wait for her in her room. She'd just assumed he would. She checked her phone for a text.

Nothing.

Maybe he'd sent her an email?

She was about to retrieve her laptop when a shadow on the far side of the wardrobe fluttered and Jack detached himself from the darkness. Her mouth went dry and her heart pounded. She tried to tell herself it was because he'd startled her, but she had a feeling her reaction was even more primal than fear.

Dressed in close-fitting jeans and a black turtleneck sweater, Jack looked dark, dangerous and disreputable.

Delicious, some part of her mind pronounced.

She wanted to tell herself to stop being ridiculous, but 'delicious' described him perfectly. What *was* ridiculous was the fact that every atom of her being should swell towards him now, with a hunger that robbed her of breath.

But why was it ridiculous—even after five years? It had always been this way between them.

Yes, but five years ago he'd broken her heart. *That* should make a difference.

She lifted her chin. It did. It made a huge difference. Obviously just not to her body's reaction, that was all.

She pulled in a breath. 'Well…?'

She held that breath as she waited for him to produce the snuffbox. She'd get her snuffbox and he'd get his divorce, and then he could marry this new woman of his and they'd all be happy.

He lifted a finger to his lips and cocked his head, as if listening to something.

Actually, she had serious doubts on the happiness aspect. She had serious doubts that Jack was in love.

Not your business.

Jack moved in close, leaned towards her, and for a moment she thought he meant to kiss her. Her heart surged to the left and then to the right, but he merely whispered in her ear.

'Go and check the corridor.'

His warm breath caressed her ear, making her recall the way he'd used to graze it gently with his teeth…and how it had driven her wild. The breath jammed in her chest. She turned her head a fraction, until their lips were so close their breaths mingled. She ached for him to kiss her. She ached to feel his arms about her, curving her body to his. She ached to move with him in a union that had always brought her bliss.

His lips twisted and a sardonic light burned in the backs of his eyes. 'Caro, I didn't come up here to play.'

His warm breath trailing across her lips made her nipples peak before the import of his words hit her. From somewhere she found the strength to step back, humiliation burning her cheeks.

'You should be so lucky,' she murmured, going to the door and checking the corridor outside, doing all she could to hide how rubbery her legs had become. 'All clear,' she said in a low voice, turning back and closing the door behind her. 'What did you hear?'

He merely shrugged. 'It's better to be safe than sorry.'

She did her best not to notice the breadth of his shoulders in that body-hugging turtleneck or the depth of his chest. 'Do you also have a balaclava?'

He pulled one from the waistband of his jeans.

She rolled her eyes and shook her head, as if having him here in her bedroom didn't faze her in the least.

'Did you get it?' She kept her voice low, even though Barbara's room was at the other end of the house and Paul's was another floor up, and he used the back stairs to get to it anyway. Nobody would be passing her door unless they'd come deliberately looking for her.

'No.'

'No?' She moved in closer to whisper, 'What do you mean, no?' She had to move away again fast—his familiar scent was threatening to overwhelm her.

'If it'd been in that room I would've found it.'

She didn't doubt him—not when he used that tone of voice. Damn! Damn! *Damn!*

She strode to the window, hands clenched. 'Where can it be?'

'Did she have a handbag or a purse with her at dinner?'

Caro swung around. 'A little clutch purse.' In hindsight, that *had* been odd. She hadn't had any plans to go out this evening, so why bring a purse to dinner in her own house?

'It's in there, then.'

'So…what now? You can't creep into her room with her in it.'

'It wouldn't be ideal,' he agreed, moving to the window and raising it. In one lithe movement he slid outside.

'So?'

'So now I go home and ponder for a while.'

She should have known it wouldn't be that easy. She planted her hands on her hips. 'Jack, you *can* use the front door. Everyone else is in bed. No one will see you.'

'But you've made me eager to try out your cat burglar method.'

So he'd heard her conversation with Paul about that…

She leaned out to peer at him. 'Be careful.'

He moved so quickly that she wouldn't have been able to retreat even if the gleam in his eyes *hadn't* held her captive. His lips brushed her hair, his breath tickling her ear again. She froze, heart pounding, as she waited for him to murmur some final instruction to her.

Instead his teeth grazed her ear, making her gasp and sparking her every nerve ending to life.

CHAPTER THREE

'I *KNEW THAT* was what you were remembering earlier. And your remembering made *me* remember.'

Jack's voice was so full of heat and desire it made Caro sway. 'So…' Her voice hitched. 'That's my fault too, is it?'

Jack, it seemed, considered everything to be her fault.

He ignored that to lean in closer again and inhale deeply. 'You smell as good as you ever did, Caro.'

She loathed herself for not being able to step away.

He glanced down at her and laughed—but it wasn't a pretty sound, full of anger and scorn as it was. She sensed, though, that the anger and scorn were directed as much at himself as they were at her.

He trailed a lazy finger along the vee of her blouse. Her skin goosepimpled and puckered, burning at his touch with a ferocity that made her knees wobble.

'If I had a mind to,' he murmured, 'I think I could convince you to invite me to stay.'

And the moment she did would he laugh at her and leave?

The old Jack would never have enjoyed humiliating her. And yet that finger continued trailing a tantalising path in the small vee of bare flesh at her throat. Heat gathered under her skin to burn fiercely at the centre of her.

She made herself swallow. 'If I had my heart set on you staying, Jack, you'd stay.'

That finger stopped. He gripped her chin, forcing her gaze to meet the cold light in his. 'Are you sure of that?'

She stared into those eyes and spoke with an honesty that frightened her. 'Utterly convinced.'

Air whistled between his teeth.

'You want me as much as you ever did,' she said. And, God help her, the knowledge made her stomach swoop and twirl.

'And you want me.' The words ground out of him from behind a tight jaw.

'But that wasn't enough the last time around,' she forced herself to say. 'And I see no evidence to the contrary that it'd be any different for us now either.'

She found herself abruptly released.

Jack straightened. 'Right—Barbara. Now I've had time to think.'

He'd *what*? All this time his mind had been working? It was all *she'd* been able to do to remain upright!

'If she's keeping that trinket so close then she obviously has plans for it.'

'Or is she looking for the first available opportunity to throw it into the Thames and get rid of incriminating evidence?'

He shook his head. 'Barbara is a woman with an eye on the main chance.'

She found herself itching to slap him. 'You don't even *know* her. You're wrong. She's—'

'I've come across women like her before.'

Did he class Caro as one of those women?

'And I'm the expert here. You've hired me to do a job and we'll do it my way—understand?'

She lifted her hands in surrender. 'Right. Fine.'

'Can you get us an invitation to this country party of Lady Sedgewick's?'

She blinked. 'You *heard* that?'

'I thoroughly searched Barbara's room and your father's study, as well as checking the safe.'

She stared at him. 'You opened the safe?'

He nodded.

'But you don't know the combination.'

He waved that away as if it were of no consequence. 'And on my way to the study I eavesdropped on what might prove to be a key piece of information. By the way, it's a nice touch to keep letting Barbara think you mean to give her half of the estate. Hopefully it'll prevent her from feeling too desperate and doing something stupid—like trying to sell something that doesn't belong to her.'

Caro's fingers dug into the window frame. 'It's *not* a ploy! I fully intend to give her half.'

'Lady Sedgewick?'

She blew out a breath and tried to rein in her temper. 'I can certainly ensure that *I* get an invitation.'

'And me?'

'On what pretext?' She folded her arms. '*Oh, and by the way, Lady S, my soon-to-be ex-husband is in town—may I bring him along?* That won't fly.'

He pursed his lips, his eyes suddenly unreadable. 'What if you told her we were attempting a reconciliation?'

A great lump of resistance rose through her.

'Think about it, Caro. Your snuffbox goes missing and then the very next weekend Barbara—who's apparently hardly left the house in months—makes plans to attend a country house party. Ten to one she has a prospective buyer lined up and is planning to do the deal this weekend.'

Hell, blast and damnation!

'This is becoming so much more complicated than it was supposed to.'

'If you don't like that plan there are two other strategies we can fall back on.'

She leaned towards him eagerly. 'And they are…?'

'We storm into Barbara's room now, seize her purse and take the snuffbox back by force.'

Her heart sank. Very slowly she shook her head. 'If we do that she'll hate me forever.'

'And that's a problem because…?'

'I know you won't understand, but she's *family*.'

He was silent for a moment. 'That was a low blow.'

His eyes had turned dark and his face had turned to stone. Her heart started to burn. 'I didn't mean that the way you've taken it.'

'No?'

Jack had grown up in Australia's foster care system. It hadn't been a brutal childhood, but from what she could tell it had been a lonely one.

She glanced down at her hand, shaking her head. 'But you won't believe me and I'm too tired to justify myself. Let's just say that confronting Barbara like that is a last-ditch plan.' Exhaustion stretched through her. 'Jack, shouldn't we be having this conversation inside?' Him falling off the roof would top off a truly terrible day.

'I'm perfectly comfortable where I am.'

Which was as far away from her and her world as he could get at this current moment. 'Fine. And this second alternative of yours?'

'You go to your employer in the morning and explain that the snuffbox is missing.'

And lose her job? Lose her professional reputation and the respect of everyone in her industry? Through no fault of her own? *No, thank you!* Besides, if the police investigation—and she had no doubt that there would be one—traced the snuffbox back to Barbara…

She shuddered and abruptly cut off that thought.

'I can see you're even less enthused about that option.'

She hated the tone of voice he used. She hated his irksome sense of superiority. She hated the opinion he had of her.

That last thought made her blink.

'So, will you get us an invitation to the Sedgewicks'?'

She gave a stiff nod. 'Yes.'

'Good girl.'

'Don't patronise me.'

'And it'll be best,' he continued, as if she hadn't spoken, 'if Barbara doesn't find out that we're planning to be there.'

'Hmm…awkward…'

He raised an eyebrow.

'But doable,' she mumbled. She folded her arms and glared at him. 'You *do* know we'll have to share a room at Lady Sedgewick's?'

Everyone would take it for granted that they were sleeping together.

He gave a low laugh. 'Afraid you won't be able to resist me, Caro?'

Yes! 'Don't be ridiculous.'

'Or are you afraid I won't be able to control myself?'

'If you can't,' she returned tartly, 'then I suggest you rethink your plans to remarry.'

'Never.'

A black pit opened up in her chest. The sooner Jack was out of her life for good, the better.

She flinched when he ran a finger down her cheek. 'Never fear, sweet pea. While your charms are many and manifold, they were *never* worth the price I paid.'

She flinched again at his words, and when she next looked up he was gone.

'Right. A weekend in the country. Very jolly.'

She closed the window and locked it. And then, for the first time ever, she drew the curtains.

* * *

'Was it difficult to swing the invitation?'

'Not at all.'

It was early Saturday morning and she was sitting beside Jack in his hired luxury saloon car. It all felt so right and normal she had to keep reminding herself that it was neither of those things. Far from it. She still didn't know how they were going to negotiate sharing a bedroom. She kept pushing the thought from her mind—there was no point endlessly worrying about it—but it kept popping back again.

'Tell me how you managed it.'

So she told him how on Thursday she'd 'just happened' to bump into her old schoolfriend Olivia Sedgewick at a place she knew Olivia favoured for lunch, and they'd ended up dining together.

The house party in Kent had come up in their idle chit-chat, and Caro had confided her concerns that this would be Barbara's first social engagement since Roland had died. A bit later she'd mentioned meeting up with Jack again after all these years, and how the spark was still there but they were wanting to keep a low profile in London in case things didn't work out.

Of course things weren't going to work out.

'And…?' Jack prompted.

'Well, from there she came up with the brilliant plan of inviting us down for the weekend. We'll get a chance for some out-of-London couple time, with the added bonus that I can keep an eye on Barbara too.'

He laughed. 'You mean you deviously planted the idea in her mind and she ran with it!'

She shrugged. 'She's a lovely person. It wasn't hard.'

'It was masterfully done. I should hire you for my firm.'

He didn't mean it, but his praise washed over her with a warmth that made her settle back a little more snugly in her seat. 'I fear I'm not cut out for a life of subterfuge and undercover intrigue. I don't know how you manage it without getting an ulcer.'

His chuckle warmed her even more than his praise had.

'Barbara has no idea that we're coming?' he asked.

'None whatsoever. I told Olivia I didn't want Barbara thinking she was being a burden to me. I asked her if we could say that we'd met up only last night and she invited us down to her parents' for the weekend on the spur of the moment.'

'Excellent. I've had her tailed over the last few days, but there's nothing suspicious to report. It appears you've not had any suspicious visitors for the last couple of days either.'

'Oh, well…that's good.'

And at that point they ran out of conversation.

'I've…um…taken most of next week off as leave from work.' Just in case they had to do more sleuthing.

'Right.'

She itched to ask him about the woman he had back home in Australia—the one he planned to marry. How had they met? What was she like? Was she very beautiful? Did they set each other alight the way she and he once had? Or…?

She folded her arms. Or was this other woman simply a brood mare? A means to an end?

She couldn't ask any of that, of course. What Jack did with his life was no longer any concern of hers. It was none of her business.

She lifted her chin. 'We're having a glorious summer so far.' She gestured at the blue sky and the sunshine pouring in the windows.

At the same time he said, 'I take it you're not seeing anyone at the moment?'

She stiffened. None of *his* business. 'What does that have to do with anything?'

He sent her a sidelong glance, his lips twisting. 'Let's just say it could be awkward for all concerned if we happened to run into your current squeeze in Kent.'

She laughed. It was either that or cry. 'That would be terribly bad form indeed. We're safe, Jack. I have no current paramour.'

Unlike him.

For heaven's sake, let it go!

She shifted on her seat. 'You'd better fill me in on the plan.' She bit her lip. 'You *do* have a plan, don't you?'

'My plan is to watch and listen. I'm good at my job, Caro. And I'm very good at reading people.'

He'd been terrible at reading *her*.

'I can nose out a fishy situation at fifty paces.'

'Fine, but… What am *I* supposed to do?'

'Be your usual charming self.'

From anyone else that would have sounded like a compliment.

'Don't forget our cover story. We're supposed to be attempting a reconciliation.'

She had no hope of forgetting *that*.

'So the odd lingering look and a bit of hand-holding won't go astray.'

She swallowed, her mouth suddenly dry and her pulse suddenly wild. 'Absolutely.'

'And just be generally attentive.'

To him? Or to what was going on around them?

'Take your cues from me.'

Suddenly all she wanted to do was return to her tiny flat, crawl into bed and pull the covers over her head.

He sent her another sidelong glance and then reached out to squeeze her hand. 'Whenever you feel your resolve slipping think about the consequences of not getting that snuffbox back.'

Worst-case scenario? She'd lose her job with no hope

of another and she'd be visiting Barbara in jail. She shuddered. No, no, *no*. She couldn't let that happen.

She squeezed his hand back. 'Excellent advice.'

'With the two of you, that brings our numbers up to a merry dozen,' said Cynthia—Lady Sedgewick—leading Caro and Jack into the drawing room, where she introduced them to several of the other guests. 'Olivia should be here any moment. Oh, and *look*, Barbie dear…' Cynthia cooed as Barbara walked in from the terrace. 'Did you know that Caro and Jack were joining us this weekend?'

Barbara pulled up short, her mouth dropping open.

'It was all very last-minute,' Caro said, going across to kiss her stepmother's cheek. 'I never had a chance to tell you.'

Jack moved across to shake Barbara's hand. 'Lovely to see you again, Barbara.'

For an awful moment, Caro had the oddest feeling that Barbara meant to snub Jack completely, but at the last moment she clasped his hand briefly before slipping her arm through Caro's and drawing her away.

'Why don't I help you to unpack? You can fill me in—' she glared over her shoulder at Jack '—on all the gossip.'

'I've put them in the room next to yours, Barbie.'

'I'll see that Caro's safely settled.' With that, Barbara led Caro out of the drawing room and up a rather grand staircase.

'Doesn't it set your teeth on edge, the way she calls you Barbie?' Caro asked in a low voice.

'It's just her way. More pressing at the moment is the question of what you're doing here with Jack?'

'Ah…'

'No, no.' Barbara held up her free hand. 'Wait till we've gained the privacy of your room.'

So arm in arm they climbed the stairs in silence and

walked along the grand gallery with all its family portraits until they reached the wing housing their bedrooms.

'Are you completely out of your mind?' Barbara demanded, the moment she'd closed the bedroom door behind them. 'That man broke your heart into a thousand little pieces and stamped all over it without so much as a by-your-leave. Have you taken leave of your senses?'

Caro opened her mouth. Closing it again, she slumped down to the blanket box sitting at the end of the bed—which, thankfully, wasn't some huge big four-poster monstrosity.

'How long?' Barbara asked.

She and Jack should have discussed their cover story in a little more detail. She decided to go with the truth. 'Only a few days. I… I didn't know how to tell you.'

'A few *days*! And already you're spending the weekend with him?'

Caro grimaced at how that sounded. 'Well, technically we *are* still married. And I thought coming down here this weekend would…would…' She trailed off, wishing this all felt as make-believe as it actually was.

Barbara sat beside her and reached out to halt the constant twisting of her bangle. 'Caro, darling, I know your father's death came as a very great shock to you, but do you *really* think this is the best way to deal with it?'

'You think I'm making a mistake?'

'Don't you?'

Her shoulders sagged. 'You're probably right. Why are we so attracted to the things that are bad for us?'

Barbara opened her mouth and then closed it, her shoulders sagging too. 'It's a very strange thing,' she agreed.

'Seriously, though,' Caro said, strangely close to tears, 'what hope does a woman like me have of holding the attention of a man like Jack?'

Barbara stiffened. 'Don't you *dare* sell yourself short! Any man would be lucky to have you.'

Her stepmother's concern warmed her to her very bones. Surely Barbara wouldn't steal from her? She'd just got herself into a fix and she didn't know how to extricate herself. That was all.

She met Barbara's gaze. 'You really do care about me, don't you?'

'Of course I do. What on earth would have you thinking otherwise?'

'Father.'

'Look, darling, the will—'

'Not the will. I meant before that. All Father's disapproval and disappointment where I was concerned.' She lifted a shoulder and then let it drop. 'You must've resented all the…disharmony I caused.'

Barbara patted Caro's hand. 'I was married to your father, and I loved him, but it doesn't follow that we agreed on every point.'

She stared at the other woman, wondering what on earth that meant.

'And now Jack's back in your life…'

Not for long.

'And you think the spark is still there?'

She huffed out a breath. 'No doubt about that…'

Barbara went to Caro's suitcase and flung it open, rummaged through its contents. 'Here.' She pulled out a pair of tight white Capri pants and a fitted blouse in vivid blue. 'Slip into these. They'll be perfect for croquet on the lawn later.'

Caro grimaced. 'There's nowhere to hide in that outfit.' She normally wore a long tunic top with those Capris. 'And there's no denying I've put on a little weight in the last few months.'

'Despite what torture we women put ourselves through

in the name of beauty, men appreciate a few curves on a woman. Jack won't be able to take his eyes off you.'

Barbara smiled at her and Caro found herself smiling back. Dressing to attract Jack suddenly seemed like the best idea in the world.

And fun.

Besides, *he* was the one who had insisted on their ridiculous cover story. She was only doing what he'd insisted was necessary. No harm in enjoying herself in the process…

Jack watched Caro ready herself to take her next shot and had to run a finger around the collar of his shirt when she gave that cute little tush of hers an extra wiggle. He wasn't the only man admiring her…uh…feminine attributes. His hand tightened about his croquet mallet. It was all he could do not to frogmarch her up to the house and order her to put on something less revealing.

Except what she was wearing was perfectly respectable! The only bare flesh on display was from mid-calf to ankle, where her Capris ended and her sand shoes started. Those sand shoes made her look seriously cute. The only problem was they kept drawing his attention to the tantalising curves of her calves.

Who was he trying to kid? Her entire ensemble made her look cute. Not to mention desirable.

Barbara trailed over to him, a glass of fruit punch dangling elegantly from her fingers. 'Caro is looking well, isn't she?'

He couldn't lie. 'She's looking sensational.' But then he'd *always* thought she looked sensational.

Some things never change.

Barbara smiled up at him pleasantly. 'May I give you a word of warning, darling?'

'Of course.'

'If you break her heart again, I will cut *your* heart out with a knife.'

Whoa!

With a bright smile, she patted his arm. 'Enjoy your game.'

He stared after her as she ambled off again.

'You're up, Jack.'

He spun around to see Caro pointing to the hoop that was his next target. Croquet? He scowled. What a stupid game!

'Cooper!' Caro called to one of the other players. 'Have you added any new pieces to your collection recently?'

Good girl.

'Dear me, yes. I picked up a rather splendid medieval knife at the quaintest little antique place.'

Don't tell Barbara that. It might give her ideas.

'I must show it to you next time you're over.'

How well did Caro know these people?

He took his shot and tried to focus as the conversation turned to collectibles and antiques. He entirely lost the thread of it, though, when Caro took her next shot. Did she *practise* that maddening little shimmy?

He glanced around, gritting his teeth at the appreciative smiles on the other men's faces. He couldn't frogmarch her up to their bedroom and demand she change her clothes! If he marched her up to their bedroom he'd divest her of those clothes as quickly as possible and make love to her with a slow, serious intent that would leave her in no doubt how much he, for one, appreciated her physical attributes.

Every cell in his body screamed at him to do it.

He ground his teeth together. He was here to do a job. He was here to put the past behind him. It had taken too long to get this woman out of his system. He wasn't letting her back into his life again. Regardless of how cute her tush happened to be.

Find the snuffbox.
Get the divorce papers signed.
Get on with your life.

He kept that checklist firmly in the forefront of his mind as he turned his attention back to the conversation.

Croquet was followed by lunch. After lunch it was tennis and volleyball. A few of the guests went riding, but as Barbara was lounging in a chair on the lawn, alternately chatting with their hostess and flicking through a glossy magazine, he and Caro stuck close to the house too. Besides, Jack didn't ride.

It suddenly struck him that he had no idea whether Caro rode or not. Just another of the many things that hadn't come up during their short marriage.

Caro smiled a lot, chatted pleasantly and seemed utterly at ease, but it slowly and irrevocably dawned on him that while she'd always been somewhat reserved and self-contained that was even more the case now. She seemed to hold herself aloof in a way she never had before. She'd become more remote, serious...almost staid.

Dinner was followed by billiards for some, cards for others and lazy conversation over drinks for the rest. The other guests were a pleasant lot, and despite his low expectations he'd found it an oddly pleasant day.

Except for the lingering glances Caro sent him. And the secret smiles that made him want to smile back...and then ravish her. He'd lost count of the number of touches she'd bestowed on him—her hand resting lightly on his arm, her fingers brushing the back of his hand, her arm slipping through his...

Goddamn endless touches!

He raised his hand to knock on their shared bedroom door, but then pulled it back to his side. He had to get a grip. Caro was only following his instructions. Even if she *was* in danger of overdoing it.

Overdoing it? Really?

He ground his teeth together. No. She'd struck the perfect balance. He just hadn't realised that her flirting with him would stretch the limits of his control so thoroughly.

Be cool. Keep a lid on it.

Hauling in a breath, he knocked. He'd given her a good thirty minutes to get ready for bed. He hoped it was enough. It would be great if she were asleep.

The door opened a crack and Caro's face appeared. *No such luck.* She moistened her lips and opened the door wider to let him enter. She wore a pair of yoga pants and an oversized T-shirt…and her nerves were plain to see in the way she was pushing her bangle up and down her arm. It sent an answering jolt through him and a quickening of his pulse. If she'd had access to some of his earlier thoughts she'd have every right to her nerves.

He resisted the urge to run his finger around his collar again. He had to get his mind off the fact that they were in a bedroom. Alone.

He draped his jacket across the back of a chair. 'I've been meaning to ask—has Barbara ever exhibited any signs of violence?'

Caro settled on the end of the bed, her feet tucked up beneath her. 'Heavens no. Why would you ask such a thing?'

He raked both hands back through his hair, trying not to look at her fully. 'During croquet she threatened to cut my heart out with a knife if I broke *your* heart.'

'Ah.' She bit her lip and ducked her head. 'So that's what put you off your game.'

He could have sworn her shoulders shook. He settled himself in the chair—the only chair in the room. It was large and, as he'd be spending the night in it, thankfully comfortable.

'Are you laughing at me?'

'Not *at* you.' Her eyes danced. 'But she's such a tiny little thing, and you have to admit the thought of her doing you any damage is rather amusing.' A smile spilled from her. 'And it's kind of sweet for her to fluff up all mother-hen-like on my account.'

That smile. He had a forbidden image of her sprawled across that bed, naked...wearing nothing but that smile.

A scowl moved through him.

She shrugged. 'It's nice.'

Nice? He stared at her, and for the first time it occurred to him that extracting Barbara from this mess—one of her own making, he might add—might, in fact, be more important to Caro than her job. Which was crazy. He'd had firsthand experience of all Caro would sacrifice in the interests of her career.

'That's why she whisked me away the moment we arrived. She wanted to warn me of you—to tell me to be careful.'

He stared at her. 'Careful of what?'

'Of *you*, of course. Of getting my heart broken again.'

'*Your* heart?' He found himself suddenly on his feet, roaring at her. 'What about *my* heart?'

Her jaw dropped. '*Your* heart? *You* were the one who walked away without so much as a backward glance!' She shot to her feet too, hands on hips. 'You mean to tell me you *have* a heart?'

More than she'd ever know.

He fell back into the chair.

She folded her arms and glared. 'Besides, *your* heart can't be in any danger. You're in love with another woman, right?'

He moistened his lips and refused to answer that question. 'Are you saying *your* heart is in danger?'

She stilled before hitching her chin up higher. 'When you left five years ago I thought I would die.'

He wanted to call her a liar. Her heart was as cold as ice. It was why he'd left. He hadn't been able to make so much as a dent in that hard heart of hers. But truth shone from her eyes now in silent accusation, and something in his chest lurched.

'I am *never* giving you the chance to do that to me again.'

For a moment it felt as if the ground beneath his feet were slipping. He shook himself back to reality.

'Sending me on a guilt trip is a nice little ploy, Caro, but it won't work. I *know* you, remember?'

'Oh, whatever...' She waved an arm through the air, as if none of it mattered any more, and for some reason the action enraged him.

He shot to his feet again. She'd started to lower herself back to the bed, but now she straightened and held her ground.

'You!' He thrust a finger at her nose. 'You made it more than clear that while I might be suitable rebellion material, to put Daddy's nose out of joint, I was nowhere near good enough to father your children!'

That knowledge, and the fact that she'd taken him in so easily, should have humiliated him. He wished to God that it had. He wished to God that he'd been able to feel anything beyond the black morass of devastation that had crushed him beneath its weight.

All he'd ever wanted was to build a family with this woman. A family that he could love, protect and cherish.

Before Caro, he hadn't known it was possible to love another person so utterly and completely. When he'd found out that she didn't love him back, he hadn't known which way to turn.

One thing had been clear, though. He'd had no intention

of leaving her. He'd blamed her father, with all his guilt-tripping emotional blackmail, for stunting Caro's emotional development. He'd figured that half or even a quarter of Caro was worth more than the whole of any other woman.

That was how far he'd fallen.

She'd stamped all over him—and he'd spread himself at her feet and let her do it.

When he'd asked her if they could start a family, though, she'd laughed. *Laughed.*

He dragged a hand down his face. He would never forget the expression on her face. He hadn't been able to hide from the truth any longer—Caro would never consent to have a family with him.

So he'd left before he could lose himself completely.

He'd fled while there was still something of him left.

'*Your* heart?' he spat. 'What use did *you* ever have for a heart? Stop playing the injured party. You haven't earned the right.'

CHAPTER FOUR

'I HAVEN'T EARNED the right…?'

Caro's hands clenched and she started to shake with the force of her anger. He watched with a kind of detached fascination. Back when they'd been married—*they were still married*—Caro had rarely lost her temper.

In fact, now that he thought about it, she might have got cross every now and again, but he couldn't recall her *ever* losing her temper. To see her literally shaking with anger now was a novel experience…and bizarrely compulsive.

Her eyes flashed and a red flush washed through her cheeks. She looked splendid, alive—and tempting beyond measure. There was nothing staid or remote about her now.

He loathed himself for the impulse to goad her further.

He loathed himself more for the stronger impulse to pull her into his arms and soothe her.

He watched her try to swallow her anger.

'In your eyes, my not wanting children made me unnatural. Having children was more important to you than it ever was for me. It's a very great shame we didn't discuss our views on whether or not we wanted children *before* we married.'

He stabbed a finger at her. 'What's a *very great shame* is that your job—your stupid, precious job—was more important to you than me, our relationship and the potential family we could've had.'

The old frustration rose up through him with all its associated pain.

'What's so important about your job? What is it, after all, other than vacuous and frivolous? It can hardly be called vital and important!'

Her eyes spat fire. 'What—unlike *yours*, you mean?'

He swung away and raked a hand through his hair, trying to lasso his anger before swinging back to face her. 'When you get right down to it, what do you *do*? You sell trinkets to rich people who have more time and money than they do sense.'

Her hands clenched so hard her knuckles turned white. 'While *you* find things rich people have lost? Oh, that's *right* up there with saving lives and spreading peace and harmony throughout all the land.'

He blinked as that barb found its mark. 'My job's saving your butt!'

'Not yet it isn't!'

They stared at each other, both breathing hard.

'If people like me didn't care about our jobs, Mr High and Mighty, *you'd* be out of work.'

Touché.

'Sometimes jobs aren't about performing an important function in society. Sometimes they're about what they represent to the people doing them.' She thumped a hand to her chest, her voice low and controlled. '*My* job is the only thing I've ever achieved on my own merit. Against my father's wishes, strictures and censure *I* chose the subjects *I* wanted to study at university.'

She'd chosen Art History rather than the Trust Law and Business Management degree her father had demanded she take. He'd wanted her groomed in preparation for taking over that damn trust he'd set up in her mother's name. Caro had always sworn she wouldn't administer that trust, but her father had refused to believe her, unable to countenance the possibility of such rebellion and defiance.

'*My* job,' Caro continued, 'has provided me with the means to pay the rent on my own flat and to live my own life. How dare you belittle that? My job has given me independence and freedom and the means—'

'I understand you needing independence from your father.' Fury rose through him. 'But you didn't need it from *me*! I'm nothing like your father.'

'You're *exactly* like my father!'

She'd shouted at him, with such force he found himself falling back a step. His mouth went dry. She was wrong. He was nothing like her father.

'You wanted to control me the same way he did. What *I* wanted didn't matter one jot. It was always what *you* wanted that mattered!' Her voice rose even higher and louder. 'You didn't want a wife! You wanted a…a *brood mare*!'

The accusation shot out of her like grapeshot and he stared at her, utterly speechless. He couldn't have been more surprised if she'd held a forty-five calibre submachine gun complete with magazine, pistol grip and detachable buttstock to his head and said, *Stick 'em up.*

He found himself breathing hard. She was kidding—just trying to send him on a guilt trip. That couldn't be how she'd felt all those years ago.

The bedroom door flew open and they both swung round to find Barbara standing in the doorway, her face pinched and her eyes wide. 'I will *not* let you shout at Caro like that!'

Him? Caro had been the one doing most of the shouting.

'Come along, darling, you can bunk in with me tonight.'

She moved past Jack to take Caro's arm and tug her towards the door. She shot a venomous glare at him over her shoulder.

Caro didn't look at him at all. Not once. His heart started to throb. He opened his mouth to beg her to stay.

To what end? It was madness even to consider it. He snapped his mouth shut, clenching his hands into fists.

'Oh, *really*, Caro…' He heard Barbara sigh before the door closed behind them. '*This* is what you wear to bed to attract a man? It won't do.'

He wanted to yell after them that there was absolutely nothing wrong with what Caro was wearing, that she looked as delectable as ever. But, again, to what end?

He collapsed back into the chair, his temples throbbing and his chest burning.

'You wanted a brood mare!'

Behind her calm, composed facade, was that what she'd really been thinking? He rested his head in his hands. Was that truly how she'd felt? Was it how *he'd* made her feel?

'Are you okay, darling?'

Caro managed a shaky smile. 'This will probably sound stupid, but that's the very first time I've ever yelled at Jack.'

Barbara lowered herself to the bed. 'Coming from any-one else I would be surprised—shocked, even—but not from you. You've always been a funny little thing.'

'Funny?'

'Very controlled and self-contained. You have a ten-dency to avoid confrontation. It can be very difficult to get a handle on how you truly feel.'

Caro blinked and sat too. 'I'm sorry. I didn't realise.'

'Oh, I know you don't do it on purpose. Besides, you're getting better.'

She rubbed a hand across her forehead. 'Fighting like that doesn't feel *better*.'

'So things with you and Jack aren't going so well?'

She recalled, despite their fight, that she and Jack had

a cover story to maintain. She forced a shrug. 'That fight has been brewing for five years.'

'Well, then, maybe it's cleared the air,' Barbara said briskly. 'In the meantime, it won't hurt him to stew for a night. Now, come along—jump into bed. Things will look brighter in the morning, after a good night's sleep.'

'Are you sure you don't mind me sharing with you?'

'Not in the slightest.'

Caro climbed under the covers. Just before the light clicked out she noticed Barbara's clutch purse, sitting on the dressing table on the other side of the room like an unclaimed jackpot.

She blinked, her mind growing suddenly sharp. With a heart that pounded she lay still, staring into the dark, willing Barbara to fall asleep. The sooner she retrieved the snuffbox, the sooner Jack would be out of her life.

It seemed an age before Barbara's slow, steady breaths informed Caro that she was asleep. As quietly and smoothly as she could, she slid out from beneath the covers and stood by the side of the bed for a couple of moments, holding her breath to see if Barbara would stir.

When she didn't, she made her way carefully around the bed to the dressing table. Reaching out a hand to its edge, she nearly knocked over the can of hairspray sitting just behind the purse. With a dry mouth she righted it and waited. When nothing happened, she edged her fingers forward until they skimmed across the purse.

With her heart pounding so loudly she was sure Barbara must hear it, she opened the purse and pushed her hand inside. At the same moment the bedside light was flicked on.

'Caro, what are you doing?'

Caro stared into the clutch purse, afraid that if she turned around her expression would betray her. *No snuffbox.* 'I was… I was looking for some painkillers.' She turned and blinked in what she hoped was a bleary fashion.

'Here you go.' Barbara handed her a pill from a bottle on the bedside table beside her, along with a glass of water.

There was nothing for it but to take the headache tablet, even though she didn't have a headache. Granted, Jack was a major headache, but she'd need something stronger than an aspirin to get rid of *him*.

'Thank you, and I'm sorry I disturbed you.'

She climbed back into bed, her stomach feeling suddenly odd. Seriously, she wasn't cut out for all this sneaking around.

She wondered if Jack was sleeping soundly next door. She wondered what would have happened if she'd stayed there. Would they have made wild, abandoned love?

She tingled all over at the thought.

Just as well she was on this side of the wall!

The fuzziness of sleep settled over her, but when Barbara slipped from the bed Caro tried to push it away. What was Barbara doing? This could be a *clue*!

The other woman padded over to the window. Caro tried to rouse herself from the darkness trying to claim her.

As if from a long way away, she thought she heard Barbara say, 'Oh, Roland, why did you have to make things so hard?'

Caro wouldn't mind an answer to that question herself. She tried to lift herself up onto her elbows, but her body refused to comply with the demand.

'Why are you making me do this?'

Do what?

Caro opened her mouth to ask, but the words wouldn't come. Her last coherent thought before a thick, suffocating blanket descended over her was that Barbara hadn't given her an aspirin. She'd given her a sleeping tablet.

* * *

Caro found it nearly impossible to shrug the fog of sleep from her brain, but she did manage to push herself upright into a sitting position.

What time was it?

Sunlight flooded in at the window, but finding the energy to locate a clock in this unfamiliar room seemed beyond her at that moment. She turned her head a fraction to check the bed. No Barbara. At least not in the bed.

'Barbara?'

She barely recognised that voice as her own.

She cleared her throat and tried again. 'Barbara?'

The result wasn't much better. Eventually she forced herself to sit on the edge of bed, and then to stand and turn around. It only confirmed what she already knew—Barbara wasn't in the room.

She hoped Jack knew where Barbara was.

She pulled in a breath. *Right.* She needed to go next door and dress and then join everyone else for the day's activities.

She made swaying progress across to the door. She had to rest for a moment before opening it, forcing herself through it and then closing it behind her. She'd almost reached the door to the room she and Jack shared when his voice sounded behind her.

'Caro?'

She rested back against the wall—needing its support—before turning her head in his direction. *Heavens.* A sigh rose up through her. With his height and his breadth, Jack cut a fine figure. A pair of designer denim jeans outlined his long lean legs and strong thighs to perfection. She'd bet the view looked even better from behind.

It suddenly occurred to her that if he'd come in a few minutes later he'd have almost certainly caught her in a state of undress. For some reason she found that almost unutterably funny, and a giggle burst from her.

'Morning, Jack.'

His eyes narrowed as he drew nearer. 'Have you been drinking?'

'Most certainly not.' She tried to straighten, but only lasted a couple of seconds before she found herself slumping again. She pointed a finger at him. 'Barbara gave me a pill last night.'

His face darkened. 'You accepted a pill from Barbara? Are you *insane*?'

She didn't like his opinion of Barbara, and she *hated* his opinion of her. 'I thought it was an aspirin. And I had to take it to maintain my reason for why she'd caught me with my hand in her purse.' She frowned. 'I think it was a sleeping tablet... I'm still feeling kind of fuzzy.'

His nostrils flared, and he made a move as if to pick her up, but she held up both hands to ward him off.

'Ooh, please don't do that. My stomach is feeling...um... queasy. A bathroom would be a very good idea about now.'

He took her arm with a gentleness that had the backs of her eyes prickling. 'Come on—it's just a couple of doors this way.'

She tried not to focus on his strength, his warmth, or how much she was enjoying the feel of him beside her. It was this physical craving for him that had been her undoing before. It was something that went beyond sex. It had brought her peace and a sense of belonging that she'd felt right down in her very bones.

And it had obviously been a lie. So she needed to ignore it now.

'Where's Barbara?'

'She and a couple of the other women have gone into the village. Apparently there's a little boutique Cynthia has been gushing about.'

'Then why are you here?'

'I have an operative tailing them.'

She stopped and blinked up at him. 'You have *operatives*?'

His lips twitched. 'I have several, and this one is female. Believe me, she'll blend in much better than I ever could on a shopping trip.' He gestured to the door where they'd stopped. 'Do you need a hand?'

'Certainly not.'

'Then you have to promise me to not lock the door.'

'Will *you* promise not to come in?'

He crossed his heart. 'Unless you call me.'

'Deal.'

She wasn't sick, although it felt like a close run thing for a minute or two. Splashing cold water on her face had helped. So did the glass of water Jack pressed on her once they reached their room again.

He fluffed up the pillows and then helped her onto the bed to sit up against them. It made her feel oddly cared for.

'I'm sorry to be such a bother,' she mumbled. 'I've never had a sleeping tablet before.' She wouldn't have had one last night either if she'd known what it was.

'They don't agree with everyone.' He touched the backs of his fingers to her forehead. 'But your colour is returning and you don't feel hot.'

Don't focus on his touch! 'That's good, right?'

One side of his mouth hooked up. 'That's good.'

Don't focus on his smile! 'The snuffbox wasn't in Barbara's purse.'

He eased away from her, all businesslike and professional again, and she tried to tell herself that she was pleased about that.

'I'm going to go and check her room.'

'What? *Now?*'

'No time like the present.'

She swallowed and called out, 'Be careful.'

But as he was practically out of the room by the time she'd uttered the caution, he probably didn't hear it.

Sitting there, with her pulse racing too hard and her ears primed for Barbara's return, was even more nerve-racking than the night he'd searched the house in Mayfair.

She wondered why he was doing this when he didn't have to. She'd made it clear that she'd sign the divorce papers whether he helped her or not.

Because he wanted closure?

She rested her head back against the pillows. Things had grown so complicated between them five years ago. It occurred to her now that she hadn't moved on from then—last night's argument had proved that. She'd only pretended to. And this morning proved that she needed to stop craving that sense of belonging she'd only ever felt with him. She had to put that behind her too.

It was time to stop feeling like half a person. It was time to get on with her life.

And there was only one way to achieve that.

The door opened and Jack moved back inside. She raised an eyebrow.

He shook his head. 'Nothing.'

'I'm starting to think she's telling the truth—that she didn't take it.' She frowned. 'Except…'

He sat in the chair on the other side of the room. 'Except…?'

'Before I fell asleep last night, I heard her talking to my father.'

He raised an eyebrow.

'Not a hallucination—give me some credit, Jack. She was staring out of the window, talking to the dead like we all probably do from time to time.'

'Speak for yourself.' He shuffled forward an inch. 'What did she say?'

'She asked my father why he'd made things so hard, and…' She frowned trying to remember more clearly. 'And something about why was he making her do this…or something along those lines.'

'Your father left you *everything*?'

'Everything.'

'Without a single condition?'

'Condition-free.'

He shook his head and settled back in the chair. 'I could've sworn he'd make the management of your mother's trust a condition of the will.'

'I told him not to bother—that I refused to be dictated to that way.'

'And he believed you?'

She almost laughed. 'He ought to have done. I told him often enough. Why?'

'Just trying to get a handle on why he did what he did.'

She'd given up on that. It was an impossible task.

She and Jack both fell quiet. Her heart started to pound. She recalled Barbara's words from last night—about the way Caro was controlled and self-contained, and how she avoided confrontation. Five years ago she'd thought Jack had *known* how much she loved him. Maybe he hadn't. Maybe she hadn't been demonstrative enough.

'I'm going to talk about the elephant in the room,' she announced, her mouth going dry.

'What elephant?'

'The termination I had five years ago.'

Every muscle in his body bunched, as if she'd just hit him and he was waiting to see if the blow would fell him. Her heart burned so hard it made it difficult to continue. Except she had to continue. If Jack knew the truth maybe he wouldn't hate her so badly—maybe he wouldn't carry such a great weight of bitterness around with him. And…

and maybe he'd find happiness with this new woman he had in his life.

The thought reduced her heart to ashes.

She moistened her lips, ignoring the blackness welling inside her. 'I spent hours and hours in those first weeks after you'd gone trying to work out why you'd left the way you had.'

She'd returned from work one evening to find every trace of him removed from their shared flat and a note informing her that he'd realised they wanted different things and he was returning to Australia. He'd left her no contact number, no way for her to get in touch with him. It had taken her months before she'd finally believed that he was never going to ring.

'And did you come to any conclusions?'

Oh, his bitterness! How could it still score her heart so deeply?

'Of course I did. I do have a fully functioning brain in my head.' Her voice came out too tart, but she couldn't help it. 'I decided that you must've somehow found out about the termination I was planning to have.'

He gave one terse nod. 'The clinic rang to confirm your appointment.'

'They *told* you?' That shocked her. They'd assured her of confidentiality.

'No, Caro, they didn't. But I'm a detective, remember? It didn't take much for me to put two and two together.'

'And yet you still only came up with three and three-quarters of the answer.'

He didn't yell, he didn't storm around the room flinging out his arms and accusing her of killing their child, but the way he stared at her with throbbing eyes didn't feel much better.

He tilted up his chin. 'I understand your right to make your own decisions when it comes to your body. I don't dis-

pute that. But to get rid of a child I so desperately wanted...'
He turned grey. 'That was when I realised you'd *never* have
children with me.'

The children that had always been more important to
him than she'd ever been.

'That was when I realised you'd meant it when you said
you didn't want children.'

'I said I wasn't *ready* for children.'

There was a difference. Why had he never been able to
understand that? She'd asked him to give her three years.
Not that she'd been able to promise him for certain that
they'd have children after that time either, but she'd needed
time to consider the issue, to make sure in her own mind
that she was up to the task of being a mother.

The thought of becoming a parent in the image of her father had filled her with horror. Jack's idea of family hadn't
helped much either—it had seemed more like a fantasy
she'd never be able to bring off. The whole issue of creating a family had left her all at sea, and it had been too big
a decision to get wrong.

'Caro—'

'Jack, my pregnancy was ectopic.'

He froze. If silence could boom, it boomed now.

'Do you know what that means?' she ventured.

'Yes.'

She barely recognised the voice that croaked from his
throat. She wanted to cover her eyes at the expression of
self-disgust that spread across his features, millimetre by
slow millimetre.

'It means the fertilised egg implanted itself in your tubes
rather than in your uterus.'

She nodded and swallowed. 'In an ectopic pregnancy
the foetus has no chance of surviving.'

'And if the foetus isn't removed it will kill the mother.'
Her surprise at his knowledge must have shown, because

he added, 'I had a foster mother who had an ectopic pregnancy.' He lifted his head. 'You had no choice but to have a termination.'

'No,' she agreed.

He shot to his feet, his body shaking and his eyes blazing. 'Why the *hell* didn't you tell me?'

'I was trying to find a way, but you left before I could! Why didn't you confront me about it as soon as you took that call from the clinic?'

He paced the room, a hand pressed to his forehead.

Caro pushed her bangle high up onto her arm, where the thin metal cut into her. She loosened it and tried to get her breathing back under control. 'I was trying to find the courage to face your disappointment,' she said.

He swung back to stare at her.

'To tell you I was pregnant in one breath and then to take it away in the next...' She shook her head. It had seemed unnecessarily cruel. 'It brought my most frightening fears to the surface. I couldn't help wondering if, down the track, it ever came to a question of my life or a baby's—which would you choose?'

He fell down into the chair.

'When you walked away I had my answer.'

Jack stared at Caro, his heart feeling as if it had been put through a grater and then the pieces collected up and shoved back into his chest willy-nilly. Had he ever really known her?

He'd walked away from his marriage believing Caro had betrayed him and his dreams...and in the end it was he who'd betrayed *her*.

'You should've told me.' He didn't yell the words this time, but they shook with the force of emotion ripping through him.

'And *still* you blame me.'

Her remote smile troubled him. 'No!' His hands clenched. 'I'm just as much to blame. I can't believe I walked away over such a stupid misunderstanding.'

'That misunderstanding wasn't *stupid*, Jack. And with the benefit of hindsight it wasn't unforeseen either. Maybe you *should* blame me—because God knows I was glad the decision had been taken out of my hands. I was glad I wasn't faced with the choice of working out what to do with an unexpected pregnancy.'

It didn't change the fact that he'd walked away from her at a time when she'd needed his support.

'I'm sorry you had to go through that alone.'

She blinked, and her surprise at his apology hurt.

She moistened her lips. 'Thank you.'

He rubbed the back of his neck, silently calling himself every dark name he could think of.

'Was the procedure…gruelling?'

She shook her head. 'It was very simple keyhole surgery. The procedure was performed in the morning and I was home again in the afternoon.'

But he hadn't been there to cosset her afterwards.

She lifted a hand to push her hair off her face. Her hand shook and his heart clutched.

'I had a couple of stitches in my belly button and—' She swallowed. 'It didn't seem like much to show for… for all that was lost.'

Her words ran him through like a knife. He had to brace his hands on his knees to fight the nausea rising through him.

'I'm sorry I wasn't there for you. I'm sorry I left like I did.'

She glanced away, but not before he'd seen the tears swimming in her eyes.

In two strides he was in front of her and pulling her into

his arms. She pressed her face into his shoulder and sobbed silently for a few seconds.

'When I first found out I was pregnant, there was a part of me that was excited.' One small hand beat against his chest. 'For a few moments I thought I could make everything work.'

His eyes and throat burned. She wrenched herself out of his arms and he felt more bereft than ever.

She seized a handkerchief from the nightstand and dabbed her eyes. 'You want to know something funny? If I ever *do* decide I want children I now have less chance of conceiving.'

His head rocked back. 'That's not funny! It's—'

'You leaving like you did…' She swung around. 'Maybe it was for the best after all.'

Did she really believe that?

She lifted her chin. 'What you said in your letter was true. We did want different things. We probably still want different things. You still obviously want children.'

His heart thumped.

She lifted a hand and let it drop. 'Me…? Even after all this time I'm still not certain I do. That would never have worked for you in the long run, Jack.'

In five years his desire for a family had never waned. If anything, it had grown. And in his pursuit of that he'd hurt this woman badly.

'I know it's a moot point now, but I wonder if you'd have married me if you'd known I couldn't have children.'

He stared at her and shook his head. 'I can't answer that. I haven't a clue.'

And now they'd never know.

He pulled in a breath. One thing was clear—this time he wasn't leaving until the job was done and he and Caro had said everything they needed to say.

Five years ago he'd misjudged her and her actions. He'd

make that up to her, and then maybe he'd be able to draw a line under this part of his life and move on. Without bitterness and without blame.

CHAPTER FIVE

'WHAT DO YOU MEAN, you believe Barbara drugged me on purpose? You really are set against her, aren't you?'

Jack kept his eyes on the road, but his every sense was attuned to the woman sitting next to him in the car. She smelt like caramel, and with every agitated movement she sent another burst of sweetness floating across to him.

It would take less than seventy-five minutes to reach Mayfair from the Sedgewick country estate, but he had no faith in his ability to last the distance with that scent tormenting him.

'She wanted nothing more than to comfort me after the fight you and I had, and to make sure I got a decent night's sleep.'

'She wanted to make sure you didn't find the snuffbox.'

His hands clenched about the steering wheel. He'd put Caro in danger. He'd underestimated Barbara's desperation and the lengths she'd go to in an effort to not get caught. His jaw tightened. What if Caro had reacted adversely to the sleeping pill? What if—?

'Barbara *cares* about me.'

His knuckles turned white. 'Barbara is determined to save her own skin! Why can't you see this issue in black and white for once, instead of a hundred shades of grey?'

The words burst from him more loudly than he'd intended and they reverberated through the car with a force that made her flinch. He cursed himself silently.

Except… 'You need to be on your guard around her, Caro. You need to tread carefully where she's concerned.'

He glanced across and her deep brown eyes momentarily met his. The confusion in them made his chest ache. Her gaze lowered to his hands and his white-knuckled grip on the steering wheel. He tried to relax his fingers. He wanted her on her guard—not frightened witless.

'Regardless of what you think, this issue is *not* black and white.'

He had to bite his tongue. This had always been a bugbear between them. She'd always claimed he was too quick to make snap judgments. He'd retaliate by saying she lacked judgment.

'I think she has a lover,' he bit out.

Barbara had buried her husband three months ago—a husband she claimed to have loved. If she had taken up with another man so soon after Roland's death it wouldn't add credibility to her claims of devotion.

Caro straightened and swung towards him. It was all he could do to keep his eyes on the road and his hands on the wheel.

'What makes you think that?' she asked.

'She bought lingerie on her shopping trip to the village this morning.'

To his chagrin, she started to laugh. 'Heaven forbid that a woman should buy pretty undergarments for her own pleasure.'

'In my experience—'

'*Your* experience?' She folded her arms. 'Exactly how many lovers have you had in the last five years, Jack?'

His head rocked back, the question barrelling into him and knocking him off balance. No doubt as it had been intended to.

His heart thudded. 'You first.' The savagery that ripped

through him made his stomach churn. 'If you really want to know the answer to that, then you answer first.'

Spots appeared at the edges of his vision while he held his breath and waited for her to answer. That was what the thought of Caro with another man did to him. Even after five years.

'It's none of my business,' she said after a long pause. 'I'm sorry.'

At her apology, it was as if a hand reached out and squeezed his chest in a grip that stole his breath. One moment he wanted to rip her apart and the next he wanted to draw her into his arms and never let her go. It made no sense whatsoever.

'It doesn't feel that way, though, does it?' he growled. 'Our *business* still feels intertwined.'

'I know.' Her chest rose and fell in a sigh. 'Which is ludicrous after all this time.'

He swallowed the ball of hardness doing its best to lodge in his throat. 'It could be because our relationship had no formal ending.' He'd just…*left*. 'There were no last words, no proper goodbyes.'

'Perhaps,' she agreed, her voice full of dejection and… and secrets?

'One,' he snapped out.

'I beg your pardon?'

He didn't need to turn his head to imagine in technicolour detail the slow blink of her eyes and the cute wrinkle of confusion that would appear between her eyebrows.

'In the last five years—since I left you—I've had one lover, Caro.'

One. He didn't turn his head. He didn't want to see the surprise that would be plastered across her face.

She coughed. 'One? *You—one?*'

He almost smiled then, because he knew that in about five seconds she'd be internally beating herself up for revealing her surprise, her shock. She'd deem it rude and insensitive.

'One,' he repeated.

'But…' Her hands made agitated movements in the air. 'But you like sex so *much*!'

He'd loved it with Caro.

'So do you.'

He couldn't continue this conversation and keep driving at the same time.

On impulse he turned in at a small pub. 'Hungry?' At a stretch they could make this an early dinner.

'Not in the slightest.' She unbuckled her seatbelt and opened her door. 'But a glass of burgundy would go down a treat.'

They sat at a table by the far wall, nursing their drinks.

'And I can hardly call her a lover,' Jack said.

Caro shot back in her seat, one hand pressed to her chest just above her heart, drawing his attention to the pale perfection of her throat.

'Please, Jack, you don't have to explain. You don't owe me anything.'

Yes, he did.

'It was a one-night stand,' he continued, 'and it was a disaster.'

The entire time the only person he'd been able to think about had been Caro. It had been Caro's touch he'd craved, and he'd used another woman in an attempt to drive Caro from his mind. Not only hadn't it worked, it had been unfair. The encounter had left him feeling soiled, dirty and ashamed. He hadn't been eager to repeat the experience.

Caro brought her wine to her lips and sipped. Her hand shook as she placed the glass back to the table. 'It's only been the once for me too. I wanted to get on with my life. I wanted to feel normal again.'

He could tell it hadn't worked.

'It was terrible. It left me thinking I should join a convent.'

He grimaced.

She stilled. He glanced across at her. She twisted her bangle round and round with sudden vigour.

'What?' he demanded.

'You don't have a woman waiting back home for you in Australia, do you?'

He glanced away.

'You want to remarry, and you still want children...' She let out a breath. 'But you don't have anyone specific in mind yet.'

Something inside him hardened. 'Why are you so relieved about that?'

'Because I *knew* you weren't in love. I thought you were about to make another mistake.'

He stared at her, at a loss for something to say.

'You want to feel normal again too. That's what all this is about.'

He thrust out his jaw. 'It's time to draw a line under us.'

She stared down into her red wine, twirling the glass around and around instead of her bangle. 'So...we're working towards—what? An amicable divorce?'

Acid burned in his stomach. He took a sip of his beer in an attempt to ease it. 'And getting your snuffbox back.' He owed her that much.

She suddenly straightened, and although she leaned towards him he couldn't help feeling she'd erected some emotional barrier between them.

'Barbara doesn't have a lover, Jack. She bought that lingerie for *me*. I'm afraid she doesn't subscribe to the view that yoga pants and a T-shirt are suitable attire for the bedroom. She thinks I should be making more of an effort to attract you.'

A groan rose up through him.

'So, in case you need to know this in support of our cover story, it's a long gold negligee with shoestring straps and some pretty beading just here.'

Her hands fluttered about her chest and it took an effort of will for him not to close his eyes. 'Right…'

Her eyes grew sharp. 'And yet you still think she could hurt me?'

He straightened too. 'Why don't you just throw her to the wolves?' The woman was a thief, for God's sake!

'I care about her. She…she and Paul…are like family to me.'

She said the word *family* carefully, as if afraid it might hurt him.

He gulped back a generous slug of beer. 'Some family!'

She sipped her red wine, but her jaw was tight. 'You *do* know your idea of family is too romantic, don't you?'

That was what happened when you grew up without one of your own.

Her eyes narrowed, as if she'd read that thought in his face.

'I hope you find what you're looking for, Jack. I really do. I hope it makes you as happy as you seem to think it will.'

He sensed her sincerity. And her doubt. 'Not all families are as screwed up as yours, Caro.'

'That's very true. But Barbara…' She shrugged. 'I feel a certain affinity with her. My father turned her into a trophy wife, never correcting the widely held view that people had of her. Probably because he found the depth of his feelings for her too confronting. So he tried to control her…and she let him. Unlike me, she did everything he asked of her—everything she could to please him. And if you think that was easy then you're crazy.'

He could feel his mouth gape. He snapped it shut. 'You're *nothing* like Barbara.'

'That's where you're wrong. All I'd have had to do was agree to have children with you, Jack, and I'd have been exactly like her.'

'That was totally different!'

'How?'

'I *never* tried to turn you into a trophy wife.'

'No—just into the mother of your children.'

He ground his teeth together. 'Asking you if we could start a family was not an unreasonable demand.'

'My father didn't see ordering me to take over the administration of my mother's trust as an unreasonable demand either. He thought it a worthy goal. And he was right—it is. But it's not a role I want in life.'

In the same way, she obviously didn't want the role of mother.

'For God's sake, Caro, I *loved* you!'

'But not unconditionally! It was clear you'd only continue to love me if I bore your children.'

His hand clenched about his glass. 'What you're saying is that what you wanted was more important than what *I* wanted.'

She lifted her glass, but she didn't drink from it. 'I don't recall you ever offering to be the primary caregiver. I don't recall you ever making any attempt at compromise.'

Each word was like a bullet from a Colt 45.

'I was the one who was expected to make all the sacrifices.'

Bull's eye. For a moment Jack could barely breathe.

'But that's all old ground.' She waved a hand in the air and sipped her wine. 'Do you seriously think Barbara could present a physical danger to me?'

It took an effort of will to find his voice...his balance... his wits. 'I'm not ruling it out.'

'Then let's call the search off.'

She drained the last of her wine and he found it impossible to read anything beyond the assumed serenity of her countenance.

'For God's sake, why?'

'I don't want to force her into actions she'd otherwise avoid. If she's as desperate as you're implying, then she's welcome to the snuffbox.'

'But your job…?'

'I'll have to explain that I've lost the snuffbox, make financial reparation to the seller, and then tender my resignation.'

She'd sacrifice her *job*? She *loved* her job.

'I could go back to university.'

'To study what?'

'Something different from my undergraduate degree, obviously. Or I could enrol in a doctorate programme. It's not like money will be an issue.'

But there'd be a cloud hanging over her head, professionally, for the rest of her working life. Regardless of their differences and their history, she didn't deserve to take the blame for someone else's wrongdoing. Caro was innocent and he was determined to prove it.

'No!'

She raised an eyebrow and rose casually to her feet, though he sensed the careful control she exerted over her movements.

'I believe we're done here.'

He rose too. 'Give me until the end of the week, Caro. Like we planned. Give me until Friday. It's only five days away.'

She opened her mouth and he could see she was going to refuse him.

'Please?'

His vehemence surprised her, but he couldn't help it.

'I swear I won't put Barbara in any position that will incite her to violence.'

She glanced away and then glanced back. Finally she nodded. 'Okay—but then it's done, Jack. It's finished.'

He knew what she really meant, though. They'd be done. Finished.

The resistance that rose through him made no sense.

He nodded, and then took her arm and led her out to the car. 'Am I taking you back to the house in Mayfair or to your flat?'

'The flat, please.'

Good. He didn't want to run into her when he bugged the Mayfair house tonight…

Caro frowned at the knock on her door. She dumped her notepad on the sofa before seizing the remote and clicking the television off.

Daytime television, Caro? How low do you mean to sink?

Shaking her head, she padded to the door and opened it.

'Hello, Caro.'

Jack!

She moistened suddenly dry lips, wishing she'd bothered to put on something more glamorous than the default yoga pants when she'd dragged herself out of bed this morning.

'Uh, good morning?'

She started and glanced at her watch, huffed out a sigh. 'Yep, it's still morning.'

'Just.'

Right.

'May I come in?'

She blinked, realising she'd been holding the door open and just staring at him. 'Of course. I'm afraid I wasn't expecting to see you today.'

He entered without saying a word. He sported those same designer jeans he'd worn yesterday and the view from the back was indeed spectacular. It wasn't his physique that held her attention, though—as drool-inducing as those shoulders and butt might be—but the odd combination of stiffness and stillness in his posture that hinted at…nervousness? What did Jack have to be nervous about?

Oh, dear Lord! Unless he had news for her. *Bad* news.

She pushed her shoulders back, forced her chin up. She'd already decided the snuffbox was lost forever, hadn't she? She'd accepted the fact that she'd lose her job. She pulled in a breath.

'You've found out something? You have…bad news?'

He shook his head. 'I'm currently collecting information and analysing data.'

No, he wasn't. He was here in her flat. Her *tiny* flat.

Widening his stance, he eyed her up and down. Warmth crept across her skin and a pulse fired to life deep inside her. Soon, if she weren't careful, he'd have her throbbing and pulsing with the need he'd always been able to raise in her.

She crossed her arms, not caring how defensive it made her look. Once upon a time she'd have sashayed over to him, run her hands along his shoulders and reached up on tiptoe to kiss him—long, slow, sensuous kisses that would have had him groaning and hauling her close…

She clenched her hands. But that had been back before he'd left. That had been before he'd broken something inside her that she hadn't been able to put back together. She wasn't kissing Jack again and they most certainly weren't going to make love together. It would set her back five years!

She stared back at him. She didn't know if there was a challenge in her eyes or not, but the hint of a smile had touched his lips.

'I'm afraid Barbara wouldn't approve.'

It took a moment for her to realise he referred to her

yoga pants and T-shirt. 'Barbara never drops around un-announced.'

He took neither the bait nor the hint, just nodded and glanced around her sitting room. For once she wished it were larger, not quite so cosy. His gaze zeroed in on the plate of cake perched on the coffee table. He turned back and raised both eyebrows.

Her cheeks started to burn. Dear Lord! She'd been caught sitting around in her slouchy pyjamas, eating cake and watching daytime television. What a cliché!

She refused to let her humiliation show. 'I'm on leave this week. It's a well-known fact that when one is on holi-day, cake for breakfast is mandatory.'

He didn't point out that it was nearer to lunchtime than breakfast.

'Besides, that orange cake is utterly divine—to die for. Would you like a slice?'

He shook his head.

She pulled in a breath, counted to three and then let it out. 'I really wasn't expecting to see you today, Jack. I don't mean to be rude, but what are you doing here?'

His eyes shone bluer than she remembered. They seemed to see right inside her—but that had to be a trick of the light.

'I was hoping to take you to lunch.'

Her heart gave a funny little skip. 'Why?'

'There are some things we should discuss.'

Divorce things? She didn't want to talk about the di-vorce. Why couldn't they just leave it up to their lawyers? She wanted to say no to lunch. She wanted to say no to spending more time in his company. She wanted to resist the appeal in those eyes of his. Those eyes, though, had always held a siren's fascination for her.

'Is it really such a difficult decision?'

To admit so would be far too revealing, but to go to lunch with him…

'I just don't see the point.'

'Does there need to be a point? It's a beautiful day outside.'

Was it? She glanced towards the window.

'And maybe I'm striving for the *amicable* in our amicable divorce.'

Was she supposed to applaud him for that?

In the next moment she bit her lip. Was he worried that she'd become difficult and spiteful if he didn't recover the snuffbox?

She frowned. Surely not? Surely he knew her better than that…

Her heart started to pound. Very slowly she shook her head, recalling the expression on his face when she'd revealed the true reason behind her medical termination. His shock had swiftly turned to self-disgust and guilt. She didn't want him racked with guilt. She was just as much to blame as him for that particular misapprehension. Besides, that one incident hadn't been responsible for the breakdown of their marriage. It had just been the proverbial last straw.

'Caro?'

She raised her hands in surrender. 'Fine. I'll go and get changed.'

Twenty minutes later they were outside, walking in the sunshine. Jack was right—it was a glorious day.

She lifted her face to the sun and closed her eyes. 'I love this time of year. I wish it could be summer all year long.'

'Which begs the question, why were you cooped up in your flat when you could've been outside, enjoying all of this?'

'Maybe because my leave is for a family matter rather than a true holiday? Maybe because I don't actually feel in a holiday mood?'

'So the cake…?'

'Cake is its own reward,' she averred stoutly, trying to resist the way his chuckle warmed her to her very toes.

They were quiet until they reached the Thames. Caro turned in the direction of several riverside cafes and restaurants. The river was dark, fast-flowing and full of traffic. She loved its vibrancy…the way it remained the same and yet was always changing.

'When did you stop having fun, Caro?'

Her stomach knotted. 'I beg your pardon?' She slammed to a halt, planting her hands on her hips. 'I have fun!'

How dare he try to make her life all black and white with his judgments?

The dark seriousness in his eyes made her heart beat harder. 'I'll have you know that I have plenty of fun! Oodles of it! I catch up with my girlfriends regularly for coffee.' *And cake.* 'I see shows, go to movies, visit art galleries. I live in a city that offers a variety of endless activities. I have plenty of fun, thank you!'

'You've had nothing in your diary for the last three months.'

She clenched her hands to stop from doing something seriously unladylike. 'You went through my diary?'

'It was on the coffee table…open. I figured if it were sacrosanct you'd have put it away.'

'Or maybe I expected better manners from my visitors!' Heat scorched her cheeks. 'That is one of the rudest things I've ever heard. An invasion of privacy and—'

'Not as rude as stealing a snuffbox.'

She folded her arms and with a loud, 'Hmph!' set off again at brisk pace. 'You were looking for clues?'

'Just wondering if you'd made any enemies lately.'

She rolled her eyes, wondering why it was so hard to rein in her temper. 'I'm not the kind of woman to make enemies, Jack.'

Except of her father.

And her husband.

'Is there anyone at Richardson's who's been fired recently? Someone who might hold you responsible? Is there some guy who's been pestering you for a date over the last three months? Have you had a disgruntled client who's cross they've missed out on a particular treasure? Is there—?'

'No!'

'Caro, your diary is full of work commitments, the odd work-related lecture at London University or an art gallery, and one weekend conference in Barcelona. You didn't have a single dinner date, coffee date, movie date, *any kind of date* scheduled into your diary at all.'

'Maybe because it's a *work* diary. I remember my social engagements. I don't need to write them down.'

It struck her now that there were so few invitations these days they were easy to remember. She went cold and then hot. When had that happened? She'd once had a full calendar.

'You always were a good liar.'

He said it as if it were a compliment!

'I'm sorry to say, though, that I don't believe you.'

'And that should matter to me because…?'

He flashed her a grin that set her teeth on edge. 'Getting under your skin, aren't I, kiddo?'

'Don't call me that!' It had been a pet name once. Jack had drawled it in Humphrey Bogart fashion and it had always made her smile.

Not any more.

'You were only ever that rude when you were fibbing or hiding something.'

'And it seems you can still try the patience of a saint.'

God knew she wasn't a saint. But his perception had her

grabbing hold of her temper again, and her composure, and trying to twitch both into place.

'You wrote *everything* down. You were afraid you'd forget otherwise. You were big on making lists too.'

'People change. Believe it or not, in the last five years even *I've* changed.'

'Not that much.' He pulled a folded sheet of paper from his pocket. 'You still make lists.'

She snatched it from him, unfolded it and started to shake. 'This… You…'

'That's a list you're making of options in the eventuality of losing your job.'

'I know what it is!' She scrunched the sheet of paper into a ball. 'You had no right.'

'Maybe not, but it brings us back to the original question. When did you stop having fun, Caro?'

Before she could answer, he marched her to a table for two at a nearby riverside restaurant and held a chair out for her. For a moment she was tempted to walk away. But that would reveal just how deeply he'd got under her skin, and she was pig-headed enough—just—not to want to give him that satisfaction.

Besides—she glanced around—the sun, the river and the warmth were all glorious, and something deep inside her yearned towards it. She didn't want to turn her back on the day—not yet. For the first time her flat suddenly seemed too small, too cramped.

Blowing out a breath, she sat. For the briefest of moments Jack clasped her shoulders from behind in a warm caress that made her chest ache and her stomach flutter.

He took the seat opposite. 'Caro—'

'Pot.' She pointed to him. 'Kettle.' She pointed to herself. 'When was the last time *you* had fun?'

The waitress chose that moment to bustle up with menus. *Manners, Caro.*

'They do a really lovely seafood linguine here.' The Jack of five years ago had loved seafood. She figured he probably still did.

'Oh, I'm sorry,' the waitress said, 'but that's no longer on the menu. We've had a change of chef.'

Jack glanced at Caro and then leaned back in his chair. 'When did you change chefs?'

'It'd be four months ago now, sir.'

Caro swallowed, staring at the menu without really seeing it. 'My…how time flies.'

Jack said nothing. He didn't have to Had it really been over four months since she'd been down here for a meal?

They ordered the prawn and chorizo gnocchi that the waitress recommended, along with bottles of sparkling mineral water. When the waitress moved away, Caro hoped that Jack would drop the subject of fun. She hoped she could simply…

What? Enjoy a pleasant lunch in the sunshine with her soon-to-be ex-husband? That didn't seem likely, did it?

She gestured to the river, about to make a comment about how fascinating it always was down here, watching the river traffic, but she halted at the expression on his face.

'You're not going to let the subject drop, are you?'

'Nope.'

'Why does it matter to you one way or another if I have fun or not?'

'Because I can't help feeling that I'm to blame for the fact you don't have fun any more—that it's my fault.'

He couldn't have shocked her more if he'd slapped her.

She folded her arms on the table and leaned towards him. 'Jack, I get a great deal of enjoyment out of many things—a good book, a good movie, cake, my work—but I think it's fair to say that I'm not exactly a pleasure-seeker or a barrel of laughs. I never have been.'

'You used to make me laugh. Now, though, seems to me you hardly ever laugh.'

'Has it occurred to you that it's the company I'm currently keeping?'

He didn't flinch—not that she'd said it to hurt him—but his gaze drifted out towards the river and she couldn't help feeling she'd hurt him anyway.

Their food arrived, but neither one of them reached for their cutlery. She touched the back of his hand. His warmth made her fingertips tingle.

'I didn't say that to be mean, but neither one of us should pretend things are the same as they used to be between us—that things aren't...difficult.'

She went to move her hand, but in the blink of an eye he'd trapped it within his. 'When was the last time your soul soared, Caro? When was the last time you felt like you were flying?'

Her mouth dried. She wasn't answering that.

The last time had been on a picnic with Jack in Hyde Park. They'd packed a modest meal of sandwiches, raspberries and a bottle of wine, but everything about that day had been perfect—the weather, the world...them. They'd gone home in the evening and made love. They'd eaten chocolate biscuits and ice cream for dinner while playing Scrabble. That day had felt like perfect happiness.

Had that day been worth the pain that followed?

She shook her head. She didn't think so.

He released her hand. 'I see.'

Did he?

'Just as I thought.'

She forced a morsel of food into her mouth. 'The gnocchi is very good.'

'I bought a boat.'

She lowered her cutlery with a frown. *Okaaay.*

'I go boating and fishing. And some days when I'm

standing at the wheel of my boat, when I'm whipping along the water at a great rate of knots and the breeze is in my face, sea spray is flying and the sun is shining, I feel at peace with the world. I feel alive.'

He lived near water? 'What made you get a boat?'

'A couple of friends, tired of my…grumpiness, dragged me out on their boat.'

Her jaw dropped. 'Grumpiness?' Caro felt like an idiot the minute the word left her. She tried to cover up her surprise by adding, 'You obviously enjoyed it enough to buy your own boat.'

'When I left you and returned to Australia I threw myself into work.'

He'd made such a success of his firm that only an idiot could accuse him of wasting his time.

'But I didn't do anything else—just worked. I didn't want to be around people. I just wanted to be left alone.'

She could relate to that.

'Apparently, though, being a bear of a boss isn't the ideal scenario.'

Ah…

'A couple of friends dragged me out on their boat, where I was quite literally a captive audience, and proceeded to tell me a few home truths.'

She winced. 'Ouch.'

'They pointed out that I had no balance in my life.'

'So you bought a boat?'

He shrugged. 'It helped.'

'I'm glad, Jack, I really am. But…' She leaned back, her stomach churning. 'Why are you telling me this?'

'Because I want to help you find *your* boat.'

CHAPTER SIX

HE WANTED TO help her rediscover her passion, but she was suddenly and terribly afraid that they'd simply discover—*re*discover—that *he* was her passion. What would they do then?

You could offer to have a family with him.

No! She didn't want to live with a man who placed conditions on his love. She'd had enough of that growing up with her father. Why couldn't *she* be enough?

Oh, stop whining!

Jack stared at her, as if waiting for her to say something, but she was saved from having to answer when a little girl moved close to their table, her face crumpling up as is she were about to cry.

Caro reached out and touched the little girl's shoulder. 'Hello, sweetie, have you lost your mummy?'

The little girl nodded, her eyes swelling with tears.

'Well, I'll admit that's frightfully easy to do,' Caro continued in her usual voice—she hated the way adults put on fake voices where children were concerned, 'but shall I let you into a secret?'

The child nodded.

'Mummies are very good at finding their little girls.'

'You think Mummy will find me?'

'Oh, yes, I know she will.'

Caro was aware of Jack's gaze—the heaviness in it, the heat…his shock.

'The trick, though, is to just stay put and wait.' She glanced at the food on the table. 'Would you like a piece of garlic bread while you wait? My friend here—' she gestured to Jack '—thought I was hungry and ordered a lot of food, but…' She started to laugh. 'I had cake for breakfast, so I'm not really hungry at all.'

The little girl's eyes went wide. 'You ate *cake* for breakfast?'

'Uh-huh.'

'Is it your birthday?'

'Nope—it's just one of the good things about being a grown-up.'

In no time at all the little girl—Amy—was perched on Caro's lap, munching a piece of garlic bread. Caro didn't want to meet Jack's eyes, so she looked to the left of him, and then to his right.

'You might want to keep an eye out for a frantic-looking woman.'

'Right.'

She turned her attention back to the little girl. It was easier to look at her than at the yearning she knew would be stretching through Jack's eyes.

The sight of Caro holding that little girl, her absolute ease with the child, burned through Jack. A dark throb pulsed through him. They could have had this—him and Caro. They could have had a little girl to love and care for. If only Caro hadn't been afraid.

If only I'd been patient.

The thought slid into him, making his heart pound. She'd asked him for time but he'd thought she was putting him off, making excuses. So he hadn't given her time. In hindsight he hadn't given her much of anything.

Unable to deal with his thoughts, he stood and scanned the crowd, doing as Caro had suggested and trying to locate a worried mother in the crowd. It took less than a minute for a likely candidate to appear. He waved to get the woman's attention, and in no time flat—with a multitude of grateful thank-yous—the pair were reunited.

He sat.

Caro reached for her mineral water. 'Stop looking at me like that.'

'Like what?'

'Just because I don't know if I want children of my own it doesn't mean I don't like them.'

'Right...'

She glared at him then, before skewering a prawn on the end of her fork. For some reason, though, *he* was the one who felt skewered.

'Why on earth did you—*do* you,' she amended, 'want children so much?'

He shrugged, but his chest tightened, clenching in a cramp, and for a moment he couldn't speak.

Eventually he leant back. 'I've always wanted children... for as long as I can remember.'

'Well, now, *there's* a strong argument to convince a woman to change her entire life to fit children into it.'

With that sally, she popped the prawn into her mouth and set to picking through what was left of her pasta, obviously in search of more prawns.

A scowl built through him. 'Can't a person just want kids?'

She shrugged. 'Maybe. My next question, though, would be... Do you want children because you believe you can give them a good life and help them to grow up to be useful members of society? Or...?'

'Or...?'

'Or do you want children because you've never had a proper family of your own, have always felt lonely, and feel that children will fill that lack in your life?'

He stared at her, breathing hard. 'That's a mean-spirited thing to do, Caro—to use my background against me.'

Her forehead crinkled. 'I'm not trying to use it against you. I'm truly sorry you had such a difficult childhood. I sincerely wish that hadn't been the case. But at the same time I don't believe children should be used to fill gaps in people's lives. That's not what children are meant for.'

'Why didn't you ask me any of this five years ago?'

She set her fork to the side. 'I doubt I could've verbalised it five years ago. Your craving for children made me uneasy, but I could never pinpoint why.'

Jack wanted to get up and walk away—which, it appeared, was his default position where this woman was concerned.

'And, you see,' she continued, staring down at her plate rather than at him, 'back then it played into all of my insecurities.'

Her what?

'And that made me withdraw into myself. I realise now I should've tried to talk to you about this more, but I felt that in your eyes I wasn't measuring up.'

Her words punched through him. 'Just as you feel you never measured up in your father's eyes?' He let out a breath, seeing it a little more clearly now. 'If I'd had a little more wisdom… But your withdrawal fed into all of *my* insecurities.'

Her forehead crinkled in that adorable way again. *Don't notice.*

'Insecurities? *You*, Jack? Back then I thought you the most confident man I'd ever met.'

When he'd been sure of her love he'd felt like the most invincible man on earth.

'I saw your refusal to have children with me as a sign that I…' He pulled in a breath and then forced the words out. 'That I wasn't good enough for you to have children with.' He dragged a hand back through his hair. 'I thought that as a brash colonial from the wrong side of the tracks I was only good enough to marry so you could thumb your nose at Daddy...'

She straightened. 'I'll have you know that I've never thumbed my nose at anyone in my *life*!'

'I thought I wasn't the right *pedigree* for you.'

Her shoulders slumped. 'Oh, Jack, I was never a snob.'

He nodded. 'I can see that now.'

Her shoulders slumped further. 'I'm sorry you felt that way. If I'd known...'

'If you'd known you'd have set me straight. Just like I'd have set *you* straight if I'd known I was making you feel like *you* weren't measuring up.'

She pulled in a breath and lifted her chin. 'It's pointless wallowing in regrets. We live and learn. We'll know better than to make the same mistakes in the future...with the people who come into our lives.'

He understood what she was telling him. That there was no future for them regardless of whatever acknowledgments and apologies they made for the past now.

Beneath the collar of his shirt his skin prickled. Of *course* the two of them had no future. She didn't need to remind him!

She pushed away from the table a little. 'It's been a lovely lunch, Jack, but—'

'We were talking about boats.'

She rolled her eyes. 'I don't need a boat. I don't *want* a boat.'

'When did you become so risk-averse? *Everyone* needs a boat, Caro—a figurative one—even you. You had passions once.'

Her cheeks flushed a warm pink. His skin tightened. He hadn't been referring to that kind of passion, but he couldn't deny that as lovers they'd had that kind of passion in spades.

The one place where they hadn't had any problems had been in the bedroom. She'd been everything he'd ever dreamed of…and everything he hadn't known to dream of.

He wanted her now with the same fierceness and intensity with which he'd wanted her five years ago. The way her eyes glittered told him she wanted him too. They could go back to her flat and spend the afternoon making wild, passionate love. That would help her rediscover her passion for life.

For how long, though? Until he left and returned to Australia?

A knot tightened in his stomach. They couldn't do it. It would only make matters worse.

Caro glanced away and he knew that regardless of how much he might want it to, she'd never let it happen.

Which was just as well. His hands clenched. This time when he left he wanted to leave her better off than when he'd found her. They might still want different things out of life, but that didn't mean he couldn't help her rediscover her joy again.

He set his shoulders. 'You said you'd give me to the end of the week.'

'To find my snuffbox!'

'We need people to believe we're reuniting…we don't want them suspecting that I'm working for you.'

That was a lowdown dirty trick, but he could see that it had worked.

She folded her arms and glared at him. 'To the end of the week,' she growled.

He had to hook his right ankle around his chair-leg in order to remain seated rather than shoot to his feet, reach across the table and kiss her.

The fingers of her right hand drummed against her left arm. 'What I'd like to know, though, is what *precisely* does this entail?'

'That you be ready when I come to collect you at six o'clock this evening.'

He shot to his feet. He needed to breathe in air that didn't smell of Caro. He needed to clear his head before he did something stupid.

She blinked. 'Where are we going?'

'You'll see.'

'What should I wear?'

He'd started to turn away. Gritting his teeth, he turned back and tried to give her a cursory once-over. But his hormones said *To hell with cursory* and he found himself taking his time. Her heightened colour told him she wasn't as averse to his gaze as she no doubt wished she were.

'What you're wearing now will do nicely.'

With a half-muttered expletive, he bent down and pressed his lips to hers, refusing to resist temptation a moment longer. The kiss lasted no longer than two beats of his heart—a brief press and a slight parting of his lips to shape his mouth to hers, a silent silky slide—and then he stepped away.

Stunned caramel eyes stared back at him.

'Please excuse me if I don't walk you home.'

Walking her home would be asking for trouble.

He turned and left before he could say another word— before he did something dangerous like drag her to her feet and kiss her properly. One touch of his lips to hers hadn't eased the need inside him. It had turned it into a raging, roaring monster. Her scent and her softness had made him hungrier than he'd ever been in his life before. He needed to get himself back under control before their date tonight.

Caro changed from her earlier outfit of jeans and a peasant-style top into a pair of white linen trousers, and then flipped through her selection of blouses.

The blue silk, perhaps?

No, Jack had always loved her in blue. She didn't want him thinking she was dressing to please him.

The red?

Good Lord, no! She swished that along the rack. Red and sex were too closely aligned, and that wasn't the signal she wanted to send.

The black?

Low neckline—not a chance!

What about the grey?

She pulled it out, but shoved it back into the closet almost immediately. It showed too much midriff. She needed something asexual. She didn't want Jack kissing her again.

Liar.

Even if that lunchtime kiss had only been for show…in case anyone had been watching.

Don't be an idiot.

He'd kissed her because he'd wanted to. End of story.

A breath shuddered out of her, her fingers reaching up to trace her lips. Lips that remembered the touch and taste of him as if it had been only yesterday since she'd last kissed him. Lips that throbbed and burned with a violence she'd thought she'd managed to quell. That was bad news. *Very* bad news. She had to make sure he didn't kiss her again.

Or if he tried to she had to take evasive measures—not just sit there like a landed duck, waiting and hoping for it to happen.

Now choose a blouse!

In the end she decided on a soft pink button-down with a Peter Pan collar. As it wasn't fitted, no one could possibly accuse it of being sexy. With a sigh, she tugged it on. And not a moment too soon either, as Jack's knock sounded on the door while she was still buttoning it up.

How do you know it's Jack? It could be anyone.

She shook her head, slipping the strap of her purse over her shoulder. It would be Jack, all right. Nobody else knocked with quite the same authority. Besides, he was bang on time. He'd always had a thing for punctuality.

She took a deep breath and then opened the door, immediately stepping outside and pulling the door closed behind her. She did *not* want Jack in her tiny flat again, with its temptation of a bedroom a mere door away. The less privacy Jack and she had, the better.

'Hello, Jack.' She prevented herself from adding a snippy *again* to her greeting.

'Caro.'

The heat from his body beat at her. He wore an unfamiliar aftershave, but it had the same invigorating effect as dark-roasted coffee beans. She breathed in deeply, her nose wrinkling in appreciation.

He gave her a flattering once-over. 'You changed.'

'Just freshened up.'

'You look nice.'

She went to say thank you, but he reached out to flick one of her buttons—the second button down...*the one right between her breasts*.

'These are kinda cute.'

She glanced down and then groaned. The buttons were bright red plastic cherries! 'If you knew the lengths I went to tonight to choose an appropriate shirt you'd laugh your head off.'

'Appropriate? You'd best share. I enjoy a good laugh.'

She moved them towards the elevator. 'I wanted to choose a shirt that was...demure.' She jabbed the elevator button and the door slid open.

'So I wouldn't kiss you again?' he said, ushering her inside and pushing the button for the ground floor.

She couldn't look at him. She moved her handbag from her right shoulder to her left. 'Something like that.'

'You hated it that much?'

'Can…can we continue this conversation once we're outside, please?'

They travelled the rest of the short distance in thin-lipped silence. At least, *his* lips were thin.

'You hated it that much?' he repeated, once they stood outside on the footpath.

She pulled in a breath of warm evening air. It didn't do much to clear her mind. 'No, Jack, the problem is that I liked it too much.'

He swung to stare at her, his lips going from thin-lipped sternness to erotic sensuality with a speed that had her tripping over her own feet. He reached out to steady her, but she held both hands up to ward him off. Although he didn't actually turn around and stare back the way they'd come, she could practically feel his mind moving back to her fifth-floor flat.

'Not going to happen,' she said, wishing her voice had emerged with a little more resolution.

'We still generate heat, kiddo.'

'What good did heat do us five years ago?'

A slow grin spread across his face, turning him into a rakish pirate and her insides to molten honey. 'If I have to explain that to you then—'

'Hey, mister!' a taxicab driver shouted from the kerb. 'Do you want the cab or not?'

Caro gestured. 'Is that for us?'

Jack nodded.

She set off towards it at a half-trot. 'He wants it,' she called back to the driver, trying not to run. But she wanted to be away from her flat *now*.

Jack followed, a scowl darkening his features. He gave the driver directions, closed the dividing window and settled on the seat beside her.

'We're five years older and wiser, Caro.'

Older, maybe—but wiser? She wasn't so sure about that.

'What good do you think it would do us? We generate heat. So what? It's the kind that burns, and you know it.'

He stared down at his hands for a moment. 'Maybe this time we could make it work.'

Their marriage? She wanted to cover her ears. He *had* to be joking! She gave a hard shake of her head. 'No.'

His eyes flashed. 'You won't even think about it?'

She told herself that thin-lipped and forbidding was better than steamy sex-on-legs pirate. Not that she managed to convince herself about that.

She shook the thought away. 'Do you really believe I've been able to think of anything else since I saw you five days ago?'

She recognised the quickening in his eyes but she shook her head again, awash with a sorrow that had her wanting to curl up into a ball.

'Hell, Caro,' he ground out. 'Don't look at me like that.'

She dragged her gaze back to the front, not wanting to make him feel bad. She'd never wanted him to feel bad.

'Even though you told me you wanted a divorce, I haven't been able to stop wondering—what if we came to understand each other properly this time around? Could we make a go of it? Could this be the second chance I craved and fantasised about in those first few months after you left?'

Her throat closed over. Beside her, waves of tension rolled off Jack in a silent storm of turmoil. She passed a hand across her eyes and swallowed.

'The thing is, Jack, I keep circling back to the same conclusion. I don't believe I have what it takes to make you happy.'

'I—'

She held up a hand to cut him off. She met his gaze. 'And with you I would always be wondering… *Is he only with me because I agreed to have children?*'

He slumped back, pain tearing across his features, and she ached to hold him, to wipe that pain away and tell him that they could work it out—but if she did she feared she'd only hurt him worse later, and that would be unforgivable.

She forced herself to continue. 'I can't see things between us working out any better if *you* were the one to make the big sacrifice either. If we didn't have the children you want so much I'd be riddled with guilt.'

She clenched her purse in a death grip on her lap.

'I don't believe love and marriage should be all about self-sacrifice. It should be about two people making compromises, so they can both be happy.'

She didn't think that was possible in her and Jack's case.

'It's about both people being equally important.'

She tried, unsuccessfully, to unclench her hands from around her purse.

'I can't help feeling that in either scenario the things that drew you to me, the things you loved about me, would fade…and in the end you'd leave me anyway.' She stared at her hands. 'I'm not saying this to be mean. I'm saying it because this time I want to be completely honest with you.'

She finally turned to look at him. His eyes were alternately as soft as a kiss and as hard as adamantine.

His lips finally twisted with self-mockery. 'You really have thought about it, haven't you?'

She wanted to cry. When he'd come searching for closure had he pictured *this*?

He turned to gaze out of the window. 'No amount of mind-blowing sex can compete with that.'

A chasm opened up inside her. 'I wish I could have that great sex without paying the price.'

'But that wouldn't be the case. Not for either one of us.'

It helped a little to hear him admit it too. 'Some people subscribe to the view that the loving is worth the losing, but

I don't believe that. It took me too long to get over you the last time, Jack. And I know now it was just as hard for you.'

'You don't want to risk it again?'

Did he? *He couldn't!* She shook her head. 'The odds are just too high.'

He took her hand, pressed it between both his own before lifting it to his lips and placing a kiss to her palm. Her blood danced and burned.

'I'm so sorry, Caro. For everything.'

The backs of her eyes stung. 'Me too.'

He laid her hand back in her lap with a gentleness that had her biting her lip. How could she still want to throw herself at him with such fierceness after the conversation they'd just had?

'I swear I won't kiss you again.'

She closed her eyes and concentrated on her breathing. 'Thank you.'

'I only want to make things easier for you. Better. It was all I ever wanted.'

She couldn't speak. She could only nod. She knew that too. It was why she'd fallen so hard for him in the first place.

The taxi stopped. Caro glanced at her watch. It felt as if a whole lifetime had passed, but in reality it had been only ten minutes. She slid out from the door Jack held open for her and waited as he paid the cab driver, pulling in deep breaths to try and calm the storm raging through her.

She'd hoped such a frank conversation would ease the storm. That wasn't going to be the case, evidently. She was at a loss as to what else to try.

She glanced around, searching for distraction. She'd paid next to no mind to where they'd been going, but their location looked vaguely familiar.

Jack moved up beside her. 'Do you know where we are?'

The taxi pulled away and drove off into the warm summer evening. She had no right to feel abandoned.

Huffing back a sigh, she pointed to a sign. 'That says this is Red Lion Square. So…we're in Holborn?'

He nodded. 'We're heading for a building on the other side of the park—and then my dastardly plan will be revealed.'

He smiled, but she saw the effort it cost him. Reaching out, she pulled him to a halt. His warmth immediately flooded her, daring her to foolishness, and she reefed her hand back.

'Are…are you sure you still want to do this?' She wouldn't blame him if he wanted a time out. It wasn't his job to help her find happiness again, her relish for life.

'Of course I still want to do this.' He stared at her for a long moment before shoving his hands into his pockets. 'I have no desire, though, to force you into something *you* don't want to do. If you want to leave, Caro, just say the word.'

She didn't even know what *this* was yet, but that wasn't really what he was referring to anyway. He wanted to see her smile and have fun again. She wanted the same for him. And she sensed that by helping her he'd be helping himself.

From somewhere she dug out a smile. 'I'm game if you are.' The force of his smile was her reward. She turned away, blinking. 'Lead on, Macduff.'

He led her into the headquarters of one of London's premier Scrabble clubs. Her jaw dropped as she took in the sight of the boards and players set up around various tables.

A young man brimming over with energy came bustling up. 'You must be Caro Fielding. I'm Garry.' He turned to Jack. 'You're—?'

'A friend,' he supplied, with a wink at Caro. 'I rang yesterday.'

'I remember. You said Caro might be interested in joining our club.'

He had, had he? 'I—'

'She's a brilliant player,' Jack inserted.

Good grief! 'I haven't played in an age. And he exaggerates.' She elbowed Jack in the ribs but he just grinned down at her, utterly unrepentant.

'Well, why don't we set you up with Yvonne? She's pretty new to the club too.'

Before Caro knew it she found herself deep in a fierce game of Scrabble. She'd loved the game once. She and Jack used to play it—though he'd never really been a match for her. He'd only ever played to humour her. But when had *she* stopped playing?

When Jack had left.

Her heart thudded.

At the end of the game she sat back and stared at the neat rows of tiles. 'You just wiped the board with me.' A thread of competitiveness squirmed its way to the surface. 'Again?' She wanted a chance to redeem herself.

They started another game. Caro was vaguely aware of Jack strolling around the room, watching the other games, but she had to block him out to concentrate on the game in front of her.

'You might be rusty,' her opponent said, 'but you're picking it up again at a fast rate of knots.'

Caro lost the second game as well—but not by a margin that made her wince. An old fire she'd forgotten kindled to life in her belly. 'Best of five?'

Yvonne simply grinned and started selecting a new set of tiles.

Caro was amazed to find that three hours had passed when a bell sounded and they were instructed to finish up their games. Where had the time gone?

She glanced about, searching for Jack. When she found

him, leaning back in a chair at a neighbouring table, he grinned at her, making her heart pitter-patter.

'Ready?' he said, standing and ambling over to her.

'Just about. I have to hand in my registration form and pay my club dues.'

He started to laugh. 'You don't want to think about it for a bit, then?'

'Heavens, no.'

For some reason that only made his grin widen.

'Do you know they hold competitions—and there's a Scrabble league? Did you know there are world championships?'

'You have your eye on the main prize?'

'Not this year.' She tossed her head, a little fizz of excitement spiralling through her. 'But next year could be a possibility.'

'C'mon.' Throwing an arm across her shoulders, he led her outside. 'Let me buy you a burger.'

'Ooh, yes, please! I'm starved!'

'And I owe you a meal.' He grimaced down at her in apology. 'I didn't realise until much later that I'd left you holding the bill for lunch today.'

They both remembered the reason why Jack had left so abruptly.

He removed his arm from her shoulders and she edged away from him a fraction. She cleared her throat and tried to grab hold of the camaraderie that had wrapped itself around them so warmly just a few short moments ago.

'It's a small price to pay for this.' She gestured back behind her to indicate the Scrabble club. 'I had a great time tonight. I'd forgotten how much I enjoyed Scrabble. It was an inspired idea, Jack. Thank you.'

The burgers were delicious, but while they both did their best to make small talk the easy camaraderie had fled.

'Where are you staying?' she asked him afterwards.

He named a hotel in Covent Garden. 'Oh, Jack, you could walk there from here. Please—you don't need to see me home.'

'But—'

'Truly! I'd prefer it if you didn't.' She wanted to avoid any fraught goodnight moments on her doorstep. 'But I'd appreciate it if you'd flag me down a cab.'

'You insist?' he asked quietly.

She gave a quick nod. He looked far from happy, but he didn't argue. He hailed a cab and insisted on paying for it.

As he helped her inside he said, 'Tomorrow. Six p.m.'

A ripple of anticipation squirrelled through her. 'Again?'

'Wear a dress and heels. Small heels—not stilettos.'

She did everything she could to prevent her breath from hitching. 'Will we be cabbing it again?'

'Yes.'

'Then I'll wait downstairs for you. Goodnight, Jack.'

With that she sat back, before she did something daft… like kiss him.

CHAPTER SEVEN

'SALSA CLASSES?'

Caro's mouth dropped open, but Jack kept his concentration trained on the expressions flitting across her face rather than the temptation of her lips, shining with a rose-pink lipstick.

Lips he ached to kiss fully and very, *very* thoroughly. Lips he wanted to tease, tempt and taste. The longer he stared at those lips, the greater the need that built inside him.

Who was he trying to kid? What he wanted was Caro, warm and wild in his arms, wanting him just as much as he wanted her.

Except he wasn't supposed to be thinking about that!

He dragged his attention back to her expression, trying to decide whether she was excited or appalled. Maybe a bit of both.

'What do you think?' he found himself asking.

They'd attended dance classes once—back before they were married. At the time he hadn't been all that keen—except on the thought of holding Caro in his arms. He hadn't let on, though. He'd been too intent on wooing her. To his utter surprise, the dance classes had been a blast.

She frowned up at him. 'I'm really not sure this is such a good idea.'

She was afraid of the physicality of the dance, afraid of where it would lead…and maybe a little afraid of herself and her own body's yearnings. He needed to put her mind at rest and reassure her that they could survive one dance class together.

The results of the few enquiries he'd made into Caro's life since returning to London—showing the extent of her withdrawal into herself—had shocked him. That was the price she'd paid for the breakdown of their marriage. It was a price she should never have paid and it was time for it to stop.

He touched a finger to her temple—gently and very briefly. 'The Scrabble is for your mind and the dance classes are for your body. A healthy mind and a—'

She blew out a breath that made her fringe flutter. 'And a healthy body,' she finished for him. 'If you say one word about me eating too much cake...'

'Wouldn't dream of it. Cake is necessary too. I don't see why you should feel guilty about eating cake.'

She rolled her shoulders. 'I don't.'

'Then stop being so defensive.'

He moved them to one side as a couple bounded up the steps to push through the door.

The young woman turned just before entering. 'Are you thinking of joining the class? You should. It's great fun—and a really good workout.'

'My friend here is,' Jack said, before Caro could pooh-pooh the whole idea. 'The problem is that I can only attend tonight.'

'That's not a problem. There are two guys in the class who are currently looking for partners—Marcus and Timothy.' She leaned in closer. 'I'd go with Tim. He's a bit shy, but really lovely. See you inside.'

With a smile, she and her partner disappeared through the door.

Jack turned back to Caro and spread his hands, saying

nothing, just letting the situation speak for itself. She bit her lip, glancing once again at the flyer on the door.

Her uncertainty pricked him. 'You loved dancing once.'

'Yes.'

He wanted to ask her what she was afraid of. He didn't. He decided to try and lighten the mood instead. 'It's either this or rock wall climbing.'

She spun back to him, her eyes widening. 'I beg your pardon?'

'There's a gym not too far from your flat that has a climbing wall. I bet it'd be great fun. A great workout for the arms too.'

A laugh shot out of her. 'You can't be serious?'

'Why not?' He grinned back at her. 'Except as we're here, and not there, I did come to the conclusion that you'd prefer this to that. If I'm wrong, just say the word.'

When had she become so risk-averse?

With another laugh, she took his arm and hauled him into the hall.

She wore an amber-coloured dress with a fitted bodice and a skirt that flared gently to mid-calf. It looked deceptively plain until she moved, and then the material—shot through with sparkling threads of gold and bronze—shimmered. Beneath the lights she sparkled, until he had to blink to clear his vision. He led her to a spot on the dance floor before moving away to speak to the dance instructor for a few moments.

He drew in a fortifying breath before returning to Caro and waiting for the class to begin.

He was insanely careful to keep a respectable distance between their bodies when the music started and the instructor began barking out instructions, but her warmth and her scent swirled up around him, playing sweet havoc with his senses. The touch of her hand in his, the feel of her through the thin material of her dress where his hand rested at her waist, sent a surge of hot possessiveness coursing through him.

He had no right to that possessiveness.

He gritted his teeth. He only had to get through one night of salsa. Just a single hour. He gritted his teeth harder. He could do it.

'I can't believe how quickly it's all coming back,' Caro murmured, swinging away and then swinging back.

Her throaty whisper told him that their proximity bothered her too. *That* didn't help. He pulled in a deep breath, but it only made him draw in more of her scent. That *really* didn't help. *Don't think about it.*

'I was worried your feet might be black and blue after an hour of dancing with me.'

'Liar! If you were worried about anybody's feet it was your own. You were always better at this than me.'

'Not true. I mastered the moves quicker, but once you had them down pat you were a hundred times better.'

Their gazes snagged and locked. They moved across the dance floor with an effortlessness that had Jack feeling as if they were flying. Staring into her dark caramel eyes, he could almost feel himself falling...

Stop! a voice screamed through his mind.

With a heart that beat too hard, he dragged his gaze away. He had to swallow a couple of times before he trusted his voice to work. 'I checked with the teacher and found out that's Tim over there.' He nodded across the room to a slim, well-groomed man with light hair and a pleasant smile.

Caro mistimed her step and trod on Jack's foot. 'Oops.' She grimaced up at him in apology. 'It's a challenge to count steps, talk and look round all at the same time.'

Fibber. But he didn't call her on it.

'Why don't we introduce ourselves at the end of the lesson?'

One of her shoulders lifted. 'Seems to me he's found a partner.'

'She's an instructor here. She's filling in to make up the numbers.' He glanced across at the other man again. 'He seems pleasant enough. He's not tramping all over her feet either, so that's a plus.'

'For heaven's sake, Jack! Do you want to give him my phone number and set me up on a date with him too?'

He snapped back at her biting tone. 'Don't be ridiculous.' He glanced across at the other man again. This Tim wasn't her type…was he? 'Your private life is your own to do with as you will.'

It suddenly occurred to him that encouraging Caro to get out more would throw her into the company of men. Men who would ask her out. Men she might find attractive.

He had a sudden vision of Caro in the other man's arms and—

'Ouch!'

He pulled to an abrupt halt. 'Hell! Sorry!'

He bent down to rub her foot, but she pushed him away, glaring at him. 'What are you doing?'

'I was…um…going to rub it better.'

'Not necessary!'

Those amazing eyes of hers flashed cinnamon and gold fire and all he could think of was kissing her foot better, and then working his way up her leg and—'

'Come! Come!'

The dance instructor, who had a tendency to repeat everything twice, marched up to them now, clapping his hands, making Jack blink.

'You must concentrate! *Concentrate*, Jack. Take your partner in your arms.'

He adjusted their positions, moving them a fraction closer to each other, pressing a hand into the small of Caro's back to force her to straighten. The action thrust her chest towards Jack. Jack stared at those delectable curves, mere centimetres from his chest, and swallowed convulsively.

Good God! Torture. Utter torture.

'You must maintain eye contact,' the teacher barked at them.

With a superhuman effort Jack raised his eyes to Caro's.

'This is the salsa!' The man made an exaggerated gesture with his hands. 'This is the dance of flirtation!'

Caro's eyes widened. It was all Jack could do to swallow back a groan.

'So…you must flirt.' He performed another flourish. *'Flirt!'*

Caro's eyes started to dance, and Jack could feel answering laughter building inside him. The instructor moved away to harangue another couple.

'You *will* flirt,' Caro ordered in a mock authoritarian tone. 'We have ways of *making* you flirt!'

He gulped back a bark of laughter.

'It's quite a conundrum,' Caro continued, this time in her own voice. 'How exactly *does* one flirt while dancing?'

She made her eyes innocent and wide. Too innocent. He felt suddenly alive.

He grinned and nodded towards their teacher. 'According to him, lots of eye contact.'

She eyeballed Jack, making him laugh. 'Tick,' she said. 'We have that down pat. But we can't accidentally brush fingers when we're already holding hands.'

'And with your hands already engaged you can't do that cute twirling of your hair around one finger thing, while giving me a come-hither look.'

She snorted back a laugh. 'Ah, but I *can* lasciviously lick my lips in a suggestive fashion.'

She proceeded to do so—but she did it in such an over the top fashion he found himself hard pressed not to dissolve into laughter.

'Your turn,' she instructed. 'You *will* flirt!'

He copied her move in an even more exaggerated way, until they were laughing so hard they had to hold onto each other to remain upright.

'Excellent! Excellent!' The instructor beamed at them. 'Now, *dance*.'

The rest of the hour flew by.

'That was fun,' Caro said a little breathlessly when they stood on the footpath outside afterwards.

Jack put her breathlessness down to the unaccustomed exercise.

'Night, Tim,' she called out when the other man bounded down the steps.

'See you next week, Caro,' the other man called back, with a smile that set Jack's teeth on edge.

He refused to put Caro's breathlessness down to the fact she'd made a *new friend*.

'Stop glaring like that,' Caro chided. 'It was your idea.'

Not one of his better ones, though. It felt as if he was handing her over to another man. Without a fight.

He scowled up at the sky. 'Just remember I don't want an invitation to your wedding.'

'I'm not even going to dignify that with an answer.'

He shook himself. He wouldn't blame her for simply walking away. 'Sorry. Uh…hungry?'

She eyed him for a moment before finally nodding. 'Yes.'

Excellent! He refused to dwell on why he wasn't ready for the night to end. 'There's a great little restaurant around the corner that has—'

'No.'

He frowned at her. 'No?'

'A restaurant meal is too much like a date, Jack, and we aren't dating. C'mon—I know a better place.'

The dance school was in Bermondsey, just a couple of

stops on the tube from Caro's nearest station. He'd chosen it for the convenience of its location. He'd wanted to make attending classes there as easy and trouble-free for her as possible. He scowled down at his feet. He hadn't meant for it to be that easy for her to hook up with another man, though.

He tried to shrug the thought off. It shouldn't matter to him. He wanted a divorce, remember?

Ten minutes later he found himself in a large park, with people dotting the green space, making the most of the summer evening.

She pointed. 'There.'

He grimaced. 'A fish and chip van?'

'You can get a burger if you prefer.'

Without further ado she marched up to the van and ordered a single portion of fish and chips. She shook her head when he reached for his wallet. She paid for it herself. She didn't offer to pay for his meal.

He received the message loud and clear.

He ordered the same, and then found them a vacant park bench. He figured her dress wasn't made for sitting on the grass.

'So, if this isn't a date,' he said, unwrapping his fish and chips, 'what is it?'

'The kind of meal friends would share.'

Was this how she and Tim would start out—sharing a friendly meal in the park? Maybe they'd eventually progress to dinner in a pub, and then romantic candlelit dinners for two in posh restaurants?

Stop it! Caro deserves to be happy.

He closed his eyes. She *did* deserve to be happy.

'Are you okay?' she asked quietly.

It was one of the things he'd always appreciated about her—she never made a fuss, never drew attention unnecessarily.

He shook his head, and then nodded, and finally shrugged, feeling oddly at sea. 'I wanted to say that I've thought about what you said the other day.'

'Hmm…?' She popped a chip into her mouth. 'You might need to be a bit more specific than that.'

'About my reasons for wanting children.'

She paused with a chip halfway to her mouth. 'You don't have to explain anything to me, Jack.'

'If not to you, then who?'

She lowered the chip back to the packet. 'To yourself.'

He stared around the park, at the family groups dotted here and there, and his soul yearned towards them. To belong like that, to be loved like that…to *create* that—it was all he'd ever really wanted.

He turned back to Caro. 'It's occurred to me that I'm better prepared for fatherhood now than I was five years ago. You were right. I wanted children too much back then.'

'I'm not sure it's possible to want something like that *too* much,' she said carefully.

'You were spot-on. I wanted them for *me*—to make me feel better and…and whole.'

She stilled, staring down at the food in her lap. 'Even if that was the case, I don't doubt that you'd have been a fabulous father.'

'Maybe—but I'd have had a few rude awakenings along the way.'

She went back to eating. 'That's just life.'

'I wanted you to know that, after looking back, I don't blame you for the misgivings you had.'

She slumped, as if her spine no longer had the strength to support her. She stared at him, her eyes sparking copper and gold. 'That…' She swallowed. 'Thank you. That… It means a lot.'

She deserved to be happy.

He forced himself to continue. 'You've also made me confront my own selfishness.'

Her head rocked back.

'When I said I wanted to have a family, what I really wanted was for you to *give* me a family. I expected you to give up work and be a full-time mother.' He stared down at his hands. 'But if someone had asked *me* to give up everything I was asking you to give up when I was twenty-five, I wouldn't have given it up without a fight either. I'm… I'm sorry I asked that of you.'

She reached out to grip his hand. She didn't speak until he turned to look at her. 'What you wanted wasn't a bad thing, Jack. Stop beating yourself up about it. Apology accepted, okay?'

Her words and her smile made him feel lighter. She released his hand and it took all his strength not to reach for her again.

'Wow…' She shook her head. 'When you say you want closure you really mean it, huh?'

He didn't want closure. He wanted her back.

The knowledge he'd been trying to ignore for two days pounded through him now.

'For my part…' She pushed her shoulders back. 'I'm sorry I withdrew into myself the way I did. I should've tried to talk to you more, explained how I was feeling. You're not a mind reader. It was unfair of me.'

But she'd been scared—scared that he'd reject her. Just as she was too scared to take a chance on them again now.

'I am truly sorry for that, Jack.'

'Likewise—apology accepted.'

Could he change her mind? His heart beat hard. Could he find a way to make her fall in love with him again? What about the issue of children? Could he give that dream up for Caro?

* * *

Caro tried to ignore how hard her heart burned at the care-worn, almost defeated expression on Jack's face.

She tried to dredge up a smile. 'We're a classic example of marry in haste, repent at leisure.'

They should have made more time to get to know each other on an intellectual level, discussed what they wanted out of life. Instead they'd trusted their instincts—had believed so strongly that they were fated for each other. Because that was what it had felt like—and they'd ignored everything else.

Being with Jack had felt so *right*. The world had made sense in a way it never had before. The fact of the matter, though, was that their instincts had led them astray. They'd wanted to believe so badly in the rightness and the *uniqueness* of their love that they'd left logic, clear thinking and reality behind. Arrogant—that was what they'd been…too arrogant.

'You don't believe what's been broken can be fixed, do you?'

He was talking about *them*. Her stomach churned. He wasn't thinking clearly—muddled by a combination of hormones, nostalgia and an aching sentimentality that she could—unfortunately—relate to. The fact that he found himself liking her again had rocked him—shocked him to his marrow. It was no surprise to her that she still liked *him*.

She glanced across and a chasm of yearning opened up inside her. Not liking each other would make things so much easier. If only…

She bit back a sigh. No, she couldn't think like that. One of them had to keep a clear head.

'No.' She made herself speak clearly and confidently. 'I don't believe we can be fixed.'

His shoulders slumped and it took all of Caro's strength

not to lean across and hug him, unsay her words. Jack hated failure. He always had. But in a day or two he'd see that she was right—that she was saving both of them from more heartbreak.

'Eat your chips,' she ordered. 'They'll make you feel better.'

He cocked a disbelieving eyebrow. 'Chips will make me *feel better*?'

'Deep-fried carbohydrate cannot help but boost the soul.'

Five years ago Jack had left angry—in a white-hot fury. And he'd stayed angry for all this time. It was what had fuelled him. Now that the anger was dissipating it was only natural that he should find himself grieving for their lost love. She'd already done her grieving. He was just catching up.

It was odd, then, how she found herself wanting to be there for him as he went through it.

Dangerous.

The word whispered through her and she acknowledged its innate truth. She had to be careful not to get sucked back into the disaster their marriage had become. She couldn't go through that a second time.

She went back to diligently eating her chips. Wallowing wouldn't do either one of them any good. What they needed was a sharp reminder of their differences.

'You know,' she started, with a sidelong glance in his direction, 'I always envied your confidence that you could make a family work.'

His gaze grew keener. 'What do you mean?'

She munched a chip, desperately searching for a carbohydrate high. 'My own experience of family wasn't exactly positive. It didn't provide me with role models of any note.' She gave a short laugh. 'Let's be frank, it was totally dysfunctional. You met my father. For as long as I can remember he was remote and controlling. Paul tells me he was different when my mother was alive, but…'

'You don't believe that?'

She shrugged. 'I don't have any strong memories of my mother before she died.'

'You were only five.'

'In the same vein, I don't have any memories of my father being different before she died.' She couldn't recall *ever* connecting emotionally with him. 'Although I don't doubt her death affected him.'

Her mother had died of breast cancer, and she knew, because Paul had told her, that her mother had been seriously ill for the eight months prior to her death. It must have been hell to witness.

She shook herself and glanced at Jack. The look in his eyes made her mouth suddenly dry and she didn't know why.

'You think he loved her?' he asked.

She tried to get her pulse back under control. 'I guess the fact it took him fourteen years to remarry is probably testament to that.'

He frowned. 'You're saying you think you'd take some of that dysfunction into your relationship with any children you might have?'

'Well…yes. It seems plausible doesn't it? I mean, in my kinder moments I tell myself my father was simply a product of his own upbringing…'

'But doesn't the fact that you're aware of that mean you'll take extra steps to make sure you're *not* like him?'

She shoved a chip into her mouth and chewed doggedly. 'I don't know. It all seems such a…*gamble*.'

What if she couldn't help it? What if she made those hypothetical children's lives a misery? The thought made her sick to the stomach.

She turned to face him more fully. 'Jack, your child-hood was far worse than mine.'

He shook his head. 'I'm not so sure about that.'

'I grew up with wealth. Money makes a big difference. It couldn't buy me a family, granted,' she added, when he went to break in. 'But it was a hundred times better than being in the same situation and struggling financially. A *thousand* times better. I've been lucky in a lot of ways.'

Lucky in ways Jack had never been. She'd done nothing to earn those advantages. He'd deserved so much better from life.

He'd deserved so much better from her.

'You think my confidence is misplaced?'

'No!' She reached out to grip his arm, horrified that he'd interpreted her words in such a way. 'I *always* believed you'd be a wonderful father. I just wished I could believe in my own abilities so wholeheartedly. That's what I meant when I said I envied you. I... I didn't understand where that confidence came from. I still don't.'

He glanced down at her hand. She reefed it back into her lap, heat flushing through her. 'I...uh...sorry.'

'You don't need to apologise for touching me, Caro. I like you touching me.'

His words slid over her like warm silk, and for a moment all she could do was stare at him. Her breathing became shallow and laboured. Had he gone mad? She eyed him uncertainly before shuffling away a few centimetres. He couldn't be suggesting that they...?

Don't be daft. He'd promised to not kiss her again. *You didn't promise not to kiss him, though.*

She waved a hand in front of her face.

Jack scrunched up what was left of his dinner and tossed it into a nearby bin. His every movement reminded her of his latent athleticism. He'd always been fit and physical, and he'd been very athletic in bed.

Don't think about that now.

He settled back, stretching his legs out in front of him and his arms along the back of the bench. His fingers toyed with her hair. He tugged on it gently and she tried not to jump.

'There was one particular foster family that I stayed with when I was twelve…'

She stilled. Jack had rarely spoken about his childhood, or about growing up in foster homes. All that she knew was that his mother had been a drug addict who'd died from an overdose when Jack was four. But whenever she'd asked him questions or pressed him for more information, he'd become testy. The most she'd ever extracted from him was that he hadn't suffered any particular cruelties, but he hadn't been able to wait until he was an adult, when he could take charge of his own life.

As for the rest of it… She'd automatically understood his loneliness in the same way he'd understood hers.

'What was this family like?' She held her breath and waited to see if he would answer.

'They were everything I ever dreamed a family could be.' He smiled, his gaze warm, and it made something inside her stir to life. 'Through them I glimpsed what family could be. Living with them gave me hope.'

Hope?

He told her how Darrel and Christine Jameson hadn't been able to have children of their own, so they'd fostered children in need instead. He described picnics and outings and dinner times around the kitchen table when the television would be turned off and they'd talk—telling each other about their day. He laughed as he told her about being grounded when he'd played hooky from school once, and being nagged to clean his room. He sketched portraits of the two foster brothers he'd had there, and how for twelve short months he'd felt part of something bigger than himself—something good and worthwhile.

Something he'd spent the rest of his life trying to recapture, she realised now.

Envy swirled up through her. Envy and longing. 'They sound wonderful. Perfect.'

'They were going to adopt me.'

Her heart dipped and started to throb. This story didn't have a happy ending.

'What…what happened?' She had to force the words out. Jack had deserved to spend the rest of his life enfolded within this family's embrace. Why hadn't that happened?

'Darrel and Christine were tight with a core group of other foster carers.'

That sounded like a *good* thing. They'd have provided each other with support and advice.

'One of their friends' foster sons got into some serious trouble—taking drugs, stealing cars.'

Her heart thumped.

'It was a mess. He became violent with his foster mother.'

She pulled in a jagged breath. 'That's awful.'

'Nobody pretends that taking on a troubled child is going to be easy, but common wisdom has it that the good gained is worth the trouble and the heartache.'

'You don't believe that?'

He pulled in a breath. 'Seems to me that all too often "well-intentioned" and "idealistic" are merely synonyms for "naive" and "unprepared".'

She swallowed, wanting to argue with him but sensing the innate truth of his words.

'The incident really spooked them—especially Christine. And when my older foster brother was caught drinking alcohol, we were all farmed back to Social Services.'

Although he didn't move, the bleakness in his eyes told her how that had devastated him.

She pressed a hand to her mouth for a moment. 'I'm so sorry.'

He shrugged, and she didn't know how he managed to maintain such an easy, open posture. All she wanted to do was fling herself against his chest and sob for the thirteen-year-old boy who'd lost the family of his dreams. She could feel his fingers in her hair, as if touching it brought him some measure of comfort. She held still, willing him to take whatever comfort he could.

'You never found another family like that one?'

He cocked an eyebrow. 'How do I grieve, Caro?'

She stared at him and then nodded. 'You get angry.'

'I stayed angry for the next five years. I acted out. Got a name for myself within the system. I spent my last two years in a group home.'

She swallowed. 'A detention centre?'

'No, it wasn't that bad, but it wasn't really a…a *home*, if you catch my drift.'

She did. And everything inside her ached for him.

'It was a place to mark time until I became an adult and the state could wash its hands of me.'

She tried to control the rush of anger that shook through her. 'Boarding school was a hundred times better than that!'

He twisted a strand of her hair around his fingers. 'I'm glad.'

She bit her lip, the touch of his hand in her hair sending spirals of pleasure gyrating deep in her belly. She shifted in an attempt to relieve the ache. 'Why aren't you bitter about losing that family?'

'I was for a long time, but they taught me that my dream could come true. I'll always be grateful to them for that—for providing me with a yardstick I could cling to.'

She moistened her lips. He zeroed in on the action, his

eyes darkening, and a groan rose up through her. The pulse at the base of his jaw started to pound and her heart surged up into her throat to hammer in time with it. She tried to draw a steadying breath into her lungs, but all she drew in was the scent of him.

'Have you…have you ever considered becoming a foster carer yourself?'

His fingers in her hair stilled. 'No.'

'Maybe you should. You'd know the pitfalls and understand the stumbling blocks. You'd be brilliant.'

He'd be a wonderful father.

'I…'

He faltered and she shrugged. 'It's just something to think about. Obviously not the kind of decision you'd make on the spur of the moment.'

'But worth considering,' he agreed slowly.

She had no intention of wasting such a rare opportunity when he was in such an amenable mood. 'So you didn't feel you belonged anywhere again until you joined the police force?'

When she'd first met Jack he'd been working for the Australian Federal Police. He'd been stationed in London, on secondment to the British Intelligence Service as a surveillance instructor.

Those blue eyes of his sparked and grew even keener if that were at all possible. 'The police force gave me a direction in life. But, Caro, I didn't feel I belonged anywhere again until I met *you*.'

CHAPTER EIGHT

CARO'S MOBILE PHONE RANG, making her jump. Her fountain pen corkscrewed across the page in an example of less than elegant penmanship. She glared at the blot of ink she'd left behind. *Botheration!*

The phone rang again. She pressed it to her ear. 'Hello?'

'Are you home?'

Her hand about the phone tightened. 'Good morning, Jack. How are you? I'm well. Thank you for asking.'

His chuckle curled her toes. 'Caro, as ever, it's a delight.'

She wanted to stretch and purr at the warm amusement in his voice. *So* not good.

'I'm running up your stairs as we speak.'

He didn't sound the slightest bit breathless. If she walked, let alone jogged up the stairs, she'd huff and puff for a good five minutes.

'Really, Jack, is running necessary?'

This time he laughed outright.

Don't bask. Stop basking!

'Your door has just come into view.'

She snapped her phone off and turned to stare at her door. What was he doing here? If they had to meet, why couldn't they have done it somewhere public?

The snuffbox!

Her stomach tightened. With reluctant legs, but a madly beating heart, she moved across to the door and opened it. She tried not to look at him too squarely as she ushered him in. 'To what do I owe the pleasure?'

'Your manners are one of the things I've always admired about you, Caro.'

Was he laughing at her? Or did he sense her resentment at his intrusion? 'Do you have news about the snuffbox? Have there been any developments?'

He glanced down at the table and frowned. 'What are you doing?'

A scowl she didn't understand started to build inside her. She swallowed and sat. 'You're the detective. What do you *think* I'm doing?'

He lifted the sheet of paper she'd been practising on. *'"My darling Barbara. Wishing you many happy returns for the day. May you always be happy. To my darling wife. Love. Much love. All my love. Roland."'* He turned the paper sideways to follow her scrawls. *'"Your Roland. Roland. Your loving husband, Roland."'*

She grimaced. Would her father ever have signed himself as Barbara's loving husband? How on earth could she gush it up a little and still sound sincere?

Jack set the sheet of paper down and lifted one of the letters her father had sent to her while she'd been away at university. She'd received one or two missives from him every semester. Cursory things that never actually said much. She didn't even know why she'd kept them.

Dropping the letters back to the table, he reached for the jewellery catalogue and sales receipt sitting nearby. His nostrils flared, but whether at the picture of the diamond necklace or at the amount on the receipt, she wasn't sure.

'That is worth…'

'A significant amount of money,' she agreed.

'It's hideous.'

'Very true. However, it's not its beauty that matters, but

its value.' Besides, it was the kind of piece her father would have admired. If he'd still been alive to admire it, that was.

Jack tossed the catalogue and the receipt back to the table. 'My detective brain informs me that it's Barbara's birthday soon.'

'Today.'

'And that you're faking a gift to her from your father… from beyond the grave.'

She summoned up her brightest smile. 'I *knew* you were more than just a pretty face.'

He didn't smile back. 'When were you going to tell me about this?'

His lips thinned when she blinked. She pushed her bangle up her arm. 'I wasn't. I don't see how it has any bearing on…on other things.'

'You try and guilt Barbara into giving the snuffbox back and you don't think that's relevant?'

No, she wasn't! This—

'How much more is this worth than the snuffbox?'

She could tell from the way he'd started to shake that he was getting a little…um…worked up. 'It's…' She moistened her lips. 'It's probably worth about three times as much, but that's beside the point. I—'

'You really think Barbara is the kind of woman who can be worked on like this? Have you lost your mind completely? She'll take the necklace *and* the snuffbox and run!'

Caro shot to her feet. 'Stop talking about her like that!' She strode around the table and stabbed a finger at his chest. 'You're wrong! I know her far better than you do, and yet you automatically assume your assessment of her is the right one and that mine is wrong!'

'You're too close.' The pulse at the base of his jaw ticked. 'Your emotions are clouding your judgment.'

'No!' she shot back. 'It's your prejudices that are colouring your judgment. You're just like my father.' She whirled away. 'You think because Barbara is young and beautiful she must've married my father for his money.'

'If your father thought that, then why the hell did he marry her?'

She swung back. 'He didn't think that about her. He thought it about *you*!'

A silence suddenly descended around them. All that could be heard was the harsh intake of their breath.

Caro forced herself to continue. 'When you married me, you married a potential heiress. There are some people who would insinuate that your showing up now, like you have, is so you can collect your cut of the spoils. That's how people like my father and his lawyers think.'

His eyes grew so glacial the very air grew chill. 'I thought we'd already covered this.'

'I *don't* think like that. I *don't* believe you ever married me for my money and I *don't* believe money is the reason you're back in London. Why do I think that? Ooh, let's see…' She cocked her head to one side and lifted a finger to her chin. 'Could it be because I'm a good judge of character?'

Jack closed his eyes and dragged a hand down his face.

'Believe me, Jack. If there's one person who clouds my judgment, it's you. Not Barbara. I *know* she didn't marry my father for his money.'

He slammed his hands to his hips. 'But you believe she stole the snuffbox?'

'Not out of malice or for vengeance! It was a stupid spur-of-the-moment thing, done in a fit of pique and hurt, and now… Well, I expect she's bitterly regretting it and trying to find a way to get it back to me.'

He blew out a breath. 'May I sit?'

Good Lord, where were her manners? 'Please.' She gestured to a chair.

He fell into it and then motioned to the paraphernalia on the table. 'And this?'

She lowered herself back to her own chair. 'This has nothing to do with the rest of it.'

'I don't understand.'

She could tell from the low timbre of his voice that he wanted to. She moistened her lips. It meant talking about love. And talking about love to Jack…

She pushed her shoulders back. 'Believe me when I tell you that Barbara loved my father. She believed that he loved her too.'

It took a moment or two, but comprehension eventually dawned across his face. 'And when he cut her out of his will…?'

She nodded. 'I mean, *we* know the reason for his sudden coldness.'

'But she has no idea he thought she was stealing from him?'

'I can't tell her the truth. She and Paul have no warmth for each other. With him, I fear she would retaliate. To be honest, a part of me wouldn't blame her.'

'Damn it, Caro. Part of me wants to say not your monkeys. Not your circus.'

'But it's not true, is it? I know they're not the kind of family you've always dreamed about, but they're all I have.'

Jack lifted the sheet of paper she'd been working on, stared at it with pursed lips. 'You're pretty good, you know.'

'Yes, I developed quite the reputation among my school friends.'

He glanced up, his eyes alive with curiosity. 'You'll have to tell me about it one day.'

When? At the end of the week he'd be gone and she'd never see him again. There wouldn't be any cosy nights in, laughing over reminiscences. Not for them.

'You're hoping this necklace will reinforce the fact that your father did love her?'

'Yes.'

He stared at the sundry messages she'd written when copying her father's handwriting. 'Men are less verbose than women.'

She leaned towards him. 'What are you trying to say?'

'I think you should just sign the card *Love, Roland* and leave it at that—leave all of this other stuff out.'

'Are you sure?'

'Positive.'

She glanced through the letters her father had sent her and realised Jack was right. Her father had never been demonstrative. At least not in his letters. Pulling the card towards her, she carefully wrote *Love, Roland.*

'Utterly authentic,' Jack said.

'It seems I've developed an unfortunate taste for deception. I've made the jeweller swear on all he holds dear that should Barbara contact him he'll say he was acting on my father's wishes—that all this was organised months before he died.'

'You've covered all bases?'

She hoped so. 'All I have to do now is drop this card in at the jeweller's and the package will be ready for delivery this afternoon.'

He stared at her for a long moment, making the blood pump faster around her body. It took a concerted effort not to fidget.

'What?'

'You're a woman of hidden talents, and at the moment that's to our advantage.'

'What are you talking about?'

'Can you forge Barbara's signature as well as you do your father's?'

'I don't know. I've never tried.' She'd never had to forge

her stepmother's signature on a permission slip. Not that it had ever really been necessary to forge her father's either. It had just been easier than asking him—quicker and cleaner. It had saved her from having to look into his face and be confronted anew with his disappointment.

She pushed the thought away and pursed her lips. 'From memory, though, Barbara's isn't a difficult signature.' Unlike her father's, which was all bold strokes and angry slashes. 'I'd have to see it again before…'

She trailed off when he whipped out a form. Barbara's signature appeared at the bottom.

'Right…' She stared at it. After five attempts she had it down pat. 'How is this going to help us?'

He pulled a key from his pocket and set it on the table. 'Do you know what this is?'

'A key, obviously, but I have no idea what it's supposed to unlock.'

'A safety deposit box.'

She pulled in a quick breath. 'Barbara's?'

He nodded and handed her the appropriate paperwork.

'Good Lord, Jack! Where on earth did you get this?'

He raised an eyebrow and she held both hands up, palm outwards.

'You're right. I don't want to know.' She studied the paperwork. 'This isn't held at the bank my father did business with.' Her father had dealt with a bank in the city. This branch was in Chelsea.

'Do you know anyone who works there?'

She stared at the name of the bank and nodded. 'Lawrence Gardner—in another branch of the same bank. He's the father of an old school friend.' She shook her head. 'I'm sorry, Jack, but I can't ask him to check this safety deposit box. I—'

'What I'm trying to assess is the likelihood of us running into anyone you know if we were to go to that branch with you posing as Barbara.'

'I… What? Oh, God! I think I'm going to hyperventilate.'

He didn't turn a hair. 'We have two days to reclaim the snuffbox.'

Two days before a police inquiry descended on her head.

Caro swallowed. Barbara might have made a mistake, but she didn't deserve a police record and jail. 'You think the snuffbox is in that safety deposit box?'

'I can't think where else it'd be.'

'But…but I don't even *look* like Barbara,' she croaked. Barbara was tall, thin…gorgeous.

'You're both blonde.'

'She's ash-blonde.' Caro was a honey-blonde. 'And her hair is long.' So were her legs…

'I can get you a wig. And if you wore one of those sharp little power skirts she fancies, with a twinset and dark glasses…'

'Those things won't make me tall and thin.'

'No, the disguise won't hold up to close scrutiny,' he agreed. 'Not for someone who knows you or her…like this Lawrence Gardner. Would he recognise you?'

'Oh, that won't be a problem. He works from the bank's main office, which is in Knightsbridge.'

Her heart pounded hard.

She stared at him. 'You believe that if I go in there with this key, the ability to forge Barbara's signature and a blonde wig that I could pass for her?'

'Especially if you have some additional ID.' He handed her a credit card and an ATM card.

She squished her eyes shut. 'I'm not going to ask…'

'I'll have them back to her before she even knows they're missing.'

She hoped he was right.

'But, yes, I believe all of those things combined will gain us access to the box…if you dare.'

The way he said it reminded her of the way he'd challenged her on not having fun any more, on being *risk averse*. She pushed up her chin. She wanted that snuff-box back. She wanted Barbara in the clear. She dragged in a breath. *And* she wanted to keep her job and her professional reputation.

She folded her arms. Mostly to hide how badly her hands were shaking. 'When do we do it?'

'Today.'

Dear Lord!

Nerves jangled in Caro's stomach when Jack switched off the car's engine. She pulled down the sun visor to scrutinise her reflection in the mirror again.

'You look perfect,' he assured her.

He'd parked in an underground car park not too far from the bank. He didn't want to rely on taxis or public transport. He didn't want them to be seen. Which made her nerves jangle harder.

She pushed the visor back into place. 'I've been thinking. I should go in on my own.'

If she didn't pull this off then at least Jack wouldn't get into trouble too. She refused to dwell too deeply on the kind of trouble *she* could get into if this didn't go to plan. If she did that she'd freeze.

'Not a chance, kiddo. I'm in charge of this operation. I'm not sending you in there alone.'

She wanted to weep in relief. *Coward.*

'I'm not letting you have all the fun.'

She turned to gape at him. *'Fun?'*

'You and me—we're partners in crime.'

'Fun?' she repeated. *'Crime?'*

He grinned, exhilaration rippling in the depths of his eyes. 'Besides, we're not doing anything wrong. Not really.'

'Tell that to the judge.'

His grin widened. 'We don't want to steal anything. We don't want to hurt anyone. We just want to right a wrong.'

His words made her feel like a cross between Robin Hood and the Scarlet Pimpernel.

'To achieve that end we have to pit ourselves against the system—a worthy adversary. Are you going to tell me you're not experiencing even the tiniest flicker of anticipation?'

'Adrenaline junkie,' she accused, but there was no denying the fever that seemed to be working its way through her blood. *Keep breathing.* 'Any last instructions?'

'Do your best to channel Barbara.'

'That won't be difficult, darling.'

'Perfect.' He rubbed his hands together. 'Once inside, try and keep your head down. Stare at your hands or feign preoccupation with the contents of your purse. I don't want the CCTV cameras getting a good shot of you.'

Dear Lord!

There were two people ahead of her in the queue, and Caro's nerves steadied as they waited their turn. The fact that no alarms or sirens had sounded when they'd entered through the bank's sliding glass doors helped.

She twirled the wedding band Jack had suggested she wear round and round her finger. *Her* wedding band. She'd taken it off two years after Jack had left. Wearing it again now, she felt as if a missing part of her had been reclaimed. Which was an utterly crazy notion, because the thin circle of gold was nothing more than an empty symbol.

Don't think about it. Stay in character.

She pursed her lips and tapped her foot. She didn't watch a lot of thrillers, preferring dramas and comedies, but she did her best to summon a list of kick-ass heroines to mind. There was that Lara Croft *Tomb Raider* character—she was pretty handy in a tight situation. Oh, and Julia Roberts's character in *Ocean's Eleven*—very suave. They were women who strode out confidently and held their heads high.

She was about to toss her hair and lift her head when she recalled Jack's strictures to keep her head down. Hmm, on second thoughts they might not be the best archetypes to use as models in this particular situation. Still, she made a resolution to watch more movies with capable, efficient, devil-may-care, thrill-seeking female protagonists. And now that she thought about it, amateur dramatics might be a spot of fun. Maybe she should look into—

'We're up.'

She started at Jack's words, but her preoccupation helped her not only to keep her legs steady, but her voice steady too. 'Good afternoon,' she greeted the teller. 'I'd like to access my security deposit box, please.'

She handed over the paperwork Jack had procured. Heaven only knew when or how he'd done it, but she had visions of him dressed in black, prowling silently through the house in Mayfair.

Mind you, the vision wasn't without merit…

'If you'd like to follow me, Mrs Fielding?'

A thrill shot through her. This was working! They were going to get away with it.

'Certainly,' she said, following the teller along the length of the counter to a door. This was almost too easy. It occurred to her then that she could become a bit of an adrenaline junkie too.

The teller had started to punch in the door's code when it opened from the other side and a man strode out. Caro's heart leapt into her throat. She ducked her head, using Jack's body as a shield.

Please, please, please...

'Caro!'

Her heart thundered so hard she thought her whole body must pulse with the force. What on earth was Lawrence doing *here*?

The teller frowned and glanced down at the paperwork. 'Caro...?'

Think fast!

'Lawrence, darling, it's *Barbara*.' She made herself beam. 'You do that every single time—mix me up with Caro. We're not even related. It must be the blonde hair.' She reached up to kiss his cheek. 'Please don't give me away...' she whispered. Throwing herself on her sword was the only option.

He stared at her for a long moment, before taking her hand and bringing it to his lips. 'That was clumsy of me. How have you been coping since the funeral?'

To Caro's utter horror she could feel tears start to prick the backs of her eyes. She gave an awkward shrug. 'Oh... you know.'

'What are you here for?'

Caro let the teller explain, while she tried to gain control over the pounding of her heart. What on earth was Lawrence doing in Chelsea rather than Knightsbridge?

'I'll take care of Ms Fielding,' Lawrence told his underling.

Caro swallowed a wince at Lawrence's use of Ms rather than Mrs.

Taking Caro's arm, he led her and Jack back the way he'd come, not releasing her until they reached an office. He closed the door before swinging back. 'Caroline Elizabeth Fielding, what on *earth* do you think you're playing at?'

She swallowed. 'Hello, Uncle Lawrence.'

* * *

Uncle Lawrence! Jack closed his eyes. What on earth had he got Caro into?

He cleared his throat and stepped forward. 'Sir—'

'Uncle Lawrence, this is my husband, Jack. I don't believe the two of you ever met.'

As she spoke she led Jack to a chair and pressed him down into it. She squeezed his shoulder briefly—a not so-subtle signal to keep his mouth shut. Jack fully intended on taking the complete blame for whatever trouble was about to rain down on their heads, but he'd let her have her way for the moment. He was curious to see what she'd do.

'Jack, this is my Uncle Lawrence. It's an honorary title, of course.' In the same fashion as she'd led Jack to a chair she now led her 'honorary uncle' to the chair on the other side of the desk. 'He's my best friend's father. I spent most of my summers at their house in the Lake District.'

Her best friend? He thought for a moment. 'Suzie?'

Her eyebrows shot up as she took the seat beside him. 'You remember her?'

'Sure I do—the super-smart brunette addicted to *Twilight* movies and Hobnob biscuits.'

She'd been at their wedding. He frowned, trying hard to remember something else—anything else. If they could soften the father through the daughter...

'Wasn't she relocating to Switzerland, to run a department of some trading bank?'

Both Caro and Lawrence laughed. 'She's practically running the entire operation now,' her father said with pride, and Jack gave thanks for the tack Caro had taken.

'Good for her. I'm glad she's doing so well.'

'Well, she is now,' Caro said. 'Things were a bit bumpy there for a while, after her second little girl was born. Suzie had postnatal depression, but she's doing great again now.' She shot Lawrence a smile. 'We had a long, slightly wine-fuelled chat the week before last. She's doing wonderfully. You must be so proud of her.'

'I am.' He paused, his eyes keen. 'You know I'll always be grateful to you, Caro, for taking leave like you did, to be with her for those first few weeks after she was released from hospital. It made all the difference.'

It struck Jack how much pressure career-minded women who wanted children were put under. Men rarely suffered the same pressures. He eyed Caro now, his lips pursed.

'It's what friends do…and godmothers.'

Caro was a *godmother*?

'I'd do anything for Suzie and her family. Just as she'd do anything for me and mine.'

That was a masterstroke of emotional manipulation. Jack wanted to shoot to his feet and give her a standing ovation.

'Caro—'

'Uncle Lawrence, I find myself in something of a pickle…'

Without further ado Caro told Lawrence the entire story. By the time she finished the older man had taken off his glasses and was rubbing his eyes.

Caro leaned towards him. 'You *have* to see that I can't let Barbara go to jail.'

He pushed his glasses back to the bridge of his nose. 'Caro, if I take you through to that safety deposit box I will be breaking so many codes of conduct, not to mention laws, that I wouldn't be able to hold my head up in public and—'

'*I* don't actually want to look inside her safety deposit box.'

Jack swung to her. *What on earth…?*

From her bag she pulled out a photograph. 'This is a picture of the missing snuffbox. I don't want to know what else Barbara is storing in the deposit box—that's none of my business. But maybe *you* could check the box to see if that's there.' She pressed the photo into his hand. 'I'm not asking you to remove it—just to see if it's there.'

She stared at her Uncle Lawrence with pleading eyes and Jack held his breath right alongside her.

Lawrence stared at them both for several long moments. 'Do *not* move from those seats.'

Caro crossed her heart. Without another word, Lawrence rose and left.

Caro turned to Jack, sagging in her seat, her hand pressed to her heart. 'I'm so sorry. I can't believe he turned up here today of all days.'

Jack shook his head. 'Not your fault. And this may, in fact, work out better.'

Her shoulders drooped. 'Except now I've involved someone else in my life of crime.'

He meant to say, *Nonsense*. What came out of his mouth instead was, 'You're a godmother?'

A smile suddenly peeked out and he had to catch his breath at the way her face lit up. 'Twice over. To both of Suzie's little girls. Would you like to see a picture?'

'Love to.'

His heart thumped madly when he glanced down at the picture of Caro sitting on a picnic blanket with a toddler in her lap and a baby in her arms. She looked…so happy. His chest twisted. Had he ever made her that happy?

He *wanted* to make her that happy. He wanted—

He blinked when Lawrence came back into the office. Caro reached across and took the photo from his fingers, flashing it towards Lawrence with an abashed grin before slotting it back into her purse.

They all stared at each other and then Caro shuffled forward to the edge of her chair. If he didn't know better he'd think she'd started to enjoy all this subterfuge and intrigue. 'Well?'

Lawrence slumped down in his chair. 'I didn't find the snuffbox.'

Damn! Jack's hands fisted. Had Barbara managed to dispose of it in that half-day before he'd come on the case? He'd had her tailed ever since. He'd had all the guests at the country house party thoroughly investigated, and had come to the conclusion that Barbara hadn't even taken the snuffbox with her that weekend. Instinct told him she'd gone there to make initial contact with someone. He kept waiting for her to visit one of those guests…or for one of them to turn up at the house in Mayfair. So far, though, there'd been nothing.

'I did, however, find this.'

Jack snapped back to attention when Lawrence placed a locket on the desk in front of Caro.

She stilled, before reaching out to trace it with one finger. 'Mother's locket…'

'That belongs to you.'

Exactly! What on earth was Barbara doing with it? It must be worth a fortune.

'Although I have no real memory of her, all my life I've felt overshadowed by my mother.' She stared at the locket with pursed lips. 'My father set that charity up in her name and then expected me to devote my life to running it. He turned my mother into a kind of saint, and there's not a living, breathing woman who can compete with that. It wouldn't surprise me in the least to find that Barbara has felt overshadowed by the first Mrs Fielding too.' She scooped up the locket with its heavy ornate gold chain and put it in Lawrence's hand. 'Put it back. I have so much. I don't need this.'

Lawrence stared down at the locket, his face grim. 'There are some rather interesting items in that deposit box…'

Caro shook her head. 'Barbara is entitled to her secrets.

I have no right to them. I have no desire to pry further than I already have.' She moved to where Lawrence sat and pressed a kiss to his brow. 'I can't thank you enough for all you've done. May I come to dinner some time soon?'

'You know you're welcome any time. Your Auntie Kate would love to see you.'

He rose and kissed both Caro's cheeks. As he did so he held his business card out to Jack behind Caro's back. Jack pocketed it before Caro could notice the exchange.

'It was nice to meet you, sir.'

'I'm reserving my judgment,' Lawrence said in reply.

Jack and Caro walked back to the car without exchanging a single word. As soon as they reached it, however, Caro started hopping from one foot to the other. Her eyes glittered and her cheeks flushed pink with what he guessed was an excess of adrenaline.

'That was…' She reached out as if to pluck a word from the air.

'A close call,' he finished for her. 'If Lawrence Gardner didn't hold you in such high esteem we'd be toast by now.'

She grabbed his arm, all but dancing. 'Jack, I can't remember the last time I felt so…*alive*!'

'And you call *me* an adrenaline junkie.'

He kept his voice teasing, but all the while he was aware of her grip on his arm and the warm smile dancing across her lips. An ache as big as the Great Barrier Reef opened up inside him. His every molecule screamed at him to kiss her.

'I could get addicted to that.'

Addiction? He stared down at her luscious mouth. Yes, he understood addiction. He thought he might explode into a thousand tiny pieces if he didn't kiss her.

You can't kiss her. You promised.

'Thank you.'

'What for?' he croaked.

'For believing I could pull that off.'

Tenderness rose up through him, warring with his desire—and they entwined, forming something stronger and brighter. 'You were brilliant.' It was nothing less than the truth. 'You saved the day.'

'I can't remember the last time I had to think quickly on my feet like that. For a split second I didn't know whether to lie or to confide in Lawrence.'

'You followed your instincts and they didn't let you down.'

She reached up on tiptoe and kissed his cheek. He bit back a groan.

'I…'

Her voice trailed off at whatever she saw in his face. Her eyes met his and darkened. Her gaze lowered to his lips and her own lips parted ever so slightly—as if she were parched, or as if she couldn't quite catch her breath. Wind roared in his ears. She wanted him. With the same desperate hunger that ravaged him. He'd promised not to kiss her, but…

He moved in closer, traced a finger down the soft flesh of her cheek. Her breath hitched. Her eyes never left his.

'You…' She hiccupped again as his finger moved down the line of her throat. 'You promised,' she whispered.

'I promised not to kiss you,' he murmured. 'I don't recall promising not to touch you. You can tell me to stop any time you want to and I will.'

Her lips parted, but no words emerged.

A surge of something hot and primal pulsed through him. 'And I don't recall *you* promising not to kiss *me*.'

Her breath hitched again. Maintaining eye contact, he took her hand and raised it to his lips, nibbled on the end of her ring finger and then her middle finger, drawing it ever so slightly into the warmth of his mouth.

'You didn't promise you wouldn't kiss me,' he whispered

again. 'And I want you to kiss me, Caro. I want that more than I've ever wanted anything in my life.'

A shiver shook through her. He went hard in an instant.

'I didn't promise that I wouldn't put my arms around you...'

Very slowly she shook her head. 'No, you didn't promise that.'

Very slowly he backed up until he was leaning against the car. He drew her towards him to stand between his legs—not quite touching, but their heat swirled and merged and another shiver shook through her.

He kissed the tips of each of the fingers of the hand he still held. 'I didn't promise not to place your arm around my neck...'

He put her hand on his shoulder, snaking an arm about her waist and pulling her closer. The feel of her in his arms was familiar and strange both at the same time. Her other hand slid about his neck too.

'Jack...' she whispered.

He moved his face to within millimetres of hers. 'I didn't promise not to ask you to kiss me...'

'Oh...'

The word was nothing more than a breath and it whispered across his lips, drawing everything inside of him tight. Her hands tightened about his neck.

'I'm not asking, Caro,' he groaned. 'I'm begging. Please kiss me. I—'

She leant forward and pressed her lips to his.

CHAPTER NINE

THE MOMENT HER lips touched his Jack had to fight the torrent of need that roared through him. It took all his strength to let her take the lead and not crush her to him. He didn't want to overwhelm her with his intensity. He didn't want to frighten her with his hunger. He wanted her to remain right here, where she belonged—in his arms.

His hunger was all about *him* and he wanted this kiss to be all about *her*—he wanted to give her everything she needed, everything she craved. He wanted their kiss to tempt, to tease and to tantalise her on every level.

He didn't want the kiss ever to stop. He wanted it to whet her appetite—for him, for *them*. He wanted it to challenge her belief that they couldn't be fixed.

She pressed in closer and a groan broke from him. 'You're killing me.'

She laughed, her breath feathering across his lips. 'And here I was thinking I was kissing you.'

He grazed his teeth across the sensitive skin of her neck, just below her ear, and she melted against him. 'Jack…' His name left her on a whisper, filling him with vigour and a lethal patience.

He kissed a slow path down her throat, revelling in the taste of her and the satin glide of her skin. He moulded her to him—one hand in the small of her back, the other between her shoulderblades. Slipping his lower hand beneath the soft material of her shirt, he lightly raked his fingernails across her bare skin as he kissed his way up the other side of her throat.

She gasped and shivered and pressed herself all the more firmly against him. He wanted to give her so much pleasure it would blot everything else from her mind—the pain he'd caused her, the mistakes they'd made five years ago.

He wanted her filled—body and soul—with the promise of their future. A future he had utter faith in.

He moved his lips back to hers, pressing light kisses at the corners of her mouth, wanting to drive her wild with wanting. Her hands slid up through his hair to hold him still, and his heart pounded until he thought it might burst. She slanted her mouth over his—all open-mouthed heat and wild need—and Jack couldn't contain himself any longer. It was like coming home. It was like being welcomed home.

Fireworks of celebration exploded behind the backs of his eyes. He crushed her to him, wanting the line between where she started and he ended to blur until they became one.

Caro wrapped her arms around Jack's neck and held on for dear life as the maelstrom of desire they'd always ignited in each other rocked through her, lifting her off her feet and hurtling her along with a speed that would have stolen her breath if Jack hadn't already done so. It should frighten her, except she knew Jack would keep her safe. He would never let any harm come to her.

To feel him, to taste him again, alternately soothed and electrified her. It was so familiar, and yet so dark and dangerous. An utter contradiction. Kissing Jack was like every risk she'd ever taken rolled into one—and it was like every warm blanket she'd ever pulled about herself. Kissing Jack was like being flung out of her mind and body at the same time. It was heady and wild.

And it was frightening too—what if she never found

herself again? She didn't want to lose herself. Not completely. Not for all time. If she made love with Jack now where would she ever find the strength to be true to herself? How would she be able to resist all that he would ask of her? She would try to become everything he wanted—needed—and in the process she'd become something neither one of them would recognise.

And then she would have nothing.

Half sobbing, she reefed herself out of his arms. Backing up a couple of steps, she leaned against the car to try and catch her breath. Jack closed his eyes and bent at the waist to draw in great lungfuls of air. She forced her gaze away from him, tried to stamp down on the regrets rising through her, tried to ignore her body's insistent demand for release.

An hour of heaven was not worth another five years of hell.

She started when two arms slammed either side of her on the car, trapping her within their circle. 'You are the most divine woman I have ever met.'

And he was the most divine man she'd ever met—but she wasn't going to say that out loud. She hitched up her chin. 'That could be a sign that you need to get out more.'

He stared down at her, and she didn't know what he saw in her face, but it left her feeling naked.

One corner of his mouth hooked up. 'You never were a pushover.'

Could've fooled her.

'We need to talk, Caro.'

'About the fact we're still attracted to each other?' What was the point of that?

'We could start there.'

She shook her head. 'I can't see there's much we can do about it.'

'Really?' he drawled, cocking a suggestive eyebrow.

She found it hard to stamp down on the laugh that rose through her. In the back of her mind the salsa teacher's voice sounded: *You will flirt!*

'Not going to happen, Jack.'

He raised that eyebrow higher.

She shook her head, but it was harder than it should have been. 'An hour of pleasure is not worth a lifetime of regrets.'

He leaned in closer. 'I can make it last longer than an hour.'

God forgive her, but her breath hitched at the promise lacing his words.

'Do you really think we'd have been able to stop if we'd been at your flat or in my hotel room rather than in a car park?'

She didn't know the answer to that, and she had no intention of finding out. 'I never thought I'd say this, but I'm glad this happened in a public place.'

He reached out and brushed his thumb across her oversensitised lips. It was all she could do not to moan and touch her tongue to him.

'You still want me.'

'With every atom of my body,' she agreed.

His eyes darkened and his breathing grew shallow at her admission.

'But I am not a mindless body controlled by impulse. I possess a brain, and that brain is telling me not to just walk away from this, Jack, but to run.'

'You're frightened.'

'You should be too! You didn't emerge unscathed the last time we did this.'

He made as if to cradle her cheek, but she snapped upright.

'You're crowding me.'

He immediately dropped his arms and moved back. She

paced the length of the car before coming back to stand in front of him.

'We have no future together, and I cannot do some kind of final fling with you. I've worked too hard to get over you to risk undoing all my hard work now.'

He stared at her for a long moment. 'I beg to differ with you on one point, Caro.'

She folded her arms and tapped a foot. 'Really?'

'I believe we *could* have a future together.'

Her arms slackened. Her jaw dropped. 'You *can't* be serious.'

His eyes grew keen and bright. 'I've never been more serious about anything in my life.'

Fear, raw and primal, scrabbled through her, drawing her chest tight.

'What makes you—' he leant down so they were eye to eye '—so certain we *don't* have a future?'

'Our past!' she snapped. He was being ridiculous! Nostalgia was making him sentimental.

'We can learn from the mistakes of our past.'

'Or we could simply repeat them.'

He shook his head. 'I'm smarter now. I know what it is I really want—and that's you.'

No! She wouldn't believe him. She *couldn't*. 'What about children.'

'I don't care if we have children or not.'

How long would that last? 'I don't believe you.' This time she moved in close, invading his personal space. 'I think you want children as much as you ever did.'

His eyes flashed. 'I want you more.'

She stepped back. She wouldn't be able to live with him making that kind of sacrifice.

'Does *nothing* of what I say make any impact on you?' he demanded, his voice ragged.

She swung away and closed her eyes against the pain

cramping her chest. 'Jack, for the last five years you've held me solely responsible for the breakdown of our marriage. In the last eight days you've been confronted with your own culpability. I understand your sense of guilt, I understand your desire to make amends and to try and put things right, but…' She turned, gripping the tops of her arms tightly. 'We cannot be put to rights. There's no longer any *"we"* that can be salvaged.'

Her words seemed to beat at him like blows and each of them left her feeling bruised and shaken.

He seized her by the shoulders, his face pale though his eyes blazed. 'I love you, Caro. Doesn't that mean anything to you?'

Yearning yawned through her. To have…

No!

She hardened her heart and shook her head. 'I don't wish to be cruel, Jack, but no, I'm afraid it doesn't.'

Turning grey, he let her go, his shoulders slumping as if she'd just run him through with a sword. She had to bite her lip to stifle the cry that rose up through her.

Why had he ever come back to London?

Why hadn't he simply sent the divorce papers through the post?

She'd rather he'd continued to blame her—hate her—than put him through this kind of emotional torment.

She had to leave before she did something stupid, like hurl herself into his arms and say sorry, tell him she loved him too. Love wasn't enough. It never had been. It was better they face that now than another twelve months down the track.

She pulled herself up to her full height. 'I'll see myself home.'

He stiffened. 'Get in the car, Caro. I will take you home.'

Her hands clenched. 'I am not a child who can be ordered about or cajoled. I have a free will, which I'm choosing to assert now. I would much prefer to see myself home.' She tried to pull in a steadying breath. 'But thank you for the offer.'

He stared at her, shoved his hands in his pockets. 'Right.'

She moistened her lips. 'I think it'd be for the best if we didn't see each other again.'

His head jerked up. 'The snuffbox—'

'Is lost forever, I expect.'

'I haven't given up hope.'

She had.

'At nine o'clock on Friday morning—' the day after tomorrow '—I'll be informing my boss that I've lost the snuffbox and I will tender my resignation.'

The pulse in his jaw jumped, but he didn't say a word.

'I'd like you to send me a bill for your time and expenses, though I suspect you won't.'

'You suspect right.'

'I'll sign the divorce papers and have them sent to your lawyer.'

She couldn't say any more. Her throat ached too much from saying the word *divorce*—it lodged there like a block of solid wood, its hard edges pressing into her with such ferocity it made her vision blur.

She spun away and made for the exit. 'Goodbye, Jack.'

The letters on the car park exit sign blurred, but she kept her focus trained on their neon glow rather than the throb at her temples or the pain pressing down on her chest. It took all her strength to remain upright and to place one foot in front of the other.

This was for the best. She could never trust Jack again. She could never be certain that the next time she failed to measure up to his expectations he wouldn't just walk away again. And she wouldn't be able to bear that.

She hadn't made him happy five years ago. Oh, they'd had great sex—there was no denying that—but a solid mar-

riage needed stronger glue than great sex. She and Jack…
they didn't have that glue.

The sunshine made her blink when she finally arrived
outside. She scowled at it. How dared the day be so…*summery*?

She caught the tube home. *Please, please, please, don't
be one of those people who cry on the train.* She couldn't
bear the mortification of that.

She might not be able to turn the pain off, but she could
try and corral her thoughts. She recited the alphabet silently
until she reached her stop. On wooden legs, she turned in
at Jean-Pierre's bakery.

He spun with a smile that faded when he took in her expression. *'Ma cherie.'* He shook his head. 'Not a good day?'

'Dreadful, dreadful day,' she agreed tonelessly. 'The
worst.' She gestured to his counter full of cakes. 'I'm looking for something that will make me feel better.'

Sugar wasn't the answer. They both knew that. But
she blessed his tact in remaining silent on the subject. He
packed her up an assortment. She trudged upstairs to her
flat and sat at the table. She stared at the cakes for several
long minutes—a chocolate éclair, a strawberry tart, a vanilla slice and a tiny lemon meringue pie.

She couldn't dredge up the slightest enthusiasm for a
single one of them.

The longer she stared at them the more her eyes stung.
A lump lodged in her throat. Shaking her head, she lifted
the chocolate éclair to her lips and bit into it. She chewed
and with a superhuman effort swallowed. She set the éclair
back down. Its dark brown icing gleamed the exact same
colour as Jack's hair—

Slamming a halt to those thoughts, she picked up the
lemon meringue pie, bit into it, chewed and swallowed.
She did the same with the strawberry tart and then the vanilla slice. With each bite the lump in her throat subsided.

It lodged in her chest instead, where it became a hard, bitter ache.

She stared at the delicacies, each with a dainty bite taken out of them, and pushed the cake box away to rest her head on her hands.

Jack started when he realised darkness had begun creeping across the floor of his hotel room. He barely remembered returning here earlier in the afternoon, but the stiffness in his muscles told him he'd been sitting in this chair for hours.

He glanced across to the window. The grey twilight on the other side of the glass complemented the greyness stretching through him.

He closed his eyes. Every fibre of his being ached to go and find Caro and change her mind—to fight harder for her—but…

He rested his head in his hands. The look on her face when he'd told her he loved her… He'd wanted to see joy, hope, delight. He'd wanted her to throw her arms around his neck and tell him she loved him too.

Instead…

He dropped his head back to the headrest of his chair. Instead she'd stared at him with a kind of stricken horror that had made his heart shrivel.

He understood now how out of character it had been for Caro to fall in love with him so quickly six and a half years ago. How out of character it had been for her to marry him after knowing him for only four months. By nature Caro was a careful person, but she'd loved him back then. She'd trusted him completely, and when he'd left he'd not only broken her heart, he'd broken faith with her, he'd made her doubt her own judgment.

He should have fought for her five years ago!

He'd misinterpreted her reserve as meaning she didn't

love him. Instead of challenging her, though, he'd run away. *Like a coward.*

He'd blown it. He'd get no second chance with her. She'd never let him close again, regardless of the promises he made her.

What promises have you made? What exactly have you offered her?

He frowned at the gathering darkness. With a curse, he leapt to his feet and switched on the lamp before reaching for his laptop. There were no promises he could make that Caro would believe, but he had promised to do all he could to retrieve that damn snuffbox. That was one thing he *could* do for her.

Settling earphones over his head, he tuned in to the listening devices he'd placed in the house in Mayfair earlier in the week. *Give me something!*

Two hours later he pulled the earphones from his head and flung them to the desk.

Eureka!

He backed up the files in three different locations, emailed them to each of his email accounts, burnt them to a CD and loaded them on to a thumb drive as a final precaution. Next he researched the government's National Archive. Forty minutes later he tossed both the CD and the thumb drive into his satchel. Throwing the bag over his shoulder, he set off on foot for Mayfair.

'Mr Jack,' Paul boomed when he opened the door. 'It's very good to see you.'

That wasn't what the treacherous snake in the grass would be saying in ten minutes' time.

'Jack?' Barbara appeared in the doorway of the drawing room. 'Is Caro with you?'

'No.'

He might have misjudged Barbara—just as Caro had

said—but she was still as treacherous as Paul in her own way. Though at least now he understood her.

Barbara moved more fully into the foyer, a frown marring the china doll perfection of her face. 'Is everything all right, darling? Is Caro all right?'

'Caro is fine, as far as I know.' And he meant to keep it that way. 'But everything is far from all right. I need the two of you to listen to something. Do you have a CD player?'

Barbara swept an arm towards the drawing room and directed him across to the far wall, where a stereo system perched on an antique credenza.

'Don't go, Paul,' Jack added, not turning around but sensing the older man's intention to withdraw. 'I want you to hear this too.'

He put the disc into the player, surreptitiously retrieving one of his listening devices as he did so. He'd retrieve them all before he left this evening. He pressed the play button.

'You might want to sit,' he said, gesturing to the sofas.

Barbara and Paul both remained standing.

'This necklace didn't come from Roland, Paul, and we both know it.'

As her voice emerged from the speakers, Barbara sank down into the nearest chair with a gasp, her hand fluttering up to her throat.

'There's only one person who could possibly be responsible for this, and that's Caro.'

A short pause followed, and then Paul's voice emerged from the speakers. *'Yes.'*

Jack could almost see the older man's nod as he agreed with Barbara.

'I don't want to do this any more, Paul. I want Caro to know the truth.'

'We can't! We promised her father! And there's your

mother to think of. You could never afford her medical bills on your own.'

Jack reached over and switched the CD player off. 'I could let it keep running, but we all know what it says.'

Barbara lifted her head and swallowed. 'I'm glad the truth will come out now.'

And yet only a couple of hours ago she'd submitted to Paul's bullying.

'Are you *utterly* faithless?' Paul shot at her.

His words were angry, but everything about him had slumped, as if he were caving in on himself.

'Faithless?' Jack found himself shouting. 'What about the faith you should've been keeping with Caro? She loves the two of you! She considers you her family. And this is how you treat her?'

Barbara wasn't a woman easily given to tears, but she looked close to them now. He sensed her regret was genuine. And, considering the bribery Roland had used to sway her, he could almost forgive her. *Almost.*

He shoved his shoulders back. 'Shall I share the conclusions I've come to?'

Barbara spread her hands in a *please continue* gesture. Paul said nothing, but his back had bowed and he'd lost his colour.

'Sit, Paul,' Jack ordered.

The other man's head lifted. 'I'm the butler, Mr Jack. The butler doesn't—'

'Can it! You lost all rights to butler etiquette the moment you started this nasty little game.'

Without another word, Paul sat. Jack stared at them both, trying to swallow back the fury coursing through him.

'Before he died, Caro's father made the two of you promise to sabotage Caro's job at Richardson's in an attempt to have her fired—so you could force her hand and have her finally take over the administration of that damn trust.'

Barbara hesitated, and then nodded. 'He thought that by making her the sole beneficiary of his will it would soften her attitude towards both him *and* the trust.'

'And of course the two of *you* were to do everything you could to encourage that softening?'

She winced and nodded.

'I also know that if you succeeded, you were both to be rewarded.'

Barbara's head came up.

'I suspect your mother's hospital bills and her care were to be guaranteed if you succeeded.' He named the medical facility where Barbara's mother resided. 'I know the kind of care she needs, and I know how much that costs.'

She shot to her feet, visibly shaken. 'How do you know about that?'

'I'm a private investigator. I'm trained to follow a lead.'

He'd found out Barbara's mother's name and had tracked her to a private medical clinic in Northumberland. A phone call had confirmed that she had a severe dissociative personality disorder and needed round-the-clock psychological monitoring. She was receiving the very best of care. The fees, however, were astronomical.

Barbara sat again, brushing her hand across her eyes. 'I can't even visit her. It upsets her too much. Making sure she gets the best of care is the one thing I *can* do.'

He couldn't imagine how difficult that must be. 'I'm sorry about your mother, Barbara.'

'Thank you.'

'Roland blackmailed you?'

She glanced up and gave a strained shrug. 'In a way, I suppose. But you see I *did* love him. Ours wasn't a wild, romantic relationship, but… I wanted him to be happy. It didn't really seem too much to ask of Caro, to administer that wretched trust, but…'

'But?'

She lifted her head. 'But, regardless of what the rest of us think or want, Caro has a right to make her own decisions in respect to her life.'

His heart thumped. 'I couldn't agree more.' He just wished she'd made the decision to include *him* in her life. Pushing that thought aside, he turned to Paul. 'What I don't understand is why *you'd* agree to Roland's games. I thought you cared about Caro?'

'I do!'

Nobody spoke for several long moments.

'He just loved Caro's mother more,' Barbara finally said, breaking the silence that had descended.

Jack fell into a seat then too. Paul? In love with Caro's mother?

'I went too far.' Paul rested his head in his hands. 'What are you going to do, Mr Jack?' he asked.

If Caro didn't care about these two so much he'd throw them to the wolves. But she *did* care about them.

It occurred to him then that his idea of family had been utterly unrealistic—a complete fantasy. Family, it appeared, was about accepting others' foibles and eccentricities. It was about taking into account and appreciating their weaknesses as much as their strengths.

He leaned towards the other two. 'Okay, listen carefully. This is what we're going to do…'

Caro was brushing her teeth on Friday morning when Jack's knock sounded on her door.

She knew it was Jack. She refused to contemplate too closely *how* she knew that, though.

She rinsed her mouth and considered not answering.

'Caro? I have the snuffbox.'

His voice penetrated the thick wood of her door. She stared at it, and then flew across to fling it open. 'If you're teasing me, Jack, I'll—'

He held out the snuffbox, and for a moment all she could do was stare at it.

'Oh!'

She could barely believe it. Maybe…maybe disaster could be averted after all.

With fingers that trembled she took it from him, hardly daring to believe this was the very same snuffbox she'd lost. She took Jack's arm and pulled him into the flat, and then ran to get her eyeglass. She examined it in minute detail.

'What are you doing?'

'Making sure it's authentic and not a replica.'

'Well…?' he asked when she set the eyeglass to the table.

She wanted to dance on the spot. 'It's the very same snuffbox I lost last week.'

She wanted to hug him, but remembered what had happened the last time she'd let her elation overcome her reserve. She pressed a hand to her chest to try and calm the pounding of her heart.

'You've saved the day—just as you promised you would. How? How did you do it?'

He shuffled his feet and darted a glance towards the kitchen. 'Is that coffee I smell?'

She suddenly realised he was wearing the same clothes she'd last seen him in, and that he needed a shave. She padded into the kitchen and poured them a mug of coffee each. She set his mug to the table.

'Have a seat.'

With a groan, he unhooked his satchel from his shoulder and dropped it to the floor, before planting himself in a chair and bringing the mug to his lips. 'Thank you.'

She frowned at him. 'Have you had any sleep in the last two days?'

He made an impatient movement with his hand. 'It's no matter. I can sleep on the plane.'

He was returning to Australia *today*? An ache started up inside her.

It's for the best.

Except the misery he was trying to hide beat at her like a living, breathing thing.

She sipped coffee in an attempt to fortify herself. 'How did you find the snuffbox? Who had it?'

'It was all a comedy of errors, believe it or not, and frankly you needn't have hired me in the first place.'

She frowned. 'What are you talking about?'

He eyed her over the rim of his mug. 'You have an army of cleaners coming in to the Mayfair house twice a week, yes?'

'Yes.'

'It appears that when Barbara made her midnight raid on the safe she dropped the snuffbox on the stairs.'

So why hadn't she or Paul found it?

'The next day the maid dusting the staircase found it and placed it in the sideboard in the dining room. She thought it was some kind of fancy spice pot, or something along those lines.'

'And therefore thought it belonged with the dining ware?'

'Of course she forgot to mention to anyone what she'd done.'

She gaped at him. 'So it was never Barbara? Oh, I should burn in brimstone forever for thinking such a shocking thing of her!'

His lips pressed together in a thin tight line.

'It's such a simple explanation! But…how did you find all of this out?'

'I rang the cleaning service you use, spoke to the woman in charge and asked her to check with the staff.'

Amazingly simple—and yet…

'I'd never have thought of that. I did right in hiring you,

Jack.' She swallowed. 'You've saved the day and I can't thank you enough.'

'I'm glad I could help.'

He rose and her heart started to burn.

'It's time I was going.' He barely looked at her. 'Good-bye, Caro.'

She couldn't make her legs work to walk him to the door. It closed behind him and she had to blink hard for several moments and concentrate on her breathing.

Last night's cake box still sat on the table. Seizing it, she strode into the kitchen and tossed it into the bin. Sugar wasn't the answer. Nothing but time would ease the pain scoring through her now.

She limped back to the table and picked up the snuff-box, clasped it to her chest. 'Thank you, Jack,' she whispered to the silent room. 'Thank you.'

She went to turn away—it was time for her to dress for work—when something black and silver under the table caught her attention. She reached down and picked it up. A CD. Had she dropped it? Or had Jack?

It wasn't labelled. With a shrug, she slotted it into her CD player. If it belonged to Jack she'd post it to him in Australia. She glanced at the case again, but it gave no clue.

And then two voices sounded from the speakers and her mug froze halfway to her mouth.

'I don't want to do this any more, Paul. I want Caro to know the truth.'

'We can't! We promised her father!'

CHAPTER TEN

CARO PLANTED HERSELF in a chair and listened to the CD twice more.

'So…' She drummed her fingers against the table. 'The maid never put it in the sideboard after all…' She pressed her fingers to her temples. Paul and Barbara had joined forces to take the snuffbox *together*. She stared up at the ceiling. 'I didn't even think they *liked* each other.'

Actually, the recording didn't change her mind in that regard. Obviously her father had compelled them to sabotage her career. No doubt in the hope that she'd take over that damn trust. What did he have on them? Why would they agree to do such a thing to her? She'd thought they cared about her!

She shot to her feet to pace about the room. Why had Jack lied? Why hadn't he told her the truth? For a moment she wanted to throw things at the walls and shout *No one can be trusted. No one!*

She passed a hand across her eyes. Except that would be histrionic—not to mention an unwarrantable generalisation—and she didn't do histrionics.

With the most unladylike curse she knew, she spun away to storm into her bedroom. She'd just had over a week's leave. The least she could do was get her butt over to Fredrick Soames's house in Knightsbridge and sell him this rotten snuffbox.

* * *

Freddie set the snuffbox to his desk and pursed his lips. 'It's a pretty piece, I grant you.'

'It *is* pretty.' Caro crossed her legs. 'But…?'

'The price is rather steep.'

'That's nonsense, Freddie, and you know it.' She'd known the Honourable Frederick Robert Arthur Soames for her entire life. Her father and his father had both been at Eton together.

He pulled a notepad towards him. 'I'd be prepared to pay…' He jotted down an amount, turned the pad around and pushed it across towards her.

The sum was significantly lower than the price she'd just quoted him.

Freddie loved to play games. And he really loved a bargain.

Caro crossed out the amount and jotted down a significantly higher figure. 'In all conscience I cannot allow my client to accept an amount lower than that. If you choose to pass at that price then we'll take our chances at auction.'

His face dropped comically. 'But…but that's the original asking price.'

She smiled. After all the trouble this snuffbox had caused, she had every intention of getting the best price possible for it.

'Listen, Caro, I know it's your job to do the best for your client, but we've known each other for a long time and—'

'Don't you dare say another word, Freddie Soames. We may have known each other forever, and we may indeed be friends, but I am *not* cutting you a deal on this snuffbox. You should know better than to even ask.'

His shrug was completely without rancour. 'You can't blame a guy for trying. You have a hard-nosed reputation in the industry.' He said it in such an admiring tone that she had to laugh. 'It's so at odds with your personality outside of work that I just...wanted to try my luck,' he finished with a grin.

At odds with her...? That made her grow sober again. Was that why Paul and Barbara had thought they could walk all over her? Was that why...? She gulped. Was that why Jack had left her five years ago?

If she brought the same backbone and strength of purpose to her personal relationships as she did to her work, would it make a difference? If she'd put her foot down and stated, *This is what I expect from all of you—honesty, respect and acceptance. And if you can't promise me that then...then...*

Jack had said he could give her all of those things.

But she hadn't believed him.

Out of nowhere her heart started to thump.

'Caro, are you okay?'

She started, and shot Freddie a smile. 'I'm simply tickety-boo, Freddie.'

It occurred to her that now she had the snuffbox back in her keeping she was curiously reluctant to let it go.

Time to force Freddie's hand. 'Richardson's has given you first option on this beautiful example of a seventeenth-century snuffbox, but you must understand that interest in these items is always high. I'm going to count to three. You have until then either to accept at the asking price—' she touched a finger to the notepad '—or to decline.'

'No need to count, Caro.' He leaned back, fingers clasped behind his head. 'I'm going to chance my luck when it goes to auction.'

She laughed at the light of competition that sparkled from his eyes. As she'd known it would. '*If* it makes it to auction, Freddie. Don't count your chickens.'

She wrapped the snuffbox in a soft cloth, placed it into

a protective box and slipped it into her purse. 'It was lovely to see you.' She shook his hand and left.

She stood on his doorstep for a moment. Freddie Soames lived in Knightsbridge…maybe that was why Law-rence Gardner popped into her mind. She glanced at her watch. The interview with Freddie hadn't taken nearly as long as she'd thought it would. On impulse, she dialled Lawrence's number.

'I wonder if you have a moment or two to spare for me?' she said after their greetings.

'Absolutely, my dear girl. I'm in the Knightsbridge branch today.'

'I'm about two minutes away.'

'So this is the offending item that caused all the trouble.' Lawrence handed the snuffbox back to her. 'I'm very pleased you recovered it.'

'Oh, yes, I am too.' She told him the story Jack had given her.

His gaze slid away. 'All's well that ends well, then.'

She folded her arms. 'You don't believe that story any more than I do. I *know* Paul and Barbara were behind the snuffbox's disappearance…at my father's behest.'

'Ah…'

'Has Jack been to see you since our…uh…unscheduled meeting at the bank on Wednesday?'

He hesitated and then nodded. 'I believe that boy has your best interests at heart, though, Caro.'

She pulled in a breath and nodded. 'I do too.'

'Right, well… Jack came to see me this morning. He wanted a couple of bank cheques drawn up.'

She listened closely to all he had to tell her and her heart started to burn. 'Father blackmailed Barbara and… and threatened to cut off the funds for her mother's care? That's…diabolical!'

Lawrence winced.

'Why didn't she come to me? She had to know that I'd take care of it.'

She suddenly recalled Barbara's words from the night they'd spent in Kent. *You've always been a funny little thing... It can be very difficult to get a handle on how you truly feel.* Maybe...maybe Barbara *hadn't* known.

She cursed her own reserve. And Barbara's.

'I can't imagine, though, why *Paul* would agree to do such a thing.' Lawrence sighed. 'He dotes on you.'

'Oh, that's easy.' She rubbed a hand across her chest. 'He was in love with my mother. I believe she's the only woman he's ever loved.'

'Good God!'

She smiled at the appalled expression on Lawrence's face. 'No, no—I don't believe for a single moment that there was anything between them other than mutual respect and friendship.'

'Thank God!' He sagged back in his chair. 'But if you're right it would explain why he'd be so set on you taking over management of the trust.'

'I can't believe I never saw it before now, but all my life he's tried to gently guide me towards it. I thought he was simply trying to be conciliatory—to improve matters between Father and me.'

A sense of betrayal niggled at the edges of her consciousness, but she pushed it away. It would be easy to retreat behind a sense of outrage and betrayal, but what would that achieve? The last time she'd done that it had led to five years of misery.

'So Jack's taken it upon himself to try and put this all to rights?'

Lawrence spread his hands and nodded. 'What are you going to do? Is there anything I can do to help?'

She leaned across his desk to clasp his hand. 'You have

already done so much and I will be eternally grateful.' She pulled in a breath. '*I'm* going to make things right—that's what I'm going to do. Although I could use some help with a couple of practical matters.'

He straightened. 'I'm a practical man. Fire away.'

Three hours later Caro let herself into the house in Mayfair. A voice emerging from the room to her left informed her that Paul, at least, was in. She moved across to the doorway of her father's study and her heart hammered up into her throat, before settling back to bang and crash in her chest.

Jack!

Jack was here. He hadn't left for Australia yet. Somewhere inside her she started to salsa.

The internal twirling faltered when she remembered that flights to Australia didn't usually depart Heathrow until the evening. Her heart nose-dived to her toes. Jack's flight was probably six or seven hours away yet. He still had plenty of time to make it.

Unless she managed to change his mind.

She moistened suddenly dry lips. Her happiness was in her own hands. All she had to do was reach out and take what she wanted.

If she dared.

'Caro, darling!' Barbara shot to her feet, a look of dismay settling over her features. 'Darling, I…' She fell back into her chair, her words trailing off as if she had no idea what to say.

Caro didn't blame her. Squaring her shoulders, she strode up to the desk. 'I'd like to take the floor for a moment, if you don't mind,' she said to Jack and Paul.

She pointed to the two chairs on either side of Barbara, and after a moment's hesitation the two men moved to them.

Paul could barely meet her eye.

Jack stared at her with such undisguised hunger it made her blood rush in her ears, but his gaze snapped away when he realised she'd surveyed him and he shuffled the papers he held in his hands instead. An ache swelled through her.

She slid up to sit on the desk, but had to swallow a couple of times before she could risk speaking. Her voice jammed in her chest again when Jack darted a glance of frank appreciation at her legs.

That sealed it. She knew *exactly* what she was going to do.

But first…

She reached into her purse and pulled out the CD. 'I believe this belongs to you, Jack.'

Barbara closed her eyes. Paul paled.

Jack's eyes darkened as he took it from her outstretched hand.

'It must've fallen from your bag when you visited me earlier. You really should learn to fasten the latches on that thing.'

She could see his mind flicking back to this morning. 'I pulled the snuffbox from it and…'

'And then dropped said bag to the floor when you had your coffee.'

'Without fastening it again.' The pulse in his jaw pounded. He raised the CD slightly. 'Did you listen to it?'

'Oh, yes.'

All three of them winced.

She reached out and plucked the documents Jack held from his other hand. Cheques. One made out to the facility where Barbara's mother resided and the other made out to her mother's trust. Both for huge sums. *Oh, Jack! This isn't your mess to clean up.* Shaking her head, Caro tore the cheques into sixteen fragments apiece.

Barbara pressed the heel of her hand to her mouth to stifle a sob.

'Okay, so here's the deal,' Caro continued calmly, dumping the scraps of paper on the desk behind her. She opened her folder and brought out the first in a series of documents. 'Barbara, this paperwork here, as you'll see, is a contract between the facility where your mother is kept and me. It ensures that your mother's care is guaranteed. I do wish you'd trusted me to take care of this in the first place.'

God, she was magnificent.

Jack stared at Caro and his skin tingled as a rush of warmth shot through him. He hadn't been sure how she'd deal with the truth of all this, but he could see now that he should have trusted her with it. She was all class.

'Oh, I…' Barbara had to wipe her fingers beneath her eyes, to mop up the tears that had started to fall.

'I understand that my…reserve has made you unsure of me. I am sorry for that. I also understand that your loyalty must've felt torn between my father and me as well.'

The other woman lifted her chin. 'The fact of the matter is I did marry your father for his money, darling. I wanted my mother taken care of properly.'

Caro nodded. 'And in return for that my father received a wonderful wife who always went the extra mile for him. I still think he received the better part of that deal. I want you to know that I've had several million pounds transferred into your account—'

'That is absolutely unnecessary! I don't—'

'Humour me, Barbara. I've also had the deeds to the villa in Spain transferred into your name.'

Barbara swallowed. 'You'd like me to move out?' She nodded. 'Of course you do—'

'Absolutely not! I just know how much you love that villa. You and Father honeymooned there.'

'Oh, but, Caro darling, it's all too much.'

'Nonsense.' Caro turned from Barbara to Paul. 'Now, Paul.'

Jack leaned back, folding his arms and enjoying the show.

'It's occurred to me that if my mother's trust means so much to you then *you* are probably the perfect person to manage it. This document here—' she held up a sheaf of papers '—names you as chairman of the trust's board.'

'Miss Caroline, I—'

'Caro!' she ordered.

Paul swallowed. 'Caro, I… I don't know what to say.'

'Say you'll accept the position and that you'll do your best to execute the duties of the post.'

'You have my word,' he croaked, falling back into his seat.

'I've also arranged for a pension for you. Something my father should've taken care of before he died. It will be in addition to the salary you draw from administering the trust.'

The older man's head shot up. 'I won't be drawing a salary from the trust! It will be an honour to administer it.'

Caro didn't look the least surprised by this avowal. Jack would bet she'd factored that in and had made sure that his pension was very liberal.

'Good grief, Caro! I can't accept this,' he said when she handed him the paperwork outlining the details of the pension. 'This is far too generous.'

'You've earned it. You gave my father sterling service for over thirty years. Besides, I can afford it…and it's what I want.'

Caro drew in a deep breath, and such a roar of longing spiked through Jack, his hand clenched about the seat of his chair to keep him there.

'Now, I want you both to know that these things I've set in motion today are set in stone. They cannot be changed.

I cannot revoke or undo what I've just promised you. You are both free to simply walk away from me now, without the fear of any reprisals.'

The room went so still that all Jack could hear was the tick of the grandfather clock out in the entrance hall.

Caro pressed her hands together. 'So now it's time for me to cast aside my wretched reserve and for us to speak plainly with each other. Barbara and Paul—I consider the two of you my family.'

Jack's heart burned that she hadn't included *him* in that number.

'I care about the two of you a great deal. I was hoping my affection was returned.'

'It *is*, darling!'

'I love you like my own daughter!'

'But that didn't stop either of you from trying to sabotage my happiness. If the two of you really care about me then what I demand from you is respect, loyalty and acceptance for who I am. If you can't give me that, then we need to go our separate ways.'

Paul shot to his feet. 'You will have it to my dying day,' he vowed.

'Yes, darling, you have *my* word too.'

Caro's smile was sudden, sweet and utterly enchanting. 'Then we can continue on as we've been doing. I mean to give up my flat and we can all live here in this ridiculous house like the mismatched dysfunctional family that we are.'

Barbara stood in swift elegant motion and pulled Caro from the desk to fold her in a hug. 'Darling, that sounds marvellous.'

Paul waited beside them, impatiently moving from foot to foot, until he had a chance to engulf Caro in a bear hug. 'Splendid! Splendid!'

With a heart that throbbed Jack slipped the strap of

his satchel over his shoulder, stood and turned towards the door.

'Where do you think you're going?' Caro called after him, before he'd had the chance to take two steps.

He pulled in a breath, but didn't turn. 'I have a plane to catch.'

'In what—six hours?'

Acid burned his stomach at the thought of flying away from her. He met her gaze briefly. 'I have to be at the airport in four hours' time and…and there are things I need to do before then.'

Number one on that list was: save face and maintain whatever pride he could.

'I was hoping… Please, Jack, could you spare me ten more minutes?'

He should say no. He should toss a casual *sayonara* over his shoulder and walk away from her with a jaunty stride.

Casual? Jaunty? *Impossible.*

Saying no to Caro? Also impossible.

His shoulders slumped. His satchel slid to the floor.

'Sure. What's ten minutes?'

But they both knew what havoc ten minutes could wreak. Six and a half years ago on a reckless impulse he'd asked her to marry him. On impulse she'd said yes. It had taken less than a minute for them to promise to build a life together.

Five years ago, when he'd thought she meant to abort their baby, it had taken him ten minutes to pack his bags and walk away.

When he'd told her he loved her yesterday, it had taken less than a minute for her to shatter his hopes.

What was ten minutes? It could be the most hellish time of his life, that was what.

Or the most heavenly.

He pushed that thought away. He could harbour no hopes.

He snapped back to himself to find Barbara slipping her arm through Paul's and leading him from the room, murmuring something about tea and cake.

He forced his gaze to Caro's. 'You want to take me to task for keeping the truth about the snuffbox from you?'

She shook her head, her smile spearing into the centre of him. 'It was kind of you to want to protect me from the truth, even if it *was* misguided. It was even kinder of you to offer such large amounts of money to both Barbara and Paul in an attempt to make things right.'

He'd hoped by buying their gratitude it would help offset some of the damage Caro's father had caused.

'If it's not that, what *do* you want to talk to me about?'

Her gaze dropped to her hands and she looked so suddenly uncertain that he took a step towards her. She glanced up and then away again. Finally she reached into her purse and pulled a wrapped object from it. He knew immediately what it was—the snuffbox.

She unwrapped it, placed it on her palm and stared at it for a long moment. 'I bought this earlier today.'

She what? 'You mean to tell me that blasted Soames bloke didn't want it after all?'

'Oh, he wanted it all right.'

Her laugh washed over him and it was all he could do not to close his eyes and memorise it—to help him through tomorrow…and all the days after that.

'But he decided to play games instead—hoping for a lower price—and I found I didn't want to part with it. Regardless of the price offered.'

She held it out to him. 'Jack, I'd like you to have it.'

His jaw dropped. 'That's absolutely not necessary. I told you I didn't require payment, and—'

'It's not payment. I know enough not to challenge you on that. This is a gift. A…a symbol.'

He snapped his mouth shut. He found himself breathing hard, as if he'd just completed the obstacle course at his old police training college. 'A symbol of what?'

She placed the snuffbox in his hand and backed up again, to lean against the edge of the desk. She pushed her bangle up her arm as far as it would go and twisted it.

'I've only just admitted this to myself, but…my heart was lost in the same way that this snuffbox was lost. You found the latter and somehow that helped me to find the former.'

His heart pounded a tattoo against his ribs. He was too afraid to hope. Caro didn't like risks. She avoided them where possible. It would be folly to think she'd risk her heart on him a second time.

'I'm not precisely sure what that means.'

She bit her lip and then looked him full in the face. Her uncertainty almost undid him.

'I never ask for what I want. I'm not sure why that's the case. Habit, I suppose. What I wanted never mattered much to my father, so I guess I thought what I wanted wouldn't matter much to anyone else either.'

'It matters to me,' he said, moving a step closer. 'Caro, are you saying that you want…*me*? That you want to give our marriage a second chance?'

Her eyes suddenly flashed. '*I* want to be the one to state what I want, Jack. I don't want to leave it up to you. I don't want to leave it up to anyone! I don't want to place people in a position where they have to guess at what I want. I want to overcome this hateful reticence of mine and say exactly what I mean—at least around you, Barbara and Paul.'

She'd just put him in the same category as the rest of her family and his heart all but stopped. It took a moment for him to catch his breath.

'What *do* you want, Caro?'

She met his gaze. 'I want *you*, Jack. I want to spend my life with you. I love you.'

He couldn't contain himself a moment longer. He closed the distance between them and hauled her into his arms. 'You know I'm never going to be able to let you go again, don't you?'

Her eyes throbbed into his. 'I like the sound of that. I also very much want you to kiss me.'

He stared at her infinitely kissable mouth and something in his chest shifted.

'You don't need to ask twice.'

He lowered his mouth towards hers and a fraction of a second before their lips met she smiled, as if she suddenly believed that she could have everything she asked for.

Her hope and delight bathed him in a warmth he'd forgotten that he needed. Cradling her face in his hands, he kissed her. Slowly. Thoroughly. Sweetly.

Her hands slid up either side of his neck and she pressed herself to him, kissing him back with the same thoroughness, the same passion and tenderness, and with the same intent to reassure and pour balm on old wounds.

He savoured every moment, something inside him filling up and easing. Then, in a flash and a touch of tongues, the kiss changed to become hungry, hot and demanding. Jack gave himself up to the heady abandon and the flying freedom of it.

He didn't know how long the kiss lasted, but when they finally eased away from each other it seemed as if the very quality of the light in the room had changed—as if a brand new day had dawned.

Caro touched her tongue to her lips, which did nothing to quieten the hunger roaring through him.

'Wow…' she breathed.

A grin stretched through him. 'You should ask for what you want more often.'

Her eyes danced. 'I mean to.' She reached up to touch his face. 'Jack, I promise to be more open and upfront with you. I know that my reserve played a big role in our troubles five years ago.'

He took her hand, kissed her fingertips. 'We can put that all behind us now. It's in the past.'

She shook her head. 'It's only in the past if we've learned from the mistakes we made back then.'

Ah.

She bit her lip. 'Jack, can you promise me honesty from now on?'

He recalled the promise she'd extracted from Barbara and Paul. 'I can promise you honesty, loyalty and acceptance.'

She smiled. 'I never doubted the second and third of those for a moment. But your urge to protect me...'

He pulled in a breath, knowing he couldn't give this promise lightly. Finally he nodded. 'I promise you honesty, Caro. Even if it's hard for me to say and hard for you to hear.'

'Thank you.'

'You promise me the same?'

'I do,' she said, without hesitation.

She bit her lip again, and while her eyes didn't exactly cloud over the light in them dimmed a fraction.

'What?' he demanded, immediately alert.

'I understand your desire for children and a family, Jack, but hundreds and thousands of couples work it out—negotiate it somehow—so I'm sure we can too, and—'

He touched a finger to her lips, halting her rush of words. 'I've been thinking about this a lot, and I think I've found a solution.'

Her eyes narrowed. 'I don't want you making any unnecessary sacrifices.'

'I don't want you doing that either.'

'Okay…'

She drew the word out and it made him smile. 'If you're not totally against the idea of having children—'

'Oh, I'm not. Not now. Being exposed to Suzie's two—being their godmother—has made me realise that I'll never become the kind of remote parent my father was.'

He stared at her. 'I wish you'd told me that was what you were afraid of five years ago.' He didn't want to make the same mistakes ever again where this woman was concerned. He pushed a strand of hair back behind her ear. 'Why didn't you ever tell me?'

One of her shoulders lifted. 'I didn't want you to laugh at me.'

'I would never laugh at you.'

'And I didn't want my fear dismissed as nonsense.'

He nodded slowly. 'The fear isn't nonsense, but the idea that you could be anything less than a loving mother seems crazy to me,' he admitted.

'I'm confident enough in myself now to see the difference.'

He touched the backs of his fingers to her cheek. 'We married too soon, didn't we?'

Five years ago he'd wanted all his dreams to come true then and there.

She caught his hand in hers and kissed it. 'I understand we needed a trial by fire to cement what was really important. I only wish it hadn't take us five years to get through it.'

He wanted to wipe the sadness and the remembered pain from her eyes. 'I promise to never walk away from you the way I did five years ago. I should've stayed and fought for you back then. I will always fight for you, Caro.'

The brilliance of her smile almost blindsided him. 'I think I'm going to have to ask you to kiss me again.'

He laughed. 'How does this sound? When you're ready, we can start a family…and if you want to return to work then that's what you'll do, and I can be the stay-at-home parent.'

Her eyes widened, brightened. 'Really?'

'I'd love it.' He would too. 'My business is doing brilliantly, and I'm proud of it, but it's just something to fill in the time. I can hire a manager to take over operations, or even take on a partner. I might do the odd bit of consultancy work, just to keep my hand in, but building a family with you, Caro, is what I really want to do.'

She smiled back at him with a mistiness that had him throwing his head back and laughing for the sheer joy of it. 'We both have more money than either one of us will ever conceivably need. We can hire all the help we need or want—housekeepers, nannies, gardeners.'

Her eyes shone so bright they made him feel he was at the centre of the universe.

'Would you like to remain in London?' He didn't care *where* they lived.

'Oh! I hadn't thought about it. I love London, but I'm sure I'd love Australia too, and—'

'It's just—' he glanced around '—this house is huge. If we stayed here then maybe, down the track, we could think about fostering kids in need.'

He'd barely finished before she threw her arms around his neck and held him tight. 'That sounds perfect—absolutely perfect! Now, as it appears you won't kiss *me*, I'll just have to kiss you instead.'

His heart expanded until he thought it would grow too big for his chest. Her lips moved to within millimetres of his—

'Darlings, there's tea and cake if you'd like some.'

With a smile that set his blood on fire, Caro eased away to glance at Barbara. 'I'd love cake, but there's some paperwork I need Jack to go over…uh…upstairs.' Taking his hand, she led him out of the room, past a bemused Barbara and up the staircase. 'Make sure you leave us some!' she shot over her shoulder.

He started to laugh when they reached her room. 'You're not fooling anyone with that story, you know.'

'I know—but you can't expect a lifetime of reserve to simply vanish overnight. And the odd polite fiction keeps the wheels turning smoothly.'

He stared at her, barely able to believe he was there with her. 'I love you, Caro. I will cherish this and keep it safe—' he opened his hand to reveal the snuffbox '—in the same way I will always cherish your heart and do all I can to keep it safe.'

Her eyes burned into his. 'I love you, Jack. I will do everything I can think of to make you happy.'

'You promise to always tell me what you want?'

She nodded and then grinned. 'Want to know what I want right now?'

His mouth dried at the look in her eyes. 'What?' he croaked.

'You,' she whispered, moving across to stand in front of him. Reaching up on tiptoe, she pressed a kiss to the corner of his mouth. 'I want *you*.'

'You have me,' he promised, his lips descending towards hers.

'Forever?'

'Forever.'

* * * * *

COMING SOON!

We really hope you enjoyed reading this book. If you're looking for more romance, be sure to head to the shops when new books are available on

Thursday
6th September

LET'S TALK
Romance

For exclusive extracts, competitions
and special offers, find us online:

f facebook.com/millsandboon

⊙ @millsandboonuk

🐦 @millsandboon

Or get in touch on 0844 844 1351*

For all the latest titles coming soon, visit
millsandboon.co.uk/nextmonth